To Dena,

Happy reading!

THINGS GRAK HATES

PETER J STORY

THINGS GRAK HATES

ISBN: 978-0-9907493-0-1

Library of Congress Control Number: 2014949488

Printed in the U.S.A.

Text type set in Adobe Garamond Pro
Book design by Marie T Story

To Alvi.
If it weren't for you, this book wouldn't exist.

Things Grak Hates

1 - Olives

Grak hates olives. Truly. If there were one point of supreme importance to understand about his habits or character, this would be it.

Admittedly, a detail of this sort appears on the surface to be a mere quirk. Thus, one might feel tempted to dismiss it as an insignificant ingredient in Grak's nature. But that would be an erroneous assumption.

Only upon closer examination can one discover the trait's true value. Much like a root, it both feeds the man and reveals a profusion of information about his very essence.

Perhaps greatest among these insights is the rationale behind Grak's antipathy for the fruit. His chief source of complaint stems from the berry's abundance. As is often the case with things of plenty, olives have become routine. And Grak does not like routine.

Though, to be fair, he does appreciate *certain* routines. If circumstance prevents his evening dip in the hot springs, he gets cranky. This is especially true if that day consisted of hunting or some other equally taxing activity. Grak describes his "hot spring dip" routine as "enjoyable."

But some routines only bring grief for Grak. Whetting his toenails falls into this category. And yet he finds the practice as unavoidable as rising from sleep. And nearly as deplorable, which is saying a lot. He would do away with waking if it were possible, but has yet to find a suitable approach.

Likewise, as much as he disdains crafting his toenails before the day begins, Grak finds the chore inevitable. And not because it reduces the occurrence of torn nails. While a pleasant benefit, that was never his aim.

No, his purpose has always been for the sharpened point itself. By his estimation, it provides a hidden advantage should he find himself in an unfair fight without the upper hand.

Needless to say, the tribe does not ask this of him. In fact, when others noticed the habit, they agreed without dissent that they considered it "rather queer."

But Grak is not keen on sharing the reasoning for his secrets with the camp. He fears that doing so might rob him of that needed edge. Thus, the tribe has no choice but to assume the practice derives from his "rather queer nature."

And, of course, comments such as these only serve to renew his determination (and bolster his contempt) for the task. Grak describes his "toenail whetting" routine as "regretfully necessary."

But olives ... now there's another beast altogether. Grak has never liked olives. Even as a boy, he found them "awfully bitter" and "poorly textured." And if that weren't bad enough, they also had a cruel way of leaving his face in an abnormal puckering state.

The other children would, of course, make matters worse by calling him names. "Puck" was their first choice, and perhaps the least derisive. In fact, Grak's longing to be considered "good natured," even led him to occasionally admit it carried a ration of humor.

But when they began to address him as "Tum-Tum," that poured a sadness into his being. It whispered, "Your friends are looking down on you. They think you're weak," and Grak considers that to be cruel and unfair. Especially since he finds himself faultless in the circumstances surrounding the name's origin.

It grew from the handful of incidents where his stomach turned when he spotted the vile berries being served. On the first of these occasions, after a public display of vomiting, Grak became embarrassed. Attempting to redirect blame, he pointed toward a spreading illness as the cause.

And much to his surprise, that approach found success. But only at first. By the third occurrence or so, it had been some time since anyone else was unwell, and his guise crumbled. The name began soon after.

Grak believes this series of events was also responsible for the development of his most hated nickname: Olive. The constant reminder of something so despised was bad enough. But when one mother heard the teasing, she liked the name so much that she bestowed it on her soon-to-be-born daughter.

Within a few snows, the moniker became a trend among girls. Though none call *him* by the name anymore, he still hears it often, and his heart twinges ever so slightly.

But even a tragedy like that might have been bearable were it not for the fruit's unrelenting presence. No matter where his people set up camp—olives! Several times he thought he had a run of fortune, but then a foraging party would return days later and suddenly—olives!

And not just a few olives turn up, but an overwhelming supply. "Yay! We have so many olives to eat!" the tribe declares giddily. But this only drives another pin into Grak's soul.

Even when the days turn cold, he finds no relief. Hysteria drives his clan to gather every olive they can find and submerge them in clay jars filled with brine. "We don't want to run out of olives!" whimpers the worried bunch. And Grak feels alone in his knowledge that this only makes the things more repulsive.

No. No escape from olives for him. Grak describes the "forced olive consumption" routine as "appalling" and "abominable." But most often he simply refers to it as "depressing."

Of course, there's much more to know about Grak than his contempt for olives. Such as his love of the color blue. Or its connection to his roughly equal feelings of fascination and fear toward the sea.

Or his guilty pleasure of seeing children scolded, embarrassed, or falling down. Though if they're more than mildly hurt, he *does* feel concern; he's not a monster.

Or his love of ponies. Grak does love ponies.

Or his hyper focus on every detail, especially ones he deems unpleasant or disruptive of the few pleasures he does find. Like when someone reprimands a pony for biting a child.

Or the collection of leaves he keeps stashed away in a leather pouch under his pillow. While they tend to get damaged there, it's the only place he's found that's so secret even Doran won't stumble upon them.

Or his best friend, Doran, who was the only one to resist calling him anything other than "Grak." Although, the man *did* privately express a concern for his friend's "severe and unusual hatred of olives."

Because that's what it always comes back to with Grak: olives. Really, that just sums him right up. More than anything else. By far. He hates them. A lot.

But while this period of Grak's life begins with olives, this day's events do not. They start with a chair. A plain, unadorned, wooden chair.

And though it lacks the usual flair and quality of other chairs in camp, Grak doesn't mind. He's looking at his new chair with an odd sort of delight that he doesn't normally derive from such things.

And that's because this chair is different. It's the first one he's made successfully. Which is to say, it can support his weight and doesn't wobble *too* much.

Admittedly, it's a limited definition of "successful." Especially since Grak bestows this description on all his handiwork. But he'll usually admit to himself that it's an exaggeration (however slight), and he's not doing so here. No, he's quite proud of *this* chair.

Even qualifies as a masterpiece, I think. Can't imagine I'd be alone in that thought, either.

Grak opens the tent flap for more light. Not too wide an opening, of course. He has a fear that if someone were to see his work before its completion, they might think it inferior. Then the resulting humiliation—while entirely unfair—would be too much to bear.

Grak sits on his bed roll and leans against the deerskin wall with his hands behind his head. This immediately causes a fairly uncomfortable bend in his back, given the wall's slant.

Why do I always sit like this when I think? It's rather painful. What other options are available?

Grak leans forward, resting his elbows on his crossed legs.

Much better. No pain, and I have a closer view of the chair. Remember this posture, Grak. Remember this posture. Remember this posture.

This is his personal memory trick. He finds three times is sufficient. Four is just excessive.

With that important detail out of the way, Grak returns his focus to the matter of inspection. Spotting a small bump on the otherwise smooth chair leg, he attempts to scrape it down with his fingernail.

Grak surveys his finger, wrapped with a suspiciously discolored scrap of cloth found under the foot of his bed roll. The bleeding appears to have subsided, so that's comforting.

He looks around for the splinter. This proves a challenging task, given the clutter of dirty garments and useless items strewn about his tent. Grak opts for a different approach and attempts to retrace his movements.

Would be a shame if it ended up in my foot later.

Given its size, the thing could cause serious damage if left to its own devices. Then he'd have to hide an embarrassing hobble, and that wouldn't do.

Ah, there it is.

The splinter is resting just next to his bedding. Though in all honesty, that could describe any location in the tent. Size constraints limit his decorative ability.

He picks up the sliver and holds it close for further analysis. The dried blood and bit of nail stuck to it must have acted as a camouflage of sorts. Nonetheless, Grak's keen eye proved superior once again.

Not this time, splinter. Not this time.

He tosses the sliver outside, taking care to ensure it lands far from the entrance.

Now where was I? Ah, the chair.

Grak settles back into his new thinking posture. On further inspection, he's undecided whether the new gouge is too noticeable. He settles on leaving it be.

I suppose it adds character. Well, quite a good job, I must say. The tribe would probably want to see its quality.

Not enough good chairs in camp and all.

But last time I showed a chair around, everyone was so critical. Probably just jealous. Probably just wanted to find something to hate about it. Yes, I'm sure that's all it was.

I imagine I could avoid that by not directly asking for opinions. If I simply act like I don't care. Yes, that makes sense. So how would I do that?

An instant later, Grak's mind clicks. He rushes into action and throws on the nearest of his three tunics, leaving it open due to the heat.

Some continue to question the need for so many garments, but Grak has responded to them so many times that he's run out of patience. "You wouldn't understand," is his only reply these days, accompanied by a shake of his head and a pitying smile.

The reason is simple enough, though. Having several on hand not only provides greater variety to choose from, but also makes it possible to find one when in a hurry.

In fact, Grak's trousers are currently demonstrating this point. He only has one pair of those, and he's certain that's the reason they're proving so elusive at the moment. But he's not losing hope. In a tent this small, they can only stay hidden for so long. Sure enough, a bit more digging soon reveals them beneath his pillow.

Unlike the tunics, Grak didn't make his trousers. Padded leather is far too tricky. Instead, he convinced Doran to do it for him. In secret, of course.

And while Grak suspects that no one *truly* believed he was responsible for such fine work, no formal accusations were ever made. Several individuals posed questions, but more out of curiosity than suspicion.

Besides, Grak managed to put those to rest with relative ease. He persuaded Doran to claim witness of the event, and that did the trick. Shoulders were shrugged and the matter was soon dropped.

Fortunately, Grak's cap requires no searching. It's crumpled there where the trousers recently lay, just next to the soup bowl. This reminds him, and he finishes the broth.

Despite the day's warmth, Grak dons the head covering. No matter the occasion, he always makes sure to wear it when stepping out. He has to show the thing off, after all, since it's the best example of his handiwork. Which is to say, the hat fits, more or less, and doesn't have *too* much of a point at the top.

But he's certain *that* part isn't his fault. "Fitting cloth to the shape of a head is simply a difficult task," he reminds himself often. Though he has to do so while ignoring the rounded caps all throughout camp.

And it's not like he didn't *try* to do away with the point. He put sincere effort into it. The one he's wearing now is the best of thirty-two attempts. But by the time he reached that count, realization hit that he would soon run out of room to hide the mistakes.

Thus, he opted to refocus his efforts. Which is to say, Grak then tried to convince everyone that the point made for a more comfortable fit. But that never caught on. Neither did his insistence that it added character.

Still, aside from the comparison some draw to female anatomy, he's quite proud of the thing. "My *good* hat," he calls it.

Armed with the added confidence his cap provides, Grak steps outside, chair in hand, and sets off toward Groka's tent. He feels that's the best place to begin his plan, given her expertise in crafting wood and the central location of her dwelling.

Of course, it doesn't hurt that she's his second favorite person in camp after Doran. But that's no surprise, since they have so much in common: their names are similar and they both make chairs.

Plus, she's pretty, so that's three. Especially her neck. So long and elegant. Quite fetching. And not too thin, either. Very graceful overall.

Grak hides a smile upon finding her home. "Hello, Groka!" The tone betrays his concealed excitement. He tries for something more nonchalant. "How are you today?" Much better.

She looks up from her woodwork, glancing at the hat before settling on his eyes. That hardly bothers him anymore. Now he just attributes it to habit.

"Oh hello, Grak!" At least her enthusiasm matches his own. "I'm doing well, thank you! And you?"

"Just fine, just fine." This seems like a decent time to introduce his strategy. "Sorry, I can't chat right now. I'm looking for Doran. Have you seen him?"

Groka stares at the ground in thought for a long moment, scratching her neck enticingly. Finally, she looks up and shakes her head. "No, I can't say I have."

She isn't mentioning the chair. Grak didn't expect his plan to fall apart so quickly. And try as he might, no alternative ideas are coming to mind.

"Alright ... Well, I'm looking for him ... If you see him, I'll be walking around ... looking for him ..."

"Sure, I'll send him off to you. But wait, if you're walking around, how will I know where to send him?"

Grak is confused now. He's not sure how this went so wrong. It seemed like such a simple plan initially.

"I guess ... I don't know ... I guess I'll just keep asking around ..."

He chides himself for not preparing a backup strategy. In his defense, he didn't think it would be necessary. He usually finds it simple enough to think on his feet.

Must be Groka. I'm too distracted by her.

That's truer than Grak realizes. His wits have a habit of napping when she's around. Even more so when her neck glistens with sweat like this. Unfortunately, her charms also impair his ability to overcome the problem.

Grak opens his mouth in a daring attempt to speak whatever comes to mind. Nothing does, however, and the two stand in awkward silence for a moment longer.

"Hello, Groka. Grak."

Grak is caught off guard by the newcomer. She must have sneaked up from the side. "Oh ... hello, Jafra."

He finds himself strangely relieved to see her. Under normal circumstances, Grak loathes the woman without remorse. But in this situation, he's glad for the third person to help ease the tension. So much so that her uneven eyebrows are hardly bothering him right now.

An idea pops to mind and quickly takes shape. He usually tries to exclude her from his plans, but she might serve a purpose here.

"Jafra, have you seen Doran?" He makes a show of looking uncomfortable, and switches the chair to his other hand.

Jafra's eyes follow his movements. "Oh look, you made a chair! Not bad."

Fortune! She walked right into that one. Though she almost seems too excited.

Grak is unsure whether to be suspicious. He decides against it for the time being, focusing instead on how pleased he is with the plan's current success.

"Oh, this? Well, thanks. It's really not finished yet, but that's nice of you."

Jafra grows confused. "Oh? What's left to do?"

There's another angle he failed to foresee. "You know ... just ... chisel ... level ... wood ..." Grak hopes that if he mumbles enough chair-crafting words, she'll just nod and return to her day.

Fortunately for him, Groka interrupts. "Yes, it's very nice, Grak. Well done!"

Jafra adds her mind. "Definitely better than your last one. Oh, what's that gouge there?"

Grak fervently looks for a way out. He never meant for this to become a lengthy conversation. "Oh, you know, makes the chair look aged ... anyway, Jafra, have you seen Doran? I wanted to get his opinion on it."

"Yes, I have. He was heading down to the shore. The view's lovely today. Even more than usual. I think you'd enjoy it."

Grak resents the woman assuming she knows what he'd enjoy. Though she *did* compliment his chair. He decides that earns her a crumb of courtesy.

Not too much, of course. Can't have her thinking everything's better between us.

"Well, I wouldn't be so sure of that if I were you," he replies.

Jafra is confused once again, but says nothing more. Her furtive eyes seem to be searching for a way out, but finding none. Groka looks much the same.

Though prettier, obviously.

Finally, Grak musters up the courage to break the awkward silence. "Alright, I'd better go and find him. I'll see you later, Groka!" He decides to give the other woman a little more courtesy. "And you too,

Jafra." Compliment or no, she'll have to earn the cheer he uses when addressing Groka.

Grak heads for the path that leads over the hill and down to the shore on the other side. He'll have to abandon the plan for now. If he keeps asking around, Groka and Jafra might realize what he's doing. And besides, all the questions they posed are making him rethink the brilliance of his strategy.

Perhaps they'll spread the word for me. Tell everyone how wonderful the chair is. Yes, I could see that happening. They seemed excited enough about it.

That'll have to do until he can come up with something else. Grak ponders alternative ideas as he walks. Much to his dismay, the thick, moist air is making both tasks more difficult than usual.

Hmm, perhaps after I talk to Doran, I can head over to the hot springs. Yes, definitely in need of a dip. That should clear my head right up.

Grak reaches the hill, and his pace slows. The slope seems steeper than before. And the chair seems bulkier than a moment ago. He begins to regret having made it so heavy.

Grak sets his chair down with an exaggerated breath. No response. Too far away. He moves closer and repeats.

Doran's head turns, his face mimicking an abrupt waking. "Grak!" He relaxes. "Good day! I apologize. I didn't hear you approaching."

Grak tries to hide his annoyance. "Apparently not," he grumbles.

"The sea has that effect on me. Mesmerizing, isn't it?" Doran's gaze follows his attention back toward the horizon. "How far do you suppose it stretches?"

Grak is too annoyed to discuss the view at the moment. "Well, I didn't mean to interrupt your reverie with my silly chair."

Doran's focus returns. "Oh, of course. You're right. I apologize for that too. Here, let's see your latest work." He bends over for a closer view. Not once have his eyes grazed the cap.

Good man. Absent-minded at times, but a good man.

"Yes, please do. I'm interested to know your opinion." Surprised by his own sincerity, Grak reviews the statement in his mind.

Hmm, I suppose I am. Well, he is a good man, after all.

Doran squats down to inspect the chair's seat. Grak finds his posture quaint, but suppresses a smile so as not to offend the man.

After a long moment of careful examination, Doran stands with a look of wonderment. "I'm impressed, Grak. This is almost up to *Groka's* standard." He furrows his brow in confusion. "But tell me, why do you insist on perfecting your chair crafting? Some say we have too many as it is, moving around as often as we do."

Grak's ears are still buzzing with the compliment. "*Groka's* standard? You think?"

"Oh yes, I thi—" Doran squints and bends over. "Oh, what's this gouge here?"

Grak is quicker this time. "And what of this seat? How does it compare to hers?"

Doran tests it. "Hmm. Regretfully, not as good. Perhaps if it didn't wobble so much. Hers usually have fewer splinters too." He pulls one out of his thigh.

"Fewer, you say?" Grak wonders if he can pass it off as intentional. "So you believe I should make it like every other chair? You think that would be an improvement?" He's feeling a little offended now. "Who would want a chair like *that*?"

Doran nods as he mulls it over. "Well, I suppose that's one way to look at it. Though, I wonder if comfort is more important in this case." He shrugs. "Either way, excellent crafting. Definitely your best yet."

Grak inspects his friend's face for traces of evasion. While undoubtedly well-intended, it's still important to be aware of.

None ... None!

He scrambles to fill the silence before more problems can be identified. No need. Doran's mouth hangs open, his eyes wide and distant.

Grak follows his friend's stare to the rippling water beyond the shore. "Wh ... what are we looking at?" Part of Grak hopes the man might just be in awe of his quality woodwork.

Doran's focus returns, dashing Grak's optimism. "Did you see that?

What was it?"

Grak rolls his eyes. "Again with the sea, Doran? It's water. We drink it. Well, not saltwater ... but you know what I mean. Anyway, it's not very interesting."

That last bit wasn't true, but Grak doesn't care. He's too upset right now. And hurt, if he's being honest. But mostly upset.

"No, it wasn't just the ocean! How did you not see the thing? It rose up as tall as the sky! Way out in the distance. And it splashed back down with such force!"

Grak's keen empathy catches a whiff of frustration in his friend, which he considers more than a little unfair. "Well, I was kind of looking this way at the time. Toward you. So, I didn't turn my head until you said something. But I will point out that I'm the only one who seems committed to our conversation right now."

"Grak, man! Are you listening to me? I saw something out there! At sea ... on the horizon! Something incredible ... and terrible!"

Grak sighs and looks again. Nothing but waves. And one sad cloud. And a seagull. Grak hates seagulls; he hates anything loud and bossy.

"Well, it's gone now, Doran. Whatever this thing was. Though I can't imagine it being worth the fuss you're making."

"Can't ... not worth the *fuss*?"

Yes, definitely frustration. Best to try a new approach. "Well, do you think it's dangerous? This ..." Grak attempts an awkward hand gesture, but nothing relevant emerges. "This *thing* ... you saw?"

"I ... I can't say. How would I know? Maybe? Maybe not. Either way, it's fascinating. And important! I have to tell the tribe!" Doran races off along the path back to camp.

Grak isn't sure how to categorize his friend's reaction to the chair. On the one hand, he approved of it, but on the other hand, he clearly wasn't in awe. Grak ponders the matter for a moment longer before settling on "positive." He smiles.

All in all, a good day so far.

"No … please … look …" Doran sighs in frustration.

Grak sympathizes with his friend's annoyance now that it's channeled at the surrounding crowd. And quite a large crowd at that. Grak was shocked to see such a gathering on his return from the hot springs. And even more surprised to learn what they were gawking at.

Doran takes a deep breath and tries once more. "Please, listen carefully. I'll attempt to explain it again, but as I do, please keep in mind that I *have* seen waves. I am aware of their usual shape and potential sizes. *This* was not a wave."

While Grak initially found it amusing to watch the tribe getting so confused, that enjoyment is already waning. His hunger is demanding too much attention now. Which reminds him. The sun is already setting. He should get going.

Grak slips out of the crowd and heads for his tent. If he acts now, while most of the tribe is distracted, he won't have to wait in line.

Through extensive testing, he's found that food has a far greater tendency toward flavor when warm. Unfortunately, everyone else seems to have discovered this too.

Thus, since the serving pot gets fired up once more just before dusk, this proves an especially busy time on most nights. But not this night. No, this is Grak's opportunity to eat a truly hot meal. He allows himself a chuckle.

Fools.

Grak enters his tent and squints through fading light. The dish hasn't moved. He grabs it and sets a quick pace toward the cook site, sniffing the bowl as he walks.

Should be good for another day. Maybe even two if I'm fortunate.

Grak arrives at his destination. He was correct: no lines. And the stew looks as appetizing as it smells. He serves himself.

A successful chair, a dip in the hot springs, and now a hearty meal with no wait: a very good day indeed! If I can manage to keep this goin—

Grak gulps and stares at his food. A smooth, black lump just surfaced. He may have been premature in his excitement.

He plucks out the olive and tosses it to the ground, sucking his fingers to cool the burn. But the stirring surfaced another lump. And another.

And … He moves the bowl closer to the fire for better light.

Chunks too! And finely chopped! Meant as a personal insult, I'm sure. I knew he was offended yesterday. No matter what he said to the contrary. Foolishly offended. And unfairly!

Grak sips at the meal with a heavy heart, attempting to filter the proper from the wretched. His teeth squish a flavor he knows too well … and again … and again … Grak sighs.

No hope for this meal.

And again … and again …

He makes his way toward Doran's gathering.

And again … and again … He resigns himself to swallowing each sip as quickly as his valiant stomach can manage.

Grak reaches the crowd's perimeter and scans the faces for his foe.

Doran rambles on in the background. "No. Much bigger than that."

Grak spots the cook. Lago is standing nine feet or so to the left, scratching his generous stomach absentmindedly. The man's attention is split between Doran's words and his own conversation with Jafra.

What is this deviousness? Was she a part of this? Did they plan it together … out of their mutual resentment toward me? Would she do that to me? After everything she's already put me through?

While that much is unclear right now, Lago's culpability is obvious enough for the moment. Grak reaches deep and channels the sum hatred of his existence at the man.

But it doesn't last long. Jafra spots him and waves. This alerts Lago, who turns to follow her gaze. Upon recognizing Grak, the man raises his cap with a slight nod and a broad smile.

The audacity! Rubbing it in, is he?

Grak grits his teeth, appearing controlled only in his mind.

Vengeance will require something particularly inventive.

Doran's excitement is on the rise. "Here, follow me to the cliff face, and I'll draw it for you."

The crowd obeys without fuss, accompanying him to the rock wall on the edge of camp. Grak joins them, but only to keep an eye on Lago.

So, how to get my vengeance? It has to hurt. Deeply. What does he love? A shame he never had any children of his own …

Grak quickly shakes that one off. Not even in his current state.

He loves cooking! Of course he does. He never has to lift a finger on hunts. Just sits back, filling his belt while we do the hard work!

As Doran finishes the drawing, a question is shouted out. He looks at the torch-lit wall in confusion. "Well, sort of. But it's not."

Perhaps I could replace Lago as cook. That would have a just sting to it!

Doran rubs his brow in frustration. "Well, because I know what a crab looks like, and this wasn't a crab!"

But the tribe loves Lago. No one would just stop eating his food in favor of mine.

Doran holds his hands up in appeasement. "Alright, look ... I admit the drawing is lacking ..."

Perhaps if I can rile the tribe against him. Get them to hate Lago with me. But how, without revealing my intent? The idea can't come from me. They'd catch on. They might not be sharp, but they're smart enough. Is it even possible?

Grak surveys his clansmen. A nearby woman shouts above the other voices. "*I* believe you! I'd like to see it! Will you show us tomorrow? At first light?"

It's one of the Olives: Olive Thirteen, if Grak's not mistaken. Of all the names on his list of the daft, hers is near the top. He feels that she too often dribbles words out of her mouth with no thought for sense.

Certainly true here. Too eager to follow—that's her problem.

An idea hits. Grak looks around once more.

They all are, aren't they? Indeed. Abundantly eager. Given proper motivation, of course ...

2 - And Lago

To say that Grak hates Lago would be an understatement. It's not a greater loathing than what he feels for olives, of course, but close. And, to no surprise, this disdain stems from a longstanding disagreement on the fruit.

What Grak has always asserted is that olives should be avoided in meals. At the least, he reasons, they should be served on the side for those in camp who choose to forgo them.

Lago, on the other hand, has always held the opinion that he doesn't care about Grak's opinion. Or at least, that's Grak's understanding of the cook's feelings. He often finds it difficult to interpret the man's meaning.

Yet throughout their regular disagreements, the conversation has always been tame. Matters have never escalated into anything more than a mild argument. That is, until several nights ago.

That evening, after serving himself and finding olives once again, Grak approached the cook. While he feels his own demeanor during their subsequent discourse was calm and rational, he can't say the same for Lago. The man's response was bitter and frigid. Some vague reasoning having to do with "not enough food" and "everyone else likes olives."

Of course, Grak felt forced by the man's provocation, and had no choice but to escalate the matter by presenting a new solution. He suggested that Lago should consider suddenly ceasing to live.

His proposal reasoned that this would be more beneficial to the tribe than any alternative. Fewer olives, to be sure, plus none need be offended any longer at the sight of such greasy neck rolls.

Grak also pointed out the added benefit of losing the man's pungent odor. He estimated it would improve the camp's smell by nine times or more. "Clearly the superior choice," he summarized.

But to Grak's annoyance, Lago was not only unwilling to try the proposition, he also appeared unbothered by it. Still, Grak wasn't fooled: it must have had an effect. From that point on, he began watching for the impending retaliation.

But Lago's reprisal last night was far more blatant than expected. The cook managed to work a record number of olives into every part of the stew. Worse yet, many were diced so small, they proved nearly impossible to remove.

And Grak is certain that's the cause behind his growing illness this morning. It seems reasonable to him that his body was simply disgusted at having to eat the vile berries. So repulsed, in fact, that it's now fighting him in an effort to prevent repetition of the heinous act.

At least that's the gist of it. He's still working on the details. Primarily how the pieces being so small might have contributed.

Size definitely had a hand in it. Just have to deter—

Grak sneezes. That was the most violent one yet. His arm is even tingling from it. He takes a moment to recover.

All this sneezing is getting annoying. He's certain that's his least favorite part of this sudden illness. That and the rampant coughing.

Though far more horrible than either is the way in which his sense for strategic scheming is so dulled at the moment. Just yesterday he pulled off an exquisite plan involving a chair. But today ... well, nothing really. That is to say, plenty of scheming but nothing strategic.

His best idea yet involved a fish and Lago's bed roll. Something to do with worsening the man's stench, though details are hazy due to Grak's current state of minor delirium. And while it may seem like a mediocre plan, the other schemes were far worse. "My good idea," he calls it, though with understandable hesitation.

But, despite the sickness and its accompanying miseries, the morning isn't *all* bad. Grak is glad for the rain at least. Not only is it cooling the air, but the sensation as it dances on his face is comforting.

Grak removes his cap to give his hair a greater drink. His heart yearns to stop and sit for a while. To ponder the rain and nothing else.

This has always been one of his favorite pastimes. As a child, Grak would spend whole days with almost no activity aside from watching the drops fall. He finds it a shame there's so little time for simple pleasures these days. Too busy honing his crafts and all.

Grak's thirst beckons to him from a nearby puddle: the one with a particularly refreshing look just ahead and to the left. He walks over to it and squats down for a sip, but the sudden appearance of his face causes him to stop short.

The reflection reveals that his beard has taken a wild turn since he last noticed. So wild, in fact, that Grak is finding it difficult to spot any two hairs growing in the same direction. He leans in.

Ah, there's a group. Still, should probably take more time to smooth it all out each morning.

Comforted, Grak sets the bow down to free up his hands. He cups both together for a larger scoop. The liquid provides instant cooling as it washes down his throat. One of the greater pleasures in life, no doubt.

Grak splashes his face and makes a final review of his appearance. A slight flattening of the eyebrows and straightening of his hair, and he's quite satisfied.

Wait, a spot of mud on his cheek. Grak makes quick work of it. Quite satisfied.

Wait, a spot in the crease of the nose. It's proving more stubborn than the last. Closer inspection reveals a freckle.

Hmm, I don't remember that being there. Oh look, another just a bit farther up. Well, best not to get caught up in this. Could take all day, and I have other matters to handle right now.

Grak's mind returns to the task at hand. From his squatting position, he surveys the surrounding forest. The rest of the hunting party must have gone ahead. No sign of the deer they were tracking either.

I'd better catch up before they get too far away. Can't have them saying I fell asleep again.

Grak slowly rises to his feet, taking great care to prevent dizziness. He looks to the right not a moment too soon. An arrow whistles just beyond his face, no more than an eyelash away. This snaps him out of his reverie as instinct pulls his body down and aside.

He's shocked. Too shocked to respond in the instant. He feels his face, checking for wounds. None. So far as he can tell. Grak realizes that in his current state he may lack the sense to make a proper analysis.

Of course, he might be dead so far as he knows, which would also limit any analysis. This raises an alarming question.

How would I know if I'm dead? Could be an imperceptible difference.

Grak allows himself a slight panic. Which is followed by a surprising calm. And that, in turn, is followed by a shouting coming from his near right.

"Grak! Are you alright?" It's Frolan—Grak ranks him among the camp's greatest dullards.

"Yes, I'm fine. I think. It seems to have missed me." Looking around, Grak spots two other tribesmen.

Gaping fools.

He remembers to be angry. "Who did that?"

No, not angry enough. Two levels higher should do it.

"Who's responsible?"

No, now it's too shrieky. Almost hysterical. Needs to be louder, deeper, and less of a question, I think.

"Who shot at me!"

Perfect.

Frolan hesitates with his mouth open for a moment. "Well … to tell the truth, it wasn't like I was shooting *at* you. There was a deer just ahead, and I only noticed you rising when it was already too late."

Grak wonders if they'll make assumptions about why he was crouching. "Well, I happened to be laying a trap for that same deer!"

Well done, Grak. Quick thinking.

"And you just ruined it." He remembers to be angry again. "And nearly stuck an arrow in my ear while doing so!" Grak feels he's clearly winning here.

Someone calls from the other direction. "We got it! Everyone! We got it!"

Grak squints, but can't quite make out who's shouting. It sounds like Jafra, though.

Makes sense. It would be just like her to scare off any other potential kills.

Frolan dons a look of excitement. "Fortune! That's the last one we needed. We've finished early!"

Hmm, still, Jafra's shouting probably scared other animals out of the area permanently.

The group closes in on the spot where the creature fell. As Grak draws nearer, he takes in the sight. Not as messy as usual. Most likely because no one had to slit the thing's throat. An arrow must have hit something vital, though it's hard to tell which one was successful. Several shafts protrude from the carcass: all generic and none the obvious culprit.

Grak remembers to keep up appearances and points to one at random. "Ah, there's mine. I guess you didn't ruin my trap after all."

Jafra's response is swift. "How can you tell?"

Of course she'd say that. She's always plotting against me.

Grak tears the arrow from the animal's neck and slyly scratches a slender groove with his thumbnail. "I always mark mine. See? Right there."

Frolan is impressed. "Wow, good eyes!"

Grak basks in that compliment, even though he knows it's undeserved. He's just so proud of himself for thinking quickly there.

Perhaps the illness is wearing off. Well, if I'm on a roll.

Grak reaches for a way to throw Lago into the mix. A partially formed idea pops to mind. He decides to run with it and figure the rest out as he goes.

"I just hope Lago isn't too upset," he says.

Jafra takes the bait. "What do you mean? Why would he be upset?"

Grak attempts the most indifferent expression in his repertoire. "Oh, nothing. I shouldn't have mentioned it."

To his dismay, Jafra simply shrugs and sets about tying the deer's legs for transport. Everyone else seems to have lost interest as well.

Perhaps my ruse was too good. Have to keep that in mind for next time.

Grak sighs with exaggeration. "It's just … well, I told him I wouldn't talk about it."

Frolan tilts his head. "Talk about what?"

Grak appreciates that he can always count on the brute to follow blindly. "Well, since we're all friends here." He tries not to look at Jafra while saying that word. "Lago told me he hopes the hunting fails today. He says meat is harder to prepare, and he doesn't like having to work so much. Says he's upset at the camp for forcing him to cook all the time."

Grak pauses for effect. "I don't know. It's Lago. You know how he can be. I guess he's never really liked the rest of us."

The instant Grak finishes those words, he regrets having gone quite so far with them. This plan might prove too difficult to maintain.

A slight furrowing of Jafra's thicker eyebrow indicates concern. "I wonder if he's working too hard. Maybe he needs a change. Maybe one of us should switch with him for a bit."

Grak ignores the woman's misplaced sentimentality. After all, she's showing herself useful here.

Of course, I'm sure the strategy deserves most of the credit. It's working even better than I imagined.

Time for step two of his scheme. "You may be on to something, Jafra. I've done some cooking in my day, and it can be a real challenge. I can only imagine how difficult it would be to do that *every* day."

Jafra's expression shows genuine interest. Even the dwarf eyebrow is climbing half her forehead. "I didn't know that about you, Grak! So full of surprises." Her eyes go wide. "Oh, there's an idea! Would you want to trade places with him? He might really appreciate it."

And there's the opening for step three. In light of her pleasant demeanor today, Grak considers altering his "hatred of Jafra" policy.

But Frolan's mind is still spilling out. "Why are we trying to help Lago? Sounds to me like he's just lazy. How much does he even *work* in a given day? Nowhere near as much as *we* do, that's for sure!

"And why would we want him on a hunt? He's so lazy he wouldn't be of any use. Or he might get himself killed. Or worse, he might get one of *us* killed!"

Grak isn't sure where the brute is going with this, but he appreciates the vitriol aimed at Lago. "Don't forget, he's fat too."

Frolan nods emphatically. "You're right. He is fat, isn't he? Really fat. You might be a little on the small side, but you're far better suited for hunting than *he* is."

Grak lets that comment slide. "I'm also strategic. Remember, I got the closest to this deer without being seen."

"You're right!" Frolan turns to Jafra. "You can keep Lago as cook. I prefer Grak and his strategies by my side on a hunt."

Grak suppresses a smile.

The fool's wisdom is astonishing today. Perhaps I haven't been giving him enough credit.

Jafra seems a little offended now. "Well, I don't think we should get so upset at Lago. Maybe a change would help him lose weight and work harder."

Her point reminds Grak of his true purpose. "Well, perhaps you're right. We could at least try it. I'd be happy to prepare the deer tonight."

Frolan grows excited. "Did you say beer? Or deer?"

"Deer."

"Ah. Wait. With a d or a b?"

"D."

Frolan pauses. Utter confusion. "D as in …" He channels intense effort toward the act of thinking. "Dark? Or b as in …" More thought. "Bear?"

Grak's incredulity leaves him speechless.

Or perhaps I've been giving the dolt too much credit. Yes, far more likely, I think.

The party emerges from the dense woods and turns right, following the sparse shoreline. Grak is glad for the change of surroundings. While the rain is a meager drizzle now, the forest floor is already covered with mud and was impeding their movement. This ground, on the other hand, is rocky enough that their steps won't be hindered.

While they're not far from camp, every moment still counts. Grak is hoping they can arrive soon enough that the hunters will still be focused on their animosity toward Lago. He feels it would be a shame to waste such potential.

But mud isn't the only thing interfering with Grak's plans. He looks back at Jafra with disdain.

She's slowing the group far more than wet dirt ever could.

As if hearing Grak's thoughts, Frolan stops and assists the woman. "A dim, but useful fellow" is Grak's current stance on the man.

Perhaps a closer bond with him would prove beneficial.

Frolan's considerable height contrasts with Jafra's small frame to make the transfer difficult. Nonetheless, she manages to hoist the deer onto his shoulders. He situates the carcass, and the party resumes their trek.

Now there's a good speed. Much better.

Several moments later, they round the final bend. Grak isn't surprised to see the crowd unmoved since this morning and still gawking with all their might.

Doran's voice floats above the din. "Well, no ... or, at the least, I doubt that. I would think it rather unusual if it were something only *I* could see."

The tribe sounds disappointed. Grak can even make out flecks of disdain from the bits of conversation he catches.

"*I* still believe you!" shouts Olive Thirteen. "When you think about it, it's unlikely this thing would even come around again for the rest of us to see it."

That statement baffles Grak. Which comes as no surprise, as everything about this situation bewilders him. But he can't deal with any of it right now.

One thing at a time, Grak. Take care of Lago, then see about this matter with Doran's sighting.

The party makes quick work of the path over the hill and soon arrives at the perimeter tents. As they enter camp, Grak spots Lago just off to the left, chatting casually and rubbing his greasy hands on an overworked apron.

Of all things! Just flaunting his lack of work!

Grak wonders whether he should incite something now. After careful deliberation, he opts to wait a bit and see if the hunters' anger will perform the task for him.

Several moments later, they reach the cook site, and Frolan drops the carcass with a sigh of relief. He stands tall, hands at his hips, breathing into the sky. Grak feels this is all a bit exaggerated, but permits it, given his current focus.

The remainder of the team, however, has no excuse for their loitering.

And each excessive breath coming from Frolan just makes Grak antsier. He checks his shadow. It hasn't moved much since their return, though it feels like they've been back for a while.

Grak reaches for any conversational topic to get things rolling. "My, the camp is empty. I guess everyone headed down to see Doran's … uh … whatever it was. Crab, I suppose. I don't see how his drawing could have been anything else."

Jafra is quick to interject. "He said it wasn't a crab."

Grak rolls his eyes.

Always finds something to disagree with, that one.

"Fine. Then they all headed down to see Doran's … thing." This isn't the direction Grak intended. He needs to bring their focus back where it belongs. "I mean, look around. Have you ever seen it so bare? No one's working. There isn't even a meal being prepared here."

Frolan stretches his shoulders and rolls his head from side to side. "Oh, I saw Lago on our way in. He's just over there talking to Brak."

That's Brak with a "B." Grak is always eager to point out that there's no relation. He feels it's wisest to distance himself from balding individuals lest he catch that ailment.

Grak opens his mouth to say something, but Frolan isn't finished. "The lazy pig. Could have at least had a bite prepared for those of us returning from the hunt. You know, I have half a mind to go and set him straight this very instant. I mean, I'm famished! That was a long trek, and this deer isn't made of feathers!"

Under normal circumstances, Grak would feel duty-bound to point out the idiocy of that analogy. But at the moment, he decides to shake it off. After all, it seems to be agitating the other hunters to no end.

Except for Jafra, of course. "Well, we did finish unusually early today.

I don't see how he could have known we'd be back so soon."

Always ready to kill a good thing, that one.

While her calm demeanor is troubling, Grak can't resist the opportunity for self-aggrandizement. "Yes, my strategy did bring us back early."

He allows a moment for the team to reflect on his words before getting the conversation back on the right path. "But he could have had something ready just in case. He did know I was hunting today, after all. And I told him how I've been working on a strategy to make our hunts shorter."

That ignites Frolan's rage. "Exactly! I didn't even know what Grak was doing, and I knew we'd be back early. I've had it with Lago and his fat, lazy, slob ... ness! Who's with me?"

All but Jafra agree. And with considerable vigor too. Led by Frolan, they storm off to confront the cook. Grak follows, taking position just behind the brute. This seems like a good spot: close enough to influence the action, but not so close that any would suspect it was all his idea.

In a moment, they reach Brak's tent. But a portion of their fury dies upon seeing that Lago isn't there.

Frolan's annoyance is obvious. "Where did he go?"

Brak's confusion looks genuine. "Who?"

"Lago! I saw him here on our way in. Where did he run off to?"

"Oh, of course. He headed off to the forest to find some herbs. He's been working on a new recipe all morning. He's quite excited about it. I'll admit, it does sound delicious.

"He said it's something to try and mask the flavor of the olives. Said he's had a complaint about the number of them in every meal. I find that odd, though. I've never minded their taste. And Lago said most of the tribe doesn't, but he still wanted to make this person happy."

Of course that fat fool would complain about me. The wretch takes every opportunity to attack me.

Grak has always held that the man is devoid of scruples. "Must have been born without them," he often tells Doran.

But these blatant complaints are going too far. Our disagreements should be a private affair. No sense dragging others into it.

Brak dons an eager expression. "If you hurry, though, you should still be able to catch him. He headed off that way. And look, there he is, just cresting the hill toward the shore."

Unthinking haste pushes the group into action, and they trot off after the cook. Grak is annoyed at having to jog so soon after hunting, but allows it given the priority of his goal.

At least we're not slogging through wet dirt.

It's true, that does make things easier. The sun is out in full now and working at drying the ground. Mud still covers much of the area, but the bit of heat is enough to make this well-traveled path solid under foot. Bumpy, yes, but a solid kind of bumpy.

They crest the hill and spot Lago walking toward Doran's crowd.

"Look at him!" says Frolan. "Heading off to chat, like he has nothing better to do! And without a care! Just leaving his responsibilities like that!"

The dolt's anger is looking well-groomed today. I may not need to coax it any further.

Lago reaches the outskirts of the throng and begins chatting with a small group as Grak's mob approaches. With his back to the path, the cook is oblivious to his impending danger.

Frolan calls out, "Hey! Fat man! Nothing better to do with your time?"

Well-groomed indeed. I would have been hard-pressed to come up with a beauty like that.

Several pairs of eyes shift to the newcomers. It dawns on Grak that the crowd might prove useful to his purpose.

This could be a more public spectacle than I realized. That would be nice. Things are really lining up for once.

"Can't be bothered to prepare even a scrap for the returning hunters?" Frolan places a forceful hand on the cook's shoulder.

Lago whirls around. His nervous smile and confused eyes seem unsure whether to show humor or shock. "Wh ... hello, Frolan ..."

He peers around the man at Grak and the others. "Hello. Did the hunt go well? You're back rather early, aren't you?"

Now it's Frolan's turn to be shocked. "Ba ... early ...? Of course we are! And you should have known that. We had Grak with us. I'm surprised we didn't get back sooner."

Grak cheers a little on the inside while feigning humility with a slight nod and shrug. "I've been working on a new hunting strategy, and it paid off handsomely. But I told you that this morning, Lago. When we chatted just before I left. I told you we'd be back early."

Lago's shock remains, but a pinch of fear replaces his humor. "I ... um ... we didn't speak today ... did we?"

Grak realizes this might be seen as a direct challenge. The number of onlookers has already doubled, and it continues to grow. Such a large crowd could just as easily be used against him if he's not careful.

He struggles to sound indignant. "Are you calling me a *liar?*"

Frolan steps closer to Lago. "Yeah, are you calling Grak a *liar?* After all the man has done for the tribe? His new hunting strategy will change the way we live! He deserves respect, not accusations!"

Every eye is now focused on Frolan's disturbance. While Grak is happy about that, he's also worried that this "hunting strategy" is getting far too much attention. He sets it aside under "important, but not urgent" for review at a later time.

Lago's emotions melt into a pitiful fear soup. "Liar? I ... no ... I didn't mean that. I just didn't remember. But now something ... yes, yes, I think I remember it now. That's wonderful! I mean ... thank you, Grak!

"And as it so happens, I was just getting herbs for you. I know how you don't like the flavor of olives.

"But I can put that aside. I can go make something to welcome home our hunters. Something to revive your energy?"

Although Grak finds Lago's groveling satisfying, Frolan may be unstoppable at this point. The brute presses even closer. "It's too late for you. No one wants your cooking anymore. Grak is going to replace you. Immediately. You're just fortunate he was kind enough to agree."

This new information doesn't sit well with Lago. In fact, it even appears to be inciting something akin to anger in the man. "But I like cooking, and I do a good job, and ..." Fear slips back in. "And what else would I do? I don't know any other skill."

"I suggested you might join us on our hunts instead." Jafra must have followed them.

Always sticking her nose where it doesn't belong, that one.

Frolan is outraged with her suggestion. "No! That's not an option. Our kills are heavy enough as it is; we don't need to drag you around too. I don't care what you do, but it won't be hunting."

Jafra persists. "Well, then maybe you could do something else for the tribe. Surely you must have other abilities."

Grak finds her angle murky and suspicious. He opts to let it develop for the moment, but prepares to act should she try something.

Lago, however, is unwilling to let it go any further. He's growing more indignant by the moment. "No, I can't do anything else! And why should I? I haven't done anything wrong! I forgot something Grak told me. That's it!"

Several in the crowd voice quiet backing of the cook. Cordo—Grak *was* indifferent toward him—speaks up from their ranks. "Friends, this may have gotten out of hand. Let's talk about it further. Lago's done a fine job so far. Perhaps we should calm down for a mome—"

"Calm down?" Frolan's quick response pleases Grak. "I'm perfectly calm! And no! I refuse to discuss this any further! Lago hardly lifts a finger around here. The rest of us toil to provide for one another, and he complains at having to cook meat! Says he'd rather do something simpler!"

The tribe rumbles in disdain. Lago's mouth gapes at the accusation. His eyes are full of fear and disbelief.

Frolan rides the momentum. "So why should we allow a man who speaks openly of hating the tribe prepare the very food we need to survive?"

Several in the crowd grow more vocal in their disgust toward Lago. Comments of "fat pig" and something unidentifiable having to do with grease are among the loudest.

This prompts Jafra to attempt a rescue. "Wait a moment. We haven't even given Lago a chance to say anything in his defense. I'm sure we've blown this out of proportion."

All eyes turn to the sweaty cook. He gulps. "I ... well ... no ... I ..."

Grak can't risk losing support. He decides a killing shot is needed.

"You also made me ill."

The crowd falls silent. Confusion dances on every face.

Grak rolls his eyes. "You put something in my food last night to make me ill."

Sudden gasps show understanding. Even Jafra is taken aback. Murmurs of anger grow louder and voices shout several forms of "How could you?" Grak has never seen the tribe this upset.

Frolan takes over. "I thought you looked ill on our hunt."

His eyes grow more intense with each breath. He turns to Lago. "Grak is a hero. And a better friend to the tribe than you've ever been. And you? You're too lazy to do *anything*, so you chose *cooking*! And now you're even too lazy for *that*!

"What good are you to us? If you hate the tribe so much, why don't you just leave? I think we'd *all* be happier."

A hopeful agreement erupts from the crowd, solidifying Frolan's idea. "So go on! Get out of here! We don't need you. And we don't want you anymore either."

He pushes Lago toward the path. The man pauses in bewilderment. Full of sorrow, he looks around at his people, tears welling. Frolan shoves him again, much harder this time. The cook yields and stumbles toward camp.

The tribe follows with shouts of encouragement as Frolan hustles the man along. Lago attempts to plead with them, but his words bumble out onto deaf ears. Grak can't help but feel a shred of guilt.

And yet, this is what Lago forced me to. He struck first. Besides, he was never there for the tribe. Only for himself.

And I'm really not responsible. The others obviously hated him more than I ever did. That's so true. Look at all the anger they were holding just below the surface.

Very well then. Chin up, Grak. This is what the tribe wants.

They arrive at Lago's tent. The man's sobbing prevents any further pleas as he packs his few effects into a sack: a tattered, old, sad thing, much like himself.

The crowd grows quieter. They're softening from the display. Several sniffles are audible.

Grak feels a twinge of pity too. He reconsiders his rationalization from a moment ago. After all, this isn't what he was aiming for.

And yet, to back out now might rob me of my purpose. Perhaps if I could somehow keep their anger while convincing them to let Lago stay.

Grak strains for a way to do that. Nothing comes. Except a lump in his throat. He attempts to clear it. That only causes a short burst of coughs.

Grak composes himself and glances around. Every eye is watching him, and they're all dry now. The tribe turns back to stare at Lago. They're angry again, reminded of Grak's illness at the man's hands. Angry at their trusted cook and his act of malice.

But Lago can give them nothing else. Even his tears have run out. He shoulders his belongings along with their hatred, then looks around. With a heavy heart, he gives each of his people a silent and pitiful farewell.

When the cook reaches Grak, he pauses. This look is something new, something Grak hasn't seen before. There's a touch of anger in the man's brown eyes. But his graying eyebrows betray a sadness too. And not a simple one, but deep and complex. The tiny twitches in his facial muscles also tell of hurt. No, more than that. Betrayal. And it's all aimed at Grak.

Definitely not the goal I set out with ... But the goal is achieved, none-theless ... A good day ... I suppose.

Lago looks to Frolan with a final, speechless request.

The brute returns only a cold resolve. "Go," he says.

The tribe watches in silence as Lago climbs the path leading over the hill and down to the shore beyond. His back is slumped and his step is shaky. As he reaches the top, he stops for a last, remorseful look at his former people. Then, Lago turns and descends.

In this somber moment, a realization hits Grak. Well, three to be exact. Realization of the need to be more precise in his schemes. Realization that the tribe takes some prodding, but quickly becomes unstoppable. And realization that he's responsible for the tribe's meals now, but lied about ever having cooked before. This last one consumes his thoughts as he walks to his tent.

How does one turn an animal into food?

3 - And Apparently Cooking

G rak never knew he hated cooking until yesterday when he prepared a meal for the first time. His decision was not made in
haste, however. Numerous elements contributed to the sentiment.

What he found most annoying was that the choice to cook was not
his to make. At least, not in the *strictest* sense of the word "choice." Or
rather, not according to *Grak's* definition of it. He felt the responsibility
was forced on him. "No other option" was his analysis of the matter.

And yet, despite this abuse, he approached the duty with a willing
mind. After all, the process seemed simple enough at first glance:

1 - Put food things in the pot
2 - Start a fire
3 - Serve

But step one proved more challenging than it let on. Of course, as
is usually the case in situations of this sort, the first two legs weren't
the problem. They folded easily enough into the pot. The last two,
however, *those* were the *real* challenge.

*I wonder how Lago always did it. Ah, of course! The deer last night must
have been larger than usual.*

*Perhaps we just need a bigger pot, then. Yes, that's it. Lago must have
been using inferior tools. Would be just like him, wouldn't it?*

*Though, I don't know why the fool couldn't even mention it to me on his
way out. Probably wanted me to have a difficult time. Just so he can rub it
in if we ever meet again. 'Not so easy, after all, is it, Grak? Not so fun, is it?'*

No. Far from it. In fact, around the time he began cutting into the ears, Grak realized this job wasn't for him. More than that, he decided the task belonged on his list of hates.

Grak is fairly certain this is the fastest anything has ever joined the list. Fairly certain, though not absolutely. He's beginning to have trouble keeping track of all that the list holds. In fact, he often finds himself remembering only too late that he hates something.

Perhaps I could write it down. Would take a great deal of stone, though. Hmm, yes. Too heavy during a move.

Also, it'd be difficult to hide. Someone might see their name on it, and of course, they'd get offended. Then everyone would coddle the sensitive fool while ostracizing me. No, that won't do.

I suppose I could just write down the tasks I hate. After all, the people are easier to remember. Still, the weight of it. No, wouldn't do.

Grak uncrosses his legs and stretches them. The new thinking posture is good, but not great. It tends to cause a stiffness in his legs and a tingling numbness in his feet. Also, he only has two options for his back: hunched or straight. Either way, soreness always sets in before long.

What other options are available? Of course!

The answer is right in front of him. Grak steadies his chair, then timidly sits on it. He manages to keep from toppling over this time, and soon gets the wobbling under control.

That's a good deal better. Now I can think in comfort. Though what to do with my arms?

Grak tries hanging them at his sides, but that feels awkward. It also throws off his balance, which takes longer to regain than previously. He tries folding his hands on his lap.

I suppose that'll do for now. Remember this posture, Grak. Remember this posture. Remember this posture.

The memory trick undermines his balance again, but Grak recovers with ease. He congratulates himself for making such an improvement.

And a better posture found at the same time. Excellent progress so far.

Now, where was I? Oh yes. What to do about this whole cooking ordeal?

Despite sincere effort, Grak is at a loss for ideas on that subject. But this comes as no surprise. He *often* finds his creativity stifled when dealing with disagreeable circumstances. And "*the* meal," as it's now being called, clearly falls into that category.

Though I don't see why everyone's making such a fuss over it. Certainly wasn't as repulsive as Lago's cooking.

His stomach turns in apparent disagreement. Grak tries to ignore the feeling. He isn't ready to admit that the meal might be the cause of his current nausea.

I imagine Lago's poisoning the other night is still having an effect. That bears the real blame for my stomach's condition.

While far-fetched, this theory does bear a resemblance to reason. After all, Grak has yet to experience any of the more serious symptoms currently plaguing everyone else. Of course, he ate very little in comparison, but he considers that point moot.

I'm sure I ate enough to become ill from it. If the food caused all this, I mean. Which it didn't.

By "ate enough," Grak means three bites. At that point, the sound of vomiting had grown so loud that his appetite abandoned him. Then he had no choice but to pour his bowl back into the pot and retire to his tent.

Of course, it never occurred to him that he might hear more of the matter. Indeed, Grak expected a peaceful night. And he likely would have achieved as much, if not for the occasional trips to relieve himself. But alas, each outing revealed worsening conditions and greater animosity coming his way.

Still, Grak didn't let that get him down. He just learned to use the cover of darkness, blending into shadows or getting lost among those who still had use of their legs.

And it worked. For a time. But by his last excursion of the night, Grak was the only one not on the ground, writhing or unconscious. Thus, attention became unavoidable.

That's when those still able to speak began shouting to him from their sprawled positions. But only a few retained civility in their communications. The rest were just screaming crass accusations.

Of all things! At me! As if I bore some responsibility in the matter!

Nonetheless, Grak was in a forgiving mood, and opted not to scold them for their boorishness. Instead, he thought it better to mimic them in hopes of throwing off suspicion. To his disappointment, this proved unsuccessful. Still, at least it provided momentary freedom from their bitter allegations.

Awful how people become so spiteful in such a hurry. Completely unfair too. After all, I'm new to this whole cooking thing.

Grak shakes off this thought. It makes him feel like he's accepting blame, and it's become clear that even a hint of admission would invite trouble. After all, those who have regained consciousness are mad enough already. It's doubtful they would exercise restraint if he confessed.

Especially given some of the threats he's received. Cordo's, for example, sounded particularly gruesome. It involved a glowing hot blade and areas of the body that would be considerably more useful if left undisturbed.

But, he might have just been in the dementia stage of his illness. Yes, probably didn't even mean it. Though his wording choice was exceptionally robust. And it certainly seemed lucid. And yet, it was just before he entered the fever-screams stage. Yes, I'm sure I'm worrying for nothing.

The other threats, however, came from individuals in clear control of their minds. They included acts of a more specific and achievable nature, which Grak found to be an even greater cause for concern. While none were *as* terrifying as Cordo's pledge, their potential for realization made up for it.

But, truth be told, Grak would prefer not to experience *any* retaliation if he can help it. Though this again brings him back to the pressing issue.

What to do about this whole cooking ordeal? And why can't I think of any ideas? Perhaps my approach is too vague. Yes, that's it. So, what does the ordeal consist of?

Surely, the immediate danger to my body is an important part. Also, I'd like to be free from having to cook again—very important, to be sure. And I'd like to eat well again ... or uh ... rather, eat better than my food or Lago's bile.

Of course, these points would all be resolved if I could trade duties with someone. Someone who possesses greater skill, that is.

But I can't just stop cooking. Might be seen as an admission of guilt. And I'd be deemed lethargic on top of it. No, can't do that. I'd wind up in the same position as Lago. And some might even realize that I had a small hand in his banishment.

So how to do it without seeming lazy? And without getting blamed for the meal?

Something tickles the inside of his cheek. Grak maneuvers his tongue into action, but the rogue object is lodged in his teeth. He reaches two fingers in and, with minor effort, pulls out a clump of matted fur and skin.

Hmm, thought I had gotten it all.

Grak has learned not to swallow these. Instead, he tosses it out the tent flap. After allowing a moment for the chair's wobbling to subside, he summarizes his analysis of the problem.

Cooking ordeal. Avoid blame. Get new cook. One that makes good food. And don't end up like Lago in the process. Of course! The fat man is the solution!

Grak stands and pulls a splinter from the back of his knee. Under normal circumstances, this might cause further introspection, but not now. He's too giddy about his idea.

I worked alone. The events are mine to reshape.

He grabs a tunic and searches for his trousers.

So how to get the word out?

Grak rushes along the empty path, trying in vain to contain his excitement. He can't remember the last time he felt this much enthusiasm for a plan, but there's no doubt it's deserved.

In every aspect. Pure brilliance.

So ingenious, in fact, that nothing seems capable of deterring his zeal right now. Even the otherwise chilling absence of people in normal daily routines. Even the odor of bodily fluids mingled with a delicate undertone of decaying flesh that now pervades the camp. Even the death tents. Well, almost.

As he approaches *that* area, Grak once again feels the tug of intrigue. Slowing his pace, he stares in guilty curiosity at the invalids moaning in the dirt.

Needless to say, Grak considers "death tents" a hasty and unnecessary term. First of all, only one was ever completed, as those working to erect them fell ill while doing so. Secondly, and more importantly, no one has actually *died* from the meal yet. In fact, quite a few of them can still move their heads a little.

Grak shudders at the sight: their dull, milky gray eyes following his every move. Truth be told, they're probably just drawn to any shape that distorts what little light they can still see. Nonetheless, he's certain they recognize him.

Be strong, Grak. They're more afraid of you, then yo—

Grak stops. His heart trembles. He didn't expect to see her here. Sure, if he had taken time to think about it … well, why *wouldn't* she be? And yet, her appearance seems worse than most.

Grak hesitates, debating whether to approach. In the end, sympathy wins out, and he walks over to the woman.

Groka's head turns slightly. Weakly. Pitifully. As if to listen for movement in the immediate area. Her neck strains at the effort, even with such a small task. It's thinner now, less stately: almost stringy. Her jaw trembles as she forces a quiet gurgle through her crusted lips. For the briefest of moments, Grak feels remorse.

No, Grak! It's not your fault. Besides, she'll recover. Frolan almost has.

Grak resists the temptation to touch her cheek. He doesn't want to disturb her rest. Also, he doesn't want to risk catching her ailment. Besides, he has to be about his task.

She'll recover. Without a doubt. Not your fault.

At that, Grak straightens his back, levels his gaze, and resumes his purpose. But the sight of Groka so near to death is now seared in his mind. Even walking does little to scrub it out. Fortunately, he doesn't have far to go. Distraction soon consumes his thoughts as he rounds a corner and arrives at Frolan's tent.

Oh good, the flap's open. I imagine that's best in this situation. The smell was getting severe.

Probably means he's doing better too. Hmm, though it could just as easily mean he's doing worse. Hard to tell. He might have opened it to get some air before he died. Yes, quite possible, now that I think about it. Would be unfortunate, if that's the case.

It's true. Grak finds his stomach averse to dead bodies. More than most, in fact, though he's never determined the source of this unease. Also, custom would name him responsible to haul the corpse away for burning, and that would hamper his plans for the day.

And yet, without Frolan's help, his strategy has little chance for success. Grak has no choice in the matter. He takes a moment to prepare his eyes for the sight, breathes deep, then pokes his head in. Relief.

"You're looking much better, friend." Grak isn't even stretching the truth here: the yellow tinge in Frolan's skin is almost gone. "How do you feel?"

"Oh, I feel much better. Thank you. The tooth is still a little sore, but even that seems to be improving." Frolan pulls back his lip to provide a better view.

Grak tries to hide a wince. "Yes, you can hardly notice the crack. And the bleeding has slowed as well."

Frolan smiles something gruesome. "And I'm thankful for that, let me tell you!"

"I can imagine." Grak is just relieved the man is in good spirits.

He's taken the meal rather well when you think about it.

That's true. Frolan was one of the first to grow ill, and even had one of the worst cases of the illness. Yet he never complained about Grak or even associated him with the malady. And Grak reasons that this positive thinking is why the man's condition has improved so much already.

Of course, Frolan doesn't have much of a choice when it comes to blame. If anyone considers Grak responsible for the tribe's current woes, then they have to include Frolan for his part in the matter.

After all, he was the one who got rid of Lago. In a way, I even tried to stop it.

But all this talk of blame is upsetting for Grak. Besides, he came here for a reason. "Well, I'm glad you're feeling so well, Frolan. For your sake, of course, but also because I have troubling news that I had to share with someone."

Frolan's concern runs deep. "Tell me, Grak. What is it? Have you fallen ill too? I thought you were looking unwell this morning."

Grak is taken aback by that statement. He hasn't passed any puddles today, but can't imagine he looks so bad as to warrant a comment like that. Especially from one in such a horrendous state. He decides to check at the first available opportunity.

Come to think of it, I've noticed metal holds a reflection quite well. Perhaps I could find something more permanent than a puddle.

Grak hides the hurt and stores this reflection idea for another time. "No. Nothing like that. But I believe I may know the cause of this illness. Do you remember how Lago put something in my food several nights ago? To poison me?"

"Yes ..." Frolan seems to be jumping ahead.

"Well, last night, while I was preparing the dish, I had to leave to grab some ..." Grak hadn't thought of this aspect. He scrambles to fill the void.

What would you put in food? Tree bark? No, that doesn't sound right. Rocks? No, that was ill-conceived. Especially the pebbles. Wait, what was Lago looking for?

"Herbs!" Although Grak's excitement is inexplicable, Frolan fails to notice. Still, Grak brings it down a notch. "When I returned, Lago was there."

Frolan grips his bed roll. Full understanding shows in his eyes. Still, he's choosing restraint at the moment.

Grak hesitates at the man's reaction, but soon continues. "I thought he was just hungry and looking for something to eat. And I felt pity for the old man. So I sent him off with a few days' rations.

"And I thought nothing more of it until today—when I regained my strength after the illness, that is. In hindsight, it's so clear. He must have put something in the food while I was away."

Frolan's anger boils over. "That monster! That—" He grits his teeth in a strained effort to retain some self-control. "He was trying to kill us all!

"We were right to expel him. But we should have done more. We need to gather a hunting party. To go after that vile beast. To hunt him down like the animal he is!"

That was a far stronger reaction than Grak had planned for. And completely unexpected too. Though, it really shouldn't have been. Grak isn't sure how he failed to realize the obvious response to news like this.

Must be the nausea. No matter. Think Grak, think. How to redirect this new anger?

It's not that he cares for the former cook. Not at all. But that doesn't mean he wants the man to come to more harm. Grak does have a heart, after all.

Despite what some people might think. And what do they know?

Grak's growing anger over these thoughts makes its way to his face. This incites a new layer of rage in Frolan, and the brute attempts to stand. No, too much, too soon. He swoons.

Good! That should give me some time to shift focus away from Lago.

Grak dresses his expression with concern. "You're in no shape to do anything, Frolan. Just get better. And wait. Lago will still be out there when you're healthy again. Then we can decide what to do."

Frolan settles down a little. He takes a deep breath. "You're right, Grak. You're always right. We're fortunate to have your wisdom in the tribe."

Grak tries but can't restrain a smile. "Well … I mean … true …" He remembers to feign humility. "I suppose. But I'm really just like any of you. I'm not anything more elevated, or a better person or something."

Frolan mulls that over, then shrugs. "You're right. I suppose I got carried away."

That's not desirable either. Grak thinks quickly. "But I imagine you're right in a way, aren't you? I should learn to trust your gut feelings."

Flattery takes hold, and Frolan smiles. "Yes, I suppose I *was* right. You're a hero, Grak. I'm glad we have you."

That's much better. It also presents a fantastic opening for the next phase of Grak's plan. "Well, since I've recovered more than most, I feel the need to gather the healthy and coordinate our efforts. I'll be busy doing that, so I can't cook anymore. Which is rather unfortunate, because I was going to make some incredible meals."

Frolan perks up. "Oh? Like what?"

Grak sees clear value in learning to stay on topic while scheming. "Well, that's beside the point. But since I'll be so busy with caring for the tribe, I thought I might put someone else on cooking. Trying to do both would grow taxing. Then I'd be no good in either capacity.

"Anyway, I could use your help to spread the word. People seem to notice you. They listen to your opinions." Grak is careful not to mention how the man's imposing stature might bear responsibility there.

Frolan's look of confusion contradicts his nod. "Makes sense. But, wait. A moment ago you told me to stay put."

"Well, I meant you shouldn't go off *hunting* right now. But you seem fine enough to relay information to others. That shouldn't be too tiring.

"And it shouldn't take you long, either. We have, what, some two hundred people? Around one hundred or so are at the death tents, so that's a breeze. And the rest are pretty stationary at the moment."

Frolan shrugs. "Well, I suppose. If you think I'm well enough, then I trust you. You've got a good head on your shoulders, friend.

"Is anyone else— Wait. Death tents?"

Grak is running out of options, and he's beginning to worry. Doran wasn't home or at any of the spots he tends to frequent in camp. He wasn't even at "the recovery area," as Grak is attempting to rename it.

If he isn't down at the shore, then … well, then I have no idea where he might be. Did he wander into the forest during his dementia stage? Did he go out to sea, searching for his cra—

Grak is snapped away from thought by a glimpse of someone moving about behind the row of shelters to his left. He squints. Nothing's there.

Did they hide? Who was it?

The figure was too short to be Frolan, but no one else has been able to move their legs yet. One possibility pops to mind.

Might it be Lago? Returning for revenge?

Grak shudders at the thought. He scrambles for a plan. "Who's there? Show yourself!"

Hmm, not a very robust idea. Certainly less so than many of my others. Is it possible that I've used up my planning abilities for the day?

The flap on one of the smaller tents moves a bit, as though bumped by someone lacking proper hiding skills. Grak readies himself to run should the cook's bald head appear. But no need. Relief floods in as a woman steps out.

"Jafra? What are you doing up? I mean ... you're feeling better? That's ... nice." Though he can think of others more deserving of good health.

"Hello, Grak. Yes, I was so tired after the hunt that I went to sleep without eating. And now I'm glad I did. Not only was the extra rest helpful, but I also avoided this sickness."

Grak analyzes if that was meant as a personal attack.

Hmm, unclear. Still, best to assume as much when dealing with Jafra.

He attempts to refute it by shaming her with altruism. "Well, I'm not sure that's important right now, *Jafra*. I think we should concern ourselves with getting the tribe healthy again." No sense in wasting a good opening, though. "And since I was the first to recover, I've been trying to organize everyone's care."

Jafra nods enthusiastically. "Yes, Frolan told me." She switches abruptly to sorrow. "And he told me about Lago too. It saddens me to hear the old man was behind this. I wonder if we pushed him to it. If we were too harsh in forcing him to leave." She pauses to consider that for a moment.

Or perhaps she's pausing for effect. Yes, much more likely. Definitely a veiled accusation, now that I think about it.

Grak considers his options. After careful deliberation, he decides against saying anything just yet. If she's allowed to ramble on without hindrance, she might reveal her ploy.

Jafra shrugs. "Well, I suppose there isn't much we can do about it now." It appears she's sensed his trap somehow. "And we have more important matters to deal with.

"I've been checking in on people the best I can. And I sent Frolan back to rest. He wasn't looking steady on his feet. But good thing I bumped into you, since you're organizing everything. What can I do to help?"

Grak hadn't considered the possibility that coordination might require making decisions. He struggles to come up with a sensible task that reflects competence.

Should also be something tiring. And it should require a great deal of her time. To keep her out of my hair for as long as possible.

"Death tents!" Far too much excitement, given the context. Also, mistakenly called. "I mean, the recovery area. I've changed the name to inspire hope."

"Of course. Sounds wise. I could finish setting them up and get those poor people out of the dirt. Good thinking, Grak. Thanks so much for stepping in to be there for the tribe. I'm glad we have *you* around."

Grak is shocked by that comment. "W ... well ... yes ..." is all he can muster in reply.

Sounded sincere, but it might just be an attempt to deceive me. She's such a devious one.

Grak tries to fill the silence lest she wrest control of the conversation from him. But alas, no words come.

Worse still, Jafra takes the opportunity. "Well, I'd best be about it then. Thanks again, Grak." She pecks a quick kiss on his cheek and strolls away.

Wh ...

Grak is even more stunned than before. It happened too fast to raise protest.

What, in all the land, could she be up to?

Fearing the further loss of time, Grak resumes his mission, pondering the matter as he climbs the hill. Strangely enough, he's finding himself mildly impressed by her schemes. But also frightened. Clearly, this falls under both "urgent" and "imperative."

Does she know the meal was my fault? Er ... rather ... Does she think the meal was my fault? Because it wasn't. No matter what she thinks. Still, can't take any chances. Not with her. Best to handle this immediately. Well, once I find Doran and get his backing, that is.

Grak reaches the summit and surveys the view below. Waves gently lick the sand while several dunes and a few pieces of driftwood laze about on the otherwise empty shore. And a shrub of some sort, just next to one of the larger dunes. He hadn't noticed the thing at first, but squinting separates it from surrounding shapes.

Wait a moment, the shrub's moving. Yes, clearly human.

Comfort washes over him as he realizes that it must be Doran. Well, most likely. Despite the person's proximity, they still appear blurry. Grak trots down for verification, hopeful that one weight might lift from his burdened shoulders.

As he draws closer, the color of the hair poking out from behind the dune becomes distinguishable. Grak's spirits rise. It's the same shade of light brown as his friend's.

"Doran?"

"Yes? Here I am. Is that you, Grak?" Doran's goofy smile is a pleasing sight as it pops into view.

"Yes, it's me. I'm glad I finally found you. I must have searched every tent in camp."

"Oh, sorry to worry you, friend. I found the waves so peaceful … and the air so refreshing. I felt compelled to linger last night. I must have fallen asleep by accident. I even failed to eat. Come to think of it, I'm *famished*. I don't suppose there's anything left from yesterday's serving?"

"So that's why I've decided to lay aside my passion. The camp needs my organizational ability right now more than it needs my food."

While Grak is annoyed at having to fill the man in, he's glad for the opportunity to adjust the story more to his liking. He considers the new telling "positive overall," though he wonders if he went too far with some of the alterations.

Doran slowly shakes his head. "Oh my. This sounds dire. And I just slept here! How could I? When my people needed me.

"Well, Grak, I'm glad we have a person as sensible as you to … well

… to *lead* us, I suppose. Like the lead rider while we travel, but instead, you'll lead us while everyone recovers. If there's anyone I'd choose to lead us through this ordeal, it's you, friend."

Grak likes the sound of this word. He hadn't thought of it that way previously.

But I guess it's true. Everyone will look to me. And everyone will follow me. Very much like the lead rider while we travel.

He allows himself a slight smile and a moment to savor the feeling.

But Doran is unaware of Grak's morsel. He's already on his feet, brushing the sand off the rear of his trousers. "So who will cook in your stead?"

Grak stands too, still relishing the feeling in secret. "I'm not sure. Do *you* know how?"

Doran sets a quick pace for their return trek. "I've never tried, but I'm willing. Is it difficult?"

Grak struggles to match his friend's speed. "More than you'd imagine," he sighs. "Better to find someone with experience, if we can."

Doran nods. "Well, from the sound of things, Frolan isn't up to it yet. Even if he knows how, he shouldn't be on his feet at the moment. It was good of you to insist he rest. I imagine more sleep will do him some good."

Grak reviews that alteration. He estimates it's "unlikely" to come back and bite him. "True. Very true. So that leaves Jafra. Unless someone else is on their feet by now." He ponders the woman. "You know, she might be a decent choice."

In all honesty, Grak has no idea if she even possesses the skill. He just hates the task and the woman with roughly equal disdain. Thus, he assumes they would pair well together.

Doran tosses the proposal around in his mind. "Well, I would agree with you under normal circumstances, but it sounds like she's not at her best today. Her current callousness might prove dangerous if applied to cooking. With the tribe in such a dire state already, she might make matters worse."

That alteration may have gone a little too far. Grak adjusts it to be more in line with the original. "Well, I may have been too hard on her.

What I meant was that she's being somewhat rough in her care of the ill."

That doesn't appear to have helped. Doran is still apprehensive. "Sounds like a great deal more than being 'a little rough.' I can't even imagine why someone would yell at an unconscious person."

Way too far with that one. Grak decides it's best to be vaguer when lacking a direct purpose in the future. "It was probably the strain of caring for so many in such poor health. I think cooking will relieve much of that pressure."

Doran shrugs his acceptance. "Well, I suppose it's worth a try. I trust your opinion of her. And she *is* good with an ax. In case Lago returns."

Grak allows himself a moment to bask in the pleasure this idea provides. It accomplishes all his original goals and might also serve to curb Jafra's meddling.

At least for a time. So, how to categorize her now? 'Dangerous, but not timely.' Yes, that'll do.

"Well then. As the 'lead,' I suppose I'll need to let her know." Grak is enjoying that word more with each use. He rolls it over in his head as they round the hilltop.

The 'lead.' Lead of the entire tribe at that.

He pauses to view the camp below: a sea of dull, brown leather with hardened, grooved mud intersecting in haphazard curves. The only movement is coming from the person raising a tent pole at the recovery area. Grak can't remember the last time it was this peaceful.

I just might like this. I've never been very good at much else, so maybe leading the tribe is more my thing.

4 - And Lazy People

Grak's hatred of lazy people extends beyond mere frustration. And for good reason, he estimates. After all, they drain the tribe of energy and resources without giving anything in return.

Thus, he feels this is grounds for a purer sort of anger. The kind that can't easily be refuted and shouldn't even be considered "anger" in the traditional sense.

As such, Grak describes his aversion toward lazy people as "indignation." Though when he's feeling especially informative, he'll usually expound on that thought. The words "wisdom" and "tough love" often make an appearance at such times.

And this sheds a bit of light on why he's so indignant at the moment. After all, a drastic number of his people are currently falling into the category of "lazy." As if that weren't bad enough, Grak is also facing tremendous difficulty in his efforts to motivate them.

A difficulty named Jafra. She's always defending these types. And in such a defiant manner too! Seems intent on making me look irrational and angry.

Her stint thus far as cook has left Grak with mixed emotions. His initial reaction was one of pleasant surprise when he discovered she was handy with a cooking pot. Clearly, she must have learned a thing or two growing up around the old man.

She also has what he deems "an acceptable approach toward olives." She holds to Lago's view on needing the food, but has relented to Grak's request that she serve them on the side. It's not an ideal resolution, but neither is it unbearable.

In fact, Grak would deign to classify her tenure as "generally positive" if it weren't for one major annoyance. She seems to be finding a way to spread more of her opinions than ever before.

The woman has taken to serving each meal and talking to every person in the process. She claims it's a matter of kindness—with many being too weak to serve themselves—but Grak knows her nature too well.

Devious to the core. Forcing people to hear her mind under the guise of aid. Probably trying to take my place as leader. Shrewd. And devious, of course.

In fact, if not for its devious attributes, the plan's shrewdness would inspire considerable envy in Grak. As it is, he's finding it difficult to maintain a proper amount of spite in the face of such jealousy.

A shame I never came up with that idea when I was cook. But understandable. I had my hands full with Lago's treachery, after all. I'm sure I would have gotten around to it. Wish I had, though. Then I wouldn't be stuck in my current predicament.

Although, when telling Doran of this problem, Grak is quick to point out that he doesn't *dislike* others' opinions. On the contrary, he has no problem with opinions unless they're wrong like hers always are. And one viewpoint in particular—her stubborn stance on the issue of the lazy—is what has him so incensed these days.

She's even worse than they are. They might be lazy, but she's fighting my efforts to toughen them up. To make them useful. She's enabling them. That's what it all comes down to. I don't see why others can't understand.

Even Frolan hasn't been much of a help on that point. He went so far as to side with Jafra initially. Of course, this caused a considerable increase in Grak's indignation.

He, of all people, should know better. He rested less than two days before getting back on his feet. So why should others require so much care a full seven days later?

Of course, in the end, Grak found it in himself to forgive the man. After all, it only took the remainder of that day to convince the brute of his point of view. And once the issue was cleared up, Grak admitted he had been finding it difficult to "stay mad at such a simple fellow."

He's just an ignorant one. Requires careful explanation, that's all. Not a scheming bone in his body.

Although, while Frolan did end up agreeing, he still believed it unnecessary to push people to work before they could walk. Considering this an adequate compromise, Grak relented on that point.

Still, he was wary of the possibility that the man might reverse his judgment again on the greater issue. Thus, when Frolan renewed his request for leave to hunt Lago, Grak took action. He decided to strike two birds with a single stone by asking Frolan to lead a team hunting for *deer* instead.

So far, the task has kept the brute too busy and tired to track the old man. Especially with the tribe's herd moving farther south, the team has had to stay out too long for any real rest between trips. The last expedition took two full days, and this one is already pushing late into the third.

Although, truth be told, this also has Grak concerned. If the hunters stay out any longer, the tribe risks what some would call "starvation." Even with Cordo's team scrounging for rabbits in the forest each day, many still think it won't be enough.

But Grak has never liked pessimists. Especially when they hinder his plans. Thus, as a matter of principle, he's refusing to make the issue a priority. And yet, he knows deep down that the herd is crucial. So he can't ignore the concern indefinitely.

I may need to deal with it before long. But the lazy people are a greater priority right now. And so is Jafra's hold over the camp.

Fortunately, all this leading has been keeping his mind sharp for schemes. By Grak's estimation, the only thing required to break Jafra's hold is to spend time talking to people. After all, they were swayed by her words in the first place.

A little conversation, then I can go back to ignoring them. Not bad when you consider the greater good achieved. Well, a little bad, I suppose. But a necessary sacrifice for the benefit of all. And once I loosen her grip, I can focus on the lethargy issue.

However, much to his dismay, Grak has noticed himself getting irritated with those he's trying to persuade. Of course, he's unapologetic about it, as he feels they're obviously *deserving* of irritation.

The fools can't even follow my lead properly. Wouldn't surprise me if they were born without the ability. Would explain why they mindlessly repeat Jafra's views all the time.

And yet, no matter how irritating they are, Grak needs them. All of them. Or as many as he can get. And his overt displays of annoyance seem to be pushing them away.

To be expected. I should know my people well enough by now. Sensitive to a fault. Too delicate to lay aside their emotions and deal with the real issues. Still, if I'm to gain their backing, I'll need to forgive them of these defects. But don't worry, Grak. It'll be over so—

"Um … Grak?" Brak's tone conveys worry.

Grak turns his attention toward the interruption. "Yes? Do you need something? Don't be a dawdling oaf, now. Make it quick. I'm very busy these days, you know."

Perhaps this would be a good place to insert some of that forgiveness.

Grak reaches deep for a sample from Doran. "I mean, *please* don't be a dawdling oaf." Good, but missing something. "Friend!"

Brak is both perplexed by the awkward enthusiasm and touched by the show of kindness. "Um, yes … Well, I was just curious if you heard my response."

"What response? What madness are you up to?" Grak catches himself again. "Friend."

Well done, Grak. Much more natural that time.

"Um, well you asked how I was doing. And I was telling you about my cap. How it finally tore beyond use. Then you got this strange, distant look."

"Ah … that." Grak scrambles to salvage this potential supporter. Brak is well-liked in camp, after all. "I … um … sorry?"

This appears sufficient, but Grak moves to solidify. "Forgive me. All this leading has my mind wandering at times. With so many unwil … unable to pull their weight, I've been taking on lots of extra duties for them. So, sleep has been getting pushed aside."

Brak smiles something comforting. "Oh, that's perfectly understandable. Loren and I were the same way when Olive was newly born."

Grak congratulates himself for suppressing a look of obvious disdain. For some reason unbeknownst to him, parents enjoy talking about their young. Still more perplexing, they fail to discern when someone would rather not hear about it.

He searches for a relevant response. A memory of something he once overheard from Groka rises to the surface. "Those babies. They do work." Brak's confusion tells Grak the memory may be skewed. "*Are* work ... I mean." Spot on.

Grak is doing surprisingly well here. Still, he feels the need to establish himself more before parting from the man's presence.

What else might I do to win the fool over? Of course!

"Well ... here, why don't you take my hat?"

"Re ... really? That's so kind of you, Grak. But ... you don't need it?"

Grak ignores the man's exaggerated display of surprise. "Well, I'm sure you need it more. I have hair to protect against the sun." He spots an opportunity. "Besides, it's just part of leading the camp through this difficult time. Giving up comforts to help my fellow tribesmen and all."

Brak is speechless. He's on the verge of tears.

The weak and grateful kind if I'm not mistaken. So, how to feel about that? I suppose satisfaction is applicable. And enjoyment too while I'm at it. Well done, Grak. Well done.

But he isn't interested in lingering on that thought. He finds it's best to quit while ahead. "Well, Brak, I must be off. Duties and such. I'll see you around, though." He draws on a distant memory to close the conversation. "Take care, then."

He nods in an awkward fashion and steps to the side, hoping the bald man will be on his way.

And it works. "Thank you, Grak. Thank you," is all Brak manages before he turns and strolls off.

But Grak hadn't thought this far ahead. Now he's just standing in the middle of a path, looking around at nothing in particular. It's far better than talking to anyone, he surmises, but still uncomfortable.

He surveys the nearby tents. No one of any use is about. Loren is there, but Grak doesn't feel right about placing her in the "useful" category. Though he does find himself curiously drawn to the woman's vain efforts to feed her angry child.

Angry and homely, if I'm being honest.

Unfortunately, he lingers too long, and the woman spots him. She waves. Grak returns the gesture, remembering to add a polite smile. But, in the act, he realizes it might be *too much* kindness. He reins it in a bit.

Best not to welcome conversation. I've already won her husband. No need to waste time with her as well.

But this proves unsuccessful. Loren signals him over. With no other choice springing to mind, Grak obliges.

"Hello, Loren. And Olive … uhh … what are we up to?"

"Fifty-three."

"Yes, of course. Good number." Not true. Grak finds it distasteful. Though not so bad as twenty-two.

He glances down at the woman's offspring, more out of nervousness than any other reason. But it only takes a breath for Grak to realize this was a bad idea. The thing is staring blankly at him, which he, of course, finds disquieting.

And more so because of the youth's features. Most children's faces already seem rounded beyond reason, but this one goes too far. Its haphazard manner of squishing all traits into a shapeless mound disturbs him to no end.

As if sensing his trepidation, the child allows a strange, cooing noise to break free from the small hole where a mouth should be. As one might expect, Grak is thrown off by this. Unsure whether aggressive behavior might follow, he shifts his weight to disguise a step back.

With a healthy distance now between them, he turns to its mother. Though, while the woman is less threatening, she's no less distracting. Her ears are larger than average, and Grak always finds himself compelled to stare.

Perhaps because I've yet to make up my mind. How do I feel about them? They do command respect, and that's good. But they're also somewhat awk-

ward. Wouldn't they be a nuisance on a windy day? Ah, the great debate. Perhaps I'll never have an answer. But I certainly can't settle it at the moment. Duty demands I postpone the issue.

Grak blinks, shaking the thought and concentrating again on the conversation at hand. Determined to stay focused this time, he selects a spot on her forehead to keep his gaze fixed. "So, Loren, how are you?"

She lights up at his question. "We're doing well, thank you! Except, Olive won't eat her food. Will you, darling?"

Under normal circumstances, Grak would find this irksome. He thinks it absurd when people speak to children who lack the ability to reply. And when they ask questions that beg a response, he considers it no less than madness.

But that's under normal circumstances. Those feelings pale in the moment. They're surpassed by his revulsion toward the unidentifiable mush in Olive's pale, gray bowl.

And to Grak's surprise, the sight inspires more than just an upset stomach. He's feeling a certain sympathy for the small person. It's a curious sensation, but proper in his eyes.

Still, he'd rather not get used to it. Grak clears his throat and returns to the conversation. "Yes, I often had a distaste for such … food … when I was young. Mixing in berries often did the trick for me."

He recognizes a fine spot for subtle slander. "But that might prove difficult for you, with Jafra keeping a stingy grip on the food. It requires a debate every time *I* ask her for something, and I'm the leader. So you can imagine the difficulty others face."

He shrugs. "Still, it's worth a shot."

Loren's face lifts with enthusiasm, causing her ears to fan out even farther. "Oh, that's so kind! You would do that for me?"

Grak pauses, dumbfounded. He's unsure how his statement carried any sense of commitment. A second review still comes back empty. But what he does spot is another clear opportunity to strengthen the tribe's positive perception of him.

"Sure. I'll see if I can persuade her to share some food with the hungry children."

Good sting on that one, Grak. Understated, yet effective. Nice work.

It's also a perfect end to the conversation. "Well, then. I suppose I'll be off. To check on that, I mean."

Loren's excitement turns into gratitude. Her ears relax accordingly. "Thank you, Grak! And take care!"

"Yes. You also. Take care, I mean." He starts to turn back toward the cook site, but propriety tugs at him, begging for acknowledgment of the child as well. Grak forces a smile. "And you too, Olive Fifty-three."

Another cooing noise escapes its head, further confirming Grak's fears. Decorum or no, his nerves can only take so much of this. With a final nod, he departs, setting a rapid pace toward the center of camp.

Only after covering significant ground is Grak certain that danger has passed. He begins to loosen up a bit, relaxing his shoulders and rubbing his neck. A few paces later and he even feels comfortable taking a moment to reflect on the day's successes.

Well done, Grak. These berries should be a simple enough task. And they should have a significant impact too. Let's see Jafra top this one.

He focuses on the path ahead just in time to sidestep a man lying across it. Grak shakes his head.

Sando again? Now there's a lazy one. One of the laziest, in fact. And Jafra just coddles them. Of all things. You'd thi—

Grak halts and looks around. He's only just recognized the part of camp he's passing through. A little off down the path to his right is Groka's tent.

I could pop in to see how she's doing. Wouldn't take long. Then I could be about my work. In fact, that's part of my work. A large part. I have to take care of the tribe.

Besides, of all the people still claiming illness, hers is the only legitimate case. That alone seems deserving of regular visits. Even if for no other reason than to encourage proper behavior in camp.

Then it's settled. Grak changes directions, his new pace quickened with excitement. Though it proves a bit *too* energetic. He arrives only a moment later, but is forced to pause and catch his breath for twice as long.

Can't have her thinking I rushed over here. Oh look, the flap's open. That's a good sign. She's probably eager for a visit. Well, best not to disappoint her.

After one last pause to calm the flutter in his stomach, Grak pokes his head in. His heart leaps and sinks in the same beat. She's home, but asleep. Though it's an elegant sleep, with her eyelids flickering to the tranquil rhythm of her dreams.

So peaceful. So beautiful.

The aroma of her characteristic cinnamon tea wafts by. That scent takes him back. It always does. And it comforts him. Even beyond words. Though it threatens to also dredge up emotions Grak would prefer stay buried.

In one of his earliest, most bittersweet memories, his mother made him this drink. It was a rainy day when nothing was going quite his way. But she knew what would help. She always knew.

Nestling his head securely in the nape of her neck, he sipped at the hot beverage, and his problems melted away. The fragrance soothed. The steam calmed. The heat inspired. And everything looked a little brighter.

Later, when Grak was a few snows older, she passed the process on to him and his friends. But he could never get the skill to stick: a point he's always regretted. Though he considers it an even greater tragedy that Groka is the only one he knows of who still brews the tea.

And while he's willing to accept that this lends to his affection for the woman, he'll only do so with great hesitation. After all, connecting his mother to a woman he holds such feelings for seems wrong in far too many ways.

Grak takes a peaceful breath and smiles at Groka's sleeping form.

The tea must be a sign she's returning to normal health. That's good. I knew she would. Even during the blood coughs. Never had a doubt.

Frolan insists that he looked worried at that point, but Grak denies it.

I was just racking my mind for ways to help her. That's all. It just looked like worry to those lacking discernme—

Groka gently arches her back as she emits a low, guttural moan. Grak tries not to panic.

Or was it more of a whimper? Either way, that can't be a good thing.

He struggles to get control of himself. His heart is pounding in his head, and he's almost certain sweat has begun to pour out of every orifice.

But there's no time for hygiene right now, Grak. What to do? What to do? Think, Grak!

It comes to mind in an instant. He checks her breath. Still there. He feels her chest for a beat. Nearly as strong as his own. Once again, he's at a loss.

What are other ways to check a person's health? Eyes!

Yes, he remembers seeing Loren do that when checking one of the "unfortunates" a few days ago. Slowly, and with great care, he pulls Groka's right eyelid open. The milkiness is almost gone. Other than that, he doesn't know what else to look for.

Didn't Loren have the fellow move his eye up and down?

Grak opens it farther. No, he still can't see the bottom of her eye. He straddles the woman in a kneeling position, jockeying for a better angle. He pushes her head back with one hand and spreads the eyelid with the other. Still not wide enough.

Grak reasons that just the one hand isn't doing it. He positions his knee to hold her head in place, thus freeing up both hands to assist with the inspection. Very wide now. Much better. Still nothing unusual, though.

"Ow! What ... Grak?"

He falls to the side, startled.

Groka cups her eye and glares with the good one. "What, in all the land, were you doing?"

Somehow, Grak is sweating even more now. "I ... I was just making sure you were alright. You made a strange moan, and I ... I thought you might be in pain." If he's being honest, he finds it annoying that she should reprove him for trying to help.

"I ... well, yes." Groka averts her eyes. "I'm fine."

Did she just blush? Perhaps she's charmed by my care for her. Well done, Grak.

Groka takes a deep breath. "I'm sorry I snapped at you." She touches his cheek with tenderness. "I appreciate your concern, Grak."

Well done, indeed. Keep this up, and yo—

"Oh good, you're awake," says an all too familiar voice.

Grak's spine tingles. He was so focused on his friend that he didn't hear the other woman approaching.

Groka's face lights up with a broad smile. "Hello, Jafra! Good to see you!"

Grak musters up a cold and murky tone. "Jafra. What brings *you* here?" In hindsight, improper use of emphasis may have revealed too much.

Fortunately, Groka diverts attention by taking the reply on herself. "Oh, Jafra's been coming by regularly. She's been taking such good care of me."

Grak doesn't appreciate the way Groka is gazing at the other woman, though he can't quite tell what that look is. Admiration, perhaps, though it's hard to say. He has little to use as comparison.

Don't see how anyone could admire such a misshapen brow. Unless they've been tricked. What are you up to, Jafra, you sly fox? Trying to subvert one of my supporters to your side? You would be that treacherous, wouldn't you?

Nonetheless, Grak decides it's best to play naive on this one. "Well, not such good care, I think. You weren't here just now. Groka was moaning and in poor health. And I was the one who helped her."

Hmm, not quite the air of innocence I was going for. A touch more subtlety would be preferable next time.

"Oh, thank you so much, Grak! I have to say, I'm touched at how you keep coming through for everyone." Jafra's sudden gratitude suggests that the sting missed its mark.

Or was that some sort of hidden jape?

Yes, Grak can see it now. The guise was skillful, but not enough to fool him. While disgusted by her chicanery, he's also impressed by it from an artisan's perspective. He commits the nuances of her deceit to memory.

Still, I'd feel more comfortable keeping such duplicity away from Groka. Would be a shame to see her purity corrupted. And yet, how do you get rid of someone who doesn't realize when they're not wanted?

His task for Loren pops to mind as a possible solution. While it would also force Grak to leave the tent, he doesn't mind. Just so long as his foe is no longer around.

Then it's settled. "Jafra, I need some berries. For children. To eat. Go with me to get some …" Grak attempts the facade of kindness he just learned from her. "Please."

Not bad, Grak. Not bad. Though, I imagine practice would yield even greater subtlety.

Jafra tilts her head in a display of concern. "Oh? Which children? I could just bring the berries directly to them. I know you've got a lot to take care of."

Grak smiles. And not just at the unevenness of her brow. He knows her heart too well.

You'd just love to steal their appreciation on this one, wouldn't you? But you can't fool me, devious fox.

"No, that'll be quite alright, Jafra. I should be the one to do it. Don't want anyone getting confused, do we?"

"But, how would any—"

"Could you just do as I ask, please!" Not so subtle that time. Though, truth be told, Grak wasn't giving it much effort. No matter how useful Jafra's trickery might prove, he still believes in letting her know when she gets *too* annoying.

And the chastisement appears to have succeeded. Jafra nods and shrugs. "Alright. Come with me, then." She turns to Groka with a warm smile and a twinkle in her eye. "I'll check back later tonight. You take care of yourself until then."

Groka returns the smile and dons that peculiar gaze of admiration once again. Grak finds himself envious. He decides it would be best if someone gave *him* some admiration.

Grak is willing to admit he's disappointed in Loren's underwhelming response to the berries. It's been nearly a full day now, and she's only thanked him once.

If you could even call that a 'thank you.' More like a dutiful acknowledgment.

So far, Grak has found eight ways the woman's appreciation could have been better conveyed. Of these, he considers the absence of more vivid descriptors to be supreme. In fact, the only summary he's comfortable giving her gratitude is "drab."

"Is it too much to ask for more enthusiasm? Getting those berries required no small amount of work on my part. And it likely saved her child's life. You'd think she'd show a *little* more appreciation. It's not like I expected her to run through camp shouting how wonderful I am." Hoped, yes, but not expected.

Doran takes a moment to find his words. "I don't know what to tell you, friend. I wish there was some way I could help."

That's the opening Grak has been waiting for. "Perhaps you could remind her. And Brak too. That was my *good* hat, you know."

While Brak's display of enthusiasm was sufficient, Grak feels it would only be proper for the man to thank him two or three more times. After all, the replacement pales in comparison. While it's the second best of all thirty-two caps, that still isn't saying much. The point is far more prominent than on the one he gave away, and he's forced to indent it to keep that fact hidden. "My good hat," he calls it, though with furtive eyes and a noticeable lack of emphasis.

Doran nods, deep in thought. "Yes, I suppose I could. Alright, next time I see them, I'll do that. I'll let them know how important it is to you."

That certainly won't fit in with Grak's plan. He can't have others thinking he's the sensitive sort. "Well, it's not really important to *me*. I just feel it's important to the *tribe*. As leader, it concerns me."

While Grak is proud of his subtlety, Doran's confusion reveals the need for supporting details. "If we don't thank each other properly, we'll grow cold. We'll become a divided people. I've already seen it among some. Like Jafra."

Doran's response comes faster this time. "Hmm. You might be right, friend. She's changed. I wouldn't have thought her to refuse food to hungry children. She actually said she *hates* them? Or did she just say she lacks a fondness for them?"

Grak identifies the need to rein that one in. "Uh, well, it was more a feeling I got. Based on her refusal to feed them. Also, her body movements and facial expressions gave it away."

Another good save, Grak. Nice work.

Doran shakes his head in disappointment. "Well, I'm convinced. If Jafra's pleasantness can be lost, then it could happen to anyone. Increased appreciation is a dire necessity. I'll be sure to spread the word. And not just with Brak and Loren."

He places a hand on Grak's shoulder. "I'm glad you're leading us, friend. It's only been a handful of days, and the difference is already clear."

"Eight." Grak remembers to appear indifferent about that. "I mean, I think." But he can't resist a final mumble. "More than a handful, though."

"Me too!" Olive Thirteen looks up from her painting. "I'm glad for your leading. Everyone seems much happier."

Grak glances at her rock. It still looks like a crab. Though he does appreciate the vibrant blue she's added. But aside from that, it's nearly identical to everyone else's attempts. And all are equally perplexing in his eyes.

Still, they're certainly preferable to the songs. Can't imagine I'm alone in that thinki—

"There it is!" shouts an indistinct voice from the crowd.

Grak remains seated while everyone else rushes to the water's edge. They bunch together, jostling for position.

"Where?" another voice yells.

"I can't see it." That sounded like Olive Thirteen.

"Of course you can't. Doran's the only one who can." That might have been Sando, though the man was just faking illness, so it's not likely.

"Nope. Not accurate." Doran's voice is unmistakable. "As I've stated a numb—"

"Is *that* it?" Another ambiguous voice cuts him off.

"No, that's a wave. But I'm telling you, I just saw it! Not a moment ago," shouts the first voice again.

Grak tires of attempting to fix names to the shouts. And he's long been tired of these "sightings." Though he will admit the first one *did* pique his interest. But once he realized how common an occurrence they were, he decided it wasn't worth the fuss.

Be nice if Doran saw that too. Can hardly find a moment alone just to talk like we used to.

If nothing else, this whole thing's just a distraction. And lazy too, now that I think about it. We have far more important matters to deal with. I have enough to keep me busy through the snows and beyond. Could certainly do without this piled on top.

Grak's frustration gets the better of him, and he kicks Olive Thirteen's rock. It tumbles past a pair of boots that must have walked up when he wasn't looking.

Cordo lifts an eyebrow at the show of anger. The mole just under his left eye rises in unison. "I feel the same way. They've lost their minds, I tell you. This … crab or … wave … nonsense. It's not right."

While Grak agrees, he's caught off guard by the sudden appearance. Also, the man's team is something of a distraction. Each appears as though attempting to out-sad the next. And the meager game they're carrying seems to be the cause.

This sight in particular steals Grak's immediate focus. "Is that all you could find?" He hears a touch of fear in his own voice and remembers to mask it with indignation. "That won't feed the camp, you know." He's happy with how that turned out.

Cordo, on the other hand, seems annoyed, yet controlled. Even his mole is stoic. "This is what I've been saying, Grak. The pickings are slim. And getting slimmer every day."

Grak steadies his voice in advance. "Well, if Frolan isn't back soon, then we'll …" In all honesty, he's not really sure what they'll do. "Well, then we'll need to think of something." That's good enough for now.

"Even if Frolan *is* back soon, we're still in trouble, Grak." Cordo's control is showing signs of fraying. His mole quivers slightly. "The herd is moving too far and at too great a speed. This small, local game can't sustain us on these long waits. As pitiful as the hunt was today, I think we might have finally killed off the wildlife around here. We'll need to move the camp."

Grak has been fearing this suggestion. Traveling is high on his list of hates. So far, the illness and recovery have helped him dodge the subject, but now it might be unavoidable.

Worse still, the crowd is beginning to return. Several have already flocked to his conversation, and their silent concern is spreading.

Can't have them worrying. They need to think I can handle this.

Grak puts on his brave voice. "Cordo, you're such a worry ... person." He realizes the need for a properly fitting phrase there. "If Frolan doesn't get back soon, I'll think of something. No need to fear!"

"I have faith in you, Grak," says Doran. "You've led us through *thus* far. I'm sure you'll come up with something until Frolan returns."

"Well, we need one of your ideas right now," interrupts Cordo. "We don't have enough food to go around."

Think, Grak. Think. Probably have to stop feeding some. But who? The lazy would be an obvious choice.

"We have lots of olives. Haven't been using them much lately." Jafra must have sneaked into the crowd while Grak's guard was dropped.

Trying to ruin everything, as usual. Should probably stop feeding her too. Though, I suppose we might need the olives anyway. Given our lack of options. Besides, with my triple servings these days, I can still avoid the vile things without facing hunger.

Grak puts on an air of confidence. "I was just thinking that, Jafra. And was about to suggest it. Please, try not to interrupt."

He turns to the crowd. "So as you can see, I already have a solution. And we'll be fine for the time being. As I said, no need to fear."

Grak checks his shadow. It's around half past midday. "But to put your minds at even greater ease, I'll offer this. If Frolan isn't here by sundown, I'll think of a solution for the longer term."

Maybe I could send out more teams. Could bring back a greater haul that way. And they'd have to find their own food while gone. That would relieve demand on supplies here. Should leave enough to eat for those of us who stay back.

"If that's the case, we may just need to move anyway," says Cordo. "And hope to meet Frolan's team on the road."

"Yes. That's my idea. Absolutely. So you can all see that I've thought of everything. Once again, no need to fear."

Grak likes that phrase. He commits it to memory before attempting to end the dreadful conversation. "So enjoy your festivities! Olive Thirteen has a bold painting here that I think you'll enjoy. And a moment ago I heard someone singing ... something." He can't bring himself to compliment it. "So be comforted knowing that I'm back at camp planning our next course of action."

With that, Grak turns and starts up the hill. Stepping lightly, he listens carefully for developments in the crowd behind him. To his relief, they soon begin milling about again. He takes a deep, comforting breath at that sound. The distraction is working.

Or so he thought. The noise seems to be growing louder. Yes, now he's certain. The din has become more of a frenzied murmur.

Another 'sighting,' perhaps? No, it should have died down by now. But what else would get them so riled up? Arguing about food again? Quite likely. Can't even give me a moment of peace.

Grak reaches the summit and stops. He waits there a moment, unsure if he should go back to the shore or make them come to him. While he's pondering that thought, he turns and surveys the crowd below.

But something about their behavior strikes him as odd. None are focused on him. Instead, they're talking to each other while many point off toward the forest.

Grak follows their line of sight until his eye snags on movement. Realization slowly dawns. A group is leaving the tree line, walking this way. He can't make out their faces, but it doesn't matter. The wind has changed, and he can now hear clear shouts of joy coming from his people at the shore.

Grak sighs in relief. Frolan has returned.

5 - And Packing Day

For as long as Grak can remember, he's always hated packing day. But in a different way than he's used to. This contempt is simpler. "Childlike," he calls it. Though Grak is careful to clarify that he's not making any implications about his maturity level.

No, he's just referring to the uncomplicated nature of this aversion. Noise, chaos, and tiring labor are all high on his list, and this day invariably provides an abundance of each. It's as straightforward as that.

Well, almost. There's also the looming threat that once the day ends, an even deeper agony sets in: traveling. It possesses all the miseries of packing day, but amplified and over an extended period of time. "Who *wouldn't* despise it?" he tells Doran whenever the topic comes to mind.

And in many ways, this packing day is shaping up to be Grak's worst ever. The perpetual complaining and rampant lethargy are weighing on him to no end. It seems he can't go more than a moment without someone grumbling about lacking "strength" or "feeling in their limbs." And while Grak has tolerated the charade so far, it now portends to slow the tribe's travel—a risk he's unwilling to take.

Thus, he's made it a point to loudly and publicly shame anyone he catches slacking off. Of course, this requires greater effort on Grak's part, which is clearly less than ideal.

But there's no avoiding it. A 'necessary duty,' I'd say. Just part of leading the tribe: forfeiting energy and time for the betterment of all.

He is dreading, however, that this increase in work could end up stretching late into the night. If that occurs, it would rule out his final chance at a hot spring dip until they pass this way again in the next heats. And it goes without saying that he intends to avoid that outcome by any means necessary.

Still, despite his many hardships, Grak is trying to be positive about his situation. In fact, he's even found a few minor details about this packing day that make it "less awful" than previous ones. Doran's generous exaltations, for example. And Brak and Loren's increased appreciation as well. In fact, Grak has even noticed a resulting improvement in the tribe's perception of him.

Though I imagine my superior leadership at the shore yesterday is what brought that about. And it's about time they appreciated my true value. Long overdue, I say.

Better yet, Grak's new recognition has earned him some authority in the day's duties. He hasn't even been asked to carry anything yet. All he's had to do is stand here in a decisive manner with his hands on his hips. "My leader posture," he calls it, and none have refuted him.

To the contrary, people have been flocking, requesting direction. And while Grak generally doesn't know what response to give them, he's found that asking for their opinion does the trick. They give it, then he confirms the plan and gets the credit. It's a resounding win for him. Like a double win, really.

I'm not being lazy, though. Just haven't had the chance to do anything else. If anyone thinks I'm being lazy, then they're just ignorant. And uncouth. After all, I'm obviously working hard at leading.

"Grak, where should I put this?" Loren sets down the barrel, then tightens the harness strapping Olive Fifty-three to her back. The child peers over her shoulder and locks eyes with him.

There's the blank stare again. Dead stare, really.

Grak shudders. He shuffles away from the youth, leaning down to inspect the cask as a disguise for his actions.

"Well, I think that would depend on what's in it, don't you?" Grak grins as he glances up at Loren.

Her stern look and firm ears reveal that his playful wit was lost on her. "It's—"

She's interrupted by Grak's sudden recoiling. The smell is unmistakable, even through the barrel. "Never mind. Clearly olives."

Loren nods. "Yes. So where's the food cart?"

"I suppose it might be *that* cart there. The one with all the deer carcasses." Grak adds a smile, certain this one should get a laugh. Still nothing. He's getting annoyed by everyone's poor sense of humor today.

"Ah, there it is. Thanks." Loren hoists the drum onto her shoulder and turns in the appropriate direction.

"Actually. Wait for just a moment, would you, Loren?" Grak holds a hand to his mouth while resting the other on his hip. This is another posture he came up with today as a means of showing how hard he's thinking.

Every time we travel, olives end up sloshing around and spilling on the normal food. And then every meal stinks like the awful things for days after. So what other options do we have available?

"Yes, Grak? Do you need something else from me?" She sounds impatient.

Grak has been noticing that in a number of his people today, and it's growing irritating. He decides to convey displeasure in his voice. "Just give me a moment, please." That should calm her down.

So what other carts have room? I suppose that depends.

He softens his tone with a dash of mercy. "How many barrels do we have? Of olives?"

"Eh … five … I think." Her voice is oddly shaky.

Hmm, a change in tone. I wonder why. Is she hiding something? Is she questioning her support? Can't risk that right now. Best to rein her in before it's too late.

"You *think*? We need to be *certain*, Loren." He didn't want to, but was forced to add a healthy amount of disappointment there.

She sets down the barrel with a loud huff. "Sorry. Let me think." That chiding must have done the trick; the tremor in her voice has receded. "Yes, five. There are definitely five barrels."

Grak smiles in the most comforting way he can manage. "See? That wasn't so hard, was it?" While he's annoyed at the waste of time, he takes comfort in knowing that the woman learned a valuable lesson.

He takes up the thinking posture again. "Alright, yes. That should fit perfectly with Jafra's things. She's been designated to that cart over there. Next to the large rut."

Loren looks confused. "You mean where Sando's sitting? Or the one with rotted wood?"

Grak is surprised he didn't notice the man. And embarrassed that someone could be slacking off right under his nose. And furious since he's already warned Sando about this twice today. He's tempted to take action immediately.

No. Best to wait for Loren to leave. Don't want anyone jumping to defend the lazy, decrepit twit like earlier.

"Yes. The one with rotted wood." He's careful not to add pleasantries, lest it charm her into lingering.

And it works. She gives a slight nod before picking up the barrel once more. Without another word, she strolls over to the cart and unloads her burden.

But to his dismay, she follows this with a slow, elaborate stretch that Grak finds unnecessary. Still, it doesn't last *too* long. And after a daw-dling check of the harness knot, Loren finally heads back the way she came.

Grak takes a deep breath, thankful that his patience held out. Now, with all obstacles to his leading eliminated, he heads over to confront Sando, gathering his anger along the way.

I swear, this dullard takes more of my time than the remainder of the tribe combined. Some people think they can get away with anything. Lazi-ness just comes naturally to them!

Not me, though. Even when it looks like I'm not working, I'm still hard at it.

As Grak draws near, Sando spots him approaching. The man sways to his feet, then begins rummaging through some nearby sacks.

"Sando! *Still* with the sacks? How long ago did I give you this task? And you're *still* not finished? If I have to tell you one more time ..." Grak suddenly realizes he doesn't know how to follow that up. "I'll be *very* displeased."

Grak's quick thinking discerns that the man might assume *this* moment lacks disapproval. "Even more displeased than I am now. I'm upset now ... but my level of anger ... it'll be much higher." Not quite enough deprecation yet. "If you don't load those this instant!" Yes, now he's satisfied.

Sando rubs his wispy, white hair. "I'm sorry. I felt faint for a moment, but I'm better now. It won't happen again. Please, forgive me."

"*That* excuse again? You can't even be bothered to come up with something better? Well, you're right, it won't happen anymore!"

Grak looks around for the nearest person. "Zacha! Come here!" She wouldn't be his first choice, but no other option is close enough at the moment.

It's the woman's wide mouth that troubles Grak. Always has, ever since he was a boy. "Greater inclination toward biting," was his reasoning. And while the fear dissipated over time, he still feels uneasy around her.

Though, I suppose if I keep enough distance, all should be fine.

Unfortunately, the woman is approaching at a speed just slower than he'd like. Still, he's learned to limit the number of people feeling his wrath at any given time. Otherwise it just gets too tiring. So he waits. Patiently. At last, she arrives.

Grak swallows his annoyance toward her and takes a subtle step back. "Zacha, I need you to work with Sando for the rest of the day. Keep him busy. If he tries to slack off again, you have my permission to do whatever's necessary to motivate him. I'll check back later to see if his attitude has improved."

A moment of pity passes through her eyes, but is quickly replaced with acceptance. "Alright." She nods, then turns to the elderly man. "Well, come on, then. You heard Grak. Let's get to it, Sando." She gives him an arm to lean on as they pick up the final few sacks.

Grak monitors their progress for a moment. He soon realizes, however, that he has no reasonable standard for determining if their work is sufficient.

I suppose 'acceptable' might be awarded here. Hmm, more like 'good enough for now.' Yes, I think one more stern warning might be in order.

Grak turns slightly, as if to leave, then pauses. For added effect, he puts on his grim voice. "Don't forget, I'll be checking up on you." He waits a brief moment while his words sink in, then abruptly turns and heads back toward his leader spot.

Might need to keep a closer eye on Zacha. Can't have Sando's laziness spreading to anyone else. Maybe I should make an announcement. A policy of some sort. For the whole tribe.

Yes, that could work. But it would have to be done just so. Can't give Jafra any room to undermine it. And she would t—

"Grak!" Frolan's approach grabs his attention. A sizable hunting party wearing dopey grins trails behind the man.

What are they up to? Always something more to handle. I doubt anyone understands how much work it is to lead.

"Frolan? Why haven't you left yet?" Grak remembers to add exasperation to his voice. "I thought I made it clear how critical this hunt is. The tribe doesn't have enough food to survive the trip, *Frolan!*"

All are frowning now. Frolan removes his hat and hangs his head. A pitiful sight, to be sure. It even evokes a twinge of remorse in Grak.

No. Don't feel bad. You have to be impartial. Sometimes getting upset is necessary. Can't even let friends get away with lethargy. That's the burden of leading. Be strong, Grak.

Frolan's tone is properly contrite. "Sorry, Grak. I just wanted to finish this before I left." He offers up a small statue. "I wanted you to have it before you set out tomorrow. Maybe it'll bring fortune in your leading. And in your travels."

Grak takes the chunk of wood, giving it a cursory inspection as he turns the thing over in his hands. It's been crudely fashioned into the shape of a man, around one foot in height, with an arm stretched above its head. That hand is holding a rather ordinary arrow, though its standard size dwarfs the carving in comparison.

And yet, disappointingly lackluster overall.

Frolan braves a smile. "Do you like it?"

Grak hesitates. "What *is* it?"

"It's *you*, Grak! And your arrow from our last hunt together."

Grak considers it for a moment. "Oh … alright …"

He inspects the statue. Not much of a likeness at all. Though the hat is a dead giveaway. Or *was*, until he gave it to Brak—a kindness Grak is beginning to regret.

The man has been making a show of the cap and getting a number of compliments on its unique look. Grak had to make the point on his own more pronounced just to clarify that it was his idea originally. Unfortunately, this has caused "humorous" comments about the two men being related.

Through our hats. Somehow.

But the suggestion's absurdity irritates him less than the loss of exclusivity.

Perhaps if I increase the point a bit. Make it clear that mine is more unique.

"Grak?" Frolan brings him out of thought.

"Yes?"

"Do you like it?"

"Oh, right." He ponders the effigy for a moment. "And … *why* did you make it?"

Frolan grows confused. "I wanted to commemorate the event. Now that you're leading, I doubt I'll get another chance to chase game with you.

"Besides, your new hunting strategy is becoming renowned. I've been telling everyone about it. Once you teach us, our teams should be able to spend far less time away from camp.

"And that means more work getting done around here. Just like you've been pushing for. Thought we should have something to remember the day that made it all possible. To remember the *man* that made it all possible."

Hunting strategy? That again? Need to kill that topic once and for all. Could get awkward if I'm forced to teach them. Especially if I can't produce any results.

But how to keep the subject from coming up anymore? Maybe if I'm too busy? No, I'd have to maintain a stream of reasons. And look it too. No, has to be more permanent than that.

"Grak?"

"Yes?"

Frolan looks worried. "Do you like it?"

"Oh." Grak weighs his potential answers. "Yes" should win the man over more than the alternative would. "Very much. Thank you." He's proud of himself for that last touch—makes him look gracious.

Frolan grins again, from ear to ear this time. The whole team follows his lead.

Hmm, still … probably best to avoid any of them thinking we're too close. Can't let them get lazy.

Grak puts on his aloof face. "Well, you need to get going. Time is critical here."

Perhaps I should go over the plan again. Can never be too careful when dealing with these simple-minded types.

Grak speaks slowly, adding extra enunciation to vital words for greater clarity. "Remember, I'll lead the tribe toward *the river*, where it bends around *Redfist*. We should get there in *two days*." He holds up two fingers for further clarification. "Then we'll follow it *south*."

That might need clarification too. "By 'it,' I mean *the river*. We'll follow *the river* as it flows *south* from *Redfist*."

They all nod with understanding, though not necessarily with full comprehension. But Grak is fairly certain they've never understood *anything* in its *entirety*. Besides, a partial grasp of the matter is all he requires at the moment.

He resumes his normal pace of speech. "So, get as many kills as you can carry without encumbrance. Then return along that path to restock us."

Frolan beams with a youthful zeal. "Got it. Don't worry, Grak. We won't let you down."

He turns to his team. "Come on, hunters. We've got ground to cover!"

At those words, every face lights up with passion. The brute sets into a quick run, and the others eagerly follow after him. As they thunder off, Grak looks on with a certain sense of pride.

Good people. Dense, to be sure, but good. Just need someone keeping them focused.

He watches in admiration for a moment longer. And as their rhythmic footsteps fade into the distance, another noise fills the void. It's a coarse, heavy breathing, coming from just behind Grak's right side.

Startled, he turns to find Brak hunched over. The man's breath appears to have gotten away from him. Brak removes his cap to reveal a heavy layer of sweat, making the pale dome unusually reflective. He pats his scalp with the head covering, soaking up the moisture.

My good hat! This is how he treats a gift? Appalling! I certainly won't be so eager to help him out in the future.

"Grak," he barely manages between gasps. "I nee—"

"What is it, Brak?" Grak tries to remove some of the grit in his voice. "What's the matter? Is there trouble in camp?" He looks around, possibly for smoke, though any obvious signs of danger would do.

"Yes. Doran sent me to get you. We have a problem. Down by the shore."

Grak waits a moment, then motions with impatience. "And are you planning on *telling* me what this problem is?" Under better circumstances, he's certain Brak would have agreed on the amusing nature of *that* one.

The man takes another agonizing moment to catch his breath. "Oh, what *isn't* it? Where do I start? Alright. A lot of people are pushing to stay. They're causing a stir. They think the thing Doran saw will come back.

"Others think it's a sign. That we need to wait and see what it means. Still others are proposing that it means danger for our travels.

"And then there's a group of them—small, mind you, but vocal— who are saying that Doran is the only one who can see the thing. They don't even seem to be pushing for anything in particular, but they're scaring a *lot* of people.

"And it's all getting out of hand. Lots of shouting. Doran's worried it'll turn to fighting if we don't do something soon."

This is by far the biggest decision of the day. Grak needs to look extra leaderly here. "And what do *you* think we should do?" He remembers the leader posture, though a moment too late for maximum effect.

Brak takes on a pained expression as he puts his mind to work. "I have no idea." He tries again. "None. At all. We need your help. Please."

The fool's always shying away from responsibility like that. Afraid of confrontation, that's what it is. Normally I wouldn't mind, but in this case, a bit of spine would be preferable.

Grak looks back at his hunters. Too late. They've passed around the cliff face. He won't be able to catch up at that pace. Now he regrets having them take a shortcut. If they had gone by the shore, he would have been able to use Frolan's imposing stature to settle things there.

Should probably keep the man close by in the future. Yes. He's a dope, but a loyal one. Almost to a fault.

Perhaps I could give him a position in camp somewhere. Would probably get more done with him around. Certainly fewer arguments from the lazy. And from the devious. Jafra in particular. And fewer dullards getting all worked up about a crab, to be sure.

But I'd need a valid job for him. Something people would agree to. That might be difficult. I don't think he has any skills aside from killing.

Grak realizes that he's never really talked to Frolan about other matters. Certainly not about the man's talents.

Maybe he can do other things.

He considers that likelihood.

At least one other thing.

He considers that.

Well, it's worth asking him at least.

"Grak?" Brak attempts once more.

"Yes? Ah, right." He congratulates himself for refocusing so quickly this time. "Very well. Let's go take care of your problem."

"So then I said, 'Why don't we just wait a bit longer?'" Wanda rambles on without end. "Then he said, 'What's the point of waiting any longer?' But that doesn't …"

Grak stops listening again. Despite sincere effort, he's failing in his attempts to show indifference.

Too subtle, I suppose. Or maybe indifference isn't the answer. Maybe I just need to stop their drivel and do something.

Wanda's gestures are getting more excited. "So I said—"

"Yes, I get it." Grak's annoyance is a little too obvious. Best to cool it down. "Again, I understand the disagreement." Controlled breathing proves calming. "That's why I'm here. To end the discord. So give me a moment of silence to think. I'll decide what to do."

Wanda looks confused. "But why should *you* decide?" The question evokes general dissent. A few nearby hands swat at her.

And well deserved. In fact, as the main instigator of this nonsense, she deserves far worse.

Olive Thirteen turns toward the woman in anger. "How *dare* you talk to Grak that way! Don't you know what he's done for us?" She might just earn her way into Grak's inner circle if she maintains *this* level of devotion.

Cordo steps between the women. "Wait a moment. If I'm not mistaken, I believe what Wanda means is that we should *all* have a say." His point isn't so bold as Wanda's, yet it conceals a far more lethal dagger.

What's his game? Has he been talking to Jafra? I'll need to watch this one.

The demand for an immediate response means Grak has to leave Cordo's treachery on the cart for the moment. "Well, keep in mind that I never really wanted to lead. The tribe asked me to. *You* asked me to. Each one of you. It was basically forced on me. And I think I've done a good job."

He pauses for a response from the crowd. To his disappointment, they're surprisingly quiet at the moment.

No matter. Grak fills the void. "No, I *know* I've done a good job! An *incredible* job, in fact!" This time he's met with a mild cheer of support.

But Cordo remains straight-faced. "Yes, it's true. You have been leading us through this difficult time. And I'm personally grateful for that. I don't think we would have made it without you."

Well, that's encouraging. Maybe he isn't so bad after all.

The man continues. "But we're almost at full strength. And this is an important decision. One that will affect us all for some time to come. I think we have no choice but to discuss it and decide together. As a tribe. Just as we did *before* Lago's treachery."

Then again, it's hard to tell with him. Best to counter anything he says until I know for sure.

Grak pounces on the ripe target. "But that's just it, Cordo. Lago's treachery hasn't ended. We haven't caught him yet. If we had, do you think I'd *volunteer* to lead? *Volunteer* for the extra work? And the extra *pressures*?

"I'd be thrilled to go back to the way things were. I'd welcome it. But until that time, what are we to do? What am *I* to do? Should I abandon my people?

"Since I've been leading, I've prevented any further attacks, haven't I?" The crowd is mildly confused, yet agreeable. "So are you asking our people to give all that up? Who will stop Lago when he returns? What will *that* result look like? Will some die? How many?"

A number of conversations spring up simultaneously. The crowd is deeply troubled.

Wanda lifts her voice above the noise. "Look, I didn't mean to imply that we don't want you leading us. You're right. Lago attacks are down, and we owe that to you. I know I'm not alone in saying that we *need* you to lead." She looks around for support, which comes enthusiastically.

"But this *particular* issue carries *too much* significance. So before you decide, I would appreciate being able to explain our reasoning for staying. Could that be possible? Please?"

This sounds like groveling. And Grak's stance on that issue is favorable. When directed toward *him* at least.

Couldn't hurt. But can't have them thinking they've pushed their idea on me. That would catch on too quickly. An especially lethal poison. Can't risk that spreading. Especially while I'm already trying to contain several other nuisances in camp.

Grak decides "benevolent" would be the best approach here. "Well, if you had let me finish earlier, I was just going to explain this very idea. So yes, you'll have what you want. I'll listen to each side of the issue. But in the future, please trust me long enough to hear my plans."

An impeccable measure of chiding just there. Well done, Grak. Certainly put them in thei—

Wait a moment. If each one gets to speak, we'll be here all day. Definitely wouldn't have a chance to visit the hot springs. Oh my. That won't do.

Grak thinks quickly. "Ah, so here's what we'll do. I'll select one person from each of the opposing views. That person will explain the points in favor of that view. Then, they'll be silent. After all arguments are presented, *I* will decide what to do. Then, we'll do it. Is that understood?"

Nods all around confirm the plan.

"So Wanda, you can represent the view that we should wait here for Doran's cr ... thing ... that he saw. Olive Thirteen, you speak for the ones wanting to leave."

The woman suddenly looks worried. "Oh, but I want to stay."

Grak rolls his eyes. "Alright, fine. Brak, *you'll* stand for the ones wanting to leave. Olive, you'll represent the ones who think it's an omen."

Her face still wears concern. "But Tabo suggested that one. I really don't know *what* it was."

This is already proving more challenging than Grak had expected. And more frustrating. He shakes his head in exasperation. "Alright, look ... No, never mind. It really doesn't matter. You know what he was suggesting. You can explain it."

She shrugs in agreement, careful not to inspire greater wrath.

Grak continues. "Cordo, you speak for those who think it means danger for our travels."

Cordo holds up his hands in shock. "Wait a moment. I have no part in this. I just came when I heard the shouting. If you ask me, I think it's all hyste—"

"Cordo!" Grak is having trouble controlling himself now. "What did I *just* tell Olive? This will all be much smoother if everyone just accepts their assignments."

Cordo opens his mouth to speak, but decides against it, resigning himself to a mere sigh instead.

Unhindered, Grak presses on. "Alright, so that covers the sides."

"What about those who think Doran's the only one who can see it?" asks Olive Thirteen.

Grak gives it a cursory thought. "I think that's more of a supporting detail."

Cordo cuts in. "Well in that case, mine is also a supporting detail. Of Olive's view."

She's quick to respond. "Again, it's really not *my* vie—"

"Alright, fine!" That showed far too much anger. Grak takes a calming breath. "We'll allow it. Thank you, Olive. Tabo, you can speak for that interest."

Tabo suddenly realizes what's been asked of him. "Oh, no, I'm not in tha—"

"Again!" Grak's tone is still too harsh. "Please." Much better. "Remember, you're just representing. You don't have to *agree* with the idea."

Tabo nods. "Alright, but what about the view that we should build a floating cart in order to find the thing?"

Well, that's a new one. More importantly, why does Tabo feel he's allowed to speak? Oh, no matter. This has gone on long enough.

Grak has to put a stop to it. "Alright, you take that one too. But that's it. No more. If we give each speck of detail a representative, then everyone will be talking. Then this whole exercise would be useless."

Wanda cocks her head in confusion. "But, I thought your idea was for *all* voices to be heard."

Grak can feel his grip faltering. He has to act quickly. "Yes, that *is* my idea. But to a reasonable limit. If everyone talks, we'll be here all day, then we'll be late arriving at Redfist." Looks of concern among the crowd demand immediate clarification. "*If* I decide we should go, that is." That settles them.

"You could hear each person separately while the rest of us pack," suggests Cordo. "That way we wouldn't be delayed … *if* you decide we should go."

That's even worse. I'd never get to the hot springs. Is there no end to their insubordination?

Grak dons his leader posture in hopes it will provide greater authority. "No, that won't do either. I've got too much leading to do. Very busy day. We'll leave it with those representatives. More would just get confusing." Best to end this soon. "Wanda, we'll start with you. Why should we stay?"

"So, given that," concludes Wanda, "why *would* we go?"

Grak fends off drowsiness again. "Good. Thank you, Wanda."

He checks his shadow. Nearly dusk. "Brak? You're next. And please keep it brief. We're running out of time."

Brak steps forward. "Um, well … if we don't travel first thing tomorrow morning … there's a good chance we'll all die."

Grak is impressed. "Wonderful! Short and to the point." His respect for the man just grew slightly. "Olive Thirteen?"

She looks like a lost doe as she attempts to answer. "I … um … wasn't really paying attention to Tabo's reasoning earlier. So it's unclear."

Grak motions impatiently. "Just do your best."

She shrugs. "Alright. So … I suppose it could be an omen … because … well, if you see something … then you never know."

Grak is fine with that response. "Good. Cordo?"

The man rolls his eyes. The exaggerated movement causes his mole to flex in an unnatural way. "I have no idea. Travel can be dangerous … I suppose. But so can not eating. Much more so, really." Several in the crowd glare at him for deviating from his assigned viewpoint.

But Grak is just happy to have everything moving along. "Excellent points. Tabo?"

The man shrugs. "Well … I suppose if we build a floating cart, we could find Doran's creature with greater ease. If others can see it, that is."

He ponders the idea for another moment. "Also, the floating carts might make for faster travel." Several in the crowd chuckle at this suggestion.

Grak leans closer to Brak. "Travel *where*? The deer are in the *opposite* direction." This garners a suppressed laugh from the man.

Hmm, good. First proper response to humor all day. Still, that doesn't make up for these time-wasters.

Grak has had enough of that sort. He decides to end the discussion. "Alright, and that's all the sides." Best to ease the blow of his resolution. "Well done, all. I'm proud of you for participating."

That should suffice for the flattery phase of his speech. Now on to the point. "And after careful consideration, I've decided we need to leave.

So, everyone back to camp. We have a lot of time to make up for."

"*Careful?* How was that *careful?*" Clearly, Wanda is upset. "You hardly took any time for thought at all!"

Grak rubs his brow in disappointment. "Look, Wanda ..." He takes a deep breath. "We all agreed that we'd follow, no matter the outcome. Are you going back on that?"

The woman appears battered by her decision. "Well, no ... But ... I'm sorry, Grak, but I can't go with you. I'm staying behind. Something inside is driving me. I can't shake it. I have to see if I can find this thing Doran saw."

Grak puts on his most patronizing tone. "You'll take your chances *alone?* With *Lago* on the loose?"

"She won't be alone." Tabo steps up. "I'll stay with her. This floating cart is starting to sound like a decent idea. Maybe it would help." He holds her hand timidly.

A few more voices gather in agreement until a small group forms in support of the two. Grak checks his shadow again. It's creeping dangerously long.

Oh, what's the use? I don't need their kind in camp anyway. Things will be much smoother without them. Let these fools stay and starve. More food for the rest of us. But how to allow it without anyone thinking they defied me?

Grak thinks quickly. "Again, you didn't let me finish my decision. The tribe will leave, but if some want to stay, we won't stop them. Still, I encourage everyone to carefully consider the dangers in staying. Remember Lago's treachery!"

Doran finally adds something to the conversation. "Besides, we'll be back next heats. The ocean will still be there."

A gentle murmur rolls through the crowd. Some are convinced by his words and leave Wanda's group, making it even more meager. For others, however, it simply solidifies an existing belief that moving is vital. Either way, this pleases Grak.

Good thing I've got Doran. Need to remember to use him more often. Carries a lot of weight with these simple types.

Grak remembers the occasion at hand. "Good. I'm glad most are sensible." Best to look gracious. "And I hope those of you who stay are safe. May fortune be plentiful for you on your quest."

With that, Grak turns and heads back toward camp. But, despite the press of time, a peculiar thought nags at him as he climbs the hill. And try as he might, it won't shake.

Finally, at the summit, Grak stops and observes the camp below. After a moment, he looks back at the group by the shore.

Hmm, staying here would eliminate the need for constant travel. I wonder if that might have been a feasible option.

6 - And Obviously Traveling

Anyone acquainted with Grak inevitably learns of his disdain for travel. Of course, to the untrained eye, his sour demeanor on the trail might seem like mere fatigue. But most attempts to converse with him while in transit quickly reveal the contempt. And an abundance of it.

At that point, lack of recognition is inexcusable. In fact, Grak deems it "completely inept," or "utterly devoid of thought." Or simply "ignorant" when he's in a hurry.

But with this trip, given his increased stature in the tribe, Grak expected something different. And while there have been some improvements, they haven't been enough to offset the miseries. Chief of which is the fact that this is the slowest move he's ever experienced.

Four days just to get here. Four! Definitely not on schedule. And why? Because these fools can't follow simple instructions! Really, is it too much to ask for orderly movement?

No, it isn't. Grak's "all equals" policy should have seen to that. He announced it just before the tribe set out, and it appeared to go over quite well at the time.

And why shouldn't it? It's a simple plan.

It really is. It basically outlines how none are to be considered superior during the move or any time after. Grak even took care to word the speech in such a way that would bring shame to any asking for special treatment, no matter their condition.

Of course, as Grak predicted, the policy proved successful in curbing lethargy. Unfortunately, he failed to anticipate the difficulties it created.

Soon after his speech ended, the tribe fell into confusion as to why they needed to follow his lead anymore. On their first day out, things got even worse, and most of his commands were met with questions referencing the policy. Little progress was made that day, which prompted Grak to deliver a second announcement the next morning.

That was when he laid out his "follow the leader" policy, which reaffirmed their desperate need for his guidance. For supporting evidence, he once again cited their recent ordeals and how his wisdom brought them through it.

In this speech, Grak carefully avoided use of the word "superior." Though, he did use concepts such as "exceptional," "remarkable," and "preferable," among others. He also made it clear that his guidance was crucial in every detail. Especially on the trail, but even *more* so at their new campsite.

Again, this policy was well received, but poorly implemented. Many mistook "every detail" to be literal. Thus, that day brought Grak a significant increase in work. And still, little progress was made in their travels.

The following morning saw his "if it affects others" policy presented. In hindsight, he realizes that was more of an addendum, but cares little for semantics here. He feels such nuance would have been lost on them anyway, so the term sufficed.

This one simply clarified that personal routines need not be run by him. Only matters that might have an impact on one or more fellow members of the tribe require his attention.

Of course, Grak feared this might also fall victim to confusion. Thus, he gave a few examples and answered the resulting questions. While the process required nearly half the day, he considers it to have been "a sound use of time." As proof of this, he points to the smoother progress they've experienced since the announcement.

Before you know it, we'll reach the steady pace of previous moves. And beyond, now that we have order. The tribe just needs to grow accustomed to my commands. The confusion should fade after that. The mistakes too.

Then—

"You know, we named this rock, but why haven't we named this river?" The abrupt sound of Brak's voice destroys the moment's tranquility.

He isn't usually this annoying. The gloom of the trail must be affecting his thinking.

Still, Grak feels compelled to answer. The man is a valued supporter, after all. Also, no one else is around, so a failure to respond would be all the more obvious. Grak weighs the matter.

Yes, too valued. But how do I answer something so senseless?

He turns and looks up at Redfist, hoping for inspiration. But all that comes to mind is his usual objection to such a poor name.

It's just a large rock. Can't see how anyone ever compared the thing to a fist. Probably delirious from travel. Or drunk in an effort to relieve the misery. And I imagine no one else gave the name much thought, so it stuck.

Of course, "Redfist enthusiasts," as he calls them, regularly attempt to convince him otherwise. But he always finds their reasoning lacking. Especially since their greatest piece of evidence is that the large rock jutting out of the landmark's base looks like a thumb.

Such absurdity. Who makes a fist with their thumb out? At best, it resembles a hand. Which, by the way, has a much better sound to it. Redhand. Rolls right off the tongue.

Although, to be fair, the red is more of a brown really. Even in this early morning light, when it looks the most red, it's still an obvious brown.

A reddish brown, I suppose. But if you call this red, you might as well call a number of other things red.

Grak struggles to think of an example, but comes up empty. He's certain there are good ones available, though.

I'm just too tired to think of them. But it doesn't matter. The point remains. Brownhand is more fitti—

"Grak?"

"Yes, I was paying attention." Grak adds a touch of annoyance to clarify the need for patience when dealing with superiors. "Just thinking about your question. It's simple really. We name things to tell them apart."

Grak adds a fair amount of condescension to make it clear that children generally know such information. "This lets us know which rock among many. What would we be telling the river apart from? Is there a *second* river we don't know about?" He's pleased with the level of sarcasm conveyed just there.

Brak gives the question his full focus for a moment. "I don't know. The ocean?" He shrugs. "I suppose."

Grak opens his mouth to respond, but words fail. He shakes his head and searches for a new subject. The rock he's resting his feet on stands out as an interesting alternative. He leans closer for inspection.

Now that's a true red. Quite a brilliant red, even. And that protruding section looks a great deal like a mouth. At least more than Brownhand looks like a fist. And the mouth is perfectly positioned too. So it looks as though the rock is drinking from the river.

Sure enough, Grak's intent stare soon sparks an interest in Brak. No longer able to contain his curiosity, the man leans in as well.

"Heh, that looks like a mouth!" Brak's reaction seems *too* excited, though. "I never noticed before. We could call it Redmouth. The river, I mean."

The conversation still isn't going in a direction Grak appreciates. He reaches for a new topic to alter it once more. Unfortunately, he's out of options that carry intrinsic interest.

Grak does his best. "So, this water is nice." He splashes gently at the surface.

Brak nods, unsure how to respond. He settles on a simple, "That's true," then goes silent.

And it is true. True enough at least. Grak certainly enjoys dipping his feet here. Even when the river is cold like this as the heats retreat from the looming snows.

Of course, it isn't so nice as to appease Grak in the face of such a dull conversation. Very few things can do that. Thus, he decides it's time to end this excursion. He pulls his feet out and dries them with a nearby cloth.

Quick to notice the intended change, Brak tries in vain to spark up a new conversation. "Can you pass that, please?" The look he receives cautions him about his manners. "When you're done with it, of course."

Much better. Far more polite.

Still, Grak is annoyed by the fellow's original haste. He splashes his face and hair, then dries them, moving slower than usual to teach the man a lesson. For good measure, he makes an extra round to check for any remaining moisture. Finally, he passes the cloth over.

"Thanks." Brak unfurls the wadded tunic before putting it back on.

I can only hope he learned a valu—

"Grak?" Sando's voice calls out from a distance, somewhere up the riverbank behind Brownhand.

Oh, what does that decrepit fool want now? I swear, he's incapable of getting anything done without checking in about it.

There's a fair bit of truth to that. The man has been hovering the entire trip, perhaps more so than anyone else.

And now the sluggard can't even be bothered to use his eyes to find me? Just shouts crudely into the air. As though I should come to him!

"Grak?" Still the man cries out for him.

But principle alone demands silence as a response. Grak remains resolute.

Brak leans in awkwardly. "Grak, I think Sando's looking for you."

Poor fool. The ways of leading are foreign to him.

Grak puts on his most condescending expression. "I know. I can hear." He sits down on a wide, flat stone. "I'm teaching the oaf a lesson. He needs to work for things. Can't expect others to keep making up for his lack of exertion."

Brak nods. He's only pretending to understand, but Grak still appreciates the effort.

He'll learn. It just takes time. No one's born a leader.

The two drift into silence, listening to the river's gentle rhythm while waiting for Sando to arrive. But this reverie is soon broken by the sound of the old man's foot dragging on stone and grass just out of sight around the bend. Grak shakes his head.

What a fool! To think we'd be duped into believing his story. How would the meal cause lasting problems with his leg? And only his? Lackadaisical beyond belief!

Grak waits in agonizing frustration for another moment of that harsh scraping noise. Finally, Sando hobbles into view.

Startled, the man pulls back, catching his breath. "Ah, Grak! There you are! I was calling for you. When I didn't get a response, I feared the worst. But I suppose Redfist always did play with sound, eh? How are you?"

Grak has no time for mindless pleasantries. "Yes? What do you need?"

Sando takes off his hat—pointed, as the trend of recent days has gone. "Well, everyone was worried that you might be testing us in secret."

How are they finding time to make the caps while traveling?

The old man's words pour out nervously. "And you said we'd leave when the stick's shadow reached the tree."

Sando's cap especially. It's surprisingly well done.

"So everyone else, they've started on their way."

The point reaches nearly as high as my own. And it's stiff. Permanently. No need to continuously stand it up throughout the day.

"But the train is almost gone, and you didn't show up."

Strange that such skill never made its way to my own work.

"So I got worried that maybe something happened to you. So I came looking."

It dawns on Grak what the man has been saying. "Gone?" He scrambles to put on his trousers. "I never said … Why, in all the land, would I want the tribe to leave without me?" He slips on a boot and hops off while awkwardly putting on the other.

"Wait! Don't leave me behind!" Brak pleas while attempting to dress himself.

"The tribe waits for none, Brak!" Grak starts around the rock and calls back, "Be quick to catch up! We won't stop for you."

Sando shuffles after him.

Decrepit twit. Who even limps like that? Obvious farce. You'd think he'd drop it at a time like this, when we have to move quickly. At least he's walking a little faster than usual.

Grak climbs the riverbank and gingerly mounts his horse. He's never been very enthusiastic about riding. Not horses, anyway. "Give me my two feet any day," he can often be heard remarking.

Nonetheless, it wouldn't be very leaderly of him to walk when so many are up on tall steeds. If anything, he needs the highest vantage point available to keep a better watch for impending danger. At least, that was his reasoning for commanding Cordo to trade mounts with him.

Unfortunately, this new beast is also much broader than Grak's old one, which means a far more uncomfortable ride. And nowhere is this point more obvious than here in the woods where the bumpy ground is proving especially painful on his thighs.

Perhaps some sort of padding would be in order. Save my legs for more useful purposes.

Still, in spite of this difficulty, Grak survives the ride and emerges from the trees in decent condition. And that's when his heart sinks. The river trail is empty.

Too late. They've already passed.

He turns to the left, then pulls the horse up.

Which way were we headed?

He tries to remember, but to no avail. He's never been very good with directions.

Grak turns the horse around and walks through the motions he took when leaving for the river earlier. This proves of little value. He can remember the camp sprawled out between the trees, and he remembers entering the woods, but that's all.

"Curse those fools for leaving without me!" A slight panic takes hold.

Calm, Grak. They couldn't have gotten far. Just try one way for a distance. If you don't see them soon, head back the other direction.

Grak nods in agreement and grips the reins. But a second confusion takes hold.

Which way to start? Argh! Either way could be equally probable. Calm, Grak. Go with your original instinct.

He turns left and starts into a gallop.

"Grak!" Brak calls out from behind.

But Grak can't wait around for the man. "Hurry, Brak!"

No time for slow fools. He has to learn to keep up. Life doesn't wait for imbeciles to get their boots on.

Brak's voice carries over the wind once more, now fading with distance. "It's this way!"

Grak reins up. To his dismay, turning proves awkward due to his haste.

He shouts a reply. "I know. Thought I saw a wolf. Just checking it out. Wouldn't be much of a leader if I didn't keep the tribe's rear protected."

He gallops the short distance back and quickly passes the other two men. "Let's go! Hurry up!"

Ever obedient, Brak kicks his horse into a steady trot, causing Sando to cling tighter to his waist.

Always weighing someone down, the old log. I'll probably have to reprim—

Grak rounds the first bend and pulls up just in time, narrowly avoiding a collision with the tribe's tail end. Apparently, they weren't so far ahead as he thought.

While catching up is a relief, it's only a small one. The ride to the head of the line will prove far more time-consuming. Carts and horses are crammed to the trees on either side along the trail for as far as he can see.

This smells like Jafra's doing. All of it. First she convinced them to leave without me. Then she had them all spread out to stop me from leading. Even though I made it clear how important it is that I ride in front! Or perhaps because I made it so clear. Just to spite me.

But either way, Grak has no choice. Trying to move through the woods would be unpleasant in both speed and comfort. He'll have to press his way through the crowd.

Grak puts on his most authoritative voice. "Make way! Leader coming through! Make way!"

As he presses through, his people move quickly aside. And to Grak's surprise, they also take it upon themselves to inform those ahead of his coming. Which he's quite grateful for, as it allows him to save his voice for more important matters.

He's also glad to see so many eyes watching with excitement as he passes. At least, Grak *thinks* that's excitement. It could just as easily be admiration. Though a nagging thought points out the similarities between this look and one of basic annoyance.

Still, regardless of their feelings toward him, Grak is content with having their attention. Well, for the most part. Their caps are certainly proving disconcerting.

How have so many pointed hats appeared since I left for the river this morning? It's good that they follow, but I can't have them usurping. Really must do something about this.

Grak ponders his options as he rides ahead. Obvious ideas seem too brutal, and yet original ideas seem ineffective.

Something in between, perhaps. A policy of some sort.

But Grak has no more time to consider that. His thinking is disrupted when he spots Doran riding just ahead, talking with his new friends.

He's spending an increasing amount of time in their company, isn't he? Not that I mind, of course. I don't care what he does with his time. At least, I wouldn't if it weren't displacing the time we used to share.

That is, if we're even friends still. Friends are supposed to talk about each other. That crab's all he ever wants to talk about anymore. Never shuts up about it. That's not the friend I grew up with.

As if to further prove this point, Grak's approach does nothing to stir the man from his conversation. Doran continues to look intently at the map stone in Kando's lap, oblivious to everything around him.

His voice rises above the surrounding din. "If we could find a better way to draw out the areas we've visited."

Kando nods. "True. Drawing on rock is insufficient. We need to update it regularly with new theories. And compare to previous theories. We'd need a simpler surface for that."

Grak ponders the man's idea. It's interesting, but ultimately useless.

I doubt they'll find something better. I've never been able to. But let them try with their nonsense.

Grak manages to sneak by without being pulled into the conversation. Although, truth be told, he's somewhat dismayed by his success.

A simple greeting would be nice. The old Doran would have done that. And more. Would have invited me to ride with him. Before all this crab foolishness. Quite different indeed.

But Grak is determined not to let that bother him; it would only be a distraction right now. No, he just needs to remain focused and reach the head of the line. Then he can think in peace.

If these simpletons would clear out of my way!

The ripple of shouts has made passage relatively easy thus far, but a pack of riders just ahead appears oblivious. They're conversing loudly, focused on their own subject.

Unconcerned that their leader needs to pass. Too involved with themselves to bother doing anything for the tribe.

Cordo's voice rises above those of the other riders. "I'm just saying, the sea isn't so deep. Certainly not deep enough for something as large as Doran claims. I mean, at the most, it's what? How many men?"

Now Cordo's caught up in this whole crab business too? No one is safe from this illness.

"Move aside!" Grak shouts.

But they show no reaction. Ruch continues their conversation. "Maybe five men."

"Exactly. Five men." Cordo tilts his head back in thought. "Something that large wouldn't be able to move very well in such shallow waters. Too many rocks. And too much seaweed and the like.

"Plus, we would have seen it by now. And wouldn't it have a family? Everything else does. So we've got a family of sea monsters, each with incredible size, dipping their feet in the water? And only when Doran's around? I don't believe it."

Grak raises his voice along with his ire. "Your leader needs to get through!" Still nothing.

Zacha adds her mind. "Doran says this proves the sea must be deeper. He says he's going to work on figuring it out. He's already started on it with several of his people."

Perhaps calling by name will do the trick. These are a vain bunch, after all.

Grak raises his voice even louder. "Cordo!"

The man turns, revealing a sweatier mole than usual. "Oh, Grak." He signals the others to give him room. "Didn't notice you there." He clears out of the way.

Didn't notice me? What utter nonsense! How would you not recognize your leader's commands?

Cordo returns to his conversation. "Yes, but have you heard their thinking so far? Kando was theorizing that all the land together must be minuscule, and the water vast beyond belief. Sounds like more gibberish to me."

Grak is thoroughly put off by this neglect. If time weren't so demanding, he'd deal with them immediately. But the head of the line calls.

He reaches for a parting rebuke. "Then you'd best work on being more mindful!"

Satisfactory, but a more thorough reprimand might be needed. Perhaps this evening. If I can find the time. In public would be ideal. A lesson for the whole tribe on being more attentive. A strong one at that.

Should probably single out Jafra. Just to make it clear what kind of behavior is frowned upon. I'll need a reasonable connection, though, since she wasn't in that pack.

He stores this thought for later and continues pressing forward. Only a few more carts remain between him and his rightful place. Two riders are currently claiming that spot, maybe fifteen horse lengths ahead of anyone else. Grak considers their increased distance.

Could add to my leaderly look. Far out in front of the tribe. Bravely leading the way, all alone.

Grak decides it's worth trying. He breaks free of the throng and picks up his pace, calling out as he rides. "Farzo! Lumo!"

They both turn in response, but Grak has no time for scolding. A low growl is their only warning as a lion leaps on Farzo, knocking him to the ground. Lumo reacts quickly, but his ax is too slow. A second lion pounces on him.

Ever quick to identify danger, Grak gives a warning call. "Li …" The crackling in his voice threatens to reveal his fear. He clears his throat. "Lions!" Much more confident. He hopes no one noticed the first attempt.

An arrow whistles by, an arm's length away, and sticks into an attacker leaping from his left. The beast goes limp before it hits the ground—the shaft protruding from its neck the only reason Grak remains seated.

And perhaps alive. Though I'll have to see who fired it before admitting anything of the sort.

But Grak can't think about that right now. With a resolute focus, he looks around, trying to get a grasp on the situation.

Many of his tribesmen have arrived and joined the fray, adding an extra buffer between him and immediate danger. And as his personal risk fades, Grak finds his fear also dissipating. Just in time, too. He spots Jafra running forward, ax in hand and fury in eye, reminding him of the opportunity to lead here.

Grak looks about for the best way to manage his fighters. The answer quickly presents itself. Cordo appears to be in a desperate situation, swinging at a monster of an animal while narrowly avoiding its claws.

Grak puts on his brave voice. "Cordo! Kill that lion! It's a large one! Jafra! Help him!"

Jafra flows into action. She leaps and descends on the beast with a fierce blow to the skull. It collapses instantly, blood squirting a wild red. With no further thought for the fallen creature, she turns to face another nearby attacker.

Well, Cordo had it distracted. She had the easy part. Good thing I was here to tell her what to do.

Grak looks about for more available commands. He notices Zacha stringing an arrow from her saddle. "Zacha! Shoot that lion!"

She glances around in confusion, then lowers her bow. "Which one?"

Grak recognizes a good question when he hears it. He scans the area. Most of their assailants are dead now. Or being finished off. No threats rema—

Wait! Two are fleeing back into the woods.

"There!" He points. "Get the one on the left!"

Zacha fires. Her shot lands in the hind leg of the trailing creature, causing it to tumble through leaves and dirt. It attempts to get back up, but a second arrow follows fast and pierces its chest from the side. The cat collapses, twitching. Life ebbs out.

"I said, 'the left'!" Grak shouts. "How are we supposed to accomplish *anything* if you can't follow *simple* directions?"

"Sorry. I was aiming for it, but the other one got in the way."

While Grak finds her penitence satisfactory, he feels a reminder is important here. "Well, do better next time!"

An ample warning. Short and to the point. Well done, Grak.

He surveys the area once more. The remaining beasts are all dead, leaving the trail a haunting, bloody mess.

How should I lead now? Injuries, perhaps? Yes, that seems like a reasonable next step.

"Is everyone alright?" he calls out. "Are there any wounded?"

But Grak is too late with that one. Groka is already checking on them.

Too slow, Grak! Have to be faster in situations like this. Nothing to lead now. She already knows what to—

Grak's heart sinks as the woman's face goes pale. He follows her stare to the far edge of the carnage. Two human bodies lie there. Neither one is moving. A pool of blood steadily grows larger around them. Groka starts into a frenzied run.

Farzo … Lumo … No …

Grak remembers to lead, clearing his throat before speaking. "Groka, check on them. Will they be alright?"

She kneels to inspect. But the grisly mess all around leaves little doubt. Silence falls as hope fades.

Groka huddles lower. The tremble of her weeping body is unmistakable. The injured forget their wounds. All present hang their heads. "Sorrowful" would be Grak's description.

If anyone bothered to ask.

After a long moment, Cordo breaks the silence. "We've lost two of our brothers. The tribe needs to know. I'll inform them."

"No! I'll do it." Grak almost missed that opportunity to lead. "They'll want to hear it from me."

Cordo shrugs in agreement.

"We should bury them," says Jafra.

Grak rolls his eyes with incredulity.

Trying to take attention for herself. And at a time like this. Only Jafra would do such a thing.

"Yes, we should," he replies with a mild chiding in his tone. "And I was just about to tell you who should do it. Have patience."

"Cordo, I need you to handle that. Jafra can assist you." Grak looks around for other candidates. Proximity decides. "Ruch and Zacha, you can help too."

He turns to leave, but remembers something and pauses. "Groka, please see to the other wounded."

Jafra cuts in. "Groka, would you mind helping me bandage up my arm first?"

How egocentric! Astonishing, really. Others need help too, and all she can think about is herself. Well, at least it was a public display of her selfishness.

Grak takes a calming breath so as to appear controlled when scolding her. "Again, Jafra. Patience. Your arm doesn't look so bad. Be glad you didn't end up like Farzo and Lumo." While he regrets the comparison, its necessity can't be denied.

Jafra averts her eyes and frowns. "You're right. I'm sorry. I just didn't want it to get infected. It's a deep wound, and I'd hate for my arm to rot and need to be removed."

Hmm, so would I. Then we'd have another useless person to care for. Not that she's useful now, of course. But she'd be of even less value.

Besides, mercy would look good here. Especially in contrast to her self-serving requests.

Grak gives his most benevolent nod. "So be it. Groka, please stop tending to those in greater need so you can fix Jafra's scratches."

Groka nods and gets to work. Jafra simply submits, hanging her head in even greater shame. With a smug satisfaction, Grak turns and rides back toward the tribe.

That certainly knocked her down a peg or two. Well done, Grak. A resounding win.

But he has no time to enjoy the victory. As Grak makes his way down the line, it becomes obvious that the news has already spread. A few are weeping. Some ask pitiful questions about whether the danger has passed. Most simply wear mournful expressions.

That's when Grak notices Farzo's family just ahead. The man's mother is wailing on the ground among the trees. His widow is wearing a brave, yet lost look while trying unsuccessfully to console her young son in his tears.

A lump forms in Grak's throat. "Unfortunate" would be his description of the day's events. If he felt comfortable talking to those in earshot.

And foolish, I might add. The foolishness of Farzo. A wasted life.

Grak clears his throat. He passes a quick hand over his cheeks, feigning as though they've remained dry the entire time.

If I had been in the lead, I would have warned everyone. None needed to die. The leader should always be at the head. I'll need to make this even clearer.

Grak decides against approaching the grieving family just yet. He turns his horse around and makes for the front of the line.

Although ... If I had been in the front, I might not have had enough time. I could be among those lying on the ground right now while ...

He struggles for a name. Any name.

Well, I'm sure many would grieve my loss. And why not? The leader dying at such a desperate time? Would be tragic for all.

So, perhaps I should be front adjacent instead. I can keep an eye on the way ahead, but don't need to be in immediate danger.

Still might be too dangerous, though. I'd need personal protection too. A guard of sorts. A buffer between me and the wil—

Groka! She would definitely be weeping right now if I had been among the fallen. And probably Doran. Certainly Frolan. Once he returns.

An idea snaps into place.

Now there's a good solution. Perfect, even. Would also serve to keep the big oaf nearby. So that's a double win for me. And for the tribe, really.

7 - And Subsequently, Unpacking Day

Grak finds that his contempt for packing day pairs nicely with his nearly identical hatred for *un*packing day. The only real difference is that the latter isn't followed with travel, but rest. Or a semblance thereof. At the least, he's always been adept at finding original ways to sneak off before the work is completed.

But that's not the case this time. The promise of relaxation on *this* particular day is disrupted. And all due to the events that transpired on the trail.

The two deaths aren't sitting well with most. Truth be told, it's doubtful they're sitting well with anyone. *Grak* even feels a twinge of sorrow. Which, he points out, disproves the popular belief that his is "the hardest of hearts in the entire tribe and possibly in all the land."

Obviously, he resents this saying. To start, he finds its long-winded nature troubling on a deep level. But more than that, he feels the idiom lacks veracity. Grak prefers to describe his demeanor as "resolute," citing the gentle nature he exerts with friends as proof of this.

Everything else is merely for the comfort of onlookers during troubling times.

He also points to the near certainty that Jafra's heart is *truly* the purest iron ever known. Unarguably more impenetrable than his own, he elaborates.

Of course, he only reveals this sentiment in the presence of trusted company. Though he's noticed they've been receiving it in a less-than-desirable manner of late. He attributes that change to the uncanny cohesion currently running through the tribe.

If only I could direct that energy.

True. Harnessing such camaraderie does promise a sizeable amount of power. So much, in fact, that it would eliminate any possibility of ever losing his place as tribe leader. Alternatively, lack of intervention could result in a wild growth beyond his control. Or worse, a growth exploited by another. Even a foe.

Jafra! Always with her schemes! Surely this situation is no different.

Then it's decided. She's forced my hand. I'll have to find a way to turn this to my advantage. Even if only to keep power out of her greedy claws.

Unfortunately, the inherent obstacles are all too prevalent. It's not just that two deaths occurred in the same day. That would be bad enough, considering that deaths are so rare among Grak's people.

And it's also not just that the deaths were untimely. Sure, neither of the men saw more than twenty-five snows, but they weren't exactly young either.

And it's not even just that they died in a lion attack. While rare, such incidents aren't *unheard* of.

No, it's the combination of these events all happening under Grak's command. That's the prickle in his boot here. None have said as much yet, but the look on their faces gives him surety that talk will turn this direction before long.

Though perhaps worst of all, Grak finds the deaths a bit too upsetting on a *personal* level. He was the closest when the lions pounced. He saw the blood. And the fear. That's what sticks in his mind more than anything else.

Determined, yet terrified. Even resigned.

Grak shakes his head, and the memory slips away. Not completely, but out of his immediate focus at least. The thought promises to return, though. Always does. It's inevitable, really. And it's proving a thorough distraction. In fact, he can't remember the last time he's lacked so much focus for his plans.

Perhaps the incident with Groka's mother. Refused to believe I wasn't peeking. Such gall. And so self-absorbed. Sure, her neck was decent, but—

Ah, never mind that. It was long ago. As an adult, I've never seen such difficulty. As though my mind refuses to focus on anything else. Although ... perhaps I could use that feeling. My own difficulty could make me appear sympathetic.

But that's not enough. It would help me connect, but wouldn't grab hold. So then what?

Perhaps Lago again. Lago, lions, security. True enough. We've grown lax. I could see that working. I'll need a visual reminder, though. Comfort and fear at once. And perhaps that would suffice.

Would help if I could include Doran too. Benefit from his influence. Show that I'm not alone in this thinking. Worth a visit, at leas—

"Grak?" Frolan calls from outside, disrupting any further thoughts.

Grak sighs, resigned to the distraction. "Yes?" He searches for his trousers. "Come in."

Frolan ducks through the flap and pauses. His gaze falls on Grak's bare legs. "Oh ... sorry ... didn't know you were thinking." He turns away awkwardly.

"No, no, come in. I'm through." Grak pulls up his trousers. "Did you finish my cap?"

"Ah, yes. Here." He passes the hat. "But more importantly, Brak's asking for you. There's a bit of unrest. People are frightened. Or upset. Or both. He thinks trouble's coming if you don't put minds at ease."

Grak inspects his new cap. Much finer quality, to be sure. The point is nice and firm, even when given a hard flick. But the height, that's the real beauty here. It's a good hand taller than his previous. Or any in camp, for that matter. He puts it on carefully, scarcely succeeding in hiding his joy.

"Well, this is good news." Mostly the hat.

"Oh ..." Frolan's confusion is unmistakable. "Alright, I'll let Brak know. I thought you'd be concerned about the trouble."

"Yes, I am." Grak gives a quick show of emotion. "I'm very concerned. But it's good, because I was just thinking of how to improve security. So it's perfect timing."

Grak finishes dressing. "Let's see to the people, then. Though I think a quick stop is due first. Shall we?"

They exit the tent with Grak in the lead and Frolan close behind, looking around earnestly. This is part of the training Grak has been giving the brute on the desirable way to protect a leader from danger. It's just one of many lessons designed to make the man more suitable in his company.

And the training has proven useful so far. Frolan's imposing presence has made every order over the past few days significantly smoother. And this, in turn, has resulted in far more getting accomplished. Which, of course, all serves to improve Grak's stature among his people.

All the more reason why announcing this security team is so vital.

They arrive at Doran's tent. As is the man's custom, he has the flap pinned neatly to the outside, ensuring fresh air within. In fact, he's received such success with this approach that many in camp have pointed to it as a useful habit for *Grak* to pick up.

Of course, Grak wouldn't *normally* see fit to alter his mannerisms for the whims of the masses. But, on the other hand, Groka has recently taken to mentioning it as well. Thus, he feels a certain desperation to master this convention. In fact, several times already he's attempted to commit the thing to memory, but it inevitably seems to slip his mind.

Remember this routine, Grak. Remember this routine. Remember this routine. Once more couldn't hurt here. Propriety be shunned! Remember this routine, Grak.

Surely it should stick this time.

With that out of the way, he peers inside. To his dismay, he finds that Doran isn't in. Grak looks around.

"Don't forget to add squiggles." Kando is leaning over the rear of a nearby cart. "What we've already mapped has squiggles. The rest must too." He scratches the ridge of his nose.

Hmm, look at that. Never noticed how prominent that thing is. From this angle, almost looks like his nose is bent.

Opa is sitting next to the man, working a sharpened stick against wet clay. This strange behavior piques Grak's curiosity, and he moves in for a closer view. To his astonishment, she's quickly reproducing the map stone, though with obvious additions.

He rarely looked at the old rock, but the difference is hard to miss.

Their travels are consistent. Almost painfully so. As a result, the map has been the same since he first laid eyes on it as a young boy. Not coincidentally, that was also the point when he decided mapping was a waste of time.

And the feeling has only grown since. Although, he will admit that he's always admired Opa's proficiency. And this is especially true now that it's enhanced by this new medium.

It's the fingers. Must be. Long and bony like that. A bit too thin, if you ask me. Almost grotesque. Still, much more nimble. Well suited for detailed crafts like this.

He looks at his own fingers, thick and strong from so many snows of hunting and heavy labor.

There's the problem. Too much time spent on useless tasks. Never had the opportunity to work this kind of skill.

Sando's fault more than anything, really. He gave me these stubby fingers. And lacked the ability to teach me the finer proficiencies.

Opa looks at Kando. "Like that?"

"It's good, but maybe … I feel like it should have *more*. Can you do *more* squiggles? But don't undo what you've already made. Just enhance the detail further."

Opa alters her grip on the stick, moving her fingers with uncanny finesse. "Spidery," Grak would call it. She delivers a series of slight twitches at the wrist—softer and faster now—and the map takes a more detailed shape.

But in spite of his fascination, Grak soon tires of watching this. Truth be told, he's also annoyed with the pair for wasting so much time on senseless activities. He decides to act on it.

"Why aren't you two unloading? Have we run out of work?" Grak turns to Frolan, hoping to share in the sarcasm's true value. But despite the layers of meaning, it's lost on the man.

Poor, simple fellow. Missing the complexity of the humor. We'll have to go over that lesson again.

"Oh, I'm sorry, Grak." Doran approaches from the left. "I asked them to work on that since their immediate duties were completed. Did you need them further?"

Grak decides mercy might be beneficial here. "No, that's fine. If they're working for you. But I did need to ask something of *you*, Doran."

The man appears eager. "What can I do for you, friend?"

II'→➗

"I don't see how it could have been Lago," replies Jafra. "Wouldn't the lions just attack *him* instead?"

"Perhaps you didn't hear the earlier announcement, Jafra." While Grak is annoyed by the intrusion, he also relishes the opportunity to shame her in front of the gathered tribe. "Again, please remember to raise your hand and wait to be called on. If everyone just speaks whenever they want, we'll have nothing but chaos."

Jafra's face shows a semblance of remorse. "Sorry."

Satisfied, Grak continues. "So, as I was saying—before that rude interruption—Lago's treachery knows no bounds.

"He started with an obvious attempt to kill us all by poisoning the meal. And now that he knows I'm watching for him, he can't get close. That would force him to look for an alternative means of revenge. And I wouldn't put it past him to try something like the lion attack.

"And even if he *didn't* cause it, the attack showed how weak our security has gotten. We've let our guard down. We've grown weak from having peace for so long. And both the meal and the lions show that clearly."

"But, we've always had peace," Ruch interjects.

Need to teach the fool not to contradict me in public. And to better hide his chipped tooth when speaking; it's quite the eyesore.

Nonetheless, Grak has mercy on the man. "Yes, and that's a long time. But please remember to raise your hand."

Jafra's hand shoots up.

Grak hides his nervousness. "Unfortunately, we're stopping questions at this time. Too many points to cover before we lose the sun."

Jafra looks saddened by this announcement. Her hand drops.

Grak ignores her, focusing instead on the crowd. "Chief among these points is the need to increase security. To that end, I'm creating a tribe protection team and will personally oversee their training.

"This group will patrol the camp at all times, watching out for Lago and other signs of danger. If they find anything suspicious, they'll report it back to me. Through this, we'll have forewarning of potential threats: both internal and external."

A mixed murmur rises from the crowd, but Grak presses on. "I've just spoken with Frolan, and he and his hunting team have agreed to take on this duty. It's a big step up for them, but I'm sure they'll do a fantastic job."

Grak pauses, hoping for some sort of positive reaction. Instead, the crowd appears unsure. More importantly, Doran missed his cue. Grak motions to him.

The man steps forward hastily. "Oh, yes. I agree on this issue. What we need most during this time of such sorrow and fear is the feeling of security. We need stability. Perhaps more than ever before. This team should help with that."

The idea sends minor conversations rippling through the crowd. A majority are nodding. They seem agreeable. But as the conversation dies down, a hesitancy still hangs heavy in the air. Grak finds this infuriating.

Doran and his poor timing! They wouldn't be so indecisive if he hadn't missed his opening.

Grak takes a calming breath before attempting to salvage the announcement. "I think Doran makes a good point. Like you, I was shaken up by this tragedy. And yet, for the good of my people, I've set aside emotion and kept us together for the remainder of our travels.

"And now I ask the same of you. To put aside your emotions for the good of our people. Trust that I know what's best for the tribe. And before long, you'll see how this benefits us all. We'll be able to sleep peacefully at night, knowing we're protected."

Judging from the crowd, an example is needed to drive the point home. Grak spots an easy one nearby. "Loren, don't you want what's best for Olive Fifty-three?"

The woman is surprised at being called upon. "Uh … well, yes. That's true. It does sound like a good idea."

Grak smiles to the crowd. "There. See?"

"Although …" she continues, "I do wonder about something. That team is already quite good at what they do. And experienced. And it would take time to train a new group of hunters.

"And we're almost out of meat right now. We barely made it through the move, and wouldn't have survived if they hadn't been hunting the whole time. Might it be best to wait on this switch? Or maybe train another team to handle camp security?"

Hmm, not such a good example, after all. Someone a bit more agreeable next time, Grak.

Cordo cuts in. "It's true." He's rising fast on Grak's list. "I don't see how we could ever replace Frolan. He's our best hunter. By far."

Grak's temptation to refute that superlative is supplanted by caution. "You're right. Frolan is the best hunter. And that also makes him the best suited to protect our tribe.

"Also, I trust him. I know I can depend on the man. And when the leader has faith, the people can have faith."

Grak tosses that sentence around in his head. Yes, he's quite pleased with it. He makes the gesture, and Opa's lean fingers etch it into wet clay.

"And really, Grak's the *best* hunter." Frolan doesn't notice Grak's cautionary look. "Once he teaches his strategy, *anyone* will be better than I am."

The oaf needs a lesson on not volunteering the tribe's leader for hunting duty.

"When will you teach us, then?" Ruch calls out from the side of the crowd.

This sort of talk deeply concerns Grak. Too many are intent on causing trouble, and they're creating problems faster than he can solve them.

He thinks quickly. "Alright, look, let's not get ahead of ourselves here. First, we have to tighten our security. I have to oversee it. And we have to mourn our fallen brethren. Who else will organize that?"

Despite sincere efforts, Grak can't seem to stop rambling. "Also, I have to get the camp settled. We've been traveling for twenty-three days. That's a lot of days … so lots of settling to do."

The people appear uneasy in the absence of a solid answer. Grak catches his breath and reaches for something to appease them. "But never fear, I've already thought of a solution. Cordo will head up hunting now. He has experience. And so does Jafra. She'll be going with him."

Hmm, not a bad idea, I must say. That should keep these two thorns out of my side for the time being.

Jafra is confused. "I will? Then who will cook?"

Grak dons a look of indignation. "See, there you go interrupting me again, Jafra. Let me speak, and you'll find out." He's just stalling for time now. Unsure, he goes with a simple option. "Brak is taking your place."

Now Brak is confused. And shocked. And even a little scared, it seems. "I … am?"

Grak gives him a quiet rebuke. "Now's not the time for second-guessing me, Brak."

The bald man goes silent and looks to the ground with contrition.

Grak turns back to his opponents. "So, as you can see, I've thought of everything."

Best to move on quickly. Before these simpletons ask more questions.

He dons a somber demeanor. "Next, we need to discuss a troubling matter." That proves an effective silencer. "I regret having to bring this up, but the events of the trail demand it."

Grak allows a short pause while those words sink in. Once he has their full attention, he proceeds. "When traveling, you should never leave without the leader. So, I have to ask, who was the first to suggest leaving without me?"

Most of the crowd looks around blankly, hoping to spot the culprit raising a hand. Several, however, have fervency in their eyes.

Grak dons his most comforting smile. "Come on. I can tell some of you have a name on your tongues. You're afraid to say anything. I understand that. But don't worry. No one will be in trouble. I just need to correct the issue."

Still nothing.

Grak rolls his eyes. "Was it Jafra?"

Groka lifts her voice. "Cordo," she says, turning her eyes to the ground in shame.

Cordo stares disapprovingly at the side of her head. "Yes, I was the first to suggest leaving." He steps forward, brazenly claiming his guilt. "I wanted to avoid losing any more light. And I didn't think you'd mind."

Grak is stunned to find the man's treachery running so deep. He grits his teeth and attempts calm. "Well, there you go. Thank you for being honest with me, Groka. And Cordo, well, you don't get any praise because you waited until your errors had been revealed."

Grak turns to the crowd. "So, can anyone see the mistake Cordo made?"

Every face wears confusion. But Grak decides to be patient with them. He waits.

After a long moment, Frolan slowly speaks. "He was wrong?"

Grak shrugs. "Well … true. But that goes without saying. I mean, just look at what occurred as a result. Two deaths are on his head now. I imagine he'll have trouble sleeping at night.

"But that wasn't all. Something far worse. Anyone? No? Out of ideas? Or not trying? I'll give you a hint: he thought he knew …"

Olive Thirteen makes a cautious attempt. "He thought he knew what was best?"

Grak is legitimately impressed. "Very close. He thought he knew what I was thinking. And since I'm leader, what I'm thinking is what's best for the tribe. So, in that sense, you're right."

She's beaming now, staring up at Grak with an interesting look.

Admiration? Maybe. But not the same as when Groka gazes at Jafra.

Grak stores that thinking for another time. "Now, that's pretty bad on its own. But there's more. If I had been riding at the front of the line, I could have warned everyone and rallied a proper defense. But it took me far too long to get there. And do you know why?"

Jafra attempts an answer. "Because you told us to spread out wider on the trail?"

"What?" Grak is stunned by the accusation. "When did … I never said that!"

Jafra seems confused. "Yes, the second day out. Remember? You told us to stop riding in such a thin line. You said it was taking too long to move between your lead position and the food cart."

Grak shakes his head indignantly. "W … you're not even making sense. Yes, I was hungry and suggested a wider line, but I didn't mean it should block the entire trail."

He really didn't. And he finds it unfair that she would misunderstand and make such an accusation.

Nonetheless, Grak gathers himself enough to replace annoyance with vigorous disdain. "Obviously, that would defeat the purpose. And stop butting in, Jafra. Or you'll end up with the same punishment as Cordo."

That catches Cordo by surprise. "Wait, what? Why would I get punished?"

"For your disobedience. And for bringing about the deaths of two of our tribe!" Grak emphasizes this point with a look of disgust. "I would think that much is clear."

This new information has Groka worried. "But you said no one would get in trouble. I'm sorry, Cordo. I never would have said anything."

Hmm. I suppose I did. And I don't suppose the tribe would be forgiving if they mistook it for deception.

Grak attempts a humble look. "Well, you didn't let me finish. I'm not punishing him for misleading the tribe. I'm punishing him for the next point I was trying to make. He got in my way as I was trying to get to the lead. And my shouts went ignored as I tried to get by."

"You knew the lions were attacking?" asks Frolan.

"Well, no … not exactly …" Grak fumbles for an explanation. "But I had a sense that danger was near."

Brak cuts in. "It's true. When we got to the road and saw you were gone, he said something about that."

Well. He's finally learning to be more assertive. And I couldn't ask for a better time. Or a better cause.

"But Zacha and I were in your way too," says Ruch, jumping to Cordo's defense.

Grak considers the man's point. He had forgotten about that, but he's glad for the reminder. "Yes. You were. And that's what I was getting to. You're all three to be punished for that."

"Why are you talking about punishments like we're children?" Cordo is getting frustrated now. "I've seen several more snows than you have, Grak."

Well, he's certainly grown stubborn. And to a level previously only held by Jafra.

Grak stands his ground, refusing to be harassed. "You were directly responsible for the deaths of Farzo and Lumo. What madness would we be living in if we simply allowed people to kill others without retribution? Should we allow that for our most hated enemy? Hmm? If Lago returns, should we show *him* mercy?"

"Well, I've been trying to make that point for some time now." Jafra once again speaks without permission.

"Jafra! I warned you!" Grak takes a calming breath. "This is your last chance. Believe me, you won't want to be punished like the others."

"But why should *Jafra* get punished?" asks Frolan. "*She's* not responsible for any deaths."

Grak finds an answer with ease. "These others also thought they knew better than the leader, though. Didn't they? And their arrogance put the tribe at risk. *That's* what deserves punishment."

"It wasn't arrogance," Ruch pleads. "We didn't hear you. It was an accident."

Grak ignores the man's groveling. There's too much at stake here. "But that's not the sort of accident we can allow, Ruch. Just look at Lago. Perhaps if he had been punished sooner, he wouldn't have tried to kill us all. Perhaps we wouldn't even have needed to exile him."

Grak builds momentum, drawing inspiration from his own speech. "So would you prefer that? To end up like Lago? And what about the tribe? Do *we* want that? Should we just let you off with a warning and wait for the next *deaths* to occur?"

Astonishment runs through the crowd. Many are wearing concerned looks as they nod in earnest agreement.

Even Ruch seems touched by those words. His face shows deep sorrow now. "I'm sorry. I shouldn't have tried to get out of trouble. We've done something wrong. We deserve a punishment."

Grak smiles. "Good! I'm glad to see you coming to your senses. Frolan, have your men bind these three to that cart. And find a good switch."

Ruch's face shows confusion and fear. "No ... wait. I thought you meant extra duties or someth—"

"You'd give us a child's punishment on top of it?" Cordo's face scrunches in disgust, causing his mole to stand out more than usual. "Are you simply looking to *humiliate* us?"

"You should learn to yield before it's too late, Cordo!" Grak calms as an idea comes to mind. "But fine, I can be gracious." He smiles.

Ruch looks relieved. Zacha as well. Even Cordo seems to be breathing a little easier now.

"No children's punishments for you." Grak walks over to a vicious-looking thatch of brambles. "Adults need more than a simple switch." He looks it over, checking for thickness, flexibility, and high thorn count.

"This one should do." He cuts a particularly nasty-looking branch and passes it to Frolan. "And since they're adults, take it to their backs."

Frolan's men grab hold of the offenders. Ruch and Zacha struggle moderately, but are no match for the overwhelming numbers against them. Cordo, on the other hand, walks willingly to his fate.

While his men bind the three offenders to the cart, Frolan removes his tunic and wraps a portion of the thorny stem with it. He pauses, staring at this new tool of pain. There's reservation in his eyes. And concern.

He glances over at Grak. A stern look is returned, conveying the message that such thinking is unwise. Frolan nods. In an instant, he wipes away all traces of his previous emotions.

"How many, then?" he asks.

Hmm, good question. Seventy? No. Might be too many. Can't seem cruel. Sixty? Still round, but a rather heinous number in general.

"Fifty should do it. Each."

New pleading pours from Ruch and Zacha, but Grak has already

grown tired of their groveling. "Start with those two. Stop their yam-
mering. Save Cordo for last, since he thinks he's so tough. Let's see if
watching the pain he's caused helps him realize the error of his ways."

Frolan nods. He walks over to Ruch and takes a firm stance. Slowly,
the brute raises his arm, as though readying for an ax swing. He hesitates for an instant, then lowers the strike.

And again.

And again.

Frolan soon finds a steady pace. Grak would even say it's almost "melodic," only disrupted by Ruch's intermittent cries of agony. And those
are easy enough to ignore for the most part.

Though what's *not* so easy to avoid is the sight of blood. There's quite
a flow of it. Much more than Grak expected. So much, in fact, that
somewhere around twenty lashes in, his stomach becomes uneasy. He
attempts to settle it by occupying his eyes elsewhere.

*On something nearby, preferably. Can't have anyone thinking I looked
away. That would appear weak.*

A rock just next to Frolan's foot suggests itself. And it proves especially useful for Grak's purpose. That is, until a particularly heavy
stroke splatters blood all over it, forcing him to find a new focal point.

Still, he manages to move from one item to the next with considerable success. And it becomes even easier when Ruch's wailing fades
from a lack of strength. Finally, after what seems an unending length
of time, the rhythmic snap of branch to skin stops.

Grak looks back. With no energy left to stand, Ruch is dangling from
the cart, whimpering quietly. His body is bloodied, though not so bad
as Grak remembered it from moments ago.

*Not so bad at all, really. A few cuts. Some blood. And some bone? Not
sure about that one. Either way, no reason to get ill.*

Frolan moves over to Zacha. He takes several deep breaths, then
resumes his pace as though fresh to work.

Unlike Ruch, Zacha does her best to stay silent, perhaps considering
it more dignified. But she doesn't last long. Her determination is soon
overpowered, and she begins to groan in pain.

But these groans are of a different sort than Ruch's were. And not just because of the amplification that comes with the woman's abnormally large mouth. No, these are more heart-wrenching. From deeper inside, as though forcing their way through a failed show of courage. These hit closer to the heart for Grak.

They echo of his ninth snow: his mother's last. He had made the case against disrupting a good thing, but she and Sando wouldn't listen. Complications had delayed the second child for too long, and they were blinded by their own happiness. A cruel irony that the baby should be so unkind to her.

As Grak reflects on this, empathy threatens to rise up for the woman tied before him.

No, Grak. Be strong. Your people need you to be strong. Mother was Sando's fault. The man was too lazy. This is different. These ones deserve pain. For the good of the tribe.

Remember they deserve this, Grak. Remember they deserve this. Remember they deserve this.

Grak considers the possibility of leaving, but shakes that off. It wouldn't look right. Fortunately, Zacha's strength soon fails, and her voice quiets. Not long after that, her chastisement ends as well.

Grak stares at the woman's raw back, still attempting to fight feelings of sorrow. To his shock, she struggles to her hands and knees. As Frolan steps toward Cordo, Zacha rises to her feet, determined to resurrect her mask of bravery.

Remember they deserve this. What does that stubbornness gain her? Remember they deserve this. What did it gain Mother? Remember they deserve this. It gained her nothing. Bravery is the mark of fools who refuse to yield.

This provides *some* relief, but Grak needs more. He reaches for further distractions.

What duties remain for the day? Not many, really. I can have Brak oversee the unpacking for me. It'll be nice to get that off my shoulders. I'll need to begin training Frolan's team. That promises to be a challenge.

Grak checks his shadow. The meeting is running too long.

Such a time-consuming process. Must be tiring too. But you wouldn't think it to look at Frolan. Yet another reason why he's the best choice to lead tribe security. A truly impressive stamina.

I don't think I could have finished with Ruch before pausing for a breath and some water. Well, maybe I could have finished, but then I certainly would have had to take a break. Don't know if I would have been able to finish with all—

As it so happens, Grak is pulled out of this thinking by the sudden sound of Frolan calling for water. The lashes are done, and several from the crowd have come in to tend the wounds of the offenders. After careful consideration, Grak decides to allow this.

I suppose it's understandable. Their punishments have come to a close, after all. There's no need to keep them in pain.

The brute sits on the ground, leaning against the cart's wheel, catching his breath. He's still clutching the branch, though it's now battered beyond use. Which isn't surprising. Grak wonders how the thing lasted as long as it did.

I must have picked a good one. Which isn't surprising. I've always had an eye for quality.

A cup soon arrives, and Frolan drinks it down quickly. Once finished, he sets it aside and leans his head back, staring off in thought. But there's a growing sadness in his eyes, and this troubles Grak.

Hmm. That could be a problem. I'll need to settle the matter before it turns against me.

He walks over and squats down in front of Frolan. But only then does Grak realize he has no words for the man. Or actions. He reaches back in his mind for a sample of Doran's comfort in times past.

Grak places a hand on the brute's shoulder. "Well done, friend. You're keeping us all safe, and that's not easy. It never is. But that's what our duties ask of us. So I'm proud of you. And the tribe is proud of you too. And thankful. Look around."

Frolan surveys the crowd. "It looks more like fear, no?"

Grak thinks quickly. "Well, sure they're *afraid.* They're afraid of Lago … and lions … and probably other things. But they're giving *you* that fear to take for them. Because they see your *strength.*"

Frolan tilts his head. "I suppose you're right. I just …"

The man's words fade out of focus as something new catches Grak's eye. His attention follows after, drawn to the person supporting Cordo as he hobbles away.

Jafra! I knew she was responsible for Cordo's defiance. But what's her aim with all of this?

8 - And Hunting Strategies

Grak is irate about having to teach hunting strategies today. Though in hindsight, it was inevitable. Soon after the tribe settled in at their new campsite, the request became persistent. Demanding, even. And he could no longer ignore it.

But Grak *did* try to deflect it. Initially, he insisted the strategy would only help qualified hunters. Thus, he reasoned, the new team had to first learn the basics without such distractions.

This was the best scheme he could muster at the time, given the other pressing concerns taxing the plotting portion of his mind. And to his surprise, it succeeded. Though only for twenty-nine days.

After that, Grak was forced to rely on improvised solutions. But at times like these, when he's backed into a corner, he's often known to do some of his best work. Thus, through sheer brilliance and quick wit, he managed to delay the request for another twenty-four days.

But, as with all good things, Grak's ideas eventually came to an end. The constant demand for rapid thinking drained his mental stamina, and the schemes simply dried up.

He's also fairly sure the consistent lack of food contributed to his demise. Not that *he* went hungry, of course. But too many in camp did, and this caused a sharp increase in their demands.

Thus, for the last eleven days, Grak has been relying on a new strategy: hiding. But the plan's brilliant simplicity was also its most glaring flaw, and his fortune could only hold out for so long.

Sure enough, early this morning, Sabo wised up. The man noticed Frolan carrying a bowl of stew as he wandered off into the nearby rock hills to "relieve himself." Believing that to be a strange accompaniment for such an expedition, Sabo followed. Upon finding Grak, he alerted others, and they immediately began their usual request.

But this time, Grak had no way of escape. Which is why he's now improvising a hunting strategy in this small clearing in the nearby forest.

"Like this?" Frolan takes a deep, controlled breath.

Grak feigns annoyance. "Yes, but talking defeats the purpose. Now you have to start over. Back on the ground."

He looks about for other ripe scoldings. "As usual, Jafra, you're doing it all wrong. Hold the branches higher."

She grimaces. "I'm sorry. It's just ... my arms are really aching now. I don't think I can manage to hold them any higher ... or much longer."

Such incessant whining with this one. And she fails to see how it only makes her more disreputable.

Grak sneers. "Oh, I didn't realize I was inconveniencing you. I suppose I'll just have to tell our people that their starving children don't matter as much as your comfort."

Jafra replies with a frown. Grak smiles to himself.

Well done. One of your better exchanges, to be sure.

But he has no time to enjoy the victory, as the smell of dung is already growing too powerful. He steps farther away from the woman.

"Is it supposed to bleed so much, Grak?" Cordo asks meekly. "I fear I might be losing too much blood. I can't even feel the pins any longer. Or that portion of my leg."

"Yes. That's how you know it's working." Grak replies, lost in thought.

He's growing concerned about Cordo's weakening fortitude. It took a noticeable dip after his punishment, and has yet to return. Of course, the man's *subservience* has improved, but that's still not ideal. Grak would prefer to have *both* available whenever he needs them.

Cordo nods at the answer. "I was wondering something else too. And please, keep in mind, I don't doubt the value of these exercises. I'm only curious ... but, well, would you explain how any of this will help? It just seems we've been here for quite some time without any results.

And I fear we might lose the light before catching anything."

Grak sees a teaching opportunity. "You fear too much, Cordo. Especially the dark. Before we can properly *hunt* the deer, we have to *think* like the deer. Are *they* afraid of the dark? Or of *anything*?" He leaves the subject there lest he accidentally reveal too much about his admiration for the creatures.

Fierce. Undaunted. Majestic. If only our tribe were more like that. We could learn a thing or two from those animals.

Frolan offers his mind on the subject. "They run from *us* … and lions."

Grak silences the man with a gentle touch on the lips. "Shh, friend. Be the deer. Enter his thoughts."

"So, what about the ropes?" Jafra points to the elaborate cross-rigging among the trees. "I don't remember *those* when you last hunted with us."

"The Great and Pivotal Hunt of Awe, you mean?" The name still doesn't sound right. Grak will have to tweak it further. "You're right, they weren't there. The ropes are a new idea. But they won't be useful until you all learn to think like deer."

He remembers to be angry with her. "And you, Jafra, are disrupting that process. How is anyone supposed to think like a deer while you're asking so many questions? I'm taking your speaking privileges."

Jafra nods and casts her eyes to the ground. "Ok. Until when?"

Grak is astonished by her defiance. "Do you not understand the concept of lost privileges? You'll be notified when you have them back!"

She certainly shouldn't be missing the point. Grak made the policy quite clear and has reiterated it a number of times since. She gives a slow, sad nod to signify repentance.

Or rather, to feign it. Insists on questioning my leadership, this one. And while I'm trying to teach her something new. So ungrateful! But even if she can't be helped, I can prevent her defiance from spreading to these others.

Grak lifts his voice to address the whole group. "So many questions from all of you today. But that won't help you think like a deer. Do *they* ask questions? Of course not. They just *kno*—"

A sudden wind blows Grak's hat off. That's the fourth time today, and he's starting to get annoyed. Even more so, given this embarrassing disruption of his speech.

In many ways, Grak feels the thing is almost *too* tall now. Though he really doesn't feel he has a choice in the matter. Further copies in camp threatened the height of his previous cap, forcing him to have Frolan make another one several days ago.

But Grak was tired of having to replace his hat every few days, so he also decided to enact a "height limit" policy. In it, he took care not to mention head coverings while also avoiding any ambiguity in the wording. And he's quite proud of that feat. "My clever policy," he calls it.

Of course, Grak also made it clear that this policy only applies to "*standard* members of the tribe." Which, of course, does not include him. He reasoned that anyone wishing to find him for help or directions should be able to spot *his* hat from any distance with ease.

But despite the thorough nature of this announcement, confusion still arose. Many felt the wording might mistakenly ban future members of the tribe who have natural height tendencies.

As a result, Grak considered altering the policy. But in the end, he settled instead on suggesting that such members crouch "for the sake of all."

Besides, it's not even realistic. Frolan is the closest in height, and he's still a good two hands shy. Maybe if he mated with an exceptionally tall woman. Or a bear.

Grak allows himself a chuckle at that thought, oblivious to the concerned stares from everyone around him. He picks up the hat and returns it to his head. To his chagrin, he finds that perfect positioning requires both hands, forcing him to loosen the grip on his cloak. The cold seizes this opportunity and wafts in, sending a shiver through his entire body. He hurries with the cap, then renews his grasp on the fur.

Doesn't seem like it should be this cold yet. There's still quite some time until the snows. I hope. That would be a truly awful addition to all my other troubles. If the snows began earlier than usual.

But either way, that's far from his most urgent responsibility at the moment. His focus returns to the hunters. "Now, where was I? Ah, yes.

Think like a de—"

"Wait! I can hear them!" Frolan's ear is pressed to the ground, and he's wearing an excited grin.

"What?" Grak hides his disbelief. "Good. Good." He's stalling while deciding how to proceed. "You're learning."

Maybe I'm actually onto something here.

"I can hear it too!" Sabo is holding an ear to the wind.

Jafra assumes the man's pose for a moment. With sudden realization, she nods and points excitedly.

Should probably remove the rest of her communication privileges as well.

"No, Jafra, you're doing it wrong. You have to place an ear to the grou—" Grak freezes. He hears it too: a noise in the distance, growing louder, clearer.

All have stopped their exercises now to gawk at what this might be. The sound grows louder. And louder. It quickly grows into something akin to a heavy thunder. Memories of a similar noise tickle the back of Grak's mind, begging for attention.

"That's the herd!" Cordo points to the far line of trees where dense brush is waving violently.

"Stampede!" Jafra sounds the warning as the deer break into view.

Grak recognizes the opportunity to lead. "Cordo, kill some! You too, Jaf—"

The wind rushes out of his lungs as Jafra crashes into his chest. She pulls him behind a nearby fallen tree, and they stick tight to it. Surprisingly, this does the trick. Deer race by the spot, but hooves never touch either of them. It's over faster than Grak realizes.

He opens his eyes and peers around. The tail end of the stampede is disappearing through the next line of trees. To his left, Jafra rises to a seated position, staring at him as though expecting congratulations.

For her error? Such gall!

Grak decides on a loud voice to make matters clear to the others. "Jafra! I had a plan! We could have killed some deer." He rises to his feet. "But now we have nothing. Nothing but hunger."

Grak turns away, but can't resist one final comment. "And just so you know, you stink! You weren't supposed to use that much dung. It's one mistake after another with you." He didn't want to have to resort to personal attacks, but his anger got the better of him.

"I'm so sorry." She averts her eyes. "I was trying to keep you from danger."

"That's it! Your speaking privileges are gone for twice as long now!"

The stubborn fool. She forces these punishments on herself.

Grak glares at Frolan. "And why weren't *you* there to keep me from danger? Isn't that your job? Maybe if you had been doing it, Jafra wouldn't have messed everything up so badly. It's good to know I can count on you both when it matters most!"

Frolan winces as Cordo pops the brute's shoulder back in place. "Sorry." He rotates his arm timidly. "I should have been closer. It won't happen again."

Grak is taken aback. He hadn't expected quite so much obeisance. Nor did he imagine his fury would fade so quickly.

Well ... he seems sufficiently penitent. Perhaps kindness is in order. Or at least a change of subject. No sense dragging him through it when he's already lear—

A sudden commotion seizes Grak's attention. Several hunters are making their way toward a badly wounded deer some twenty paces off to the right.

Oh my ...

It only takes Grak an instant to realize his opportunity. He races off to join the others, arriving a moment later and in desperate need of air.

"Good ..." He breathes deep. "The strategy worked ..." Another breath. "Of course, we could have had *more* kills. I gave you a perfect opportunity, after all. Don't know how you failed to take advantage of it." Unsure of what other criticisms to level at them, Grak lets the topic trail off and seeks out a new point of focus.

He looks down at the injured creature. Judging by the two broken legs, it must have missed a step and taken a bad fall. The deer blinks at Grak and attempts to stand, but its legs give way, and the animal collapses. Still, this doesn't deter a second attempt. Or a third.

Grak has to turn away from the sight, masking his emotion with indifference. "Some—" He clears his throat. "Someone finish it off."

Jafra steps up. Her ax falls swift and heavy. The resulting sound sends shivers through Grak's body. He's never gotten used to it. Or the resulting splatter—some of which is now coating the leg of his trousers.

"Jafra!" Grak *just* had Brak remove a pesky grass stain. "Have you no contr—" He goes silent and ducks down, motioning for the others to follow.

While confused, the team obeys. Grak raises his head just far enough to see over the tall grass. His people look to each other, hoping someone else might have an idea of what's going on. Frolan tries to follow Grak's line of sight off to the far tree line, but only ends up more confused. Grak pushes the man's head down farther.

With his view gone, Frolan resorts to whispering. "What is it, Grak?"

"People." Grak's whisper is more of a loud, rasp. He's never been able to get it quite right. "Strangers. Over by the trees. I saw them just a moment ago. They appear to be hiding now."

Frolan abandons the silent approach. "Oh, I thought it was something dangerous." He begins to rise.

Grak shoves him back down. "It *is* dangerous, you buffoon!"

Frolan takes that surprisingly well. "Oh, sorry." But he looks confused again. "Wait, *why* is it dangerous?"

Grak fails to find suitable words for this flagrant ignorance. In the end, he settles on thick sarcasm. "Does the name 'Lago' mean anything to you? And he was a part of our tribe. We *knew* him. Why would we assume anything other than danger from someone we've never met?

"And why am I telling *you* all of this? You're the chief of tribe security! And my personal buffer of protection! A fine mess you're making of *that* job so far."

Frolan looks ashamed. "I'm so sorry, Grak. Twice I've failed you today. I understand if you need to choose someone else to take over my position."

Grak rolls his eyes and calms his tone. "Look, Frolan, I didn't me—"

"Hail there! You with the pointy hat! Are you alright?" The group of strangers has emerged from the trees and is heading their way.

Grak's team looks to him for orders. He replies with a rapid series of hand gestures. But to his dismay, their confusion reveals that they've already forgotten those lessons.

Grak attempts his whisper again. "Just follow my lead." He's both surprised and pleased at managing something quieter this time. "Be ready to attack if I give the signal." He receives earnest nods all around.

"What signal?" Obviously, Sabo was bobbing his head for no reason whatsoever.

Grak looks to the others, hoping *someone* paid attention. Nothing. Only empty stares and timid shoulder shrugs.

"Does *anyone* know *any* signals?" He's almost pleading now.

Frolan perks up. "There's the one where you point at your ear." He tends to be the most attentive during classes, though that isn't saying much. "Was that the signal to *listen*?" It really only serves to show how poorly the rest of the group focuses.

"No!" Grak takes a calming breath. "There's no signal to *listen*. That should be natural to you by now! What *else* would you be doing while hunting?"

He clenches his fists in frustration. "I give up! You see? *This* is why we can't have nice hunting strategies!"

Grak takes another breath. While he finds his anger understandable, he's worried that getting *too* riled will give away their location.

After another moment, he proceeds in a calmer tone. "Alright, I'll go over it one more time. Please pay attention. The signal to attack is if I *clap*."

Cordo looks confused. "But wait a moment." He's always had a nice whisper: clear, crisp, and quiet. "How will we know if you're telling us to attack or if you're just applauding something?"

Grak is amazed by the question. "Why would I start *applauding* in the middle of a hunt?"

"You started chuckling for no reason just a bit earlier." Sabo brings up a decent point. As much as Grak hates to admit it.

"Also, what if you only have one hand free?" asks Cordo.

Grak rubs his brow in frustration, desperate to find a resolution before the strangers arrive. "Alright, fine. Attack will be … if I start snapping my fingers. You can't possibly confuse that. Everyone got it?" This time the nods seem genuine.

"Should I rise first?" asks Frolan. "To draw their aim? If they attack us, I think it's better if their arrows are pointed at me rather than at you."

"Whose arrows?" comes a strong, throaty voice.

Grak reels about, prepared for the worst. But the newcomers only appear confused. And none have weapons drawn. Plus, the strangers are outnumbered fourteen to eight. Quickly taking all of that into consideration, Grak opts to restrain himself for the moment.

Still, best to keep a watchful eye. These people are far too silent in their movements. Could be surrounding us as we speak.

"Oh my, there are quite a few of you crouching down there. And you all have pointed hats," says the voice, now connected to a man with blond hair and a harsh, thick face. Harsh except for the man's eyelashes, that is. Those are long and delicate, contrasting sharply with his other features.

Like a woman's lashes. Still, a striking effect. Almost enviable.

The remainder of the group looks much the same. Minus the luxurious eyelashes, of course. And they're dirtier than Grak's people, though he can't tell if that's grounds for suspicion. Nonetheless, he feels more comfortable taking his "suspicion is the best policy" approach.

The stranger appears confused at the lack of a response, but quickly forgets in favor of a new focus. "Those are nice. Your hats, I mean." He adopts a look of confusion. "Um … might I ask … what are you all doing? Crouching down like that, I mean."

Grak stands cautiously. "We were hunting. Hunting *our* herd." He motions for the rest of his team to rise. "Might I ask what *you're* doing following our herd? And what you're doing so close to our campsite?"

"Oh, was that *your* herd? I apologize. I thought it wa—"

"Kunthar!" interrupts a woman with a wide, flat nose. "Where are your manners?" She turns to Grak. "Please forgive him, friend. He can be forgetful. I am called Dernue." The broad-nosed woman gives Grak a crushing hug.

Kunthar wears obvious annoyance. "Yes, Dernue, I was getting to that. If you had just let me finish, you would have known." He moves in to embrace Frolan. "I am pleased to meet you, friend."

Frolan forgets his training and returns the embrace. "And the same to you! Wow, we haven't met another tribe in … well, in a very long time. I can't even remember how long it's been. Can you remember, Grak?"

Grak puts on the most annoyed face he can muster. "No, I can't." He increases the disdain in his voice. "A long time, indeed."

It's too late now. The flood can't be stopped. Each stranger approaches, announces his or her name, and gives a strong hug.

But Grak isn't fooled. He finds their close mannerisms suspect. Also, the way they avoided his question leaves something to wonder about. Though posing it again should clarify the matter. "So … Kunthar … you were saying? About our herd?"

The man responds with exuberance. "Oh, yes. Your herd. Again, I apologize. Things have been rather off lately.

"Some days ago, our own herd changed their usual travels while heading south. Then they just stopped and waited around Redhand for days on end. As though afraid to cross the trail. We almost set up camp there, but then they set off again. Entirely new path. Not sure what's gotten into them.

"But these ones, we thought they were from our herd. Just more of their strange behavior. Didn't realize they belonged to another tribe in the area. Our apologies once again."

Grak finds the stranger's groveling nature endearing. Still, he steps back in hopes of avoiding the spit being propelled by the man's powerful inflections.

After a moment of consideration, Grak decides to avoid conflict at this time. "Well, I suppose it's not a problem if you didn't kill any." He realizes something. "Although, are you the reason for that stampede that wounded some of my team and nearly killed *me*?"

"Oh my, I'm afraid we are. We were trying to make a kill—a real beauty of a male—and he got wind of us. He took off running back to the others and got the whole group spooked.

"They tried to run west, but there were spikes in the ground … so many spikes … and many with deer heads on them. Very strange."

Grak feigns ignorance.

"That spooked them even more, so they turned east. But then they ran into this whole series of ropes. You wouldn't believe how extensive it was. They couldn't get through. So they headed north. And into you, it turns out. We're *so* sorry for any trouble caused. I hope the injuries weren't serious."

While pleased at the effectiveness of his traps, Grak refuses to drop suspicion toward these people. "So how do we know you were *actually* hunting?"

Kunthar looks around at his tribe. All are lost for answers. Dernue even sets down her deer while she thinks. But no ideas appear forthcoming.

After another moment of this, Grak finally takes pity on them. "Your kills would be a good way to prove it."

Kunthar gets excited. "Oh, good point." He grows confused again. "But wait, if you knew that, then why did you ask?" His eyelashes flutter wildly as he blinks in confusion.

Grak is unsure how to answer that, but settles on simplicity. "I just wanted to see if *you* knew."

Kunthar smiles. "Oh, I see. That makes sense." He shrugs. "I suppose."

Grak presses on, eager to resolve his remaining suspicions. "I'm curious about something, Kunthar. Like Frolan mentioned, we haven't seen strangers in a long time. And yet, you weren't surprised to meet us. In fact, you almost seemed to be *expecting* us. Why is that? How did you know we'd be here?"

Kunthar shakes his head. "Oh no, we weren't *expecting* you. But we did see one of your people several days ago. Called out to him, and he got real skittish and ducked out of sight. Pretty sure we saw him running away a few moments later. So we assumed we'd bump into the rest of your tribe before long."

Grak feels the need to refute that. "No. Wouldn't have been us. Our people never run. Maybe you saw a deer. Deer run. Or maybe a bear." This brings his earlier thought to mind, and he fights the oncoming grin.

Dernue cuts in. "No, it was a human. Had clothes and everything." She thinks for a moment. "But his hat wasn't pointed like yours. Thin fellow. Older too."

"Ah, there you go. All our people have pointed caps. Couldn't have been one of us. Must have been one of yours, then."

In truth, Grak is pretty sure they're describing Sando. Though why the man would change his hat and go for a stroll is baffling.

Might be losing his wits. Well, no matter. The cause is moot. The old fool's in for a scolding tonight. Both for not informing me of these events and for making the tribe look feeble by running like a coward.

Fortunately, Kunthar accepts Grak's answer. "That's possible. I suppose. I don't know why we wouldn't have recognized him. Or why he wouldn't have recognized us. But maybe."

Grak is getting uncomfortable with this subject. And with these people. "Hmm. Well, who can know. Anyway, if you don't mind, we really must get back to our hunting. I hope you find good fortune with your own." He tries to casually look from them to the tree line as a suggestion that it's time to part ways.

But Kunthar doesn't get it. "Oh we have! *Great* fortune, in fact. Some in the tribe even think we have *too much* meat right now." He slyly motions to Dernue. "They think we won't be able to use it all before it spoils. Or before we have to move again."

Dernue cuts in. "Hey, there's an idea. Would your people like to come for a feast? We're camped not far from here."

Grak is wary of that offer. The strangers are still far too suspicious for his liking.

And yet, the tribe's hungry. And irrational. I could see them getting upset at me for rejecting this offer. Although … if there's a reason beyond my control, then they can't blame me.

Grak thinks quickly. "Ah, well, I believe we have something else planned for tonight. We're pretty busy much of the time. Usually need several days' notice to adjust for something as time-consuming as a feast."

Frolan shakes his head eagerly. "Oh, no, there's nothing planned. Not for the tribe at least. You had me schedule a foot rub, but that shouldn't take long. We could easily attend the feast."

Grak leans in to the brute and whispers a reply, once again oblivious to his limits with that skill. "I cleared my schedule for the purpose of relaxing! And this feast *won't* be a relaxing event. I'll thank you not to volunteer me for such idiocy in the future!"

Grak dons a pleasant facade and turns back to the strangers. "Actually, I just remembered something else. We're quite low on meat at the moment. *Dangerously* low, in fact. Certainly can't spare anything for a feast right now. So we'll have to decline. I hope you understand."

Dernue waves dismissively. "Oh, don't worry! Like I said, we have plenty. We can provide enough meat for both tribes. Would your people be able to bring fruits? Perhaps some olives? Those are always a treat."

Frolan leans in and whispers, "Brak says we'll need our olives if we're to survive the winter."

Grak nods to the brute, then turns back to the strangers. "No, sorry. None of those either. It's a shame, though. That would have been great. Maybe next feast."

"Oh, well don't let *that* stop you from joining us." Dernue seems overly eager. "We can provide olives too."

Grak is out of ideas. "Oh, so good … I'm glad this is all working out … Nothing's stopping it … Good …"

Kunthar grins. "Wonderful! Then we'll see you at dusk. Well then, if you'll excuse us. We need to go prepare."

With that, he gives quick directions for finding their camp, and the strangers head back toward the tree line.

Once Grak is certain they're out of earshot, he checks his shadow. "Not enough time left if we're to gather the tribe for a feast. I suppose that's the end of our lessons for the day."

At least the strangers are helping me get out of that. Which gives me a chance to think up more strategies. Or excuses. Whichever comes to mind first, I suppose.

Grak claps his hands together. "Alright, let's be off then." He turns to Jafra and gestures toward the deer. "Well?"

She silently picks it up, and the team starts for home.

"That was pleasant," says Frolan.

Grak shrugs. "I'm not so sure. I still wonder if they were actually hunting."

Frolan grows confused. "What? What do you mean?"

"Just think. They were a bit too slow to respond when I asked about it. And really, we don't know where they got their kills. What if they keep a supply of animal corpses on hand for deceiving unsuspecting strangers?

"Might have been after our supplies, for all we know. They *were* awfully quick to invite us back for a 'feast,' after all. It's possible they just go around tricking other tribes like that. Then they invite them to a meal and kill them."

Frolan's face shows astonishment. "Wow, that's a pretty smart trick."

Grak shrugs. "Sure, I suppose. But it takes a smarter mind to see through it."

"Well, good thing we have *you*, Grak." Frolan suddenly grows confused again. "So, how do you suppose they keep the dead animals looking like fresh kills?"

Grak thinks on that one for a moment. "I don't know. Perhaps the trick is so elaborate that they make fresh kills before beginning the day's treachery."

"Oh." Frolan ponders the answer. "So then why wouldn't they just live off of those kills? They wouldn't need to take our supplies."

Grak hadn't considered that aspect. "Good. You're starting to think for yourself. That was a test. You're learning.

"And you're right. It would make more sense that they're telling the truth." Grak thinks on it further. "But we should still be careful. Just in case. We should go to the feast armed."

9 - And Strangers

Grak has never trusted strangers. Or liked them. But before today, he was content with only having encountered them on six occasions in his life. Well, according to his *public* count, that is.

When going by his *private* tally, the number jumps to six and a half, reflecting the time he saw people in the distance, but never met them. "Wouldn't be accurate to consider it a full meeting," was his conclusion on the matter.

And while each situation bore a unique flavor, they routinely inspired in Grak a deep enmity toward all outsiders. Even the partial encounter left him outraged that anyone could be so rude as to shun him and his people. And true to form, today's experiences show little promise of achieving a more favorable result.

"This way." Frolan leads the group down into a sparsely treed dell.

Grak and Doran follow close behind while the security team maintains a protective circle around the pair.

"So, as you can see, by *this* map … no …" Doran shuffles his stack of clay tablets. "Ah, here it is. By *this* map theory, our southernmost campsite wouldn't be far from the ocean."

"I see." Grak nods in an effort to appear attentive.

Truth be told, he rarely takes interest in Doran's ramblings these days. Nonetheless, he still tries to at least mimic the actions of one listening. By Grak's estimation, this is a necessary sacrifice for the man's ongoing support. And in turn, for the support of Doran's devoted followers.

Indeed, Grak finds the group's unquestioning loyalty to be quite useful. And their unbridled enthusiasm is even more advantageous. In fact, they consistently prove themselves irreplaceable when he needs a crucial policy implemented.

Of course, the security team's powers of persuasion are equally effective at such times. Perhaps even more so. But Grak finds it beneficial to transition between fear and popular endorsement to achieve his goals. "More sustainable over the long term," he reasons.

Grak attempts to stifle a yawn, but fails. Drowsiness seems to be sneaking up on him more often these days.

Doran grows concerned. "Is everything alright, friend?" He looks at his maps. "I must be boring you. I apologize. I get too carried away sometimes."

Grak had hoped to avoid offending the man, but a little honesty can't *hurt*. "Well, no. I wouldn't say you're *boring* me. It's just ... well, you've grown so distant. We used to be friends."

"We still are. Aren't we?" Doran responds hastily.

Grak doesn't know how to answer that. "I suppose." No, that might be interpreted negatively. "I mean, I *want* us to be. And *I* think of you as a friend." Relationship salvaged. "But you only ever talk about that thing you saw ... and the ocean ... and now your map theories. You're different."

Doran ponders those words for a long moment. "Perhaps I am different. And perhaps I do talk too much these days. I apologize, friend. I never wanted it to harm our friendship. I just find the topic so ... exhilarating. And I want to share that with you.

"I mean, what do we ever have in the tribe that's worth exploring so deeply? And if this all means what we think it means ... well, it could mean so much more. Imagine what else is out there."

Grak is confused now, but considers it less than prudent to admit as much. "Hmm, I see," he says, then withdraws into thought, determined to figure out what the man meant.

But his moment of reflection is short-lived, brought to an end by Frolan's sudden raised hand signaling a halt. Everyone in the immediate area comes to an abrupt stop, setting off a series of hushes louder than the voices they seek to quiet. This is followed by sounds of repeated bumping and occasional surprise. Finally, after several long moments of this, the tribe manages to cease all noise and motion.

Clearly, they need that lesson again. And probably several whippings. Just to ensure the point is understood this time.

Frolan beckons for Grak, then motions for his team to ready their bows. The immediacy with which they carry out the order is impressive.

Grak tiptoes to the front, staying squarely behind Frolan's large frame for safety. He peers over the brute's shoulder at the strangers' encampment just ahead in the next clearing.

After a thorough search, however, Grak can't spot anything out of the ordinary. Mostly just deer skin tents, simple wooden carts, and crooked mud paths. And, of course, people meandering about on their evening routines. No different from his own camp in most respects.

Although, Grak does realize *one* point of great interest. The strangers don't appear to have spotted his people yet. He takes a quick estimate.

Six … maybe seven hundred of them. Though I might be off by nine or so. Best to get a second opinion.

"How many do you count?" Grak's whisper continues to fail him.

"Around three hundred, I'd say," replies Frolan.

That was an unexpected answer. Grak quickly assesses the probability of his own tally being correct. "Yes. Three hundred. My conclusion as well. Far too many for us to take, should it come to a fight."

Frolan furrows his brow in determination. "We could send back for the rest of the tribe," he offers.

Grak looks at his young pupil with understanding. "Still so much to learn, friend. No, their punishments are more important. For the betterment of the tribe's character. Besides, even if we had our full strength, we'd still be outnumbered. No, I think the better appro—"

A rustling off to the right grabs their attention. Frolan motions to his team, and they nock arrows. Every eye focuses on the spot. Waiting. Expecting. Antici—

Kunthar steps through the brush, tying his trousers. He spots them an instant later and raises his hands with a start. "Wait! Wait! Don't shoot!"

Grak turns to Frolan and nods.

Frolan nods in reply, then turns to his team. "Ready! Ai—"

"Stop! Stop!" Grak's heart is racing. "What, in all the land, are you idiots doing?"

Frolan looks stunned. And a little hurt. "You nodded."

"I nodded to lower your bows, you ..." Grak breathes.

Frolan is confused now. "So you don't want us to shoot him?"

"No! Wh ...?" Truth be told, it wouldn't matter if they weren't so close to the man's encampment.

And if we weren't so outnumbered. Best not to provoke them before knowing their intentions.

Frolan shrugs to his team. They relax their bows, but keep arrows nocked.

"Could I make a request to clarify that signal?" Frolan's suggestion elicits nods and a few voiced approvals. "Seems like it might get us into a lot of unnecessary trouble."

Grak agrees, but admitting it here could cast a shadow on his leadership. "If you'd like to alter a signal, you know the required procedure. And I won't discuss the matter otherwise."

Kunthar catches his breath. "Whew! That was a close one, friend! Whatever didn't come out in the bushes is certainly gone now." Another deep breath. "Well, Frolan, I'm glad your people could make it."

Wh ...? Frolan? His people? What would inspire the fool to address the dolt instead of me? Clearly, there's been some confusion.

"Yes," replies Grak in a louder and more prestigious voice than usual. "Against better judgment, we came. Since you're new to the area." After an awkward and expectant pause, Grak realizes this sentence doesn't finish itself. "Well, hospitality and all. So ... consider yourself fortunate."

Kunthar accepts that answer willingly. "Well, I'm glad you could make it." His eyes return to the bows. "Though, are you hunting for the feast? You really don't have to. I meant it when I said you'd be our guests. I imagine we already have enough to share. What do you have there, one hundred or so? Yes, I'm *certain*. More than enough, in fact."

"Oh, no need. We've brought our own food." Grak points to Jafra hauling a sled piled high with meat.

Truth be told, while Grak remains suspicious toward the strangers, he's more afraid of being indebted to them. He feels it wouldn't be wise to give them the upper hand. Also, if they look too gracious in comparison, it could lead to unrest among Grak's people.

Kunthar looks at the meat in confusion, then shrugs and smiles. "Sure. If that's what you want. All the more to eat then, right?" His smile morphs into concern. "So … then why do you have weapons at the ready?"

Frolan speaks up. "Oh, we were just being cautious. We don't know you yet, so we had to make sure you didn't intend us harm."

The fool! It seems he needs another lesson on not divulging tribe secrets.

"Why would we intend you harm?" asks Kunthar.

Hmm. Seems almost too innocent. Highly suspect.

Grak cuts in, seeking to control the conversation before it gets out of hand. "I don't really know, I suppose. But you can't be too sure these days."

"Hmm, I suppose you're right …" Kunthar trails off in thought.

Grak reaches for a new topic. "So, Kunthar, are you the tribe's leader? If not, I'm eager to meet whoever that might be."

"The tribe's *leader*?" Confusion once again dances on Kunthar's face, causing his eyelashes to respond with vigor.

Grak resorts to slow explanations. "Yes. You know, someone to run everything. Make sure all is going smoothly."

Understanding slowly dawns on the man. "No, we don't have anyone who does that for the *whole* tribe. Fascinating idea, though." He thinks on it for a moment longer. "Well, come, I'll show you around our camp. And you can tell me more about this 'tribe leader' thing."

"They're just different. That's all. Who wants to be exactly like everyone else?" While Grak enjoys talking about himself, he's tired of explaining these concepts to each new stranger.

"Hmm, good point." Franzor thinks for a moment. "Though, if all of your people wear them, aren't you each exactly like everyone else in the tribe?"

Grak expects this question by now. "That's why mine is taller."

"I see." Franzor considers that. "But what's to stop someone else from making *theirs* taller?"

Also anticipated. Grak sighs. "That's why I created a policy."

"*Another* policy? Interesting." Franzor rubs his bald head and ponders the idea.

Grak rolls his eyes and looks around awkwardly. He's beginning to suspect monotony might somehow be a part of their plan.

Is it possible to die from boredom? Perhaps. Would be a slow and tortured death, to be sure. Lulled to sleep is a possibility at the least. Then they'd have an easy kill. Ingenious. And treacherous.

He forces himself to stay alert. Which isn't a problem for Olive Thirteen. She seems to have an astonishing reserve of excitement to draw upon, lavishing it on every word and awkward pause.

I really must learn how she manages such a consistent display. Would be useful when dealing with the tribe simpletons. And Doran too, if I'm being honest.

Fortunately, Kunthar soon grows impatient as well. "Thank you, Franzor. I apologize, but we must move along now. We'll see you at the feast in a short while." He leads the team off.

Curious that Kunthar's so eager to finish introductions. Perhaps he's planning an ambush at the cook site. Clever. Wait for the leader before launching an attack. Take him out first, and the rest will scatter. That's what I would do.

Kunthar rambles about his tribe as he leads the group along. But Grak isn't listening. He stopped some time ago, in fact. Now he's just following absentmindedly, catching up on his own thoughts.

Olive Thirteen, on the other hand, nods with enthusiasm at every word from Kunthar. Which, of course, proves an effective distraction for the man, and is the very reason Grak is able to spend the time in reflection. So in the end, despite his initial refusal of her pleas, Grak is glad she tagged along.

Which is more than can he say for the surrounding security team.

It's not that they've disappointed him in any way, but neither have they done anything to impress him.

Though I suppose they're doing a sufficient job of staying observant. And of keeping their circle tight. Yes, I doubt any surprise arrows could get through. At least not without first taking down several of my guards. And I imagine that would give me enough time to find cover and think of something.

Though Grak would prefer it if the circle had greater density. He regrets sending so many of his forces with Frolan to the strangers' cook site to protect the food during feast preparations.

Surely they didn't need half the security team for such a trivial task. We could always forgo eating if we had to, but losing the leader? Morale would be squashed. My people would be directionless without me. Helpless. Like children ... my helpless little children.

Grak's focus is snapped back to the present by a shifting breeze carrying an overpowering stench. He covers his mouth and looks about for the source. It concerns him more than a little to see the cook site nearby. But that's downwind now. He rules it out and continues scanning the area. Nothing obvious.

Wait. That conspicuous fellow. The tall, thin one. He looks particularly filthy. Even by this tribe's low standards.

And yet, against all reason, they're actually approaching the man. Grak attempts to suppress his growing disgust.

Though he is fascinating in a way, this human rag. So content with his filth. As though he welcomes all manner of grime. And what's this?

Several tears in the man's clothing reveal fabric blending casually into crusted skin. Grak shivers at the sight.

And what's splattered on his cheek? Clumps of mud? I hope. But how would he not feel that? And why wouldn't he wash it off? Or does he abstain from that practice? Maybe so. After all, his hair looks like it hasn't seen a rinse in ... well, ever. If that's even hair. Could just as easily be a bird's nest. Though I imagine a bird would keep its dwelling cleaner than that.

Unfortunately, wisdom doesn't prevail, and they continue toward the man. As they near him, Grak takes a deep breath and holds it.

"And this is Jorthar." Somehow Kunthar not only appears interested in the fellow, but also unaffected by his stench. "He looks after the horses. Feeds them … waters them … brushes them …" He thinks for a moment. "Forgive me, Jorthar. I believe I'm leaving out important details. Please, tell them what you do. You say it much better."

Grak exhales, now realizing his plan to be unsustainable. He discards it in favor of short breaths aimed at only sucking in air from his immediate vicinity.

"Well, what *don't* I do?" Jorthar's exuberance contradicts his appearance. "I do everything needed to look after the tribe's horses. I feed them … I water them …"

The man's meandering pace mingles with his aroma to create a truly maddening effect. Grak considers possible exit strategies.

Perhaps an illness of some sort. Or a meeting. That one's easier. Just talk to Frolan for a moment. No need to keep the ruse going after th—

Grak's attention snags on something he hadn't noticed before: the pony tethered to a nearby tree. He tries to fight his excitement, but the effort is futile. Thus, he abandons that idea in favor of a more direct approach.

"You have a pony?" Grak asks, already on his way over to see it.

Jorthar seems confused by this interest. "Oh. Yes." He looks at the creature with indifference. "Not a very useful beast. But it can carry small loads, so we keep it around."

Grak is repulsed by that statement. He refuses to look at the man.

Could probably say the same about him. And the pony undoubtedly smells better.

Which Grak confirms upon reaching the animal.

"What's …" He calms his voice. "What's its name?" Still not quite calm enough. Too much excitement in the air.

Jorthar grows excited at this opportunity to further display his knowledge. "We call him Patyr. Please be careful, though. He's a temperamental one. He's been known to bite at times."

Grak smiles in quiet admiration. "Yes, they're good biters, aren't they?"

Jorthar looks about nervously. "Um …" is all he manages in reply.

Not that it matters what the man has to say. Grak is too engrossed with Patyr now, taking particular interest in the pony's fur. It's a dull, splotchy gray with small patches missing in seemingly random spots.

But it's not random, is it? Quite artistic if you ask me. You certainly know how to give yourself character, friend.

Grak rubs a hand down Patyr's mane, careful to avoid the mounds of unidentifiable goop along the way. As he passes over a rough portion, the pony flinches.

What's this? A wound? Goodness. They don't treat you very well, do they? Not like I would treat you, that's for sure. Perhaps I can take you with me. I'm sure you'd like that. Mine's a much cleaner camp in general. And we'd give you very fine treatment. Something worthy of an animal of your calib—

Grak's reverie is broken by a growing commotion emanating from the cook site. Specific words are hard to make out, though. Just a general din and the occasional muddled shout.

Treachery! I knew it! Though starting too soon, it seems. Before I've even arrived. They must have fuddled some aspect. All for the best, then. We'll need to use that to our benefit.

He ponders the defenses of his current location.

Good, but not great. And too small a force should matters escalate while we're trying to flee. I'll need the remainder of Frolan's team.

Kunthar dons a look of concern. "Oh my. Perhaps we should see if everything's alright over there."

What a feeble lure. Any fool could see through it in an instant.

Grak turns to his nearest protector. "Seize this man! Can't have him at our backs." He weighs the benefits of taking Jorthar against the accompanying stench. "Leave that one. He'll just slow us down."

His men move instantly to follow the commands. Jorthar is shoved aside, and Kunthar is detained without resistance.

"What's going on, Grak?" asks Kunthar in bewilderment.

Grak assumes his hands-on-hips leader stance, relishing the chance to flaunt his superior wit. "Nice try, Kunthar." He adjusts his voice to something bolder and more appropriate. "We're wise to your scheme. So I suggest you keep silent lest I do it *for* you." He considers rephrasing that, but decides it's best to let the sentence be.

Somehow, Kunthar understands the threat. He closes his mouth and averts his eyes.

Satisfied, Grak signals to his team and starts toward the cook site. They pick up on the command and creep forward with an impressive combination of speed and stealth. Even Olive Thirteen is doing a decent job of it. In fact, they're all doing *so* well, Grak finds no need to correct them. Instead, he diverts his attention toward reviewing possible scenarios.

If I could stay back in the shadows and call for Frolan, perhaps that would suffice. He could just fight his way free and join up with us. I doubt it would take long. Then we'd be off. Yes, I like that plan.

Still, a backup would be nice. Just so we have it. I could have my guards launch a volley of arrows into the crowd. No, might hit some of our own. Although, it would also create confusion among the strangers, which would give our people a chance to escape.

Grak categorizes that one as "Plan 2." Still, one more would be ideal. After all, "Three plans are better than two," he's said a few times recently.

Of course! Kunthar makes for a great plan! No need to fight unless we're forced to.

Grak moves that idea into "Plan 1" and reorganizes the others accordingly. Just in time too. He motions for a halt as they reach the cook site.

"Maintain a healthy distance until I say otherwise." Grak laments having to whisper this point instead of signaling it.

Nonetheless, he shakes off that thought and looks around for the source of the commotion he heard.

"But how can this be?" shouts Kando. "How do we even know you mapped it accurately?" He shakes his head and looks at the map stone in Franzor's hands.

Grak shakes his head as well, adding an exaggerated eye roll for good measure.

A quaint peoples. Still using rock? I remember a time when we were so primitive.

"I can assure you, its accuracy is certain," Franzor replies with indignation. "We pay great attention to detail in our mapping procedures.

And, as you can see, we've traveled extensively. Especially in recent days. And much of it has been near the shore."

"I'll tell you how it can be!" Ruch's interruption is aimed at Kando. "Because you were wrong! All of you. Doran too." He's growing more aggressive as he speaks. "With your vast ocean theories. I told you it was nonsense!"

Shaken by Ruch's animosity, Franzor calms down a bit. "Look, this doesn't need to cause strife. I apologize for my part in it. Why don't we put our minds together? Let's see if we can figure out where the discrepancies are coming from."

Grak looks around for any other signs of danger. Surely this couldn't have been the entirety of the commotion he heard. And yet, nothing else of importance presents itself. Then it occurs to him.

This could easily be skewed in a way that makes me look bad. If Kunthar gets a chance to have his way with the telling, that is. A simple misunderstanding, really, but I'm sure that's not how he'd put it. And people might believe him.

Grak regrets not having prepared for such an eventuality. Still, all is not yet lost. An idea begins to take shape.

My children only need to know what I tell them. And the danger isn't any less real. Just more subtle than I originally thought. The strangers are simply lying in wait. Until we're relaxed. Vulnerable.

For his plan to work, though, he'll need Frolan and the *entire* security team. He looks about for the man, and quickly spots him nearby.

Talking to Jafra, of all things! And laughing with her! What's she up to? Attempting to subvert him, no doubt. Devious beyond devious! And he's just as guilty here. He should know better.

Grak sends his nearest man to fetch the brute and waits in anxious frustration for them to return. But rage washes over him a moment later when he spots Jafra coming back with them.

No! Why can't anyone follow orders? I don't want her involved. She'll just get in the way. Try to talk me out of my anger. Just like she always does!

Unless ... yes! If I prepare my words properly, she'll have nothing to refute. Alright, Grak, think. How would that sound?

Well, Frolan, what's this all about? No, not powerful enough.

So, Frolan, is this how you go about your duties? Good, but the sarcasm will be lost on all. Perhaps if I use less subtlety in the sting. Something more direct.

So, Frolan, I can't seem to trust you to handle your basic duties today. Oh, I like the sound of that. Though, I should probably drop the 'So' and add some obvious indignation.

As the three draw near, Grak launches into his speech. "Well, Frolan, what's this all about?" He winces at the missed opportunity.

"Are you alright, Grak?" Jafra asks in a voice of concern.

Always with the charades, Jafra?

"Oh, I'm better than alright." Grak isn't sure what he means by that. Or how to follow it up. "And so will you if you don't watch yourself!" In hindsight, it might have been best not to respond to her at all.

Grak turns to the brute. "Frolan. A word … in *private*." He shoots Jafra a cautionary glare while saying that last word.

She stares at him in confusion, but Grak refuses to be intimidated. He returns her gaze with boldness. Finally, she shrugs, then turns and walks away.

While Grak is pleased with his victory, there's no time to relish it. He keeps a leery eye on the woman until she's out of earshot, then turns to Frolan in frustration. "What were you two laughing about?"

The sight of a restrained Kunthar seizes Frolan's attention for a moment. But he quickly remembers his priorities and focuses once more on Grak.

"Oh, is *that* what angered you? I was worried." He flashes a relieved smile.

"We were just talking about the day's events. Seemed amusing how we spent the whole day hunting, but didn't catch anything, yet we'll leave here with so much food.

"Dernue insists we take their surplus, which is far more food than we've *ever* been able to catch. Even more than we could catch with your strategies, I imagine. No matter the speed of your kills, these ones are already dead."

Grak recognizes the need for a heavy tone. "Are the tribe's difficulties amusing to you? And, you're wrong about my strategy. It would have done far better."

In hindsight, Grak sees wisdom in avoiding such boasting from now on, no matter how difficult it is to resist. He just can't take the risk now that the tribe has demonstrated a persistence in seeing him uphold his claims.

"My strategy favors larger kills, so it's more efficient," Grak adds. Just that last one, but now he's done.

"Oh, yes. Surely." Frolan is properly worried. "I ... I didn't mean ... I shouldn't have spoken so boldly. I trust your strategy. I know it'll provide way more than this."

He may be simple, but at least he's honest.

Grak takes a calming breath. "Well, that's beside the point. My real concern is that you seemed too chummy with Jafra."

"Oh." The brute looks almost comical when he gets this worried. "Did you put her on the ostracized list again? I swear I didn't kno—"

"No, nothing that serious. Although, she does pose a very serious threat to our people. In her own way. She poisons others with her words. And you have one of the most important jobs in the tribe, so it's vital that you remain free from her toxins."

"Oh ..." Frolan casts his eyes to the ground. "I hadn't seen it that way." He looks lost. "I apologize."

Grak studies the man's face. "I can tell this bothers you." He's quite perceptive tonight. "Why?"

"Well ..." Frolan blushes. "I've always had something of an attraction for her."

"Uggh!" Grak catches himself, realizing the need to adjust his reaction for the brute's sake. "I mean, have you seen her eyebrows? And still? Really?" That's all he can muster right now. He'll do better next time. "That's a nauseating thought." Just to clarify.

Frolan scrunches his face in discouragement. "Well, for *you*, yes. But *I* like her."

Grak raises an eyebrow. "Well, I suppose she does have good blood ..."

He shakes off the disruption. "But that's beside the point. I'm disappointed. I've often told you of her ways. I thought you would have learned by now to avoid her devious nature."

Frolan looks surprised. "Oh. Well, I never knew you actually *meant* it. I always thought you were just ranting to relieve pressure."

Grak is careful to show his disdain for the man's lack of perception. "Well, now you know. So keep your distance. Besides, she's due for a punishment soon, and I can't have you holding back when administering it."

Frolan's disappointment is evident. "I understand. You're right. I'm sorry about that."

Grak's keen empathy detects sadness in the man. Rather than ignore it, he opts to show mercy. "But cheer up. There are other women. What about Zacha? She could be a suitable replacement for your interests." In hindsight, alternate wording may have been more comforting there.

Frolan reacts sharply as a thought strikes. "*Although*, perhaps I could get close to Jafra. I could find out some of these schemes you're always talking about."

Grak is impressed by that idea. It's so solid, in fact, that he's having trouble hiding his respect. "Yes. I had thought of that. But how do I know *you're* the man for the task?"

Frolan's expression is one of hope now. "Well, I found out a great deal about the daily goings-on here like you asked. I learned there's tension between Kunthar and some of the others, though nothing too serious."

Grak raises an eyebrow. "Is that *all* you've learned?"

Frolan looks around with uncertainty. "Yes …?"

Grak shakes his head. "Well, it seems you haven't learned *enough*. They were planning an ambush for the feast, and Kunthar was central to the trap. Fortunately, I realized before they could spring it."

Frolan's eyes go wide with shock. "Oh my! I had no idea. I … I'm so sorry, Grak. How could I have failed to see that? And I failed to protect you too! I've failed you so ma—"

"Stop!" Grak takes a calming breath. "When I want you to grovel, I'll order it. Tonight, however, I need you to gather our people for departure. In secret, though. Can't let the strangers know we're on to their schemes. And make it swift. I've gained us enough time to leave without fighting, but only if we don't delay."

Frolan nods. "Alright. And what about our food? Should I gather it first? Or the meat Dernue offered?"

"No. And *certainly* not! We don't know what they've done to it. Might this be part of their plan? To poison us like Lago did? Then they could just walk in and take our things. Is that what you'd like? No, it's best if we avoid it entirely. We can't risk bringing back poisoned meat."

Frolan's eyes are full of uncertainty. "I trust your opinion, Grak, but if I could just ask, don't we *need* that meat? All of our reserves went to this feast. They're already used. Even most of our olives.

"And what about the folks who stayed back? We didn't leave them any food. What about your father?"

Grak scoffs at the question. "The tribe can make do. And the ones who stayed back are receiving punishment. A minor fast will do them good. *Especially* Sando." He adds a stern look. "I just hope I won't have to add any *more* names to the list of delinquents."

Frolan nods in nervous understanding. "Yes. Sorry. I'll take care of it right away." He turns and heads back into the crowd.

Not a bad guy overall. Just have to occasionally remind him who's in charge.

The news ripples through Grak's people as Frolan makes quick work of his orders. Unfortunately, very few of them achieve subtle exits. Many even go so far as to drop their dishes on the spot before running over to the safety of Grak's circle. But that doesn't bother him so much. He's just glad they're quick about it. Sure enough, in a matter of moments, the whole tribe is grouped and waiting in silence behind him.

The strangers, on the other hand, are baffled. They're all standing in stunned silence, looking to one another for explanation. A number of conversations soon rise up, but none find resolution. Several shouts even ask for answers, but none are given.

Grak turns to Kunthar. "This is where we leave you. I expect you not to follow us or make any move against our camp. Should you try something, I can assure you my wrath will no longer be restrained."

Grak pauses to appreciate that speech. Yes, the more he considers it, the more he's impressed by it.

A shame Opa doesn't have her clay on hand. Perhaps I can make it a new policy. Require it of her at all times. Still, doesn't help us now. Remember that speech, Grak. Remember that speech. Remember that speech.

Grak gives the command, and his people depart with haste, shoving Kunthar out of the circle in the process. They make for the edge of camp and reach it a moment later, causing Grak to breathe a little easier as they enter the woods.

Given their rapid pace, the return trek is proving much faster. And much more silent, to Grak's delight. In fact, he's finding every aspect of the walk enjoyable, save for the constant checking over his shoulder. But even with that, he hardly notices the time, and they soon arrive back at camp.

Grak doesn't waste a moment. "Frolan. Set up a tight defense on the perimeter. And make sure your team is ready to fight at a moment's notice. Even when they're not on duty."

Frolan nods and turns to one of his men. "Mazo, g—"

"And Frolan," interrupts Grak. "Find Brak and have him fetch me some food. I'm famished after all that excitement."

Frolan looks at Grak in confusion. "Bu … um …"

Grak rolls his eyes. "What is it Frolan? Spit it out. I'm busy, you know."

"It's just …" The brute's tone is a nervous one. "Well, we left all of our food with the strangers. What would he fetch?"

That starts a thought, a curious tickle in the back of Grak's mind that grows to a nagging feeling. It dawns on him what the man was saying earlier.

Ah, I see. Yes, probably should have had a backup plan for the tribe's food.

10 - And Their Strange Maps

Grak resents that while the strangers are long gone, their absurd map lingers on in the minds of his people. Nineteen days already since Kunthar and his tribe packed up and followed after their herd. Nineteen days of steadily growing panic and chaos among Grak's people. And all due to a *map*.

Initially, Grak thought the matter could be left alone. That it would simply die out on its own. Yet the disruption the outsiders caused has only grown stronger.

Punishments aren't doing the trick this time. Maybe I need more of them. But I'm already ordering at least one a day. That's far more than ever before. What more can I do?

It's true. Before the other tribe came along, Grak had only found eight occasions where a whipping was in order. But since the encounter with the strangers, he's had to deliver twenty-eight more. In nineteen days. And all due to a *map*.

Of course, it's all Doran's fault, really. If he hadn't aligned his cause so closely to my own, I would have had room to distance myself. Instead, I'm tied helplessly to his fate.

So now what options do I have? None. I have to do him another favor. All there is to it. Seems like each day brings a new favor to help Doran out of a mess.

Grak sighs in resignation. He massages his brow and attempts to refocus on the matter at hand. "No, that's not quite it. 'I can assure you …' that was definitely the first part … Oh, what was the rest? Something to do with my fury, I think."

Opa absentmindedly drums her gaunt fingers on the chair as she waits.

"I can assure you of my fury?" Frolan is obviously just guessing now. *Always the easy way out with him.*

Kando makes an attempt. "I can assure you of my restraint?" He quickly realizes his glaring failure and hangs his head in shame.

Not as bright a fellow as I once thought. I wonder if the crooked nose has any effect. At that angle, it could be poking something vital in his head. The pain alone would likely hinder a person's thinking.

But even if Grak could prove it, that would do nothing to aid him in remembering his speech to Kunthar. As of yet, it's managed to elude him and everyone else.

He sighs and scratches his head. "Alright, this obviously isn't working. Perhaps it's just not a good time." He nods in thought. "Yes, let's set the matter aside for now and try again later. When we can look at it with fresh eyes."

While serious, the transcription isn't the purpose of this meeting. And the attendees seem to agree, each nodding in relief at the suggestion.

Though perhaps too much relief. I wonder if I've been too merciful with this group. Hmm, excellent question. Still, I'll have to consider it later. No time right now. The meeting is far too important. Have to see it through.

Grak shakes the distraction and concentrates on the people seated around him. He looks about in a deliberate circuit of the tent, lingering on each face for exactly three breaths. This is a method of encouraging suggestibility that he discovered recently. And so far, it's proven moderately reliable, though *why* it works is beyond him.

Perhaps because my children are a self-centered bunch. Yes, that sounds right. They only really listen when I focus on them.

Grak soon completes the circle. Though, to his dismay, it seems as though he finished *too* soon.

Yes, it felt a little rushed, didn't it? But I counted the proper number of breaths. Ah, I see the problem now. We're too crowded in here. So what other options do we have? Hmm, doesn't seem we have any. Mine is by far

the largest tent in camp. And we certainly can't meet outside. Not in this
cold. Not with the first snow expected any day now.

Grak shudders at this thought and wraps his furs tighter.

Awful snow. Awful, awful snow.

It's too late. The cold has a firm footing in his mind now.

Think warm, Grak. Think fire. And stew. Warm stew, mind you, not the
day old stuff. And the hot springs. Mmm, the hot springs.

This does the trick. Grak basks in the warmth for a moment.

Now where was I? Ah yes, space. I need more of it. I could enlarge my tent
again. Although, I don't normally call meetings with so many attendees.

Still, it would be good to have the space should I ever need to accom-
modate this number of chairs again. Then it's settled. Maybe four times
the current size. Just so there's walking room too. Yes, that should do nicely.

Now, where was I? Ah, yes, need to get to the purpose of the meeting.
But how best to begin the conversation? Something careful and deliberate,
I think. Though, I can't be too soft, either. It would hardly do if I fail to
show just how upset this whole affair makes me. Something in the middle,
then. Ah, I've got it.

"Those stupid strangers and their stupid map!" Grak catches himself
as numerous shocked expressions come his way.

Hmm, not quite what I was going for. Still, at least I conveyed an ap-
propriate level of urgency.

Doran crosses his arms, wearing deep concern. "What do you propose we do about it?"

"So many questions, Doran." Grak takes care to tame his annoyance toward the man. His influence is still useful, after all. "Maybe you
should try *giving* answers once in a while."

Hmm, might have gone too far with that last sarcastic bit.

But Doran simply nods, apparently oblivious to Grak's derision.
"You're right. I'm sorry, friend." He thinks for a moment. "Well, perhaps we could begin working on a new map. Alter our theories to be
more in line with what we've learned from the outsiders.

"Their squiggly lines *were* quite authentic looking, after all. And this
new map circulating around camp also looks to have substantial merit.
It's quite possible we made a mistake with the direction we took our

theories. We could simply start over. Admit we were wrong."

Grak hates that word. More so because of the swallowed "g." He's never liked those.

He gives his most menacing glare. "For old times' sake, I'll pretend you didn't just say that."

A far more urgent detail grabs his attention. "And *what* new map? Why haven't I heard of this yet? And more importantly, who would so openly defy me by making such a thing?" He looks at Opa.

She raises her hands in defense. "No, of course not."

Still, might be good to whip her. Just in case.

Doran jumps to her aid. "Yes, I can vouch for Opa. Kando and I have been taking all of her time lately. And I've seen the new map. It doesn't even compare to *her* skill."

If only the woman knew how close she just came.

Grak gives her a cautionary look before turning back to the main issue. "Well, this new map only serves to strengthen my resolve. There's no way we can change our stance on the strangers' map now. Maybe if you had suggested it sooner, Doran. Then we could have gone that route and avoided our current troubles. But since you decided to declare their map completely erroneous, we're backed into a corner."

Doran's surprise is only slight. "Well, to clarify, I said they *might* be wrong. For all *we* know."

Grak rolls his eyes. "That's a mere detail at this point, don't you think? What matters is that I understood it one way, which forced me to make an official policy. So perhaps *you* just need to be clearer in the future."

Doran hangs his head and nods in silence.

Satisfied, Grak focuses on the others. "So, all that to say, we can't change our policy at this point. But we *can* make it clear that the other tribe was wrong. And we *can* place a strong hold on all thought to the contrary."

Brak grows confused. "How might we stop their thoughts? That strikes me as impossible."

Someone needs a reminder of his place.

Grak puts on his "scolding papa" voice. "And your speaking without permission strikes *me* as impossible. Yet there you stand, tongue wagging, when I only asked you to pour water for the meeting attendees."

Brak looks properly ashamed and returns to his duties.

Once again, Grak attempts to get back to the pressing issue. "Whether or not *some* find it possible, I find it imperative. Matters are out of control. Chaos abounds. People are openly calling Doran a liar, and it's bleeding into general disrespect. That makes it harder for me to lead. And *that*, in turn, puts our tribe at risk."

Doran looks around the circle, his eyes full of hurt. "A *liar*? They *do*? Who? What have they said?"

After a short pause, Kando reluctantly breaks the silence. "They're saying you never saw anything out at sea. That since no one else saw it, there isn't much chance it actually happened." He pauses. "And so you must have made it up."

Doran's distress is painful to watch. "But *you* don't believe that, right?" He scans each face, ending with Grak's. "Do you?"

Grak couldn't care less, but appearances are vital in weathering this storm. "No, of course not. And that's why I'm trying to help you. And also why we can't go making a new map. We have to find another way to stop the panic. Any ideas?"

A thought flutters into Frolan's head. "Well, you always say punishment is the best motivator."

Grak cradles the man's cheek in his palm. "Dear Frolan. Sweet boy. Always the bowl to catch my every word. It's true. I do say that. But we've *already* been punishing people. And it works, yes, but it's too slow.

"If we wait until hearing about an incident of rebellion, then it's already too late. For every person willing to raise their voice, three others stay silent and just think it. So we need more than simple punishments. We need to cut this dissension at the base. Show them their ideas are foolish. So, how do we go about it?"

Truth be told, Grak had a plan before he called this meeting. It would be far too risky otherwise, as then any opinion might sneak its way in uninvited. Really, the only reason he gathered these people together was in hopes of getting *them* to suggest his idea. Just in case he needs to redirect blame later. To his dismay, however, all are sitting quietly, straining in thought.

Thinking shouldn't be this hard. Especially when the answer is so obvious. It's a wonder I manage to keep calm when surrounded by such simpletons.

He decides to get them started. "So, who was the first to champion this idea?"

"Oh, that was Ruch," replies Kando. "He's always opposed our vast ocean theory, so he jumped at the chance to promote the strangers' map. He's been at the source of the issue since it began."

That's new information to Grak. He was certain Jafra had instigated this disobedience.

"Alright, there we go. Ruch is the cause. So what should we do with him?" Grak goes silent, hoping someone might figure it out now.

I've certainly led them far enough.

But after a long moment, his patience wears thin. "Think about it. Your suggestion of punishment isn't working for the people *spreading* this idea. So what should we do to the person who *started* the idea?"

Frolan tenses as a thought strikes. "Kil …" He picks up on Grak's astonishment. "Punish …" He checks for Grak's nod before continuing. "Punish Ruch. We should punish him. And that would put a stop to this."

"Great idea, Frolan!" Grak can take it from here. "If we punish him, he'll get in line. With enough punishment, he'll back our ideas. Then imagine how easy it would be to get the rest of his followers to come around. Good work."

The brute beams with pride.

Doran, on the other hand, looks a little sour. "Grak … about that …" His tone brims with trepidation. "I wonder if we've been having too many whippings of late. Maybe we should reduce them. It seems they're causing a great deal of fear in the tribe, and it's growing by the day. That just doesn't seem like a good thing."

Grak takes offense. "Well, perhaps if you had given me more support in the previous whippings, I wouldn't have to continue them."

Doran nods slowly for a moment, then hangs his head. "You're so right, friend. This map problem really started with me, and yet you've had to deal with the fallout all alone."

Grak didn't expect such swift acquiescence. He decides to choose his own inference. "Good. I appreciate you volunteering to stand with me during Ruch's punishment. It's an excellent idea. Shows a strong front and puts minds at ease, all in one simple action."

Doran takes a moment to ponder how he managed to offer himself up for that. Unable to figure it out, he settles on silence for the remainder of the meeting.

"One hundred!" Brak calls the final lash.

Grak scrunches his face in skepticism. "Are you sure, Brak? I only counted ninety."

The man appears torn on whether to incite Grak's anger or look like a fool. He sighs. "Sorry ... I must have miscounted."

Wise choice.

Frolan nods and renews the punishment.

Hmm, though I did lose focus for a while there, didn't I? Maybe I shouldn't have said anything. Still, it really didn't feel like one hundred. Better to err on the safe side.

"One hundred!" Brak calls out.

Grak gently scolds himself for failing once more to count the strokes. He considers intervening again.

No. Three times would be too many. Even Brak can't mess it up thrice in a row.

Grak nods as he stands and makes his way to the front. Brak breathes a noticeable sigh of relief and returns to his place in the crowd. Even Frolan seems pleased by the decision as he sets down his whip and signals for water.

An impressive tool in Grak's eyes, that whip. Though he's even more impressed by how quickly the brute took to it. It's only been nine days, and yet his use has become so fluid that an outsider would think he was born holding the thing.

Though I'm sure my superior design deserves most of the praise. So simple, yet so elegant.

Grak isn't wrong about the whip's uncomplicated nature. It's just nine strips of leather braided into a grip at one end with jagged bits of iron tied at the other. He thought it up after running out of thorny branches, and had Aza get right to work constructing the thing. "My time-saver," he calls it, barely noticing the resulting cringes from those around him.

Not that I care what they think. What would they know about managing their time? Lazy beyond belief, this bunch.

He's gently coaxed out of his reverie by the sight of Doran's approach. The man takes his position just to the left of Grak and a pace behind.

No, that spot won't do. I swear, the fool grows more frustrating by the moment. No. Patience, Grak. He's useful. Simple, but useful.

He takes a calming breath, then motions for Doran to step farther back and to the side. This is Grak's preferred formation when delivering speeches with others. He finds that it not only gives him the prominence he desires, but also provides the crowd with a clear view of the whipping post.

With that misunderstanding cleared up, Grak begins. He decides to open with some gentle humor. "Well, that whipping certainly took long enough!"

The crowd stays silent. Somewhere in the back, a woman coughs.

Grak clears his throat. "So, let this be a lesson to you all. Ruch's initial defiance only brought him more lashes. Do not repeat his mistake!"

He walks over to the man and leans close, keeping his voice raised for the crowd's sake. "So, Ruch, do you have anything to say?"

Ruch dangles from the post, wrists bleeding from his vain struggle against the ropes. He works up the strength to mumble something incoherent.

Grak shrugs. He'll take what he can get at this point. "Good. I'm glad to hear it. I'll repeat it for those of you in the back.

"Ruch said he never actually thought our maps were wrong, and he's very sorry for leading anyone astray, let alone so many. He was just bored and wanted something to do.

"At the same time, he always knew the other tribe was lying because they lacked the character and honesty of our people and ... what's that?" Grak leans in and counts to three. "And because they lack my leadership abilities? Oh, well thank you.

"And thank you for being candid with us, Ruch. Your repentance is an honor to our tribe. How about a cheer of congratulations?"

The crowd responds in wooden obedience. Grak waits for the noise to die down before nodding to Doran.

The man immediately hits his cue. "So, with that being said, let's put this whole ordeal behind us. Let it be known that our tribe unequivocally rejects all outside maps. And this includes the one going around camp recently.

"Our official policy is to receive authorization from Grak before a map can circulate. And the only maps currently authorized, other than the tribe's original map, are the theories Kando and I have put forth. All others are hereby denounced, and any promotion of such ideas will be met with a minimum punishment of one hundred lashes."

Gasps and other signs of shock rumble through the crowd. Grak allows this for a moment, then leads the tribe in reluctant applause.

And now to raise their spirits. Best to do this part alone.

He nods to Doran, who takes his place with the rest of the tribe.

Can't have my little ones thinking Doran's responsible for the good things.

"Well, with that problem solved, it seems we have cause for celebration!" Grak pauses in hopes of receiving some form of cheer. More explanation must be needed. "A celebration and a feast!"

That did something. Obvious excitement now hangs in the air. But to Grak's dismay, the only manifestation is a sparse applause.

"I'm not so sure that's a good idea!" shouts Jafra.

Grak fumes as he mercilessly scans the crowd for her face. There, in the back and to the left. He gives Frolan a stern look, and the brute moves quickly to apprehend the woman.

She drops her deer in a slight panic. "I mean … we're low on meat … would that be our best move right now?"

Frolan reaches her and lays hold. Grak can't tell from this distance, but the man's usual brusque manner appears lacking at the moment.

I'll need to deal with that. But later. In private. Can't be seen at odds with my security team. Even if they're fools who follow emotions above orders.

Grak suddenly realizes the danger of punishing just her. "The rest of the hunting party too! Since they can't keep her silent, they'll share in her fate!"

Her team lets out a collective sigh. They drop their kills in resignation as Frolan's men grab hold.

Now there's a proper grip. All around, really. If it doesn't leave minor bruising, you're doing it wrong.

Ruch is dragged away as the newcomers are shuffled to the front and tied to the whipping post. Once they're secured, Grak raises a hand to halt the process, then turns to the crowd. He assumes his leader stance, hands on hips, and waits for silence. To convey even greater weight in the coming words, he slides his hands up until they rest on his ribs.

Once he has their attention, Grak lifts his voice. "My children! I know you've all been concerned about the lack of meat lately. And I want you to know that I'm concerned too. It's tough to cut back, and we're all having to do it." This elicits some agreement from the crowd.

"But there's only one reason for our current rations," he continues. "This team consistently brings back far too little from their hunts!" He points at the captives derisively.

"But are they on rations while hunting? No! And have they improved? Have they utilized my hunting strategies? No! If anything, they've gotten lazier. Even to the point that their recent trips have kept them out for considerable lengths of time. And the rest of us have to manage while we wait. This is why we've all been on strict rations for so long now."

Cordo interrupts. "No! I told you days ago. The herd's moving again. And they've already gone too far south. This is the cause of our extended hunts.

"We need to move with them, Grak. To our final campsite. Immediately! Before the first snow. Before travel grows too harsh for our weaker members. It's no longer a matter of rebuilding our supplies. We have to move or we won't survive the snows!"

A troubled murmur races through the crowd. This is bad. And it promises to be worse should Grak allow it any longer.

Think quickly, Grak.

He turns and strikes Cordo with the back of his open hand. This stings. Quite a bit, really. And while he does a moderate job of hiding that fact, he'd rather do without another go. Also, he's fairly certain he touched the man's mole in the process, and that concerns him to no end.

Can those things spread? Best not to find out.

Grak rubs his hand on his tunic, then turns to Frolan. "Hit him again."

The unorthodox nature of the order startles the brute, but he quickly gathers himself and obeys. His strike lands hard on Cordo's cheek, causing the man to reel back and nearly lose consciousness.

Oh, curling the hand into a fist. Of course. Well, I was trying to take it easy, but perhaps I was being too merciful. So, how did he do it exactly?

"Again." Grak watches closely this time.

Ah, much better. Yes, I could make that work.

With that punch, Cordo's senses leave him, and he crumples, dangling from his restraints. Frolan looks to Grak for further orders.

Grak nods. "That should do. Wake him up, though, so he feels the whipping."

He turns to the crowd. "I'm sorry it had to come to that, but this level of insolence will not be tolerated. Not only is the hunting team lazy and failing to bring back proper food for our tribe, but they also think they know better than me.

"And while it's true that they've prevented us from replenishing our stock, we're not in danger. I've planned things perfectly. And I'll prove to you just how superb my planning has been. And just how superb it will continue to be. I hereby declare that not only will we feast tonight, but rations will be doubled from this point forward!"

The people cheer at that announcement, though fear obviously motivates this as much as joy.

"You mean normal rations, then?" Brak asks.

The fool! He's just flirting with being on my list.

Fortunately, the crowd is too busy cheering to hear the man's question. Grak takes advantage of this by raising his own voice. "Our days of strict rations are coming to an end! I want to thank you all for having shown such discipline and fortitude during that time. Trust me, my children, all will be well!"

The tribe believes his words. Their applause grows even stronger.

Grak's pleasure at the day's events can no longer be hidden. "Frolan, if you would, please." He gestures toward the offenders, doing his best to hold back a smile.

"One!" shouts Brak above the crowd's continuing celebration.

Grak returns to his chair and gets comfortable. Or as comfortable as it allows.

No matter. At least these punishments tend to be relaxing. A time free of pressure to ponder the urgent issues.

Like the tribe's rations. How do I make them stretch over daily feasts?

And moving—there's another urgent matter. Definitely need to get going soon, but how to do it without the tribe thinking I've bent to Jafra's will? Mayb—

Grak's thoughts are abruptly shoved aside by the feeling of extreme cold on his nose. Startled, he reacts by rubbing the spot. His finger returns with a drop of moisture.

Oh dear ... No!

Grak looks up and holds out a hand. Another spot of cold hits his wrist. Another touches a finger. He squints. Several more land on his face.

There! Definitely saw it! Oh dear ...

The flurry thickens until a thin, steady veil of white pours from the sky. The snows have begun.

11 - And How There's Always a Group of Whiners Any Time the Air Turns a Little Cold

Grak abhors whiners. He would even venture to place them alongside the lazy on his list of hates. Or maybe a little lower, if he's being honest. In fact, they're the main reason behind his theory that some people have no value in life.

But it's when their complaints pile up that he really gets upset. And even more so when the focus of their grumblings is a trivial matter. At that point, the whiners become truly putrid in his sight.

A little cold, a little snow, and suddenly everything's falling apart. They forget how to walk, how to hunt, how to work. And suddenly they need more food and less time working outside? What kind of a simpleton do they take me for?

Sure the cold can be difficult. I should know. I used to complain about it too. But that was so long ago. In my youth. Adults just deal with it. That's part of growing up.

Besides, it's not even that cold. Certainly not as bad as these whiners make it out to be.

He opens his furs slightly to let in some air, then motions for Brak to move farther away with the wheeled fire pit. Grak is quite proud of that innovation: simple, yet exceptionally useful. It consists of a small, wooden cart supporting a flat stone about the length of his arm with a shallow bowl hollowed out of the center.

And contrary to Grak's expectations, its construction was no easy task. Finding the perfect rock proved the most challenging aspect. He had to give up several full days of much-needed relaxation to oversee the search teams.

Though that reminds me. I really should take those days soon. All this whining I've had to endure is draining me of vigor.

"I'm just concerned about the tribe," Cordo pleads.

"Thirty-eight!" Brak is having trouble shouting above the man's protests.

Speaking of whining … chief among whiners, really. A shame. I would have expected more from Cordo. And even worse, he's so bold about it! Clearly, he doesn't understand obedience. Either that, or the fool's growing numb to pain.

It's true, the man's boldness has returned of late. And regardless of the reason, it doesn't bode well for Grak. In retrospect, he admits it may not have been the wisest decision to whip the hunters every time they failed to bring back enough meat. It also might have been more prudent to set a smaller quota.

I suppose thirty-five kills might have been a lot to ask of them. Though it certainly seemed like a solid idea at the time. Besides, what other option did I have? Thirty? Such a repugnant number! Not while I still live and breathe. And don't get me started on thirty-one! No, clearly not your fault, Grak.

And he'd like to believe that. Truly. But the nagging feeling just won't go away. At the least, he wonders if it was necessary to whip them the few times they actually *did* make enough kills.

Hmm, yes, could have done without that. Well, hindsight's always a clearer view. Good to remember for next time.

"Our food problems aren't going to just fade on—" Cordo gasps from that lash. "They won't fade on their own. We need to take action. We need—" Another strike causes him to swoon slightly, but he quickly regains strength. "We need to institute rations again until we can replenish our reserves."

It's not that the man's point is flawed. It's actually fairly sensible. But Grak can't relent now. That would look like weakness to the tribe.

Never should have listened to him about moving here when we did. Should have trusted my original thinking. Really, I was just reacting to everyone's fear of the snows. Tried to keep all my little ones happy. But look where that got me. Only made me look weak. And now no one's happy.

That couldn't be truer. Grak has been hard-pressed of late to find someone who isn't eager to voice their displeasure. Even Frolan's loyalty has come into question. Just yesterday the man made a remark about feeling hungry and suffering from dizziness. The conversation took place in private, yes, but that didn't lessen its ominous nature.

And worse still, Grak's efforts to hide the lack of supplies from public view are becoming more obvious by the day. His method so far has been to strategically refuse feeding certain individuals so the rest of the tribe can eat to their content. Unfortunately, the further they go into the snows, the more he has to withhold for everyone else to eat their fill. Additionally, each time someone misses a meal, the next day they seem all the more hungry, pleading for extra food.

Whiners. You'd think they would have learned from my lead.

That's true. Grak did make an earnest effort to lead the way in sacrificing for the better of the tribe. Once they completed their move, he reduced his meat consumption to just above what everyone else was allowed. Of course, his growing waist also played a part in the decision, but he prefers to leave that point unmentioned.

Still, despite Grak's sacrifices, this pesky food shortage has lingered on. And it doesn't look like it's going away anytime soon. After all, they've been at this campsite for fifty-five days now, and the problem has only gotten worse.

But it's certainly no famine. Not yet. No matter what Cordo would try to have us believe.

Grak reviews the details of the situation.

Well, maybe a slight famine. Very mild. Really, if ever there were a mild famine, this is definitely it.

But not according to their complaints. Odd, really. You'd think they'd be used to a lack of food by now. But nooo, they always find something to whine about. And who do you blame when you're in a bad mood? Well, the leader, of course. Why not?

"Seventy-nine!" Brak calls the final lash.

Frolan sets the whip aside and signals for water. Zacha hurries forward with a smile and hands him a cup. He smiles in return, and the two head into the crowd, chatting casually together.

Ah, youth and their love. Good to see it blooming.

Grak stands and makes his way forward. He shoots Brak a stern glare, and the bald man scuttles over to keep the chair warm.

An obedient fellow overall. Just needs some prompting to get him going.

Grak takes his position in front of the whipping post, careful to leave room for all to view Cordo's limp and bloodied form.

Sometimes you just have to whip the rebellious streak out of them. Too much energy builds up, and it takes a poor course. Really, that's probably what's causing this defiance.

Though I'm sure that grotesque mole on his face also lends a hand. Must be awful to live like that. I imagine it would get annoying. Almost makes his defiance understandable. Almost.

Grak gathers his focus and directs it toward the crowd. He raises his hands to silence the din. "My children. Be at peace." The noise drops off abruptly. "It's true that these snows have been hard so far—"

"Not for you!"

Grak furiously surveys the sea of faces for the source of this interruption. "Who said that!" he yells.

Alas, the instigator's shout was too quick, making it nearly impossible to find his location now. Regardless, several of Frolan's security forces are moving among the crowd, making threats as they go. It's doubtful they'll find the offender, but at least they can discourage further outbursts.

Contented with their progress, Grak continues. "As I was saying, these snows have been hard, and they're far from over. And I know you're tempted to think Cordo might be right. After all, he seems to be presenting the easy way out. But his ideas only look good on the surface. In truth, his methods would just cause greater difficulties.

"No, we *must* stick with my plan. We have to see it through. Trust me, when this is over, you'll all look back and marvel at the wisdom. And that's all I ask. Just trust me, my sweet children. You won't regret it."

"But look where that's gotten us so far," says Ruch.

Frolan moves to grab the offender, but the man walks forward of his own volition.

Is the fool actually eager to join Cordo? This thirst for punishment is getting out of hand. Not to mention this crazy idea that I'm somehow at fault here.

Grak pushes his mind for an immediate way to redirect blame. "My children, please understand. The true cause of our current difficulties was the strangers. We were too nice to them.

"We never should have accepted their feast invitation. That's where it all started: having to leave our meat behind when we evaded their ambush. Perhaps that was their plan all along.

"And they caused the subsequent unrest with their stupid map. And that distracted us when we should have been storing up meat for winter. Plus they killed much of our herd while they were camped nearby."

"That's true," Frolan interjects. "We met them when Grak was teaching us the strategies. They were hunting our deer and nearly killed us with a stampede."

Grak had forgotten that point. "You see? It was only a matter of time before we felt the full effect of their malevolent behavior."

To his surprise, this actually seems to be working. Agreement runs through the crowd along with numerous affirmations of the strangers' treachery. Grak can only hope this anger holds out until a lasting solution suggests itself.

Zacha steps forward and lifts her voice. "But that doesn't do anything for our *current* problem! We still need to ration our food if we hope to survive."

With a look of apology, Frolan lays a gentle hold on the woman's arm. She begrudgingly acquiesces and walks with him to the whipping post.

On second thought, Zacha might not be the best focus for young Frolan's affections. Too rebellious. Might just turn him against me in the end. I suppose I'll have to find other possibilities for the oaf.

Grak stores that in memory and turns to the crowd. "I stress again, rationing would not be a wise idea."

"But why can't we decide on this with representatives?" asks Groka. *When did she grow so defiant?*

Frolan moves to grab her. Grak considers it for a moment, then raises a hand to stop him.

But only because this is her first offense. Not because of my feelings for her. And if she thinks I'll excuse further dissension, she's sadly mistaken.

"That's an interesting idea, Groka, but it wouldn't work." Now to figure out a reason. "If we were to do that, then where would it end?" Sound enough, given what he has to work with. Now for some sarcasm to finish it off. "Then what's to stop us from having representatives counsel me on *all* the issues?"

"Oh, that sounds like a good idea!" Opa's statement is reinforced by quite a few in the crowd.

Grak reacts hastily, managing a modest concealment of his nervousness. "No, that was a joke, dear Opa." He gives her an understanding smile and raises a hand of mercy. "That wouldn't work. Remember Lago ... and the lions ... and the strangers. That's what happens when I'm hindered in my leadership. And representatives would be nothing but a hindrance."

"But it worked well enough at the shore," interjects a shaky Cordo. "You weren't hindered, and we made the best decision in the end."

The tribe finds that point agreeable. Numerous conversations pop up to discuss its merits.

That fool! If Cordo can speak, then clearly he's strong enough for more lashes!

Grak calms the growing tremor in his stomach. "But look. The shore ... that was a special issue. And I made the final decision on that one. And that's the only reason why it ended up working ... for anyone."

Cordo's response is instant. "But this seems like an even more important situ—"

"Yes!" Grak has to settle this before it gets away from him. "Again ... you know, I don't know why everyone's always cutting me off." His tone rises in frustration. "Letting me finish would do wonders for your understanding."

The crowd slowly quiets.

Glad to have any improvement, Grak presses on. "I want your opinions. I do. In fact, I was already planning on creating a group to help me decide on this rations issue. I *wanted* to wait on announcing it, but I suppose *that's* ruined now. Thanks, Cordo. And Jafra!" He nearly forgot to blame her.

"Just to decide *this* matter?" asks Jafra, seemingly ignoring his rebuke. *There's a back begging for fresh stripes.*

"No, didn't you hear him earlier?" replies Opa. "He said we'd help on *all* issues."

Grak's furs are growing sweaty. "No. No. Remember, that was a joke."

"Yeah, don't you get humor?" Frolan is quite proud of himself for finally catching Grak's sarcasm. "He said it'll just be *important* issues."

Grak rubs his brow. "No, wait—"

"Who decides which issues are important?" interrupts Ruch.

Grak jumps at the chance to regain control of this conversation. "I would. An—"

"A simple majority makes sense to *me*," replies an eager Olive Thirteen.

Grak is quick to refute that. "No, tha—"

"See, that's where I would disagree," says Jafra. "A two-thirds majority seems more perfect to me. It prevents us from being too evenly split on an issue."

Grak's mouth gapes, unable to move. His heart pounds feverishly. He's watching his power slip away, and there's nothing he can do about it.

No, Grak. You won't lose all that you've built. Take hold! Now!

Grak takes a deep breath and bellows with all his might, "Silence! I will have silence!" A bit too shrill for his liking, but effective; all eyes now rest on him. "I will *not* have outbursts and chaos!" His voice is growing strained. "That only leads to danger, and I will *not* allow my children to see danger!" Severely strained.

Grak pauses to rest his throat. "But you needn't worry. Not only will I keep you safe, but I'll also listen to you and care for you. In fact, I brought you here for more than to witness punishments. I called this gathering to announce my new policy.

"That group I spoke of earlier? They won't just help me with *this* matter. They'll be my council. And I'll seek their advice before making a decision on all important issues. Starting with this one."

That causes a small stir of joy in the crowd. Grak sighs with relief.

Too close, Grak. Can't let it happen again.

"I suggest Kando be on the council," shouts an overeager Doran.

A wave of disapproval and derogatory comments ripples through the crowd. This is fairly common of late, as Doran's reputation took a severe hit after he laid out the map policy. People just couldn't get past the severity of the punishments compared to the offense.

But the man still holds deep sway with a few, and Grak needs that. "Yes, Doran, I was just thinking to name Kando. He has a solid head on his shoulders." He leaves out any mention of the man's nose. "But I'll thank you not to interrupt me. Need I remind you that *I'm* the one deciding?"

"What about Cordo?" blurts Aza. "He's got a good head on his shoulders too."

Grak doesn't even need to think about that one. "Definitely not! We can't have defiance on the council. We wouldn't get anything done."

Although ... while Cordo's definitely a thorn in my side, this could be a great way to keep him close. Perhaps even make him loyal. If he thinks his opinions are being heard, then he might calm down. It's settled then.

Grak puts on his gracious voice. "But, in my mercy, I will give him a chance at redemption. Cordo, you're on the council. Congratulations."

"What about Jafra? She's wise!" Groka is beginning to strain his patience.

"No!" shouts Grak. He catches himself and softens his tone. "This is getting out of hand. We can't trust just *anyone* with such an important position. And let me remind you once more that I alone will choose. If anyone else hinders the process, I'll be forced to abolish my new council policy."

The crowd promptly falls silent as all eyes fix on him, awaiting his decision. Grak could even swear some are holding their breath. He's pleased to still have *that* power at least.

So, who to pick? Ruch and Zacha might also turn loyal if their opinions are heard. But they might feel empowered too, especially with Cordo already on the council. Still, the simpletons aren't exactly hard to sway. And I always have Frolan's help when things get too tense. Really, with him around, what's the worst that could happen?

He shrugs in response to this thought. "Ruch and Zacha as well. To show just how great my mercy is."

Grak surveys the crowd. "Groka, I think you'll do well."

He considers further possibilities. Proximity proves a reasonable deciding factor. "Sabo, you can be on it too."

But not Voluilo; Grak has always hated how hard the man's name is to pronounce. Also his lips are far too flat and disturbing. "Unnatural," Grak calls them.

"Olive Thirteen. Aza." He moves past Olive Seventeen to avoid redundancy. "And Loren."

Grak counts the group.

Nine. A good number, but already pushing the bounds of propriety in this context.

"And that should do it." He considers having the crowd applaud.

No, they might get confused and think they're cheering for the appointees. Best to move things along.

"So, with that out of the way, on to the matter at hand. It seems to me there are really only two sides to represent here. Should we cut off food as Cordo suggests?" Grak needs to push it over the edge here. "Or will you trust me, your leader and greatest hunting strategist? And trust my proposal to require more of our hunting team?"

Cordo responds immediately. "Well, I think it's a bit more complex th—"

"Yes, yes." Grak waves dismissively. "We've heard this already. I'm simply summarizing the issue. To save time. That's all."

Jafra joins in again. "But why only two sides? Seems like we should let all the ideas be represented."

Grak laughs. "Like we did at the shore?" Pockets of the crowd chuckle nervously. "Let people suggest making floating carts? *That* would be productive. No, I think two is all we'll need."

Hearty laughter rises from the tribe, and Grak waits for it to die down before proceeding. "So let's get on with it then. All those opposed to food, please stand with Cordo at the whipping post. And all those who agree with me that we should work hard and prevent death, come and stand behind me."

Even with the simplified options, the representatives are still confused. After several moments of intense thought, they begin to trickle forward. Soon, the two groups are fully formed.

Most side with Grak, of course. In fact, only Ruch and Zacha have joined Cordo at the whipping post. Though it could be argued that they were already tied to it.

"Well then. See? When we follow my instructions, matters work out simply and efficiently. Then it's decided. We won't force starvation on you." Grak spots Cordo's mouth opening again and moves to stop it. "So let's hear it for food!"

The crowd erupts in adulation, causing Cordo to breathe a sigh of defeat.

Grak smiles with satisfaction. "So, with that out of the way, let's get back to the punishments!"

Grak's tent guards open the flaps for him, and he hurries past to get out of the cold.

Inside, Brak is just setting out the afternoon meat bowl. "Oh hello, Grak. Sorry about the nip in the air. I raced back here as fast as I could after the gathering, but most of the logs were still damp. Which reminds me. I know you don't want to keep them in here, but perhaps we could move them to a tent of their own. Just so they're not outside in the snow."

The man waits for a reaction, but gets none. "Anyway, I started what little fire I could, and it should be warm enough to remove your outer furs in just a bit. And I have more logs drying, so you should end up with enough to last you through the night."

Grak gives a menacing glare, but ultimately decides on mercy. "Very

well. Though I'll expect you to plan for such an event in the future."
He waves a hand in dismissal.

Brak nods and scuttles by nervously. Grak wraps his furs tighter,
bracing for the coming chill at the man's exit. Fortunately, it passes
quickly.

Finally, a moment of peace.

Grak sighs and settles into his chair. He picks up the bowl and digs
through its contents.

*The fool always buries the unappetizing pieces. Does he think I'll just eat
them without checking first?*

Grak plucks the unsatisfactory bits and tosses them behind him
toward the entrance.

*Brak can pick all that up this evening when he comes for my steam bath.
Having to clean up his own mess should teach the fool not to try and deceive
me.*

Grak makes another pass through his food. He nods. The remaining
cuts meet his standards. Now he can eat in peace without the distractions of fat and gristle.

*So, how to categorize the day's events? On the one hand, I ended up get-
ting what I wanted—both in punishments and decisions. That's definitely
good. But I also had to give in a little. That's definitely bad. But the tribe
is on my side for the most part. And that's also good. And those who oppose me should grow more loyal if my plan works out. Also good. Perhaps
'satisfactory,' then? Hmm, might be a bit too pessi—*

Grak is interrupted by the unmistakable rumpling of someone opening the tent flap. It's his only warning before a deep, cutting wind
signals a visitor.

He grips his furs. "Brak! How many times must I tell you? Call out
before entering so I can prepare for the cold! Do you need *another*
lesson in protocol?"

He turns to face the man in hopes of increasing the weight of his
words with a fierce glare. But his look takes an abrupt turn toward
shock at the sight of Jafra inside his tent.

"Hello, Grak." She seems timid, avoiding eye contact.

Appropriate, yet insufficient in excusing her presence here.

Grak gathers himself and channels his fury. "How did you get past security? And what makes you think you can just walk in here like that?"

He opens his mouth to call the guards, but stops short, unable to remember their names at the moment.

Well, that's not good. Though I imagine that was part of her plan. Trying to make me look the fool, like I'm not in control of my own men. Well, I won't give her that satisfaction.

Grak puts on a casual air. "But, I'll still allow it. Mercy and all. So, why are you here? Explain yourself. And be quick with it."

Jafra advances nervously with her head down. "Yes, well I've …" She notices the discarded scraps. "Oh dear." Wincing from her fresh whipping, she stoops and gathers the pieces. "Brak needs to be more careful. Food's especially precious right now." She brushes off the meat and hands it to Grak.

Unsure how to respond, he accepts the chunks and places them on the table by his bowl. "Yes … I'll be sure to speak to him about that. But don't change the subject. Why are you here?"

"Well, it's really the same subject." She finally musters the courage to meet his gaze. "I've come to discuss the food situation."

Grak's face twists into anger. "Did you not learn your lesson at the whipping post? You won't change my decision on the matter." A new advantage springs to mind. "Besides, the people's council has spoken."

Yes, they've given me an unexpected gift, haven't they? That group of dolts might just be useful after all. They do my bidding, and should my children grow upset, I just point to their representatives. A double win if I've ever seen one.

"Look, I didn't …" She averts her eyes again. "I don't want to cause you more pain." She begins pacing nervously. "And I didn't want to say anything before … but now the situation is too desperate. The tribe can't recover … not unless something changes." She stops at his statue table, gazing intently at the carving Frolan made so many days ago. "Our people need food, and if you won't provide it … well …"

Grak grows impatient. "Spit it out Jafra. Is this your feeble attempt at a threat?" He smiles, confident in his newly discovered power. "Do you seek to defy not only me, but the entire tribe and their chosen representatives as well?"

Her tone grows in courage. "The council only bent to your will today. As everyone has for some time now. As I have too. But nothing was resolved. I'm sorry, Grak. I placed my trust in you previously. Truly. Partially because I believed in you, and partially … well … partially out of guilt."

Grak sighs. "*This* again?" He rubs his brow. "Always trying to find a way to wiggle out of blame, Jafra. Can't you take responsibility for your actions? Just once?"

"That's just it, Grak. I *do* take the blame for what I did to you." She's on the verge of tears now. "I know her death was my fault. Even after so many snows, I still feel the guilt." She takes a breath to steady herself. "But I can't let that force my silence any longer."

Grak is confused. "So, you're here to convince me of your guilt? Because you really don't need to waste my time. You know I've always agreed. It's Sando that needs convincing."

Something else she said suddenly clicks. "And what silence? What madness are you up to now?"

Jafra picks up his statue. "This. I can't keep silent about *this* anymore."

Grak rolls his eyes. Now it's clear where she's headed. "Yes, I know. But it's not like Frolan has much experience working with wood. And it's really rather boorish of you to make fun of the fellow over it. Besides, I'd like to see *you* do better. Might do you some good to thank me for all I've done for you. And all I've done for the tribe."

"No, Grak." Her tone hints of frustration. "The arrow." She takes a calming breath. "I can't keep quiet about the arrow. Not with the entire tribe's well-being at stake."

Grak is lost again, but wherever this is heading, it doesn't sound good. "Wha …?" He swallows and regains his composure. "What do you mean?"

"This was *my* arrow, Grak." Her tone is almost cold now. "I noticed the gray streak running through the shaft when I nocked it. And I watched this arrow fly from my bow straight into the deer's neck."

Grak thinks quickly. "So? Then I must have been mistaken. Mine must have been another arrow."

"There's more, Grak." Her voice takes on a measure of obstinance. "I saw you that day. I was watching you, trying to make sure you didn't fall asleep again. Didn't want the team teasing you like they had the last time—I know how teasing hurts you. When we all fired, you had no clue what was going on."

"Th …" Grak swallows again, but his calm doesn't return in full this time. "That's not true. Not at all. If you were focused on the hunt, then how could you have seen what I was doing?" He's rather proud of such a swift defense.

"I was standing behind you, just to your left, no more than three paces away. I had a clear view of you and the deer at the same time. I took my shot just before the others. While you were still hunched over that puddle, staring at your reflection. You were mumbling to yourself, checking your beard, fidgeting with spots on your face: the usual. You never left my sight. Even when I fired. You never even drew an arrow that day."

Grak reaches for any other defense. "But …" Nothing comes to mind.

This only emboldens her further. "When the tribe finds out your hunting strategies were all a lie, they'll see there's no reason to trust you with our food anymore. And the council will see we need a new approach."

Grak gulps. This could be bad if he doesn't handle it immediately with grace and wisdom.

"You're so stupid, Jafra!" He springs to his feet as his voice rises. "You always have been! And you don't know *anything*!" A furious rasp rises with it. "You're just guessing about that day! Because you can't stand how I've become so loved!" A bit of a shriek now.

"So now you're trying to ruin this for me! Just like you *always* have!" He no longer has control of his voice. "You ruined my life by being born, and you're trying to ruin it again! You ruin things! It's all you've ever done and all you'll ever do! And I hate you!"

Frolan and two of his team rush in and assess the danger. "Grak!" Finding nothing of apparent concern, the brute's voice gentles. "Are you alright?"

The interruption breaks Grak's focus, bringing a semblance of calm to his thoughts. As does the severe strain in his throat. At least, enough to think about the next move.

Careful now, Grak. Breathe. You've solved much trickier problems than this before. You can easily do it again.

Grak lunges at Jafra, remembering to close his fist before striking. The blow lands square on her left cheek, causing her to stumble back. But to his dismay, she seems more confused than injured by the attack.

Grak strikes again. This time it dazes the woman and gives him a clear angle for her neck. He grabs firmly with both hands, pressing his thumbs to her throat. Her frantic pulse pounds against his grip in stark contrast to his own steady heartbeat.

His body feels alert, strangely good. Especially his arms, as though he's never used them to their full potential before. He flexes harder, tightening the squeeze. Aside from her feeble grasps at his forearms, she puts up no defense.

In that moment, Grak gives in to it. The feeling of raw strength flowing through him. The sensation of pure, unopposed control.

Frolan is unsure how to react. "Grak? What's the matter? Grak?" His voice grows noticeably concerned. "Grak! Y ... you're killing her, Grak!" He moves to intervene.

Grak's head slowly turns toward the man, revealing a penetrating, insidious glare. "Back ... away." No need to add a menacing tone; his voice is cold and terrible on its own.

Grak's focus returns to Jafra, his eyes aflame with hatred: pure, passionate, and remorseless. He renews his grip, though it makes little difference at this point. The woman's defense wanes further, as she struggles now just to stay awake. Her eyes slowly roll back.

Then it clicks. Now he sees it. Sando always said she bore a strong resemblance, but Grak never noticed before. Now it's unmistakable. Especially from the nose up.

And the same expression. The same as ... as when she died. Mother.

Grak releases her, and she drops to the ground with a heavy thud. He takes a few steps back and turns away, mustering all his strength to stem the oncoming tears. Frolan rushes to Jafra's side and cradles her head, gently rubbing her brow.

Get control of yourself, Grak. She's your enemy. And an enemy to your people. She's trying to take them from you. That's been her game all along. But you can't settle it this way. Everyone would call you brutal. Especially at a time like this, when tensions are already so high.

Grak straightens his chair and sits. He picks up the bowl and leans back. His gaze remains fixed on Jafra as he resumes his meal.

"Is she alright?" His tone is eerily void of emotion.

Frolan's eyes never leave her face. "Yes. She's breathing. I think she'll recover." There's a clear relief in his voice.

"Good." Grak takes another bite. "We can't go whipping someone who's already unconscious. Would lose its effect if my children couldn't hear her screams."

He takes another bite, chewing slowly this time. "Liven her up and get her ready. One hundred lashes. And gag her. Can't have her arguing like Cordo was."

12 - And the Devious Jafra

Grak can't even begin to describe the level of pure, deep, passion-ate, utter, profound, blinding, roiling, unadulterated, righteous, ardent, blistering, fervent, lofty, gut-wrenching, seething, liberating contempt he feels toward Jafra. He hates her even more than olives. By far.

Like nine thousand olives. Rotting. In a pile of manure. Covered in vomit. And decaying corpses. Such is Jafra.

And every word leaving the woman's lips inspires greater hatred in his heart. "Furthermore, Grak's charade of hunting strategies only dug us deeper into starvation. It was Cordo's planning that brought us out. Through his plan of volunteer rations combined with steady hunting, we were able to survive the snows with no loss of life." This elicits a spotty cheer from the crowd.

I should have seen the signs. Why was I so blind? I let her build power until it was too late. And now she's coming after mine.

Why did I spare her wretched life? What was I thinking? I had her throat in my hands! And I just let her go … Too merciful, that's what it was. That'll be my downfall.

"I don't have to stand here and take these ridiculous accusations!" Grak raises his voice even louder, just to be sure everyone in the back can hear him clearly. "Is this why you gathered the tribe, Cordo? So Jafra could have a rapt audience while she slings insults at me and sings your praises?"

Cordo crosses his arms. "Just listen, Grak. Please."

Grak clenches his jaw. It's all he can do to hold back an outburst. That wouldn't go over well at the moment. Not with his opponents all showing total calm.

Listen? That's all I've been doing! Listening and waiting. Eighty-four days now. Eighty-four days of subversion. Eighty-four days of loss. Loss of power and control and ... and everything! Eighty-four days since Jafra began spreading her lies! She's incapable of truth. Incapable of civility!

Even when the cold stretched longer than usual, Grak clung to the hope that warmer air might somehow bring a measure of respite. But it didn't. If anything, the complaints grew once the ground thawed.

His next hope was that moving to this middle campsite might grant him the break he sought. Of course, he didn't know *why* he thought this would help. He simply had a vague notion that a change of surroundings might bring a change of outlooks. But, again, this proved no more than wishful thinking.

With that final expectation crushed, Grak sank into fear and despondency. "Desperate" is how he describes his current predicament. He needs some sort of positive outcome—any sort, really—and he needs it soon.

"Grak has consistently shown a poor ability to lead." Jafra's face is all concern with only a trace of remorse touching her dominant eyebrow. "We saw that clearly throughout the snows. And the subsequent famine. And now that we've made it safely through, we need to decide who we want to lead us going forward."

"Why do we need *anyone* leading us?" shouts someone unidentifiable toward the middle of the crowd. "We never had a tribe leader before, and things always worked out well."

Grak attempts to answer that, but Cordo gets to it first. "And look what happened. We had Lago attacks and lion attacks. Clearly we need leadership. But a new sort. A better sort."

No, Grak! No more interruptions. This ends. Now.

Grak's fury is hardly masked. "I don't have time for this nonsense! I have a tribe to lead. To lead *properly* as I always have. A tribe to protect and provide for, just as I've always done.

"This meeting is finished! Frolan, whip Jafra! End this absurd display of defiance! One hundred lashes!"

Frolan moves haltingly, glancing at the council with uncertainty.

"Don't look at them!" Grak is nearly speechless with rage. "This is a matter of tribe security! It falls under my authority alone!"

Cordo holds up a hand, and the council discusses the matter among themselves. Grak hates when they do that—more because of the feeling of exclusion than anything else, really.

And even though he can't hear them right now, things don't seem to be going his way. Kando appears to be offering his customary disagreements in Grak's favor, but he's doing it alone this time. Worse still, the conversation is already coming to a close.

Far too quickly. That's never a good sign.

Cordo lifts his voice for the crowd's sake. "The council disagrees with you, Grak. The 'correction and mercy' policy says it requires our assent for '*every* punishment.' The *only* exception stated is when a tribe member is in 'immediate danger.' Clearly, that isn't the situation here."

Grak hates that policy. The council was crafty enough to push it through as their first action, and he's regretted giving his consent ever since.

Although, if he's being honest, Grak feels he was deceived in the matter. The only reason he allowed the guideline was because he thought it would display his merciful nature. Well, he also assumed "immediate danger" was a loose definition open to his interpretation. As it turns out, he was wrong on both points, and the policy has since proven to be the single greatest hindrance to his plans.

Besides Jafra, of course. Devious, devious Jafra.

Despite its consistent failure, Grak gives his usual objection, though with a slight alteration. "But if this continues, we're opening ourselves up to chaos and confusion. And that's exactly how we came to feel the pain of Lago's attack in the first place. And the lion attack too. And don't forget the strangers' deceit. Thus, we're in immediate danger of suffering future problems if we don't act now."

The addition of that last sentence seems to have thrown the council off. They return to whispering, though with greater disagreement this time. Olive Thirteen, for example, seems to be squarely on Grak's side now.

There's a loyal one. She could teach Groka a thing or two. That one's been teetering on the edge of betrayal lately. Constantly in Jafra's presence and yet to support me on even a single issue.

Though what pains Grak most is how Groka always finds convenient excuses to avoid even speaking to him these days.

Jafra's fault as well, I'm sure. Devious, devious Jafra.

More surprising than Olive Thirteen, though, is the sight of Loren arguing with Cordo. Of course, she does tend to support Grak on most issues, but what's bizarre is that she would come to his defense on a matter like this. After all, the woman usually opposes what she calls "cruel and undue punishment."

A nebulous term, really. Open to even greater interpretation than 'immediate danger.' Still, at least she's backing me here. Always a pleasant occurrence. And more so, given her added vehemence today. A lot of aggression on display in those ears.

The discussion concludes, and Cordo steps forward. "The council would remind you of the 'definitions' addendum to the 'correction and mercy' policy. It describes 'immediate' as 'happening or existing now.' Clearly, this danger you speak of does not meet those criteria." He hands over a clay tablet.

Grak slowly turns his head away, careful to make an obvious show of the slight. Nothing that man has to offer is of interest. Nor is it needed in this case, as Grak has every tribe policy and addendum committed to memory. He simply hoped the *council* wouldn't remember such a small detail as that definition.

Grak addresses Jafra again. "Fine. I won't whip you. Out of the kindness of my heart. But I *will* put an end to this meeting. It's an unauthorized gathering. And let me remind you of the 'tribe gatherings and meetings' policy. It strictly bans any grouping of three or more people unless specifically authorized by me. And I hereby *remove* my authorization from this meeting."

The council huddles together once more as a murmur of concern ripples through the tribe. Aza and Sabo seem firmly on Grak's side for this one.

There's a welcome sight. Maybe something's starting to turn my way.

The discussion ends quickly, and Cordo steps forward. "Very well. But let us remind you of the 'planning and scheduling' policy. It clearly states that the power to organize and schedule camp activities rests with the council. Therefore, we hereby schedule a new meeting, which will commence now."

"That's fine," Grak replies with a smile. "Just get it authorized first."

Cordo and his faithful are noticeably peeved by this. The council returns to its huddle. Aza and Sabo seem torn this time, but Kando, Loren, and Olive Thirteen are clearly behind Grak. The discussion comes to an uneasy conclusion.

Cordo speaks. "We propose a new poli—"

"Denied," interrupts Grak.

He turns to the crowd. "You still seem to be gathered in groups greater than two."

He turns back to the council. "As do you. Let me remind you of the 'tribe threat' addendum to the 'gatherings and meetings' policy. It's considered a threat to tribe security for any to remain gathered after I've disbanded a meeting. Or to put it another way, it's an immediate danger and grounds for punishment."

Worry ripples through the crowd as a trickling departure begins. But the council hesitates, each looking around at the others. After another moment, they separate too. Though just barely—some out of uncertainty, and others out of defiance.

Grak smiles. "Twenty feet." His voice carries a melodic tone. "Between each of you. As per the 'definition of gatherings' addendum."

Cordo ponders their options for a moment before nodding to the others. At that, the rest of the council starts back toward their tents. But Cordo doesn't budge. He simply stares at Grak with a fierce mettle.

"This isn't over, Grak," he finally says, then turns and walks away in frustration.

Grak's smile widens. Even a small victory is encouraging.

You need at least one every now and then. Eases the stress of leading. A spot of sun as the storm relents. Even if only for a moment.

Though Grak may have thought too soon there. His smile evaporates as he spots Jafra and Groka walking off together.

But this storm isn't over. Far from it. Not while Jafra continues her schemes. Strange, though. You'd think she'd be grateful for my mercy. I did spare her life, after all. But no. That one has no sense for gratitude.

And this new proposal of hers ... too far. Even for her. Or it was too far, at least. For the old Jafra. Now it seems she'll stop at nothing to ruin me.

Have to put an end to it. But how?

A profound, yet simple idea forms. So simple, in fact, that Grak is surprised he never thought of it before.

Of course! I simply need an accusation to throw at her. Simple, yet effective. But what? It would need some truth. Just enough to convince my children. Just enough to make her sweat.

He turns to Frolan. "What do you know about Jafra?"

The man shows some surprise at the question. "Oh ... uh, well lots, actually. Let's see ... She loves jasmines. She'll go on and on about them if you let her. And I don't know if you've noticed, but her left eyebrow is a smidg—"

"No, you ignoramus!" Grak has no time for this. "Accusations. I need something to tarnish her reputation."

Frolan is a little hurt, but quickly sets his emotions aside and thinks on Grak's request. "Nothing that I can recall." He thinks some more. "I could follow her, though. Maybe I'll find something."

Grak is pleasantly surprised by that idea. "Yes ... exactly what I was thinking." He considers it further, then shakes his head. "But the situation is too severe. Can't leave it with anyone else. I'll have to do it myself."

He turns to the brute. "Wait at my tent. I shouldn't be long."

Frolan hesitates. "Well ... shouldn't I go along to protect you? It'll be dark any moment now."

Grak looks to the horizon. It's true. The sun is nearly gone, only casting a shred of its full light now.

He pats the man's cheek. "Always keeping papa safe, eh Frolan? I like the way you think. But, no. You would stand out. And two are harder to hide than one. No, you return. I'm willing to risk my own safety for the good of the tribe. I'll do this alone."

Be calm, Grak. Brak will clean you off later. It's time for a new pair of boots anyway.

Grak stamps off what he can and continues on, rushing to make up for lost time. But the decision proves rash, and his hurried steps create too much noise. Jafra turns in response to the sound, giving him less than a breath to react and dart behind a nearby tent. His heart threatens to pound through his chest as he peeks around the corner.

Jafra is standing in the middle of the path, looking around in confusion. But she doesn't appear to have spotted him. Grak pulls his head back into the shadows and breathes a deep sigh of relief. After allowing a moment or two for his heart to catch up and return to a normal pace, he peeks around the corner again.

Too late! Hurry, Grak!

He picks up his pace and crosses the path, deftly ducking behind a cart near the upcoming bend in the row of tents. He's getting better at quickly slipping out of sight.

Shh. Careful now. There! Go!

Grak pops back out and scuttles across the path before hiding behind another tent. He peeks out again, then scurries off once more and ducks behind yet another tent. He crouches there and waits while Jafra chats with Voluilo.

Is this the reason she's out here tonight? No, can't be. She wouldn't wander around for so long just to talk with that fool. So then where is she going? And so late in the night? That fox. That devious, devious fox!

The conversation ends, and Jafra continues her stroll. Grak's body tenses, begging to follow, but forced to wait for Voluilo to depart. The man seems to be taking his time.

An inordinate amount of time, really. Who walks that slowly? Oh, and his boot suddenly interests him? The flat-lipped dolt! Now there's someone who deserves a whipping.

Though I imagine Cordo would challenge that too. What a fool. Never looks at the long term consequences of his actions.

Although ... if I could prove how Voluilo constitutes an immediate threat. Hmm ... how mi—

Jafra disappears around another bend, yanking Grak's thoughts back to the present.

No! Get on with your movement, you clod!

After another agonizing moment, Voluilo finally returns to his tent. Before the flap even settles, Grak springs forth, hurrying to catch up. He reaches the spot where Jafra turned, then pauses and peers around the corner. Nothing. Just another path with more tents.

No! Think, Grak! Where might she have gone?

But he quickly realizes that if this were an effective exercise, following the woman would be unnecessary. Thus, Grak abandons the idea. Instead, he settles on a systematic search, walking swiftly down the path and looking from side to side.

He stops suddenly.

Shh. Listen, Grak.

He can hear talking. It's a woman's voice.

No, two women's voices. Clearly two. But which women?

Grak focuses his hearing. The voices lead him forward and to the right. Passing two dwellings, he pauses at the third. Then shock hits. This is Groka's tent. His heart pinches, and his stomach twists.

What in all the land is Jafra doing? Meeting with Groka at this time of night? She must be subverting her! Turning her against me.

What a devious, vile beast, that Jafra! She's always known what I feel for Groka. And she's always sought to destroy it. But now ... now she's using it to hurt me. When I'm already at my weakest! This ... this is heartless. Even for Jafra.

Any contempt he previously held toward the woman is now surpassed by a new animosity. It's a fiercer, more engrossing thing that devours all other thoughts, leaving only a sharp focus behind. In fact, if it didn't hurt so much, Grak might even categorize this malice as "positive."

At least it's useful. Can't deny that.

The voices die down. Under normal circumstances, Grak would hide, but he's too angry right now. He's almost eager for confrontation. But none comes. This proves strangely calming. His senses return slightly.

What are they up to now? Sketching out plans? In silence lest someone overhear their schemes? Devious. So, so devious.

Grak creeps closer. He looks around to make sure no one else is about, then crouches and carefully peels back the tent flap. He shakes his head in confusion.

They don't appear to be writing anything down. Far too dark for that.

Grak strains to adjust his eyes to the lack of light. When he does, a gasp nearly escapes his throat.

That's definitely a breast! A naked breast!

He squints harder to see who it belongs to.

What in all—

He does better at holding back this gasp.

Kissing! Deep kissing. Lots of deep kissing. And ... other things ... Oh dear ...

Grak remembers to breathe. Slowly releasing the flap, he pulls back and sucks in a few quiet, deep breaths. This gives him a moment to think. His head is whirling with what this all means.

Maybe I can pretend I was stopping by to chat. Maybe they'll invite me in. It's possible ...

No! That's Jafra in there! Subverting the only woman I've ever loved. Doing things to her I've never had the chance to do. Tearing my heart out and stomping it into the mud!

His breathing follows his rising temper, forcing Grak to think calming thoughts. Patyr pops to mind first, eliciting a smile.

I miss that beautiful creature. And the hot springs. I miss those too. Won't be long before we head back there. That'll be nice.

Thoroughly steadied now, Grak ponders his next move. The answer comes in an instant.

Revenge. Definitely revenge. And I'll have to do it myself. To make sure it's done properly. End this problem once and for all. Not the Cordo problem, no, but the Jafra issue at least. Then I can decide what to do about that other rebellious fool.

But when? Tonight will have to do. Though not this instant. Groka doesn't know any better. She's innocent. No, I won't allow her to see suffering. So I'll have to wait until later. That's all there is to it. But what to do until then …?

Grak shrugs and settles into a more comfortable posture, then carefully peels back the tent flap.

Grak strolls calmly through camp, alert for anyone stirring, but making no effort to hide. He considers it unnecessary this late at night, as everyone should be sound asleep by now.

Except the security team. But they won't get in my way.

It's true. Grak told Frolan he heard wolves in the east woods, and had the man focus his whole team on that side of camp. "Just in case," was all it took to leave the entire west side open and free from any prying eyes.

I'm sure I could trust Frolan, of course. He's always been a loyal one, after all. But why get him involved? He's so young and innocent. No need to get his hands dirty with this. Besides, we shouldn't need two people for the task. It'll be quick.

Something else pops to mind, however.

Hmm. That's true. How will I move her afterward? Can I carry her by myself? Might have been possible in the past, but now?

Grak regrets letting his physique slip. He was never a large man by any standards, but he had muscle and was fairly lean. His current girth, on the other hand, tends to discourage heavy labor.

Maybe I should alter the plan. I could ask her to go for a walk. Tell her I want to make peace. Maybe if I say I'm stepping down. That might entice her out into the woods.

But then she might be on guard. No, best not to take the chance. Stick with the original idea, Grak. It'll be much easier if she's sleeping. You'll just have to make do with the rest. Yes, stick with the original idea.

Grak reaches Jafra's tent. His plan, while obviously brilliant, was partially based on the location of her dwelling. For quite a number of days now, she's had a peculiar preference for living on the west side of camp. So much so, that her tent sits at the farthest western point, save for a few carts and the occasional horse.

But never a pony. Never. Not for some time now.

Grak shakes his sadness in favor of the moment's greater urgency. He pauses to force his nerves into submission.

Come on, Grak. You can do this. She'll be asleep. The chances of her waking up and fighting back are slim. Nothing to worry about. Nothing at all.

He takes a deep breath and closes his eyes. Upon opening them, his gaze is cold, determined. He draws his dagger and carefully peels back the tent flap. But no one's here.

Grak enters cautiously, just in case she's sleeping under a pile of clothing or something. But a quick, yet thorough, search reveals no Jafra. He pounds his thigh, realizing only too late that the butt of his dagger is made of a denser substance than his leg. He bites his lip to hold back a yelp.

Curse that devious fox! What's she up to now? You never should have waited so long, Grak!

In his defense, though, he had assumed she would remain here for the night. After her rendezvous with Groka, he followed Jafra back and waited in the shadows for a long while, thinking up a plan. His hope was that he might come up with something sufficient utilizing the items he had on him at the time. To his dismay, however, nothing even came close to resembling a weapon, and he was forced to think of alternative ideas.

Finally, he left to fetch his dagger from his tent, concluding that she wasn't going anywhere else for the night. Thinking he had plenty of time, he also allowed himself several moments to consider the situation in peace. Now he wonders if he was too careless with that decision.

But I needed the dagger at least. That much couldn't be helped. And I don't know when she left, so the extra thinking time makes no difference. Well, it's not your fault, Grak. Just think now. Where might she be?

Noticing the obvious lack of chairs, Grak sets his dagger to the side and attempts to settle into one of his old thinking postures. Unfortunately, his new girth proves an unexpected and considerable obstacle. He rubs his stomach.

Perhaps I should cut back a bit. Or move around more. But then again, I don't often have need for this posture.

Although ... Cordo does have a rather impressive build. Perhaps that lends to his sway among my children. He certainly needs something to distract from that mole.

And come to think of it, popularity came more easily to me when I was in better shape. Perhaps the two are connected.

Then it's decided. I'll need to trim down a bit. Get into a fitter state. And given my lack of facial deformities, it should be simple enough to win my children back from that fool. Then they'll love me ag—

Grak freezes. Someone is rummaging around outside. An instant later, the flap opens, revealing Jafra against the moonlit sky. She enters and begins fiddling about with items just to her left. Strangely enough, though, she doesn't seem to notice him yet.

Fortune!

Slowly, carefully, Grak reaches for his dagger. With equal caution, he raises the blade above his head, readying for a swift downward blow. But that's when he pauses, a sudden realization taking shape.

From this angle, it would hit her skull. Might not penetrate on the first try. Certainly not without my full weight behind it.

So what other options are available? Hmm, the neck seems best. Yes, simple and quick.

Slowly, carefully, Grak lowers the dagger, readying for a swift slicing motion. But before he can get it in place, Jafra whirls around, leaving him only an instant to deflect her move. Or at least, the move he imagined she might be making. Instead, the woman slips back outside.

Grak's heart pounds, and his hands tremble. He takes a deep, calming breath and listens intently for Jafra's footsteps.

West ... out into the forest? Fortune!

Grak can only hope she'll wander out far enough without noticing him coming up behind. He estimates two hundred paces should do it. Then only a moderate burial would be needed to ensure that she's never found.

At least not before we move again. Shouldn't be too much longer. Maybe thirty days or so? Well, maybe a little farther out would be better. Perhaps three hundred paces.

A more pressing issue pops to mind, though.

But what's she even doing out in the woods at this time of night?

Only one possibility presents itself.

The strangers! She's working with them. She must be. She's trying to take my power and give it to them. Impressive. But also devious. So, so devious.

Half driven by curiosity and half by hatred, Grak follows after the woman. With little effort, he manages to close much of the gap. Soon, with around fifty paces remaining, he slows to a measured tread. Fortunately, the ground is relatively free of leaves and other noisy obstacles. Thus, even given his current girth, he's closing the final distance quickly.

Grak allows himself a quiet giggle.

Not very perceptive, are you, Jafra? Perhaps you should have spent more time practicing that skill instead of trying to steal my power. But, you've always made poor decisions like that, haven't you? And now it's too late.

He pauses to catch his breath.

Patience, Grak. Her time will come. Oh yes. All you have to do is make sure she doesn't hear you. Just don't spoil the surprise.

He restrains an excited chortle and continues on. Somehow, perhaps inspired by his current success, he moves even quicker this time. Soon, he's only five paces behind the woman. So close he can smell her jasmines now. He allows yet another silent chuckle.

Just like mother used to wear, eh Jafra? Were you hoping to stay my hand once again? Well, it won't work this time. I won't be soft now. I'll have my revenge. For everything you've inflicted on me. For all the pain you've caused. For everything you've taken!

He's less than three paces behind now as Jafra descends into a dell. Stunned at the exquisite nature of the setting she's handed him, Grak pauses to enjoy it for a moment.

Yes, that's an excellent location. At the bottom there, under the fallen tree. No one would find her. Who would think to dig in a spot like tha—?

He ducks behind a large rock, hoping he wasn't spotted. Someone is moving around down there, though Grak can't tell who it is. All he can see from this distance is a scrawny human form.

No! You weren't fast enough! How could you, Grak? You forgot about the strangers!

He takes a deep breath.

Calm, Grak. It's alright. Just wait until she's finished. Then you can get her. No need to change your plans. She won't be here all night. And neither will they.

He leans against the rock, focusing great effort on patience. This proves even more challenging due to the snippets of Jafra's words carried by the wind. Her voice taunts him. Irritates him. Then he realizes something.

You know, it might be beneficial to hear what she's planning. She'll be gone, sure, but whatever she's set in motion will linger. Just seems wise to have advance warning of it. Might even be able to stop her scheme altogether.

It's decided, then. Grak creeps forward, darting from cover to cover on the sparse slope. Finally, he stops behind a wide tree to catch his breath and listen.

Jafra's voice is obvious enough, but the other one also carries an eerie familiarity. It's not Kunthar's, though—Grak is certain of that. It doesn't even have the throatiness of the strangers' words.

Who, then?

Curiosity soon wins out, and he cautiously peeks around the tree. But he wasn't expecting this. He's forced to bite back a gasp at the sight. What Jafra brought from her tent was food, and she's handing it to someone. More importantly, Grak now has a clear view of *who* she's handing it to.

Lago . . .

13 - And Her Devious Schemes

Grak has always categorized Jafra's schemes as "acts of depravity nearly as heinous as their creator." And those schemes take on an even greater degree of villainy when they're as mysterious as her dealings with Lago last night.

What in all the land could that poisonous woman be up to?

While he was able to hear everything the two discussed, nothing of importance came out.

Or perhaps they used signals. Or a code of some sort. Hmm, probably so. A devious mixture of the two, I imagine. Just in case anyone happened upon their secret meeting.

Grak both applauds and loathes such a crafty system.

No matter, though. Neither of those traitors will be around much longer. If I can manage this with subtlety. And without casting myself into a poor light at the same time. Can't risk more tension with the council. Or the tribe.

After careful deliberation, Grak decided not to follow through on "the Jafra strike" last night. And he's not ashamed to admit that a portion of his reasoning had to do with hesitation. He just didn't feel comfortable leaving the safety of his cover while Lago was still awake.

If he had seen me, who knows what might have happened? Would he have attacked? Quite likely. After all, he's been living like a wild beast for some time now. And he looked a bit too wiry and unpredictable for my liking. I'm not risking my life trying to take him on in a fight, that's for sure.

Though, truth be told, Grak has never had to fight for his life. He's not even sure what that would entail. Nonetheless, he'd rather not find out if he's up to the challenge.

I'm sure I'd do just fine. Really. But why bother when I have a better plan in mind?

It's true. The other part of Grak's rationale for abandoning "the Jafra strike" was due to having forged a superior plan. In fact, he considers this the main reason, even though he didn't form this better strategy until today.

But it was in my head last night. I'm sure of it. Just didn't realize it because of weariness. I was rather tired, after all. And plans are better conceived after a good night's rest.

Though, in all honesty, it was a fitful slumber with dreams of the fervent sort. The kind that arise when thinking too much about work just before drifting off.

Grak feels a yawn coming and gives in to it emphatically. He checks to see if the other man noticed.

Nope. He's still rambling on. Though if he continues at this pace, I'll have no choice but to nap while I wait. And I'm sure he'd notice that.

Not that I'd mind, of course. Let him notice, and let him get upset. The rest would be far more useful than his support. Perhaps I'd even conjure a better idea after waking.

Ah, but the matter is far too urgent, isn't it? A shame. Don't suppose I have any other choice then.

"So?" interrupts Grak. "What's your answer? Will you do it?"

Brak scratches his head again. And once more. Grak never noticed before, but the man does that far more often than propriety allows.

Perhaps that's the source of his baldness. Remember to limit head scratches, Grak. Remember to limit head scratches. Remember to limit head scratches.

Brak finally speaks. "I don't know, Grak. Sounds risky. This seems more like a task for Doran. Have you asked *him* to do it?"

Grak rolls his eyes.

What a fool. What a bald, timid fool. Why must I always prod him to take initiative? Just once, it'd be nice to see a little more action and a little less hesitation.

Grak stifles his frustration. "No, that's not possible. Doran's in poor favor right now. Few in camp trust him after his 'map whipping' policy. And I thought of Kando too, but he's in a comparable situation. They're practically one and the same.

"I even thought of Groka, but I doubt she'd back me at this point. She's literally sucking at Jafra's teat."

"Practically."

"What?"

"You said 'literally,' but the correct word there would be 'practically.'"

"Ah, yes." Grak considers revealing more of last night's events, but thinks better of it. "Practically."

He looks around awkwardly, then continues. "And I've thought of every possibility. Truly. But who else can I trust at this point? Except Frolan, of course, but that would be the same as if *I* revealed the information. She's a sly one, that Jafra. She would just say I ordered him to lie—told him what to say as a means of slandering her."

Brak nods in thought. "Oh. I see. I suppose. But then wouldn't she be able to say that about me?"

"No. Our connection isn't as close as what I have with Frolan. That's the beauty of it. You simply run errands for me and do the menial tasks I can't get anyone else to do.

"Whereas Frolan ... well he's practically my right hand. He handles matters I wouldn't trust to anyone else. And it's not just work. We eat and drink together on a regular basis. And ..." Grak stops there, sensing a growing frustration in the other man.

"And *why* don't we do those things?" pouts Brak. "And *why* don't I have greater responsibilities? I could be just as useful as Frolan. Maybe I'm not as large, but I could handle matters that don't require size."

Grak cradles Brak's cheek. "Sweet, simple, Brak. We've gone over this before. It's only because of our people. They just don't think very highly of bald men. More than bald women, sure, but not by much. I would love to give you greater responsibility, but first we have to get your hair to grow in."

Brak takes that far worse than expected. "But I can't do anything about my baldness! And besides, it's never hindered me. I'm just as capable as anyone else."

Grak puts on the most empathetic demeanor he can muster. "*I* know that. Obviously. That's why I have you at my side, sweet Brak. But it's hard to change the tribe's mind. You've seen that first hand, haven't you?"

Brak shrugs. "I suppose."

"And I aim to prove them wrong, Brak, my friend." An idea pops to mind. "And that's why I'm offering you this opportunity. I want to show the tribe that you matter."

Brak shakes his head in sorrow and disbelief. "But I always mattered *before*. I had friends. And influence. It's only when I became cook and your servant that I lost all of that. I didn't even know what I had until it was gone."

"And you'll have it once again, Brak. You will!"

"How? As long as I'm your servant, what respect does it grant me? I need more than that."

"Absolutely." Grak thinks quickly. "Actually, I was just thinking the other day that you would do very well in overseeing the tribe's horses."

Brak looks offended now. "Wha ... why would I want to do *that*? And how would it improve my respect among our people? No, Grak. I want to be on the council."

Grak is surprised by that demand. "Well, look, Brak. There are already nine, and you know how I feel about te—"

"You alone have the power to do this, Grak!" Brak's anger is showing now. "My wife is on the council, and all I do is clean your trousers of the previous night's meal. It's a disgrace! I won't have it any longer!" He calms slightly. "Appoint me to the council, and I'll do this task for you."

Grak frowns. It seems he has no other option if he wants Brak's help here.

Ten, though. Not ideal. Sure, it's a simple number, but what other claims does it have? Nothing but pomp and bluster. Best to keep it at nine.

"Then I'd have to get rid of someone." Grak can think of several deserving candidates, but would prefer the idea come from Brak. "Who would you suggest I remove?"

The bald man shrugs. "Well, I don't know. Maybe Kando? If the tribe is so suspicious of him."

Grak rolls his eyes. This isn't going the way he wanted. "No, he's too useful."

He checks his shadow. Time is too precious to let Brak slowly deliberate through the other eight. Grak decides to push things in the desired direction.

"And Olive Thirteen and Loren are even more valuable. Cordo, Ruch, and Zacha would be at the top of my list, but it would likely cause significant unrest if I removed them. Aza and Sabo could go, but they've recently started to come to their senses and might still be salvageable." He pauses. "Sooo … who does that leave?"

Brak scratches his head for a moment. "Well, that only leaves Groka. But she's always been so kind to me. I'd hate to take *her* place."

Grak is getting annoyed with the man's indecisiveness. "Well, that's the only solution we have here, Brak. Do this task for me, and you can replace Groka on the council. Either that or quit whining about your responsibilities. Besides, if she were in your situation, I'm sure she'd do the same."

Brak hesitates. "Well … I suppose you're right." He ponders the idea for a long moment. "Alright, I'll do it."

Grak makes no effort to hide his smile. "Good. Let's get to work then. The council will meet momentarily. And we usually take our first break soon after. Watch for it and be ready."

Grak attempts a relaxed pose as he chats with Aza. But despite sincere effort, the proper way to casually situate one's hands is still eluding him. He's already on his third try: an awkward, crossed-arm approach that feels too high up the chest to be deemed "easygoing."

Around him, the council is spread out in several pockets, conversing among themselves. As usual, most of Frolan's security team is surrounding them, keeping a vigilant eye out for danger. Two of those guards are occupied with Brak, asking questions too quiet for Grak to hear. Finally, Frolan takes an interest and approaches. He asks several questions of his own, then nods, and the other guards step out of the way so the man can pass.

It's about time! What took that fool so long?

Aza rambles on. "So, this is why I think we should reorder the tents in a gri—"

"Quiet." Grak makes no apologies for cutting her off. "What's Brak talking about?"

Aza turns in bewilderment. "Well, it appears he isn't talking about *anything*."

True enough. Brak is just standing there, turning in slow circles, looking at the faces of the council around him.

Grak rolls his eyes. "Yes, but it looks like he's *trying* to say something." He raises his voice loud enough for the whole council to hear. "What is it, Brak? Are you in trouble?"

The buffoon can't even speak without assistance. And he wants to be on my council? Unbelievable!

Brak gives a slight nod and convinces his jaw to move. "Yes. I mean, no. It's just … well, I have something to report." He pauses for a moment until Grak's impatient look prods him on again. "I saw something last night. And I didn't know what to do about it." He's beginning to loosen up a bit. "But after careful thought, I decided the council should know."

Cordo takes the bait. "What did you see, Brak?"

"It's Jafra … I saw her last night … in compromising actions. Dangerous actions, even."

"Wha … what do you mean?" Groka's response is skittish at best, though the trained observer would identify sheer panic.

Cordo adds to that. "Yes, out with it, man. What was so dangerous about her actions?"

Brak gathers his words. "I saw her in the woods last night. She was bringing food to Lago. I think the two are planning something. I fear it may already be too late to stop them."

Most of the council gasps in shock. Cordo remains silent, but appears troubled on a different level; even his mole is drooping in a defeated manner. Groka, on the other hand, simply mumbles something to herself and settles into a deeper sort of worry.

She rushes to speak before anyone else can. "How do you know her actions were traitorous? What if she's simply caring for the man?" She looks about nervously.

Grak had planned on letting Brak do all the talking, but he can't help himself. "Is that any better? The old fool tried to poison us all. If she's feeding him, then she's practically approving of his actions."

Groka's response is instant. "What if he didn't do it, though? What if that was all just a coincidence?"

Kando grows suspicious. "Sounds to me like you're sympathetic toward perfidy. Is that true, Groka?"

The accusation makes her nervous. "No, not at all. It's just … well, I thou—"

"As much as I hate to admit it," interrupts Grak, "I agree with Brak on this one. If Jafra's feeding the traitor, that's dangerous news. No matter how innocent she may claim to be."

"Well … maybe …" Groka thinks fervently. "But we don't know if he even actually saw Lago."

Brak grows indignant. "Are you calling me a *liar*?"

She seems genuinely surprised by that. "No, not at all. But how do you know what you saw? It was dark, after all. And you were out in the woods … Wait, what were you doing out in the woods?" Accusation floods her tone.

"I … well …" He looks to Grak.

The fool! He'll give it away if he looks to me for his answers! Think quickly, Grak.

He does. "Yes, what were you doing out in the woods, Brak?" That should deflect any blame.

"I … well …" Brak is sweating now, looking about like a newly orphaned pup.

Still, Grak needs the man's story to work. "Oh, I apologize. Were you out there fetching the berries I asked for?" He looks around at the council. "I asked him to find some blackberries, but since his regular duties kept him busy all day, he was only able to go out at night."

Brak breathes a sigh of relief. "Yes. That was it. I'm sorry I couldn't find any."

Grak puts on his merciful tone. "Well, normally I wouldn't stand for it." He switches to commanding. "But in this instance we have a greater concern. Given Lago's past transgressions, this can only be considered 'immediate danger.'"

Grak pauses for exactly three breaths. "It pains my heart to do this, but I must. For the safety of the tribe. Frolan, find Jafra and apprehend her." His voice seems to be gaining enthusiasm of its own accord. He mellows it out for appearances. "We'll need something worse than a whipping for this offense. Any ideas?" Much better.

Cordo raises his hands in a halting gesture. "Wait a moment, now. This is all a bit too fast. And you're a bit too eager to jump behind this story, Grak. We still haven't answered the question about the darkness last night. We can't be sure you saw Lago out there, Brak. We trust you and all, but how can *you* even be sure you saw him?"

Brak considers this for a moment. He looks to Grak.

Grak rubs his brow, hoping to calm the steadily rising frustration. "Well, *I* believe you, Brak. And confirming your story seems a simple matter to me. Just take us to where you saw the traitor. Problem solved. Then we can get on with the required discipline. I think we should discuss possible punishments as we walk, though. Just so we're ready to take action." He has something in mind, but would prefer if it came from one of them.

The council seems fairly accepting of that idea. They all nod readily. Except Groka, of course.

No matter. She can't stop this now.

Grak gestures toward the west woods. "After you, Brak."

The man looks uncertain. He walks forward cautiously, looking back at Grak repeatedly.

The fool! Although, I suppose it would be best to show him the way.

Grak leaps to the rescue once more. "Don't tell me you're afraid of *Lago*, Brak." He coats his voice with concern. "Well, I suppose that's understandable. After all, he did try to kill everyone. I'll walk with you, then. To protect you."

Groka is flummoxed. "I'm just saying I don't see why execution would be in order. And public shaming and torture first? And how is it even feasible to order the tribe to forget she existed? And how is *any* of that warranted? *Jafra* certainly didn't try to poison anyone. Even if we find Lago ahead as Brak suggests, that only means she was feeding the man. A former member of our tribe. That's all."

Grak rolls his eyes.

The concept really shouldn't be this hard for her to understand.

"Look, I'll go over it one more time." He slows his speech. "By assisting him, she prevented us from having our justice for his attack. And that's nearly as bad as performing the attack." He catches himself. "*Just* as bad, I mean."

He decides a reversal of focus is due. "And I don't see why it matters so much to you, Groka. It seems to me that anyone who truly cares about the tribe and its well-being would *want* justice."

"Well … of course I do," she replies with hesitance. "But at the same ti—"

Grak spots the dell just ahead and ducks down, motioning for the others to follow. Groka seems annoyed by the abrupt interruption, but obeys nonetheless.

It dawns on Grak that he'll need to explain his actions. "I … uh … thought I saw something. Down in that dell. Brak, how far until we reach the spot where you saw Lago?"

Startled, the man looks around in confusion for a moment. Finally, a thought seems to strike, and his eyes settle on Grak, searching for confirmation.

What a simpleton! Could my hints be any more obvious?

Grak rolls his eyes and takes a deep, calming breath. He nods to the bald man.

Brak nods in reply. "Yes. This is it. Just down in that dell. Like you saw." He finishes with an obvious, knowing look to Grak.

Fortunately, no one seems to have noticed. Most are stretching their necks for a better view, and Cordo is already sneaking toward the rim. Ruch and Zacha soon follow him with everyone else close behind.

Except Grak. He lingers, hoping to let the situation grow on its own. Finally, after a sufficient length of time, he moves forward as well. Taking position next to Frolan, he settles in and scans the area. His heart sinks.

No! Where is he? This can't be. Did she somehow warn the man? How would she have known?

Grak thinks quickly. He decides it's best to deflect blame before it has a chance to come his way. "What is this nonsense, Brak? Did you lead us out here on some fool's errand?"

"I … no …" Brak looks hurt.

Kando grows excited. "Look! There. Down by that fallen tree. I see items. Man-made. And what looks like a recent fire. Yes. I see a wisp of smoke. Brak must be right."

Cordo interrupts, obviously annoyed now. "Then where's Lago?"

"There," says Frolan, his voice full of ice and hatred.

Every eye follows the man's outstretched arm as it points to the southern rim. A thin figure is descending into the dell, apparently unaware of his watchers.

Hope drains from Cordo's voice. "Well, what makes you think that's Lago?"

Grak can't resist a good joke when the opportunity presents itself. "True. Lago could have eaten two people that size and still be hungry for more."

Brak laughs nervously. Looking around, he finds himself alone in this action and trails off.

Frolan's voice is unflinching. "It's him, alright. I can make out his face from here. Council, I suggest you stay back. My team and I will handle him. We're not taking any chances with this traitor. Not this time."

Frolan gives quick orders, and his forces split into three groups of three. He leads his team down the middle while the other two flank on either side. They all move swiftly, ferociously.

Grak finds a curious sense of respect in watching their approach.

Desiring a closer view, he follows, leaving a reasonable gap to avoid any collateral danger.

The teams quickly reach a distance of thirty paces or so and hunch over, slowing to a covert stride. Not stealthy enough, though. Lago suddenly notices the ones to his right. He drops his branches with a start, and frantically looks around for a route of escape. The other two groups quickly become evident, leaving west as his only option. He darts for it.

Well, he's built up some speed. I'd say the exile has done him some good.

Regardless, the tribe's security has been training, and they're far too quick for the man. Just as he reaches the rim, a body lunges from the right, ending his dash for freedom.

Lago rolls to his side, dazed. He gasps for air as the remaining forces close in, forming a tight circle. Frolan grabs the man's hair and pulls him up onto his knees. Grak isn't far behind and reaches them only a moment later.

Lago's senses slowly return. "No ... no ... please. I di ... I didn't poison ..." Another deep, labored breath. "I didn't poison the tribe. I didn't!"

Grak smiles. "Who said anything about *poison?*" His raised voice proves unnecessary, as the remaining council arrives mid-sentence.

Lago's breathing calms. "Jafra did. She told me all about it. I told her I didn't do it. I explained what happened. What actually happened.

"I left immediately. After I was exiled. Made for Redfist. Thought that would be my best chance at survival. To follow the herd. I stayed there for some time, but I never returned to our camp! Or ... your camp, I mean. You have to believe me!"

A calm, resigned sort of desperation overtakes his voice. "I even left Redfist when I saw the tribe approaching. And Jafra believed me. You can ask her. Please."

"Oh, we'll be talking to Jafra, alright. We'll talk to her real good." Grak realizes that sounded better in his head.

He seeks to redirect the conversation. "How long have you been meeting with her? What have the two of you been planning against the tribe?"

"No. Please ..." Lago's voice takes on a heavy tone of fear. "You have it all wrong, Grak. We haven't been planning anything. I only met up with her recently. Eight days ago, to be exact. And I had to convince her of my innocence as well.

"But she finally believed me. And she offered to help. She said she even had theories about what actually happened. With the poisoning, I mean. She said I'd be useful in proving the truth. Please. I can be a help."

Grak doesn't like the sound of that. His heart picks up its pace as the council repeats the man's words among each other.

What truth? What's he referring to? Does Jafra know? How could she know? It's my word against Lago's.

Grak looks around at the others. Their murmurs have died down. Several wear sympathetic expressions.

But will my children give in to sympathy for this liar? Will they even believe me? With so many challenging my authority these days? They might just believe this worm instead. No, can't risk it.

Grak holds out a hand. "Your knife, Frolan."

Cordo reacts quickly, his nervousness on clear display. "Wait, Grak. We haven't confirmed all the details of the situation. What if he's telling the truth?"

It's already spreading. Be quick, Grak. Immediate action is required.

He opts for a simple, yet proven approach. "And are you an enemy of the tribe as well, Cordo? Are you seeking to spare this villain to wreak more havoc on our people?"

Frolan grows furious. "Grak's right. We all know of Lago's guilt." He takes an intimidating step toward Cordo. "Anyone who questions it at this point warrants suspicion as well! Grak, with your leave, I believe we should apprehend Cordo. Until further questioning."

Grak is thrilled with this turn of events. "Yes. Please do. And thank you, Frolan. Wise thinking."

The brute nods, obviously satisfied with himself, but holding back a smile. He gives an order, and two of his team place a tight hold on Cordo.

"And gag him too," commands Grak. "No sense in letting him harass us while we seek justice."

Frolan tears a strip from Lago's tunic and advances on Cordo. The man puts up a firm resistance, but is quickly overcome by greater numbers.

Grak gives the council a fierce glare. "Would anyone else care to interfere with tribe security?"

Kando smiles something slight. Ruch and Zacha consider it, but settle on restraint. The other four simply cast their eyes to the ground.

Satisfied, Grak motions to Frolan once more. The brute nods. He unsheathes his knife and passes it over, then steps back several paces to wait in silence.

Lago starts up again. "No! Please!"

Grak ignores the man, concentrating instead on the hilt in his palm. It feels different. The weight is nothing new. Neither is the sensation of bound leather on his skin. And yet, it feels different. He hesitates.

No, Grak. You must. Don't think about it. Just do it.

Lago senses the reluctance. "Don't do this, Grak! Please! You don't want to do this."

His voice melts in terror until it's nearly a sob. "I've always been there for your family. I was like a father to your sister. I cared for Jafra as my own. When it was too difficult for you and your father. I've always been a friend to your parents. To your mother."

Tears begin to flow down the man's cheeks. "I wept when she died, Grak. Do you remember? She was like a sister to me. Please! For her!"

Something unidentifiable clicks in Grak's mind. Tension courses through his body, moving into the jaw. His left eye tries to blink, but fails. A neck muscle twinges. It strains. Then the pressure begins to recede.

Ice methodically creeps through his veins, soothing every tension, calming every nerve. His face relaxes, and his eyes close slightly. He finds a keen awareness of his body, yet none at all. His limbs are numb, but still fully responsive.

He focuses on the weight in his palm. It's still there, but the sensation is passing through someone else's skin now. He can't truly feel it anymore. He can't feel anything. Grak extends his hand, pressing the blade to Lago's throat.

"No ... please ..." Lago closes his eyes. "Please ..."

Grak orders his arm to move. It obeys with a curious force, dragging the knife hard across the man's neck. The sobbing ends abruptly, replaced by a far more disturbing noise: a gurgling, wheezing sound.

Worse than that, Lago's eyes have opened in response to the sting. They're flooded with countless emotions. Grak can recognize a few: shock ... pain ... terror ... sadness. And more. So much more.

Lago's eyes begin to fade. As do the emotions. Slowly. Ever so slowly. It seems an immeasurable amount of time. Finally, life abandons the man.

Lago's captors toss his limp body to the ground. His eyes fall on Grak, but they're not the same. They're empty now. And this sends a shiver up Grak's spine—a sensation he can fully perceive, no longer as though through someone else. Feeling has returned, uninvited and unwanted. And it's far more brutal than before. This disturbs him more than he'd care to admit.

Calm, Grak. Calm.

He takes a deep breath, effectively soothing his fraying nerves. Looking around, he notices that most have averted their eyes.

Probably wisest. Not a pleasant sight. Most people don't have nerves like mine.

He looks down at what used to be Lago, now an empty shell bleeding out. The pool of blood creeps toward Grak. He steps back to avoid it, but realizes the effort is futile: his boots are already drenched. As are his trousers. On further inspection, he's hard pressed to find an area not dripping with the stuff.

No! Of all the things that could go wrong. I just had Brak clean this set of clothes!

Rage takes over, and he looks around for someone to blame. To his dismay, few options present themselves.

Maybe Jafra. If she were here. Or maybe—

A new fury enters Grak's mind. "Groka!" He scans the dell. "Where's Groka?"

Everyone looks around calmly. A few shrug, obviously missing the significance. There's only one reason she'd slip away in secret.

To warn Jafra. To help her escape.

14 - And Sore Losers

Grak reserves a special place in his heart for the unique disgust he has toward sore losers. "Pathetic" is his preferred description for such individuals. And if time allows, he'll elaborate with details and hyperbolic impersonations. Though, to his dismay, the tribe grew tired of these displays after a mere eleven days.

The council was more accommodating, but after another six days, a number of them began complaining too. "Poor taste," said some. "Far too graphic," complained others. "Contains too many clay figurines to follow," mentioned others still.

Thus, for the past ten days he's been forced to express himself solely in the presence of his personal guards. Reflecting on last night's showing, Grak allows himself a chuckle.

Frolan pauses, glancing around at the council in confusion. "Um ..." He's clearly disquieted. "I suppose it's somewhat humorous. I mean, at least he didn't die from it. So that's good."

Grak can tell he's missing something here. He looks around the tent. The council is expressing shock—that much is clear. And they're directing it at him—also clear. He ponders these details and deduces that the topic must have been one they deem important.

Grak gathers himself. "Yes. Sorry, who did you say this was?"

"Yado," replies Frolan.

Grak had hoped the brute would provide a few more details. "Yes, Yado ..." He tries again. "And so, given the aspects you've already explained, how do you think the injury occurred? Specifically, I mean."

Frolan cocks his head slightly as he attempts to comprehend the question. "Well, I suppose it happened ... um ... specifically ... when he hit the ground. His weight and the distance of the drop must have applied too much pressure on his leg, and the bone gave out."

Grak nods in deep thought. "Hmm, yes, I see. And where, specifically, did this occur?"

Frolan is prepared for that one. "Well, if you'll refer to the map I passed out, you can see it was about a half-day's journey north. By the way, thanks to Opa for making these copies so quickly."

She nods and gives the council a timid smile, then resumes her work of recording the meeting.

Grak looks at the tablet on the floor to his right. He had been wondering what that was for. He picks it up and studies the surface. That brings him up to speed nicely.

He turns to Opa. "Fine work. As always."

She replies with another modest smile before once again returning to her duties.

Grak turns back to Frolan. "And have you spoken to Yado yet? About not wandering off on his own? Especially near dangerous drops?"

Frolan looks about awkwardly. "Well ... no ... Given that the rest of our team was nearby, I didn't feel he was wandering off on his own."

Clearly, Grak is still missing something. "And what was the rest of your team doing at the time of his fall? Uh, specifically, of course." He almost forgot that last bit.

Frolan cocks his head once more. "Specifically ... we were walking in a line, spread out as you ordered, twenty paces apart."

That sounds familiar. Yes, Grak remembers ordering that better method of search. So they must have been looking for Jafra and Groka. *Now* he understands the whole situation.

Grak shakes his head knowingly, mercifully. "Sweet Frolan. You're missing my point, friend. While the spreading out was good, Yado should have been more focused. He shouldn't have been wandering off in his *mind* while on the search. Be sure to speak to him about that."

Frolan nods. "Yes sir."

With that confusion cleared up, Grak presses the main issue. "So, did you find them?"

"No sir. The search was unsuccessful once again." Frolan averts his gaze and sighs. "I apologize."

Grak suppresses a groan, though his expression shows clear annoyance with the team's failings. Fourteen search parties have gone out so far, and fourteen have come back empty-handed.

Of course, this nonsense wouldn't even be necessary if they had done their jobs initially. How the fools let Jafra escape right under their noses is beyond me.

Grak considers the brute and sighs. "I suppose I can find the mercy to spare you from punishments. And your team." He rolls his eyes. "*Again.* But my patience grows thin, Frolan. I want those two brought to justice."

Frolan nods, keeping his eyes on the ground. "Yes sir. I understand. I won't fail you again."

"You would not want that ... to hope ..." Grak trails off. Best to think that sentence through and try again later.

Truth be told, he's been finding it difficult to get upset over the matter. Obviously, Grak never wanted the women to escape, but at the same time, he sees clear value in their continued freedom. With Jafra replacing Lago as "Chief of All Enemies," the tribe's fear has only grown, which gives Grak the liberty to lead as he sees fit.

And then some. A good time to be me, that's for sure. And it doesn't hurt that I've managed to drop a bit of weight too. I think that's what really elevated me to the next level in their eyes. Not just a hunter or even a father anymore. A protector. A guardian. A savior, really.

Grak notices the numerous stares and realizes he's taking too long with his reminiscing. "So, what other business do we have?"

Brak stands and clears his throat. "As the tribe's newly appointed Master of Activities, I have a proposal. My idea is to have a regular event with music, dancing, art displa—"

Grak waves a hand and rolls his eyes. "Yes, yes. We get it. Have your festivities, Brak." He adds even more impatience to his tone. "Does anyone else have points to discuss?"

"Yes, I do," says Kando with clear excitement in his tone. He stands and passes out a stack of clay tablets. "I have the details of yesterday's theories meeting here. As usual, I've ordered the ideas by importance."

His enthusiasm rises as he reviews the list in his hands. "Now, this first one is a fascinating concept presented by Escha. She observed that leaves tend to face the sun, leading her to believe this is how they get nourishment. Remarkable notion, isn't it? So she's looking into ways we might gather that nourishment for our own use. Incredible potential there."

Kando looks around the tent for a positive response that never comes. He clears his throat and returns to his tablet. "Moving along, the next theory is an intriguing one from Hambo. He noticed that some of us have darker skin than others. This led him to theorize a connection between skin color and intelligence ..."

Grak is growing far too bored already. Normally, he can feign interest through five or six theories, but that doesn't seem likely today.

Must be the lack of sleep. Too many late nights with Cordo. Might be good to cut back. Limit interrogations to daylight. At least until I catch up on rest.

Of course, these theories are also growing duller. Yes, I imagine it's a combination. Proper sleep is required when attempting to sit through such taxing and monotonous discussions.

Still, no matter how difficult the task is, Grak has no choice but to push through it. He can't risk offending Kando right now. In all the recent chaos, the man seems to have regained much of Doran's old following.

Now there's a face I haven't seen in a while. I wonder what Doran's up to these days. Though I suppose it really doesn't matter in the end. He chose his future when he stopped caring about our friendship.

Grak shakes off the concern and turns his mind toward more pleasant thoughts. He considers this the best way to pass the time during these theory discussions, as it makes him look interested. As usual, Patyr takes precedence.

Ahh. Such a pretty pon—

The sound of a throat being cleared jars Grak's thoughts. He notices everyone staring at him and deduces that Kando must have finished speaking. He can only hope the man didn't stop *too* long ago.

Grak straightens up in his chair. "So, anything else?"

The council glances about casually. Several give slight shakes of the head.

Grak smiles. "Excellent! Then we'll end there. Be sure to pick up your meeting summary from Opa this ev—"

"I have something," interrupts Ruch. "*We* do, actually." He and Zacha stand up.

Grak doesn't like the look of this. He proceeds with caution. "Well? Out with it, then."

Zacha opts to be their voice. "We request to see Cordo."

Grak is stunned. He didn't think they'd try that in public.

Gutsy. Yet insolent.

Especially since he only allowed them to stay on the council because they swore total allegiance going forward.

He recognizes the need for chastisement. "*This* again? What did I tell you last time?"

Ruch takes that one. "You said you'd consider it."

Hmm. So I did. Best to give a more nebulous answer for similar requests in the future.

"And I have." Grak pauses to give his words greater weight. "No, you may not see Cordo. I can't trust the man. Not with him being so central in Jafra's schemes.

"And to be honest, I'm not sure I can trust the two of you, considering the unreasonable amount you've been pushing to see him. That strikes me as suspicious. Why so anxious? Do you need more orders from your master?"

Grak looks around for acknowledgement. Frolan and Kando got the humor at least. Though in all honesty, he wasn't entirely joking.

Given Cordo's attempts to protect Lago, I'm sure he was involved somehow in Jafra's treachery. And I can't risk that sort of behavior trickling down to anyone else.

Zacha replies nervously, "No. Not at all. We only seek to ensure his safety. And his health. You and Frolan are the only ones who have seen

Cordo for some time, and the tribe grows worried. That's all. He still has many friends who seek assurance of his well-being."

That sounded like a threat. But Grak isn't sure. He ponders the probability.

Doubtful. No one's likely to oppose me now. It would be folly with all the support I have in camp. And on the council.

That's actually a reasonable assessment on Grak's part. With Frolan and Brak replacing Groka and Cordo on the council, disagreement is at an all-time low.

I suppose it's really not much of a risk to just let Ruch and Zacha see the man. Might even scare some sense into them. Stamp out any further ideas of insurrection. At the least, watching the pair squirm would be a sight.

Then it's decided. Grak puts on his best, coldest, most powerful stare. "Very well. You may see Cordo."

Ruch and Zacha storm out of the holding tent with Grak following close behind. Squinting in the waning sun, he waits for his eyes to adjust, then takes in the sight before him. The two council members look quite comical in their current state, breathing deeply and trying to hold down the day's food. Grak gestures to Frolan and the four other guards, though only one chuckles in response.

Satisfied, Grak turns to his guests and nods knowingly. "Yes, it was like that for me too. The first few times after the smell set in. But don't worry. You get used to it. Isn't that right, Frolan?"

The brute nods, but says nothing. Aside from his reports, Frolan has been unusually silent of late. In fact, he's been that way since the Glorious and Beautiful Day of Grak's Decisive Defeat of the Hated and Villainous Lago.

Hmm, maybe I should speak to him. It was probably difficult for the young fellow. To watch that, and all. Poor thing. Probably just needs a shoulder to lean on.

Ruch finally masters his stomach. "That …" He points to the tent while calming a resurgent wave of nausea. "That is no way to treat a member of our tribe! That is … appalling! It's no way to treat *anyone*! Or *anything* for that matter!"

Grak is stunned by the man's comment. "Well if I had known you'd react *that* way …" He makes an obvious show of disapproval. "You know, I'm beginning to regret my kindness in keeping you on the council. And in letting you see Cordo. If this is the thanks I get. In fact, I might even regret not having you apprehended along with your leader!"

Zacha holds her hands up defensively. "Wait a moment now. Ruch's just worried. That's all. I think it was the sight of so much rope. It must have shocked him."

Ruch nods nervously. "Yes. And the leeches. I apologize."

Grak considers their explanation for a moment. He rolls his eyes and smiles. "Oh, well why didn't you say so? The rope was left over from hunting. Decided I might as well use it. No sense in wasting good materials, is there? And the leeches, well, I was trying out one of Hambo's theories." He shrugs. "Mixed results so far."

Zacha ventures another question. "And the … liberal … use of Cordo's waste?"

Grak is a little offended now. "Well you try interrogating someone as stubborn as that guy! He won't give me *anything* on Jafra. I have to try what I can."

Zacha's tone takes on a pleading quality. "That's because he doesn't know anything. I can assure you."

Hmm. Almost too quick with that reply. Was this whole thing planned?

"It's true!" Cordo's raspy voice penetrates the tent. "I have no idea where she and Groka went. But I'm willing to help you track them if you free me."

Grak is getting frustrated now. "Quiet in there!" He turns to Ruch and Zacha. "Now look what you've done! You got him all worked up, and he broke his lip stitches. This conversation is over. Be thankful I'm not apprehending the two of you."

Zacha's stubbornness flares up again. "Bu—"

"No!" Grak didn't want to, but he was forced to use his angry voice.

"Fine," mumbles Zacha—an unexpected ability, given the size of her mouth.

The two give feeble attempts at courteous farewells, then turn and stroll away. Clearly they're whispering as they walk, but Grak can't hear the content. He shrugs it off.

No matter, they're powerless without Cordo. Still, it'd be nice if they tried a little harder to work with me. Some people are such sore losers. They just need to admit defeat graciously. If you've lost, you've lost. Why get all whiny about it? Or try to run away like Jafra and Groka? Just take your punishment like an adult. Like him.

Grak looks at Lago. Or what's left of him. He was forced to move the head out of his tent when it began to stink—which took far less time than he thought it would.

But what he first believed was a problem turned out to be something of a solution. He found a nice spot for the head here at the holding tent where it has proven far more useful. Not only does it ward off unwanted visitors, but being visible from the cook site makes it a poignant reminder of a traitor's fate.

If only I could add Cordo's head. Though, I'd have to remove that abominable growth first.

But to his dismay, it's just not an opportune time for that. The sudden appearance of a spike bearing the man's head might inspire a panic among his former faithful. Still, given a long enough wait, Grak is certain he can make it happen. He rolls his eyes.

Procedures.

Grak turns to Frolan. "So, what else is on the schedule for the day?"

The brute responds with distance. "I need to prepare for tomorrow's search. We'll be leaving at dawn. But your day is empty."

Grak checks his shadow. "Well, I suppose I have time for another interrogation session. Care to watch?"

Frolan shakes his head. "No, thank you. If you don't need me, it'd be best if I start tomorrow's preparations right away and get to sleep early."

Grak shrugs. "Well, more for me then." He smiles to demonstrate a clear joke.

Regardless, the humor is lost on Frolan. The man nods his farewell, then pivots about and walks away in silence. While disappointed, Grak opts to shrug it off.

He's just feeling pressured, that's all. As soon as he finds the fugitives, he can take some time off. That should help. And before long, we'll be good friends once again.

With that weight lifted, Grak turns toward the tent and offers a quick nod of formality to the guards before slipping inside. As usual his eyes immediately begin their adjustment.

"So, Cordo. Will you give me the answers I need?" He waits for a moment as his vision fades from black to gray. "Come on. No sense holding anything back. Sooner or later, we'll find those two. And we'll get a confession out of them. Probably not Jafra, but Groka should be simple enough. So why not help us now and receive some leniency?"

Grak's eyes finish adjusting, and the sight forces a shiver up his spine. But only a slight one. While he's familiar with the view, there's always some new sore or other revulsion that catches him off guard.

He gathers himself quickly. "Well? Not saying anything again? That's not the wisest course of action. But fine, have it your way."

Grak picks up the skin rake: a new invention he had Aza put together. He's quite proud of the idea.

Grak sits up. The moments he's been able to set aside for sleep have been uneasy of late, and this afternoon is proving no exception. He thought it'd be wise to rest up after the interrogation, but that may have been unrealistic. No matter how hard he tries, he can't get comfortable enough to force sleep.

Grak sighs, straightening his tunic as he stands.

Well, best get an early start on my evening duties, I suppose. Speaking of which, where is Brak when I need him? I'm sure he's already late for my foot rub. The fool. Always running off at the most inopportune moments. And for what? Who can know with that dolt?

Grak steps outside in a perturbed state. He takes a moment to stretch while looking about, pondering where the man might be. But his gaze lingers too long while searching faces across the path, and one woman takes that as an invitation to wave. It's Itha, from the hunting team. He pretends not to notice her. It doesn't work.

She walks over. "Oh hello, Grak! I was just on my way to the cook site. Funny bumping into you like this along the way. What are you up to?"

Grak is surprised by the woman's sudden kindness. He promoted her to lead the hunters after Cordo's capture, hoping it would instill loyalty, but he had no idea his plan was doing so well.

Is she finally warming up to me? I suppose so. Well, it certainly took her long enough.

Grak remembers to answer. "Yes, well it's none of your concern what I'm doing. I don't need to explain myself to you!" In retrospect, he realizes a softer approach might have gone over better.

And yet, the woman's still here. Though she's not speaking. How bizarre. And awkward.

Itha finally breaks the silence. "So, how about those theories yesterday? Did you catch them?"

Grak has no patience for this. "Nope. I'm not sitting through another conversation about those theories. I've already had to do it once today, and I'm far too busy to repeat such a pointless endeavor." He identifies another missed opportunity.

Itha looks troubled. "Ah, yes, sorry. I didn't mean to annoy. Just found them interesting is all."

Grak feels he can still salvage this. "Yes, well I'll let it slide this time. Just don't let it happen again." A decent reversal.

Though perhaps I should have added a touch of charm. Hmm, yes. That would definitely help. Remember for next time, Grak. Remem—

He's torn out of his memory trick by incomprehensible shouting coming from somewhere nearby.

Grak looks about furiously. "Don't these fools remember *any* of my policies?" he asks no one in particular while still expecting an answer.

One of his guards, Mazo, ventures a theory. "It sounds like security is raising an alarm."

Grak freezes and cranes to listen. That *might* be true, but he can't quite tell. The system he put in place seemed simple at first, but proves more confusing by the day. It consists of each guard shouting the alarm they're trying to raise, while all guards in earshot pass the message along. But despite its beauty, Grak is now realizing the idea might be flawed.

Yes, definitely need to develop something clearer. And less chaotic too.

Mazo's hearing must be sharper, as he suddenly catches the message and turns in shock. "Cordo has escaped!" He bellows it now. "Cordo has escaped! Cordo has escaped!"

Grak covers his ears.

Hmm, and less abrasive on the ears too.

He signals for the man to stop shouting. "I don't remember scheduling any drills for today. Where's Frolan? If he did this without my knowl—"

He's interrupted by the sight of Frolan running up with six of his team. All have weapons drawn and are wearing dire expressions. It dawns on Grak that this might not be an exercise.

"Frolan! Is it true?" he yells with a mixture of rage and confusion. "How, in all the land, did he escape?" Grak adds some scolding to his tone. "Did you leave four guards at all times like I told you?"

Frolan signals for his team to halt. "Yes sir, I did. It appears they cut through the rear of the tent. I've sent security to the camp perimeter as per the protocol, and I'm heading off now to begin the systematic search. I would suggest you remain inside, sir. Just until everything's clear."

Grak weighs his safety against the possibility of more prestige from a second high profile capture. He shakes his head. "No, I'm coming with you."

Frolan shrugs and nods. "Ver—"

Yelling from the north interrupts them. The shouts are closer this time, and Grak easily catches the words.

Cordo's been captured. Impressive speed. Well done!

He runs north at a brisk pace with Frolan close behind. Grak finds himself glad once more to have lost some weight since the whole Lago ordeal. It certainly makes running easier. And faster.

They promptly arrive at the northern tent line, and Grak pauses for a moment of composure. He takes a few calming breaths and straightens his tunic. Then, with head held high, he dons his most dignified demeanor and approaches, taking in his surroundings as he walks.

Seven guards stand watch over three kneeling figures, each wearing a cloak with the hood pulled back. Of the three, Cordo is the only one Grak can identify from this distance.

That mole would be hard to miss at twice this span. And I suppose the bleeding wounds also make him easy to spot. But mostly the mole.

The other two require a moment longer to place, but as Grak draws near, he recognizes them. Nila and Quolo. From the hunting team.

It appears they're not all as loyal as Itha. Remember to speak with her about keeping her people in line, Grak. Remember to speak with her. Remember to speak with her.

Grak reaches the captives and pauses. He surveys the surrounding tribe. Many have already gathered to watch, and more are still pouring in. Some faces wear concern. Others show fear. But all are apprehensive.

Careful then, Grak. This could be a delicate matter. How you handle things will determine whether the issue results in stability or chaos.

Grak nods in agreement with the thought. Then he punches Cordo. Most of the crowd cheers, but some are clearly upset by this.

Well, that shows where my children stand on the issue.

Grak raises his voice loud enough for all to hear. "To those of you feeling sympathy for this traitor, let me remind you of what he's done. When I finally captured Lago, Cordo wanted to release him. When I gave Lago his long-awaited justice, Cordo tried to stop me. When I tried to capture Jafra for aiding Lago, Cordo helped her escape. And when I asked him why he did it, do you know what he said? He said he wanted to see the tribe suffer!"

The crowd gasps. Many conversations flare up, but sentiment is clearly in Grak's favor.

Cordo shakes his head with all the vigor he can muster. "No, please. I didn't," is all he can manage in a weak voice that only carries several feet.

Grak strikes the man again. "Keep silent or you'll make matters worse for yourself!"

He returns his focus to the crowd. "And what did I do? I showed him mercy. I decided not to execute him. Out of the kindness of my heart. And how does he repay me? He tries to escape and attack our people!"

Grak pauses, letting the tribe's anger grow into a frenzy before continuing. "So I ask you, what mercy remains for such an incorrigible traitor?"

Numerous derogatory shouts aimed at Cordo make their way through the roar. The tribe is barely contained now. In fact, Grak is fairly certain they'd rip the man apart if allowed. He considers that.

An interesting thought. But no. This honor is mine. And mine alone. I've worked too hard to share it now.

The captives increase the fervency of their pleas but are still drowned out. Grak smiles and holds out a hand toward Frolan. The brute passes his knife without hesitation, eliciting a new outburst of cheers from the crowd.

Nila and Quolo continue to solicit mercy, but Cordo goes silent. His disposition stiffens into simple resolve. Of the three, he alone was there to witness Lago's execution. He alone understands the brutality of his fate. He alone accepts it. And Grak finds that an intriguing point of view.

He knows exactly what's coming. Does that bring relief? Or does that make it worse? Well, no matter. Just be glad not to find out first hand, Grak.

He shakes off those thoughts and focuses instead on the leather hilt in his palm. It feels curiously right. Grak turns the knife over, basking in the sensation of this power. He smiles.

At last. Time to finish this.

He extends his arm, pressing the blade to Cordo's neck. The man's eyes take on a measure of fear, but they refuse to close. The crowd quiets in anticipation. Grak takes a deep breath, his smile widening. He's calm. Controlled. Fully aware of every sensation in the moment. He flexes his arm and dr—

"Stop!" screams Zacha, her voice frenzied, yet bold.

Grak stays his hand, alarmed by this new defiance. He looks around and quickly finds the woman. She's nine paces to the right, advancing slowly, with an arrow trained at his chest. By her side walks Ruch, ax in hand.

Without hesitation, Frolan steps forward, eyes fixed on the traitors. There's clear disappointment in his face, but also determination. He takes position in front of Grak and draws his ax, prepared to meet the pair head on.

Itha's voice cuts through the air. "We won't allow you to kill Cordo!" She steps out of the nearby crowd and aims her bow. "Your accusations are false. He bears no guilt."

The remaining hunters emerge as well, drawing weapons and advancing slowly. All eyes watch with rapt attention.

Grak recognizes the need to regain control. Immediately. The tribe's support pales in comparison to the threat posed to his life right now. Unfortunately, solutions are sparse at the moment.

Cordo's people halt at a distance of three paces, and Ruch takes a single step forward. "Back away!" he shouts.

Frolan refuses to budge. His team, on the other hand—outnumbered and terrified—quickly falls back to the crowd.

Grak glowers as they pass by. "Cowards!" he hisses.

Cordo stands up. His eyes reveal a curious fury mingling with the fading fear.

More of the tribe steps forward to join his group with crude weapons at the ready. In all, Grak counts twenty-eight gathered against him.

Insolent, rebellious traitors! I'm surrounded by them! Is Frolan up to the challenge? Can I risk it? Seven have already shown themselves craven. But I have thirty-two more, and they've been training for a good fight. And yet ... who else might suddenly feel inspiration to come to the rebels' aid? We might be overwhelmed ...

Cordo also appears to be reviewing his options. He takes a cautious step back and motions for his team to do the same. They move slowly, heading north toward the nearest unguarded edge of camp, weapons still at the ready.

Grak begins to panic. He searches his mind in desperation, pleading for some sort of plan. But nothing comes.

Think, Grak. Think!

Once clear of the gathering, the rebels quicken their pace and reach the tree line a moment later. Even Cordo is making good time, revealing only a slight limp in his step.

Surprising. And disappointing, if I'm being honest. Thought I had a more lasting effect on him. Guess not.

Wasn't cruel enough. That's where I went wrong. Never should have relented during interrogation. No, even earlier. Never should have been swayed by my children's opinions. Never should have let the man live in the first place.

The rebels are too far out in the woods now—hunters in their element. Giving chase would be difficult. The fight would be fierce. Grak's victory would be doubtful. He squeezes the knife's hilt with all his rage. It provides no relief.

Cruelty, Grak. That's the only way to deal with dissension. Hardness and cruelty. Remember that, Grak. Remember that.

One by one, the rebels pass through dense vegetation, concealing all but a trace of their continued movement. Soon, they're all gone from view. Except Cordo. He's simply standing there, eyes locked on Grak, saying nothing.

Finally, after a long, tense moment, the man takes a deep breath and calls out. Somehow, he manages to draw on a hidden reserve of strength to project his weakened voice with surprising clarity. Even his tone carries without ambiguity. It's full of acrimony, yet eerily calm.

Grak's ears ring with the man's chilling words. "This isn't over, Grak!"

15 - And Rebels

Grak despises rebels. Especially the cowardly kind. Sure, he was furious at Cordo's defiance eleven days ago, but at least the man was open about it. In contrast, the six that later sneaked off to join his rebellion have incurred Grak's wrath beyond words.

Those scum. Those craven, ungrateful piles of manure!

Grak grimaces with rage. This tends to happen when he thinks about the traitors. He closes his eyes and takes a soothing breath.

Calm, Grak. Calm. You're here to find relief. You'll be swimming soon, and that should ease some of the tensi—

He remembers a moment too late that blindly traversing stony ground isn't recommended. He trips, but manages to plant his staff on firm ground, avoiding an embarrassing fall. He straightens his posture and looks around to make sure no one saw the stumble. Other than Mazo, everyone is occupied with safely making their own way over the rocks. Grak gives his staff an appreciative look.

Ah, thank you, my friend. Where would I be without you?

He runs a hand down the shaft, admiring the oaken pattern. As always, its beauty steals his breath for a moment. He's impressed with how well Yado followed instructions. Even down to the intricate etchings of Grak's accomplishments.

Though why he resisted my directions about the ornament is beyond me. Can't believe he was so squeamish about the matter. Practically refused to put the thing on.

That's true for the most part. Yado did express discomfort when Grak asked him to adorn the top of the staff with Lago's head. But, in the end, the threat of brutal punishment was the only convincing the man needed.

And Grak believes the extra bit of effort was well worth it, as the ornament is easily his favorite feature. Even more so, now that the smell is almost gone.

You never fail to impress, dear Lago. It seems like each day I discover some new talent of yours. Unlike this feeble bunch.

Grak gestures to the sparse group surrounding him. Despite his rousing speech back at the trail, very few opted to accompany him down here. Only fourteen, to be exact. He wonders if he should have used fewer insults.

Or perhaps more? Hmm, well, hindsight. No matter. More room for me to relax.

After several more moments of careful navigation, Grak reaches his spot just below Brownhand. Mazo follows close behind and takes up his position three paces away.

Grak eyes the distance. "Maybe another two paces."

The guard obeys and takes up his new position. Satisfied, Grak drops his drying cloth and surveys the river as it laps seductively at the rocks below.

The water's clearer than I remember. And it even looks more refreshing. Wouldn't you say so?

Grak looks to Lago and lets out a soft chuckle.

Hmm, I suppose so. You're a witty one, my friend.

He leans the staff against Brownhand and begins to remove his tunic. But something gives him pause. Brak is standing just beyond Mazo, gazing intently at Grak's feet. Or the general area thereof.

Finding this behavior highly suspect, Grak attempts a whisper. "Mazo, watch this one in particular. There's a shifty air about him." He's definitely improving in both quietness and subtlety.

Mazo looks over his shoulder and nods in reply. Turning back, he gives Brak a nudge—a gentle one, by Grak's estimation, though he doesn't like to make a fuss over such trifles. And yet, in this situation it may have been *too* gentle, as Brak hardly seems to have noticed. He just keeps staring, lost in thought.

Grak is feeling self-conscious now. And a little annoyed. "Look, Brak, I already told you. This is my drying cloth. I don't know what happened to your tunic." He feels the truth is best left unspoken in this situation.

Brak wakes from thought at the sound of his name. "What? Oh. No, that's ... not ... just ... Well, look at the rock, Grak. Wasn't the water up to the mouth last time we were here? It looked like the rock was drinking from the river. So much so, we named it Redmouth."

Grak rolls his eyes and mutters, "I would never come up with such a poor name."

Brak either fails to hear that or ignores it. "The water level is lower now. By a whole foot it seems. And then some."

"That's strange," interjects Hambo. "Are you sure?"

Brak nods. "Oh yes. Positive. Isn't that so, Grak?"

This isn't the way Grak wants to spend his time at the river. He rolls his eyes and adds a layer of annoyance to his tone. "Sure, Brak. You're right ..." He lowers his voice. "I suppose."

But that didn't work. They only seem more interested. Worse still, several others are now flocking to the conversation.

Brak scratches his head. "What do you suppose might cause it to drain?"

Everyone falls silent, pondering his question.

Hambo turns to a nearby woman. "Escha, come here. Look at this."

She walks over, followed by even more onlookers. While their distance is sufficient, the sheer number of gawkers is making Grak uncomfortable. He'd like to ignore them, but feels odd undressing with so many watching.

"I believe it might be disappearing," says Hambo with a clear sense of pride in his theory.

Brak's face turns to worry. "You mean, we're running out of water?"

A torrent of questions follows with no apparent recipient and no immediate answers. In Grak's experience, that usually signals the beginning of a theory session.

Best to end this before it gets too boring.

He looks about for Frolan and quickly spots him another thirty paces off. The brute is pointing to the northern sky, discussing something with a handful of guards. Grak tries to follow the man's finger, but only sees several birds.

The buffoons get excited over the strangest things. Act like they've never seen birds before. And nondescript ones at that.

"Frolan!" shouts Grak, unintentionally silencing the nearby gawkers.

The brute returns a nod, then dispenses several quick orders before trotting over. He arrives promptly and pushes his way through the gathered theorists until he reaches Grak's side.

Frolan leans in and whispers, "Sir, we have a situation. We're still not sure whether it poses a threat, but there's smoke rising just ahead." He crouches to Grak's height and points. "See it there?"

Grak admires the man's sharp vision. The wisp is barely visible: a thin curl of light gray against a stark and cloudless azure. By his estimation, it's rising just beyond the hill there, where the river bends around to the west before turning east again. In fact, it almost appears as though *several* tendrils are ascending.

Very curious. And ominous, if I don't mind my saying.

Grak nods. "Ah, yes. I see it. Well, our course of action seems clear enough. Let's go see what's burning."

Frolan looks alarmed. "Sir? I ... I don't believe it's wise for you to join us. We'll only have a small scouting team. No more than five, for the sake of speed. Should Cordo choose to strike, you'd be safer here. Or back up at the trail with the bulk of our forces."

Grak rolls his eyes. He's getting tired of Frolan's timidity. Cordo's escape changed the brute, causing greater withdrawal and apprehension in him. And the man's anxiety has only increased since then—to the point where it's been bleeding into his judgment. He even insisted they postpone this move, reasoning that Cordo's roaming band posed a greater threat on the trail.

Grak shakes his staff at the brute, who cringes away from its falling debris. "Who's the leader, dear Frolan? I am. And I need to know what's taking place. And I can't be hindered by your fear."

He switches to a soothing tone. "Yet at the same time, I understand your concern for safety. I share it, in fact. But the solution is simple. Leave the five here and bring the other twenty-five with us. I see no reason why more people would slow us down. You'll see, friend. I'll be alright. Not a thing to worry about."

Frolan nods reluctantly. "Yes sir."

The brute turns and makes his way back to the other guards. Despite his reservations, he's swift in dispensing the necessary orders.

There's a good man. Can't get too upset at him. Always obeys in the end. And his concerns are valid enough. Can't blame him for voicing them. They're just ultimately unnecessary is all.

Unnecessary, as Grak reasons, because he has the clear advantage in strength. His first order of business after Cordo's escape was to increase the number of guards. Considering it wisest to err on the side of caution, he settled on seventy-two. Of course, he would have preferred more, but was limited by able-bodied tribe members who had seen at least fifteen snows. And even of those, too many were pulled away for hunting and other vital duties.

In the end, numbers will decide our survival. And not just a single swelling of our ranks. Constant increase. Beyond what the tribe is currently capable of. But how? Require a minimum number of offspring from each person? Maybe. Not an immediate solution, though.

He presses his mind further. Still nothing. He looks to Lago.

What are your thoughts on the matter?

Grak is shocked. He didn't expect to hear a response like *that*.

What? You're not even trying anymore, are you? I'm fairly sure that was your worst idea yet! How would it even work?

He listens respectfully.

Hmm, I suppose that's true enough. It's certainly a daring plan. Heh, you always were a bold one, my friend. Well, let's discuss this later. It looks like they're waiting for me.

Grak takes a final, longing glance at the water. It's still begging, waiting for him.

Soon, my sweet. Soon.

He turns to the gawking crowd and puts on his commanding voice.

"This is *my* spot!" Several heads look up at him. "When I return, I expect this whole area to still be available."

All are motionless and returning blank stares now. Several nods of fear and uncertainty reveal at least a mild understanding.

Still, Grak has to be sure. "This whole red rock here. No one else is allowed on it. Mazo, you're in charge while Frolan's gone with me. I expect you to enforce this rule while we're away."

The man nods. A bit too eagerly. Grak wonders if he can truly trust him with such an important task. He looks to Lago for counsel.

Hmm, I suppose you're right, friend. Though I wouldn't say I completely trust him with my life either. But point taken.

Grak returns the man's nod. Still, just to be on the safe side, he opts to stress the point once more. "Remember, Mazo … my rock."

Grak creeps along the ground. While his girth is no longer an impediment, the movement is still awkward. This strikes him as odd, considering that no one else appears to be having difficulty. He pauses to search for the source of his troubles.

The new knife seems a logical culprit, considering that Grak had it made at three times the normal length. Though if that *is* the cause, he'll gladly deal with the discomfort. He's quite proud of the idea, after all, and considers the thing a vital advantage in hand-to-hand combat. "My slicer," he calls it in front of others, or simply "Slicer" when it's just the two of them and Lago.

Hmm, on second thought, I don't see how that could be the problem. It's hardly in my way.

Grak's reasoning is sound. The blade is dangling unobtrusively at his side in a special belt and sheath he ordered crafted. He categorizes it as "unlikely" and ponders his other items.

Of course! Must be the staff. Difficult to carry while crawling. I suppose Frolan was right about that.

Well, no matter. He still deserved the scolding. I can handle him being withdrawn, but when he starts to think he knows better than me … well, that's getting serious.

Though I can't imagine he'd take it any further. He would never betray me. He's always been loyal. Not the same cut as Jafra and Cordo and their lot. Just needs to relax.

Grak ponders the man for another moment while fixing Lago's disheveled hair.

Still ... best to keep an eye on him. Isn't that right, my old friend? For his own good as well as mine.

Grak resumes his crawl and soon joins the others at the crest of the hill. Through keen observation, he notices they've removed their caps, so he does the same. With great care, he wriggles closer and peers over the ridge. Several intricate details immediately grab his attention.

A second river? Flowing into this one? Best not to tell Brak about that. He'd probably find some way to gloat.

"What do you make of it?" asks Frolan.

Grak shrugs. "Well, I suppose there *is* a second river after all. Best to keep that to ourselves, though. Lest the tribe get any strange ideas."

Frolan nods. "Yes sir. I'll swear the guards to secrecy." He pauses awkwardly. "But what do you make of the people there? Do you think they're Cordo's rebels?" he asks with a twinge of anger.

Grak considers the man's question while studying the view below. As the river wraps around this side of the hill, it splits wide and becomes two separate branches. The one they've always known bends north and east before disappearing around the trees, while the other runs far off to the west.

Between the two arms lies a large stretch of vivid, green land broken by numerous rows of dirt in large, square patches. Scattered around these patches are wooden tents, each rising straight up on all sides with a slant at the top. And the people walking about in all of this are doing so without any identifiable purpose.

Grak shrugs. "They're too far away. I can't make out any faces." He considers them further. "But it seems they've been there for some time. Too long to be Cordo's people." Still more consideration. "Nonetheless, we should probably deal with them before they become a threat."

"That's a good idea, sir," responds Frolan with obvious caution in his voice. "Though I wonder … Well, they're far. Far from us here and far from the river trail. With Cordo's rebels still on the loose, I wonder if we should keep our distance from these ones for now. Just so we don't take on too many enemies at once."

While Grak is miffed at the disagreement, he does detect sound reasoning in the idea. "Yes, that's where I was going. Next time let me finish. So, as I was saying, no sense making a second enemy before we've dealt with the first. We'll leave them alone for the time being. But once we deal with Cordo, we'll need to develop a strategy for these strangers."

Everyone nods in agreement. Grak appreciates the clarity of their response.

It's good to deal with a group that knows how to nod. So many these days are halfhearted at best.

The group slowly backs away from the ridge, standing and quickening their pace when able, and donning caps soon after. Upon reaching the base, Frolan sets the team in a protective formation with Grak at the center. After a quick inspection to confirm that all eyes and weapons are at the ready, he leads them in a brisk walk for the return trek.

Grak squints at the small shape of Brownhand on the horizon, estimating the distance.

Two … maybe three thousand paces.

He makes the necessary adjustments to account for his usual errors.

So, maybe around three hundred paces. Not bad. Should be swimming soon. Sooner if we had horses.

But alas, their poor balance and lack of grip wouldn't fare well on the steep, rocky descent from the trees to the river. In fact, it's already difficult enough for *humans* to navigate, even with boots. Grak once again finds himself wishing it were socially acceptable for horses to don footwear.

I imagine a pony could pull it off. Not as self-conscio—

His thoughts are interrupted by a steadily rising noise coming from somewhere off in the distance behind them. What began several moments ago as a low, indistinct rumbling, now bears an eerie resemblance to the sound of running feet.

A thousand fearful thoughts race through Grak's head as he turns to identify the source. His eyes widen and his stomach sinks. They must have come from the tree line. And they're closing in fast. Grak can't make out any faces, but he has little doubt.

"Cordo!" shouts Frolan, rage burning in his eyes.

Of course the wretch would strike now. While our forces are split. He must have been waiting for this. Probably orchestrated the whole thing with those strangers and their scum-filled smoke!

"Frolan!" Grak's shout is unnecessary, given the man's proximity, but urgency takes precedence. "Launch the defense protocol!"

Frolan removes the horn from his belt and gives it a single, powerful blow. The sound carries over the open terrain, likely to meet little resistance before reaching the guards on the trail.

A much better alarm, to be sure. With any fortune, the rest of our forces should reach us soon. Then it'll be a fair fight in our favor. Turn Cordo's strategy back on his own head. If …

Grak finishes the thought out loud. "If we can make it to Brownhand in time. Run!"

Outnumbered at the moment, reaching the river is their only hope. With the addition of those five guards, their forces would nearly match Cordo's. But more importantly, help from the trail would arrive that much sooner.

They start into a paced run, but Frolan quickly recognizes Grak's inability to keep up. He orders a reduction of speed, which causes several looks of frustration. Those are soon dropped, however, when Grak returns a fierce scowl.

Of all the terrible things one can do. Frustrated with their leader for having to protect him? After all the protection I've given them? Remember to punish them, Grak. Remember to punish them. Remember to punish them.

They reach the water's edge, and Grak pauses to gather his wits, hoping to find some semblance of a plan there. But his mind refuses to cooperate, focusing instead on the looming threat.

Fortunately, Frolan remains calm. "Sir. They're coming in too fast. They'll catch us before we reach the trail. And it would be perilous to have our backs turned when they arrive. We need to face them. Make a solid defense. It's our only chance."

Grak considers this proposal. A sound idea in most respects.

If I lose these guards, I'm too weak. My remaining forces would barely outnumber Cordo's. Wouldn't be a fair fight then. And chances of holding off a second strike would be low. Especially if we lost Frolan. Morale would plummet if that happened.

Grak nods. "My idea exactly. You hold them off here. I'll fetch the remainder at the trail."

"No need, sir." Frolan pulls the horn to his lips and lets out another long, deep call.

That wasn't the answer Grak wanted. He ponders the situation.

I have thirty here. Four fewer than Cordo. Could be worse. I should be safe enough. And I suppose it's better to be seen fighting than running. Just stay in the rear and you'll be alright, Grak.

Frolan's commands come quick and crisp. No time can be spared for bows to take aim, so he orders the guards into a tight line with axes at the ready.

Grak breathes deep in a vain attempt to force his heart to a steadier pace. His enemies close in. He can make out their faces now, full of wrath and vengeance. Closer. He measures their steps in heartbeats. Closer. He locks eyes with Cordo, trying desperately to will some courage into his glare.

The two forces collide, with Grak's side taking the brunt of the impact. Fortunately, only one of his guards loses his footing. Grak watches in desperation as the man is quickly overpowered.

Down by five now. Curse Cordo and his treachery! Curse Jafra and Grok—

Someone crashes into him from the left, and they drop together in a tangle. Grak frantically reaches for Slicer, but recognizes Mazo and breathes a sigh of relief.

Too soon, as it turns out. Itha takes the advantage, lowering her ax hard and fast toward the man's chest. Mazo sweeps his own weapon with blurring speed, knocking hers aside. She struggles to maintain balance while he scrambles to his feet. Too slow. She's already regained her footing.

The sound is terrible. Worse still is the sight. Mazo's face contorts in an instant of overwhelming pain and uncontrollable fear. He crumples to the ground with the woman's ax buried deep in his skull.

Itha draws her knife and turns to Grak with a cold, yet remorseful, look. She advances with caution, though the effect is more menacing than anything else.

Grak crawls on his back, even dropping the staff for convenience, but soon realizes it isn't fast enough to hope for escape. Remembering Slicer, he unsheathes it in awkward desperation. With less than a breath before she'll be on him, he searches feverishly for the best angle of attack from this position. Too slow.

Itha's head snaps back as an arrow pierces her right eye. She drops the knife and crumples to the ground. Grak scrambles to get clear, but the woman falls on his leg, pinning it. He pulls free without much effort and climbs to his feet, looking around for immediate danger. None. His people have the enemy occupied, even doubling up in some cases.

But none are using bows. Curious.

Another arrow flies by, causing Grak to turn about in response. His heart leaps. Their forces from the trail have arrived: three are firing from the slope while the rest are heading down to join the fray.

The remainder of the tribe seems to be here as well. Though it's unclear whether they came to lend support or simply to watch the spectacle for amusement.

Either way, better look good now, Grak. For your children.

He pulls Slicer back with a flourish and drives it into Itha's body. Grak follows this with two more superfluous stabs, then finishes with an exaggerated brow wipe to show fatigue. Pretending to just notice the crowd, he raises his blade in the air, eliciting a loud cheer. But this turns into a gasp an instant later, which is his only warning.

Grak spins around just in time to duck under Cordo's swing. He backs away with haste, alarmed and upset that his protectors would allow the man through.

Cordo closes the small space, eyes ablaze with vengeance, deep and terrifying. He pulls his ax overhead, and as it drops, Grak reacts. Drawing from Mazo's successful move, he swings at the weapon. His motion isn't as swift as the guard's was, but it does the trick, knocking Cordo's ax to the side and pulling his momentum along with it.

But Grak hesitates a moment too long. Cordo recovers with alarming speed and turns, swinging his weapon side-armed. Grak ponders how to counter that one. But he's at a loss.

In a moment that seems unending, he waits … and watches. His death creeps closer. He can make out the nicks in Cordo's ax now. Closer. Darkness consumes Grak's world.

Grak wakes slowly. Frolan's face is hovering overhead, bleeding from several shallow cuts. The man gives a slight smile and extends a hand. Grak takes a shaky hold, and the brute hoists him to a sitting position.

"How are you, sir? Feeling alright?" Frolan sounds relieved.

Still too dazed to offer a response, Grak surveys the area instead. Though part of him soon wishes he hadn't. The ground wears deep crimson, twenty paces in all directions. Strewn about, in no particular order, are numerous still bodies with matching stains.

The tribe's remaining able-bodied members are occupied in bringing resolution to the day. Many are busy stacking wood for a pyre. The rest are occupied with gathering the fallen to lay at its feet.

But no matter their task, all are filled with a deep sadness that permeates everything in reach. A few who can no longer bear it have even resigned themselves to a quiet, yet agonized sobbing.

But that all pales in comparison to what snags Grak's attention. A lone figure is gagged and kneeling by the river several paces away, surrounded by nine guards.

Grak smiles. "Cordo. You saved him for me."

Frolan fails to partake of the joy. "Yes sir. When you fainted, I—"

"Fainted? I didn't faint!" Grak realizes his tone is harsher than it needs to be. "I ducked. And must have hit my head."

Frolan nods. "Yes sir. When you ducked and hit your head, one of our people put an arrow in his shoulder. That gave me time to disarm him. Since he was the last enemy, I thought it simple enough to detain him. In case you wanted to question him further. Or what have you."

Grak pats the brute on the shoulder. "Well done, Frolan." He uses it to pull himself up. "Well done."

One by one, the tribe members notice Grak and pause to watch his next move. Many continue to show deep sorrow, but most seem relieved that he's alright. Even the weeping has subsided.

Good to see I have that effect. Still need something big, though. To lift their spirits. To give them hope ... and something to be happy about. I'll need to make this good then. Better than last time.

Grak picks up Slicer and searches the area for Lago. There, by Itha's body. He strolls over and grabs the staff, taking a moment to fix Lago's hair and clean the man's cheek.

Oh, my apologies, friend. I thought that was dirt.

Grak puts the skin back in place and looks around. All eyes are on him now, many even filling with hope. Infused with confidence from this, he dons his most stately demeanor and walks over to Cordo.

Appearances and all. Very important for these public events.

Grak reaches the captive and raises his voice for the crowd. "No escape for you this time, rebel!"

Some of the sorrowful faces turn relieved. Some of the relieved ones shout their approval.

Grak takes this as an indication to add more extravagance to his words. "Cordo ... for your attacks against our people ... and for your hatred of our ways ... I hereby revoke my mercy!"

He waits out a new round of cheering. "Let it be known to you and to *all* traitors or rebels that anyone who defies me or threatens our peace will meet with defeat! They will *feel* my vengeance! And they will rue the day they set their faces against me!"

Now the whole crowd takes up the cheer. Many, in fact, even seem fanatical about it.

And I don't blame them. That was an incredible speech.

Grak scans the crowd for Opa's face. He finds the woman a moment later and gives her a nod. She returns the gesture, then pulls dry clay from her pouch and sets about mixing it.

Good woman.

He turns back to Cordo. "And so it is with *no* sadness in my heart that I end your pathetic, treacherous life this day!"

Grak pulls back, gathers his full weight, and thrusts Slicer straight into the man's chest. Not hard enough. It bounces off, eliciting a gagged scream from Cordo as his eyes open wide.

The tribe looks on with mixed emotions. None are sure how to respond, though all show obvious discomfort.

Grak looks at Slicer. Then at the wound. Aside from the fresh tear in the man's tunic, a trickle of blood is the only indication of damage.

Hmm, yes, the bone there. Should have thought of that one. Though I do seem to recall having a harder thrust than that. No matter. It shouldn't be too difficult.

Grak pulls back for another attempt, then pauses. "You know, this would be much easier if he were on the ground. Then I could better use my weight." He makes a downward thrusting motion to demonstrate.

Frolan looks around awkwardly, then leans in and whispers.

Grak shrugs. "Well, I suppose you're right. But it was so *messy* last time."

Frolan nods. "True. But *easier*."

Grak shrugs once more. "Very well. Though maybe I'll just pierce through the throat. Seems cleaner that way. Reduces the squirting and such."

He turns to Cordo. "Close your eyes. I won't have you staring at me as you die. Too creepy."

With nothing left in him, Cordo obeys. His eyelids fall in peace, accepting his defeat. And his fate. Grak feels a tug of admiration for the man, but quickly shakes it off.

No. He's a fool! A traitorous fool! And now he'll die like the fool he is!

Grak extends his hand, pressing Slicer's point to Cordo's throat. He pauses for a moment to focus on the sensation of bound leather in his palm. The hilt feels proper. It feels good. He clenches his arm, basking in the strength flowing through him. The control he possesses in the moment.

Grak yields to it. He leans in and drives the weapon hard, producing disquieting sounds of tearing and snapping as flesh gives way. Cordo's eyes open suddenly at the sting, his whole body straining in shock as the blade slowly drives deeper. Layers of bone and muscle resist, but Grak responds with greater force. Ignoring the familiar gurgling and wheezing, he adds more weight to the thrust until metal rips through the other side.

He releases Slicer and steps back, watching Cordo closely, entranced by the emotions. Far fewer than Lago showed. Fear, yes. Pain, of course. But mostly just peace. It fades much faster this time. And in an instant, his enemy is gone.

Grak closes his eyes and breathes deep, savoring the moment.

No more defiance. No more need to be on guard at all times. Except for Jafra, of course. Still need to be on guard until we find her. And the strangers over the hill. Can't rest until we take care of them.

The list of tasks requiring his attention floods back in. Grak sighs.

He opens his eyes and looks around, hoping to find appreciation from the surrounding tribe. But it never comes. Most are terrified. Many even appear nauseous. Worse still, numerous parents are trying in vain to soothe their crying offspring.

Grak shakes his head and sighs again.

Leading is agony. Always something else to deal with. Can't even enjoy my victory properly. Can't even find time for a quick swim.

He looks longingly at the water. At his rock. At the mouth drinking from the river.

Well, not quite drinking. Actually, not even close. The water's a good foot lower, in fact. No, surely it wasn't like that before. Was it?

That starts a thought—a curious tickle in the back of his mind that grows into a nagging feeling.

They were discussing that earlier. It was something important, I seem to recall. Do you remember what it was?

He looks to Lago.

Yes, you're right. It was Hambo. He was saying something abou—
Oh dear ...

The memory roars into focus along with all of its implications. Grak scans the crowd and finds the man a short distance away.

"Hambo!" he shouts in his most urgent voice.

The theorist turns and looks around in stunned confusion.

Grak ignores the man's erratic behavior. "What were you saying about the water disappearing?"

Grak regrets those words the instant they leave his mouth. He can almost see them now, rippling through the crowd, inciting a murmur as they pass. The murmurs, in turn, breed worry. Worry soon grows into terrified shouts. Deep panic sets in.

16 - And Water Shortages

Grak begrudges this water shortage. And all water shortages, if he's being honest. Although, for the sake of transparency, he's willing to admit that this is the first one he's ever experienced.

But despite the clarity of his emotions, he's having trouble identifying what he hates most about the ordeal. A definite contender would be that it's delaying their travel. And by no small amount, either. It's been fifteen days since the Heroic Battle against Cordo's Villainous and Idiotic Rebellion.

Apparently moving wasn't bad enough. We also had to get stuck in endless transit. And all because Hambo couldn't keep his mouth shut about the shortage.

That's true, more or less. Once the shortage was common knowledge, Hambo did make it worse by expounding on the theory. And his numbers sounded realistic enough to create an ambiguous sort of fear in people's minds. Even more so when he concluded that they only had five snows left before running out of fresh water. Apparently, he failed to anticipate how great a panic his findings would cause.

Unnecessary panic really. Idiots and their idiotic concerns. They don't even know what true worry is. A few night terrors? A handful of children with fear paralysis? That's nothing! They should try my problems for a while. Then let's see what they have to complain about.

Of course, Grak is only venting. He wouldn't actually want that, as the problems go hand in hand with the title. He sighs and shakes his head.

So much pain in leading. Why didn't anyone bother telling me? If I had known, I would have refused. Even when they begged me to be their master.

At least I have a few competent people by my side. Or rather, fools with a shred of ability who are willing to relieve some of my burdens.

He's mainly thinking of Escha here. She came along just in time with a theory that calmed a portion of the hysteria before it got too far out of hand. By her reasoning, since the river emptied into the ocean, they'd be better off staying as far away from the sea as possible. Thus, she suggested the water could be prolonged by two more snows if they didn't move any farther north. And since her numbers also seemed realistic, the idea was accepted.

Sound logic, I suppose. And yet, such an unfortunate side effect. But I can't blame her. It's Hambo's fault. Him and his incessantly wagging jaw. He's the real reason we're stuck here. Doomed to a chaotic, horrendous, excrement-filled, sorry excuse for a campsite.

Grak isn't even embellishing much in that description. Due to the cramped nature of the river trail, and in order to leave a path for basic movement, they were only able to fit one long row of tents. But it soon became evident that smells took a considerable amount of time to dissipate in such a narrow space. Especially toward the middle of the line.

And things only got worse when Grak's "tales of Jafra's depravity" began to spread through the tribe. Everyone became fearful of the woods after that, and started relieving themselves on the edge of camp instead. Thus, with the heats gaining strength, the aroma has grown pungent. Now it's almost impossible to avoid. Even here in his tent, removed one hundred paces from the rest of the tribe, Grak can still smell it.

Not that anyone cares. They're all too panicked to bother seeing what I want.

He sighs.

Nothing but panic and chaos these days. And even bloodshed, of all things!

That's not an exaggeration: a surprising number of fights have broken out over the shortage. But when the death count reached three on the first day, Grak realized he had to clamp down.

His solution was to ban all access to the river except at the official watering point. To enforce this restriction, he positioned nine guards along its banks. And much to his delight, only two more were killed before people stopped trying to sneak unauthorized drinks. However, much to his dismay, violence *within* the trail camp is still rampant.

What's gotten into these people? Used to be calm and peace-loving. So different now. I can't believe how far they've gone. Can you?

He looks to Lago, but receives no reply. His adviser has been silent of late. This also adds to Grak's irritation.

Oh, who needs you? I have other friends.

That's partially true. Olive Thirteen and Kando are both here. Of course, some might say they're simply early for the council meeting, but Grak knows better.

They're just eager to spend time with me. As it should be. If only more of my friends were this thirsty for my companionship.

He sighs, recalling the old days. The nightly impersonations. Doran and his crab. Frolan and his bear.

That one hurts most of all. The brute grows more distant on a daily basis. He still shows the utmost respect, but that's where it ends. He hardly even looks Grak in the eye anymore. And he certainly doesn't show interest in spending time together. Or talking about each other. Grak sighs once more, beginning to wonder why no one is asking if he's alright.

Friends are supposed to talk about each other. Maybe … maybe I just need to get things started.

He looks up eagerly, reaching for the first topic that comes to mind. "So … this is a nice staff, isn't it? Nicely decorated and all. Very little smell."

Olive Thirteen is her usual cheerful self. "That's true. Yado did a great job."

Hmm, but no mention of my creative eye. Not a good indication.

Grak has noticed that trend. Conversations often go the route of talking about others, even saying good things about those people. It's not such a concern *most* of the time, but it gets annoying when he wants to talk about himself.

Though maybe that's just how the simpler types communicate. They don't really know any better.

He gives it a try. "So, Olive Thirteen … I've noticed you have …" He should have thought this through before speaking. "You have long hair."

No matter. She's thoroughly pleased with the compliment. "Why, thank you, Grak. I'm quite happy with it myself."

Intrigued by his newfound power, Grak thinks of one for Kando. "And you have a strong nose, Kando. Like a hawk's beak."

The man nods. "Thank you."

Hmm, not as good a reception. Still, it's something at lea—

Grak's attention is snagged by the tent flap suddenly opening. His spirits lift at the sight of Frolan entering, but hope fades when the remaining council members follow the man in. Grak sighs.

Just punctual. Not here to see me.

He pushes the thought aside and attempts to prepare his mind for the meeting. These sessions have been causing Grak deep sorrow of late, and he's hoping to avoid it this time. *Why* they evoke that emotion, though, is beyond him.

Perhaps it's more of that loneliness. Like the council's just too small these days.

After losing Ruch and Zacha, Grak found no new replacements suited to their positions. Except Doran. But that was more for social reasons, as he hoped it might serve to repair their old friendship. So far, the effort has been unsuccessful. Grak allows himself one final sigh, then attempts a more positive demeanor.

He adds a jovial tone for good measure. "So, let's see if we can resolve this whole issue, shall we?"

Doran and Kando make a show of looking away from each other. The rest of the council watches in discomfort, obviously feeling awkward about having to witness the tiff.

Grak expected this, though, and he has a new approach ready for just such an occasion. "So, Kando. Why don't you tell Doran what you told me yesterday? It made a lot of sense."

Kando rolls his eyes. "I had a good reason for it," he mutters.

Grak puts on a commanding, but gentle voice. "Come on, Kando.

I know you can do better than that. Why don't you try sitting up and *looking* at Doran?"

Kando slowly obeys. "I had a good reason for it." His voice is much clearer now, so that's an improvement. "He had to be stopped. And it's not like I did anything wrong. Grak approved it."

That's partially true. Grak did approve it, but only *after* the act was committed. Of course, he certainly *wanted* it done; he just had some reservations to sort out first. And when he learned of Kando's decision, he couldn't let word spread that the man acted without approval. Thus, it seemed best to retroactively authorize the matter and brush the remaining details to the side.

Doran clenches his jaw and mutters something incoherent.

Grak senses frustration in the man. "Doran, you're obviously unhappy about the situation. Can you tell me about that?"

Doran straightens in his chair and turns to face Grak and Kando. "There was no reason to execute him," he replies.

Grak is confused. "Execute whom?"

Doran's eyes bulge with incredulity. "Hambo! Who else would I be talking about? Have you executed anyone *else* recently?"

Kando opens his mouth to speak, but Grak gives him a subtle shake of the head. Wouldn't be prudent to delve into that topic at the moment. Not until Doran's nerves cool a little.

Grak puts on a soothing voice. "I just wanted you to say his name. It helps with the healing process." He quickly changes topics. "So tell me, Doran, why does Hambo's execution bother you so much?"

Doran stifles his frustration. "Why does that question even need to be asked? What's going on with the tribe? And with you? And with you, Kando? You've both changed! And so has the tribe!"

Grak doesn't like this kind of talk. Especially not from one of his council members. He puts on his stern demeanor. "Watch yourself now, Doran. You might be an old friend, but that doesn't give you leave to speak against me. Remember the Cordo."

Grak points to his new tent decoration. While the smell certainly hasn't grown on him, he finds it more pleasant than what's been wafting through the air of late. Also, it provides a certain amount of clout during meetings. Even the mole adds a fair bit of intimidation, which is the only reason he hasn't removed the thing.

Doran looks at it and swallows. A clear bead of sweat drips down his forehead. Grak can't tell if it's from nervousness or the heats.

Best to assume nervousness. At least until there's proof otherwise. And that's good. No one should be so comfortable as to think they can defy me.

He gives Lago a look of exaggerated surprise.

What's that? Oh, now you're speaking to me? I don't appreciate the silent treatment, you know. That's not the way to behave with friends.

Grak is pleasantly surprised to hear such a heartfelt response.

Well, thank you for that. It must have been difficult to say. And I forgive you, old friend. Honestly, I can't stay mad at you. It's just good to hear your laughter again.

Grak combs his fingers through Lago's hair, ignoring the strange looks from the council. He doesn't understand why people get so uncomfortable when he does this, but neither does he care. The habit soothes him, after all, and if it also happens to intimidate, then that only adds to its usefulness.

Doran's jaw trembles. "I … um … I think …"

Grak moves a finger to the man's lips. "Shh. Peace, friend. It can be hard to express ourselves." He gives a stern look to the others, inspiring affirmation from them. "Don't worry so much about what you *think*. Try using 'I feel' terminology. That might help."

Doran gulps and nods. "I apologize. It's just … well … I feel … or, I felt … it was important to find out more about Hambo's theory. About the water shortage. And … I feel … that it discourages further theories if we kill off our theorists when we dislike one of their ideas."

Grak gently strokes Doran's hair. "There, see? That was very good. And easy, no?"

He waits for a nod from the man. "But you're wrong. Hambo wasn't executed because his idea was *disliked*. He was executed because it was too *dangerous*.

"See the chaos his thoughts have already spread? How can I let that continue among my children? Would you have me *not* protect them? Would you have me *weakened*?"

Grak waits for the man to shake his head. "And I don't see why *you're* not troubled, Doran. Hambo's views directly opposed your vast ocean theory, but you didn't do anything to help me. And you're *still* not doing anything."

He pauses for effect. "And if you refuse to help, then I can't let you lead your group any longer."

Doran seems offended. "Well, I never actually wanted to start it in the first place."

That's not the answer Grak wanted. He imagined there would be a little groveling at least. Some sort of oath to do better would also have been nice. But *agreement* was the last thing he needed.

Unfortunately, Grak can't go back on his threat now. "Good. If you don't want the honor, then I'll give it to Kando. He'll head up the Vast Oceaners in your place."

Grak waits, but gets no reaction. "Besides, I was thinking of giving it to him anyway. He has some bold new plans for your group. Ways to calm this water shortage scare. I like his future-oriented thinking."

Still nothing. "And as for you ... well ..." Grak regrets having to do this. "Frolan, seize him."

Doran struggles, but is soon detained.

"Fifty!" Brak calls the final lash.

Grak prefers the skin rake under normal circumstances, but it would be unnecessary here. Doran's an obedient one by nature, and responds well where the more stiff-necked continue to resist. Besides, this punishment is really just for show. Grak isn't *actually* mad at his friend.

A little hurt by him is all. But not mad. How could I be? We've had so many experiences together.

He turns to Lago and chuckles, pushing the man's face away playfully.

Don't make me laugh. I have to look serious at these things. For my children.

Grak takes a moment to regain his composure, then stands and strolls to his spot in front of the crowd. After waiting the required nine breaths, Kando walks forward and takes a position three feet behind Grak. As opposed to the standard seven. Grak considers saying something, but shakes it off.

He's too valuable. No sense risking offense over such a small matter.

Grak turns to the crowd. "Now, I'm sure many of you are wondering why I just had Doran whipped. And that's a fair question, so long as it's not expressed in public. Or out loud. But, in my mercy, I've decided to answer it both in public and out loud."

Grak pauses, waiting for a cheer. After a moment of silence, he decides to just move along. "The answer is simple. Doran was whipped because of his dissension. He's fortunate it wasn't defiance, though. The punishment wouldn't have been so light if *that* were the case.

"But even a minor amount of dissension cannot be tolerated. And no trace of it can be allowed in any position of importance in camp. As a result, he can no longer be trusted to head the Vast Oceaners.

"From this time forward, Kando will lead the group in his stead. He's been at Doran's side the whole time, and I'm sure he'll do a fine job with it."

Kando interrupts. "Thank you, Grak. And if you don't mind, I've prepared a little something I'd like to say."

Grak is thrown off by this request. And fairly upset.

The dolt wasn't supposed to speak! Calm, Grak. Calm. He's not defying. Simply asking. And his influence is too valuable. Not such a big deal to allow him this one thing.

Grak takes a calming breath. "Yes, I was just going to see if you had anything to say. But be brief. We haven't got all day for you to drone on." He chuckles and slaps the man on the shoulder.

Kando nods and turns to the crowd. "I simply want you to know how honored I am by your confidence in me. Grak's right, of course. I have been by Doran's side the whole time. But I've also been by *Grak's* side, and I've learned much from him about leading. As a result, I'm confident in my ability to succeed."

Grak cuts in. "Succeed in leading the Vast Oceaners, that is. Just to clarify."

Kando nods, but gives no further support to that clarification. This troubles Grak. Deeply.

Calm, Grak. Calm. I'm sure he's loyal. The man's a friend, after all.

He turns to Lago with a look of concern.

Hmm, you're not wrong there. I suppose it would still be wise to speak with him.

Grak nods emphatically.

Oh yes, of course. I'll be very polite. Just have to make sure he understands the importance of clarity and showing me due respect.

Grak puts on a stony voice. "Thank you, Kando." He chooses not to request applause for the man.

That should teach him. Now where were we?

He gives Lago an appreciative nod.

Ah, thank you. I swear, sometimes my mind just gets so cluttered. But you never lose focus. I tell you, I don't know what I'd do without you, old friend.

He gestures, and Frolan walks forward, supporting a badly bruised and hobbling Escha.

Grak switches to a lighthearted tone. "Hello, Escha. I hope you've been enjoying the day's activities."

She seems confused about the direction his voice is coming from. "Yes …?" Her good eye finally spots him, and she nods.

Grak chuckles with as much good nature as he can muster. "Well, enough with the simple pleasantries. Tell us, Escha, what news on Hambo's water shortage theory?"

The woman strains to project her voice beyond the first row of attendees. "We've found …" She coughs. "We've found conclusive evidence that the water shortage theory was *untrue*."

"Then why are we rationing our water?" shouts a voice from the crowd.

The guards are quick to identify the offender, despite his attempts to hide. They soon drag a nervous Voluilo forward.

Oh good. If anyone deserves a punishment, it's him. Been a long time coming for that fool.

Grak puts on his calm face. "It seems fortune is with you today, Voluilo. Before I pronounce your punishment, I will have mercy and respond to your question. The reason we're rationing water is just so we'll have it if we ever *do* run into a shortage at some point in the future.

"If you'll recall, the famine we experienced was caused by Cordo's opposition to rations until it was too late. And because I care about you, my children, I refuse to leave such important matters in someone else's hands this time. So I'm forcing these water rations until we can build up a surplus."

Other than a few questionable murmurs, the tribe seems mellowed by that response.

Well, a little mellowed. Good enough for now, at least. Well done, Grak. Well done. And you too, friend. Don't think I've forgotten about you.

Grak nudges Lago's chin, creating more debris than usual.

He wipes it on his tunic and turns to Frolan. "Skin rake. Nine strokes."

Voluilo pleads, but several solid punches quickly knock the vigor out of him. Thoroughly subdued now, he's dragged to the whipping post and tied up.

Grak returns to his seat, pleased with the proceedings so far. After a long, thorough stretch, he allows himself a moment to reflect on the day's accomplishments.

Satisfactory. Quite satisfactory.

He leans back, closes his eyes, and breathes a sigh of relief. The rhythmic sounds of the skin rake immediately begin soothing his troubled thoughts.

Now maybe I can get a little peace.

"Fire!" comes the shout from many voices at once.

The alarm sounds again: seven blows to signify "an urgent threat posed by an individual or group." Grak sighs.

Maybe we should change the alarm system. Far too complicated as it stands.

He sighs even deeper.

Oh, but what does it matter? I've lost control, Lago. Eighth fire in five days. And how many unauthorized killings in that time? I've lost count. Perhaps you were right. But I was so certain Escha's announcement would calm things.

Grak peers outside. He's learned it's best to stay in his tent when danger abounds in camp. Too many people running around. Too much violence. He closes the flap.

Yes, best to avoid it. Frolan will keep us safe in here. Now there's a good fellow. I was thinking we should invite him over to dine with us. What do you think?

He looks at Lago in shock.

Well, that was uncalled for. You know, you're not exactly the prettiest face in camp either. Though I do enjoy how you've recently taken to wearing fresh jasmines in your hair. It's very becom—

Grak turns in surprise at the sound of his tent flap opening. He breathes a sigh of relief. "Oh, Kando, it's you." Reproach enters his voice. "You didn't announce yourself … again."

Kando shows only moderate concern. "I apologize. I assumed that since you called for me, I was already invited."

Grak ponders this reasoning. While it appears sound, his patience for the man's accidental defiance is growing thin.

He puts on a cold demeanor. "Then let me make it clear. Even if I invite you, announce yourself outside and wait for me to call you in. Is that understood?"

Kando nods. "Completely."

Hmm. A bit too calm in his response. Seems he should have more fear.

A voice calls from outside. "This is Frolan, requesting to enter Grak's tent."

Grak gives Kando a pointed look while he waits his customary five breaths. "Enter!"

Frolan ducks through the flap and nods at the two men.

'Grak's tent.' Doesn't sound very prestigious, does it? Perhaps if I added some flourish to my name. Any thoughts?

He gives Lago a heartwarming smile.

Well, thank you. And I think you're right: 'The Tent of Grak the Mighty and Powerful Leader' does sound much better. But I think it's still missing something.

Grak scratches his chin. "Let's mull it over for a few days and see if we can come up with something better," he says.

Turning back to the others, Grak notices a strange expression on their faces. Uncertain of its cause, he ignores it for the time being.

"So, Frolan, what news of the fire?" he asks.

"I ... uh ..." The brute gathers his thoughts. "Uh, yes. The fire." He returns to his usual distant manner. "We've put it out, sir. Only one cart was damaged, though beyond repair. One of the new offshoots from the Vast Oceaners is taking credit for the act. I have their leader in custody. We're awaiting your orders on how to handle the matter."

Grak nods. "Very good." He decides this is a fine opportunity to teach Kando a lesson. "You're a loyal one, Frolan, my friend. You always wait for my orders and never act behind my back. I appreciate that." He shoots Kando another pointed look.

Frolan nods without expression. "Thank you sir. And what would you have us do with him?"

Grak ponders the matter. "One of the new offshoots, you say? Which one?"

"I ... believe they call themselves 'Hambo's Truth,'" replies Frolan.

Grak scrunches his face. "Not very catchy compared to some of the other ones. But wait, didn't we execute their leader yesterday?"

Kando cuts in. "If I might. I believe that was the leader of 'Hambo's Faithful.'"

Grak remembers now. "Ah, quite right. Quite right. Hard to keep track with so many popping up."

He pauses in thought. "Now, Kando ... I seem to recall putting you in charge of the Vast Oceaners for the purpose of bringing order. But these offshoots of your group ... well, they're far from orderly."

Kando shows slight nervousness. "Yes, but *my* group is the very definition of orderly. And fanatically loyal. The increased punishments and executions have done wonders to bring that about."

He pauses for affirmation that never comes. "And ... well, I certainly can't be expected to keep everyone in line. Can I?" His eyes grow more furtive. "I mean, the offshoots can't be considered a part of *my* group any more than they can be considered ... well, *horses*."

Grak remains skeptical. "Hmm, perhaps. But I don't have time to deal with you right now. Consider yourself fortunate."

At least I managed to make the man sweat a bit. Good to know we still have that effect on people, eh Lago?

Grak smiles and shakes his head with a playful eye roll.

Oh, please! You're too kind, old friend! We both deserve equal shares in the credit. And that's all I'll say on the issue.

Grak dons a somber expression and turns to Frolan. "Take me to your captive. I'd like to speak with him."

"Doran never would have approved of this madness!" shouts Umo to the cautiously gathering crowd.

Grak raises an eyebrow, pondering the young man. He's close to Grak's own height, though a shred shorter. And while he lacks any real muscle or other visible claim to authority, something about the fellow begs intrigue. Something almost mesmerizing.

Perhaps it's just his backdrop: a smoldering cart with smoky haze swirling about. Or maybe it's the soot around his piercing blue eyes, showing a willingness to handle the dirty work personally. Or perhaps those elements only stand out in contrast to the complete absence of the marks of age.

Hardly could have seen more than seventeen snows. Couldn't possibly be coming up with such seditious ideas all on his own. Could he?

Grak turns to Lago and nods in thought for a moment.

Hmm, good point. And good idea.

He motions to Frolan, who punches the youth again. This one sends Umo into a daze. He tries to stand, but only achieves a wobbly imitation. The two guards holding him steady are the only reason he's still upright.

Grak waits until the young man regains coherence. "Where did you get these ideas? Who put you up to this?"

Umo shakes his head resolutely. "No one. Truth is evident enough to be seen without prompting."

Hmm, just the lie I would give in his position. He's a clever one. So who's he protecting?

Grak looks at Lago with shock.

Well, I never thought of that possibility. I think you might be right, friend.

He searches the crowd and spots the man. "Doran! Come here this instant!"

Doran breaks out of thought at the sound of his name. After a brief moment of uneasy realization, he quickly limps over.

Grak dons his angry face. "Doran. Did you put this idea in Umo's head?"

"Well ... not directly, no." His voice trembles. "Though ... I suppose when I was still in charge of the Vast Oceaners, I did say that often." He raises his hands to protect his face. "But I've already been punished for that ... please."

The youth cuts in. "It's true, sir. These are *my* ideas. Mine and my group's. We know what Doran originally intended, and it was not this chaos." He raises his voice as these types always do. "Nor did he intend for us to be stuck on the exact dimensions of the shoreline! Hambo's theory never opposed Doran's ideas! Doran would have understood that!"

Doran nods to himself. "That's true. I never really wanted any of thes—"

Grak smacks him on the back of the head, and the man recoils in apology.

Umo grows even more emboldened. "Doran meant for us to understand that the shoreline stretches farther out. That the ocean is actually very small. And that the water truly is in danger of disappearing completely!"

Doran's expression is one of shocked disagreement, but he opts to hold his tongue at this point.

A voice from the crowd yells out, "Doran meant for us to remain by the shore! Wanda and Tabo had it right!"

Doran's concern overpowers his fear. "Well, not really. That's certainly not ... you know what, though, I'm still here. I can just tell you what

I meant."

Grak strikes the man again. "I will inform you when you're allowed to spe—"

A single horn call echoes through the air.

Grak makes no attempt to mask his frustration. "Stop that awful, ridiculous, abrasive alarm! We have the fire under control!"

That got him more worked up than he would have expected. He pauses to calm his breathing. Much to his delight, the noise seems to have stopped.

"Well, that was fast." Grak considers waiving punishment, given the immediacy of their obedience.

But Frolan shows great concern. "No sir. I don't believe it was meant to be an alarm for the fire. That came from Brownhand. One horn. Urgent danger. Someone's threatening the tribe. And our water!"

The brute races off with many of the guards following close behind. Grak stands in stunned silence, bewildered at the speed of the man's reaction. He gathers his wits and assesses the situation.

Well, I'm already outside, so I suppose it can't get any more dangerous. And I still have nine guards. Should be relatively safe either way, whether I return to my tent or follow Frolan. And I am the leader, so I might as well see what's going on.

Grak gives Lago a comforting look.

What? No, of course not. You're such a worrier. We'll stay far enough back. Trust me, I wouldn't let anything happen to you.

Grak signals to his guards and calmly leads them toward the river. Lately, he's found himself favoring a leisurely walk over a hasty jog. It's not that he minds the exercise, of course. In fact, with the excess weight all but gone, his knees have been hurting much less these days.

No, it's just … well, why bother? Alarms are such a constant thing now. I don't know. It just … well, I guess it just grows tiresome. I can spend all my time rushing to the next problem, or I can simply get there when I get there. You know what I mean?

He looks at Lago and nods thoughtfully.

Yeah, I thought you might.

Grak holds his breath while passing the river barrier: a row of corpses tied to trees marking where the restricted zone begins.

Hmm. I seem to remember the bodies being spread out more. Yes, I'm certain a few of them are new. Definitely not executions I authorized.

Or did I? Can't quite remember anymore. Still, probably wisest to err on the side of caution. Remind me to reprimand Frolan, would you?

The trees are starting to thin out now. They must be getting close to the water. Grak breathes deep. It's safe to do so out here, as the camp's odors almost never make it this far. That's one of the reasons why he likes coming here: it feels like a completely different place.

And I feel like a completely different person. Something about Brownhand that just melts the weight of leadersh—

"Sir!" comes a whisper from just ahead.

It's unclear which of his guards spoke, but they've all stopped. Grak pushes two of them aside to clear a view. He freezes.

They've reached the riverbank and have a direct line of sight down to the water. The alarm was accurate: the situation is urgent. Grak's guards have their bows trained across the river at a force of equal size doing the same. Tension hangs in the air; the slightest misstep is all it would take to spark a panicked bloodbath.

The opposition's leader notices Grak's arrival and calls out, "Hello, my friend! Why don't you come and join us? The water's lovely in these heats!"

Grak's eyes might be poor, but there's no mistaking the strong, throaty sound of those words.

Kunthar!

17 - And Nosy Tribes

Grak abhors people who stick their noses in his affairs. And he's all the more furious when strangers do it. Which explains his current rancor toward Kunthar's presence here at the river.

He's obviously just being nosy. What other reason would he have? Just passing through? Not likely. They must know something about the water shortage. And about our current troubles.

Really, their timing couldn't be more suspect. And it puts Grak in a very awkward position. The last thing he needs right now is to lose more of his people in battle. The tribe is already in a state of regular panic, and that could set them off to no end.

Seems like there's no way around it, Lago. We'll have to handle this one peaceably. At least for the time being. Until we have an opportunity for a fairer fight.

Grak whispers to his guards, "Advance. But slowly. And keep your current formation. And keep it tight! No spaces except this one for seeing across the way."

They obey, and the group descends the riverbank, reaching the water's edge in a matter of moments. As they draw near, Kunthar gives a hushed order, and his guards respond by forming a similar grouping around him. Grak chuckles at this.

Stupid fool. Has to copy me. Can't even come up with an original formation of his own.

Kunthar calls across, "Glad you could join us, Grak! As I was trying to tell your people here, we're not looking for trouble. Simply came down for water and intend to be on our way quickly."

Grak projects a laugh across the river. "You expect me to *believe* you? If that's true, then why did you come fully armed with bows at the ready?"

Kunthar takes on a defensive tone. "Just being cautious. Can't be too sure these days."

Grak finds that response unsettling. He looks to Lago.

Can you see anything from up there? Anything of importance? Unusual behavior? Or better yet, anything to give us an advantage? Oh, sorry.

Grak raises the staff to give his friend a better view. But to his dismay, the report he gets back is basic, only consisting of four points:

1 - The strangers are around thirty paces away in a tight line on the opposing bank.

2 - Their numbers are slightly greater than Grak's own.

3 - They're all wearing familiar pointed caps.

4 - Kunthar's hat is the tallest by far.

But still not as tall as mine, eh? By a whole hand, it seems. The fool. Can't even copy me accurately.

Grak looks to Lago, his smirk fading into realization.

Hmm, good point. It might be shorter as a show of reverence. Though there's no doubt he's copying me.

But never mind all that. Those points are obvious from down here. What other information can you gather?

Grak gives his friend a skeptical look.

What? How can that be all? Look around some more!

He's getting frustrated now.

Well, no. I just don't think you're really trying. All I'm hearing from you are excuses.

Grak has had enough. He's truly upset now.

Really? That's your response? Oh, what's the use? You're awful at reconnaissance. You know that, don't you?

Grak lowers the staff. After a tense moment of silence, he takes a calming breath.

I'm sorry. I didn't mean it. You're nervous. I understand. Who wouldn't be? Given the situation.

He gives his humblest nod.

Well, you're right. I guess I'm not. But really, I mean other than me. My experience and fortitude are rare. They help me stay calm during moments like this.

But I shouldn't expect you to be skilled in reconnaissance. You're an adviser. That's your specialty. You were never trained in the art of reconnoitering. Though it might be good for you to learn. Given your height and subtle nature.

Grak smooths Lago's hair, careful not to disrupt the jasmines. That's when realization hits: their usual aroma is absent. He leans in for a sniff.

When did they lose their scent?

He dons a warm expression.

What? Then why didn't you tell me days ago?

Grak puts on his comforting face.

Oh, of course it's no trouble. Not at all! Please, tell me sooner next time. I won't let it be said that I don't take care of my friends.

He chuckles. "Good point. And an apt observation, I might add. Well, remind me to replace them as soon as we get back to camp."

One of the guards shoots him a nervous glance. Grak ponders the man for a moment, but ultimately attributes his strange behavior to the tense situation.

Which reminds me. Enough about jasmines. We need to settle this stranger problem immediately. Any thoughts?

He looks at Lago with equal parts surprise and fascination.

Hmm, well, that's a gutsy plan.

Grak shrugs. "Can't hurt to try it, though." He lifts his voice. "Well, Kunthar, I don't know about you, but I could use a swim. Though I'd be more than happy to let your people jump in first. You know, being our guests and all."

Kunthar considers the offer. "No, we're fine here, thank you. But you can go ahead and jump in. We won't stop you."

Oh, he's a clever one. Thinks he can get us to drop our bows. We'll need to keep a wary eye on him.

"No thanks," is Grak's simple response.

"But I thought you wanted to swim?" replies Kunthar.

Grak admires the man's keen strategy there. "Yes, but ..." He reaches for an explanation. "But the wind shifted. And now it's cold. So I'm not interested anymore."

Kunthar huddles with several of his people. Grak can only recognize Dernue, though she's tough to miss, given the width of her nose. Still, he scolds himself for not gathering more information about the strangers last they met.

Kunthar finishes his private discussion and shouts across the river once again. "Oh good. I'm glad to hear it was just the cold. I thought you might have changed your mind about the swim because of those lions behind you."

Fear courses through Grak's veins. He begins to turn, but stops an instant later.

You're right, Lago! The area is far too well-traveled of late. Lions wouldn't come around here. That clever fiend!

Grak shouts to his people, "Don't look! He's trying to trick you! So they can shoot us. Trust me, there are no lions behind us!"

Thanks for your quick thinking, friend. Probably saved us all. Now for retaliation.

"That was a good trick, Kunthar! But not good enough!" Grak suppresses a smile. "And it earned my people the time they needed. They're sneaking up behind you as we speak!"

Kunthar seems tempted, but makes his decision in an instant. "Don't look either! He's trying to trick us. There's no one back there!"

Hmm, clever indeed. Seems we've reached an impasse here. Any other ideas, friend?

Grak tries to control his disappointment.

Well, why not? You're my adviser. I would expect at lea—

Frolan pokes his head into Grak's formation. "Sir. This doesn't seem to be getting anywhere at the moment. Perhaps we could suggest a neutral meeting point without weapons. Just for you and Kunthar."

Grak conceals his excitement about the idea. "Hmm, yes. Just what I was thinking."

But how to word it so Kunthar doesn't argue?

He taps his lips pensively.

Ah, good idea. Thank you, friend. That almost makes up for your failure a moment ago.

"Kunthar!" shouts Grak. "I suggest you come alone and unarmed to a meeting on our side of the river."

The stranger quickly discusses the idea, then shouts back, "I don't know if I can trust you. Why don't you come over here?"

Grak didn't expect *that* reply. "Well, I don't know if I can trust you either!"

Kunthar's response is quicker this time. "Well sure, but realistically, only one of us here has held the other one captive."

Grak opens his mouth to deny that, but stops short, unable to think of a way to deflect the point. He turns to Frolan for more ideas.

The brute simply blinks. "By neutral, I meant somewhere in between."

Grak laughs derisively. "In the water? Get realistic! That's the worst idea you've had yet."

Frolan's expression remains unchanged. "Actually, I was thinking of the ford just upstream. It seems far enough away from both tribes for everyone to feel comfortable there."

Grak stops laughing. "Yes, that was my idea. Just wanted to see if you could think on your feet. Chances are, you'll have to put up with Kunthar's mocking during the meeting, so I wanted to prepare you in advance."

Frolan nods. "Yes sir."

Grak breathes a quiet sigh of relief and turns back to Kunthar. "Let's meet in the middle!"

The stranger lets out a hearty and exaggerated laugh. "In the water? Tha—" He stops abruptly as Dernue whispers in his ear.

Grak peers inside his tent. Its size made it the obvious choice for the meeting, but Kunthar would only allow it if they set the thing up on his side of the ford.

And that certainly warrants suspicion. And shows no small amount of lethargy on the man's part. Can't even be bothered to cross the water?

Seeking to teach a lesson on apathy, Grak insisted that Kunthar should be the one serving refreshments. To his surprise, the man had no qualms about this and only demanded to choose them as well.

Of course, Grak was hesitant to give him that one, as it would create an equal number of concessions from each tribe. But in the end, he relented, deciding that his victories were of a higher quality, if not a higher quantity.

Clearly, I won. Remind me to have Opa record it as such. And don—

Oh, here we go. We'll talk about that later.

Spotting Frolan's signal for "safe to approach," Grak stands tall and strolls in with confidence. But he loses some of that assurance upon entering the empty tent. Without furnishings or decorations, it feels quite a bit smaller. "Lonely" would be his description. Or perhaps "sad," save for the strong scent of jasmines in the air.

Grak sniffs Lago's hair to verify the man didn't change his flowers.

No, clearly not you. I suppose someone else has your fine sense for fragrances. And I'm not referring to myself this time.

He chuckles as he sits down.

True. So true. But enough humor. We've got important matters to deal with.

Grak adopts a somber demeanor and turns his focus toward the meeting attendees. As expected, Kunthar brought Dernue as one of his two permitted advisers. However, the bald man sitting on his other side was not anticipated.

Grak considers his own selections of Frolan and Lago.

I wonder if I should have brought Brak instead of Frolan. Just to match their bald fellow. In case that gives them an edge I don't know about. Well, I suppose only time will tell. Best to get on with this thing.

He decides to begin with simple pleasantries. "Why are you in our restricted zone?"

He glances at Lago.

Hmm, you might be right. Remind me to start with a more palatable topic next time.

He shrugs thoughtfully.

Well, maybe. Though, I'm not certain there's much to discuss about the weather.

Grak nods slowly as understanding sinks in.

Ah, I see. I suppose that would make it a decent subject to lead with. Alright, we'll go with that one next time.

Dernue looks offended, but stays silent while Kunthar responds. "We didn't know you gave the area a name. We were simply passing through."

Grak chuckles derisively. "Passing through? On the other side of the river? What? Did your herd cross the water?"

Kunthar looks troubled. "How did you know that? Have you been following us?"

Dernue leans in and whispers something. Kunthar responds with an equally quiet comment of his own. Grak shakes his head, marveling at their abilities.

Kunthar nods to the woman and turns back. "Yes, they did cross. And we followed them."

Grak finds their behavior furtive and suspicious. He rubs his chin to show careful deliberation.

They seem rather on edge, don't they?

He raises an eyebrow at Lago.

You think so? Well, that's an interesting theory. They did show up rather soon after Cordo's attack. And I imagine the strangers over the hill are probably connected too. I knew we should have killed them off right away! Well, stay quiet about this. Can't let on that we've seen through their guise. At least, not until we gather more information.

Grak puts on his formal demeanor. "So, Kunthar. I find your timing unusual." He adds his most suggestive tone. "Met anyone *new* lately? Or been involved in any *schemes* I should know about?"

Kunthar's eyes go wide for an instant. He leans in and whispers to Dernue. She rolls her eyes and releases a powerful snort before whispering something in return.

Kunthar returns to the meeting, attempting a calm front, yet betrayed by the manic activity in his eyelashes. "No. Why do you ask?"

Aha! Did you see that, Lago? Looks like you were right. But how does it all connect? You think on that one while I distract him. Let me know the moment you come up with something.

Grak rubs his chin. "No reason. No reason at all." He smiles knowingly in an attempt to make Kunthar uneasy.

The stranger begins to speak, but is interrupted by a rumpling of the tent flap. Grak whirls in his seat to spot Brak and one of the strangers entering together. It's an awkward ordeal, considering the small space of the opening and how both men are determined to hold the tray unitedly.

Good man. Following orders to the letter.

Grak turns to his enemy. "I forgot to mention one thing, Kunthar. I have to be certain that you haven't poisoned the refreshments. So my team will serve them, and you'll drink first."

Kunthar whispers with Dernue for a moment before turning back. "Alright. But only if you serve them in plain view."

Grak nods, and Brak pours the first drink. But as liquid splashes into the clay cup, an aroma rises and fills the tent, tickling the recesses of Grak's mind.

What is that scent? Do you recognize it, friend? Has a certain famil—

Now he remembers. It's a spice Grak hasn't smelled in some time. Cinnamon tea. His mind races.

Is it just a coincidence? But how could it be? How probable is it that they'd be drinking the—

He gasps. Noticing the stares, Grak attempts to turn it into a yawn. Barely passable. He adds a stretch, both to enhance the ruse and to subtly bring him closer to Frolan's ear. He whispers softly, actually managing to keep it quiet this time.

The brute's eyes go wide, and he stands. "Excuse me. I forgot to … m … p …" He leaves abruptly.

There's a good man. Swift to obey. Though now we're down by one. Two if we get in a fight. No offense, Lago, but you're in no condition to brawl.

Kunthar's worry is obvious. "Where did Frolan run off to?"

"Oh …" Grak reviews possible explanations. "He just had to switch out the river guard. End of their watch and all."

Kunthar's worry swells into panic. "What is this?" He stands in a show of anger. "We agreed not to have our forces at the river during the meeting!"

Hmm, can't have him ending things just yet. Not before Frolan reports back.

Grak raises his hands to calm the man. "Relax. It's just our standard guard. We always have a troop of nine to watch the river."

This only creates greater concern in Kunthar. "Nine? Why would you need so many there? If not to move against my people?"

Grak chuckles at that sentiment. "So *many*? Oh, was that a lot of guards? I hadn't realized."

He smiles and turns to Brak, nudging him with his elbow. The man avoids eye contact and pulls away slightly, evoking a frown from Grak.

At least tell me you got the humor, Lago.

He grins with relief.

Thank you! I can't tell you how nice it is to have someone around who enjoys a good laugh every now and then. I swear, the fools around me normally are far too serious.

He rolls his eyes at Brak and returns to the conversation. "In our tribe, nine guards isn't much." Best to clarify, just in case Kunthar doesn't quite get it. "Because we're so strong, I mean. We have a lot of guards. Far more than nine."

The stranger raises an eyebrow, but quickly catches himself and replaces it with a more aloof expression. "Oh? Like three times more? Or four?"

Grak grows indignant. "Pssh! Try six times more!" The need for caution dawns on him.

Hmm, might have been best not to give away our exact numbers. Should have exaggerated a bit. Ninety would be a solid number.

Grak gives Lago a look of pleasant surprise. "Oh, good thinking."

He rushes to implement the man's idea. "But that's just active. We have another thirty who train regularly but have other duties." Still sounds too small. "And another fifty that train, just not as regularly. So, yes, we have a lot of guards." Grak commends himself for such a smooth recovery.

Kunthar looks troubled. "Well, we have even more than that. Maybe around one hundred regular and another hundred that train but have other duties."

Grak rolls his eyes. "*Maybe* around one hundred? You're not a very good liar, Kunthar. If you're going to make up numbers, then at least be definite in them."

Kunthar whispers with Dernue before turning back. "We have *exactly* one hundred."

Grak raises an eyebrow. "Oh, and you think I'll believe you *now*? You can't just recover *that* easily after being caught in a lie."

Kunthar grows frustrated. "We *do* have that many! And I'm not the liar here, Grak. You're the one who went back on our agreement to keep your soldiers from the river!"

He's trying to change the subject now? Must be nervous. We can certainly use that. Just need to keep him arguing until Frolan returns.

Grak chuckles. "Funny thing to call them." He slowly enunciates the word. "*Sol-diers*. We just call them guards."

Kunthar calms slightly, but fails to hide his offense at that comment. "Well, 'soldiers' just sounds better."

Grak rolls his eyes and whispers to Brak, "Sure, for dumb people. Am I right?"

Brak shrugs and mumbles, "I thought it sounded nice."

Grak finds that response annoying.

Proves my point then, doesn't it, Lago?

Kunthar shakes his head in confusion and fury. "But, regardless of what we call them, I demand an answer! Why do you have forces at the river? That's in direct violation of our agreement!"

Hmm, maybe a bit too angry. Best to calm him down a little. Don't want him resorting to violence while Frolan's away.

Grak makes another calming gesture and puts on a soothing tone. "No, they're not *at* the river. They're in the woods. They're just *guarding* the river." He detects lingering confusion. "From *my* people."

Kunthar hesitates. "You post soldiers to keep your own people away from the river? Why would you do that? It doesn't even make sense."

His tone takes on a touch of indignation. "*Now* who sounds like a liar?"

It's Grak's turn to be offended. "I'm not lying! And it makes perfect sense. If we don't keep our people away, then they try to hoard the water. Obviously I'm just being a sensible leader, watching out for my people during the water shortage!"

Kunthar's eyes go wide—an effect amplified by the man's luxurious lashes. "Water … shortage? Wh—?"

Dernue angrily tugs at the man's tunic. With surprise still coating his face, he turns to the woman and leans in. The two whisper fervently for a moment while the bald man fails in his attempts to join in. Finally, Kunthar turns back and stands tall.

He's wearing an arrogant expression now. "Yes, the water shortage. We've known about that. For some time now, really."

I knew it! They do know about the water shortage! But did they cause it?

Grak rubs his chin in consideration.

Hmm, you're right. Probably need Escha's analysis if we hope to be certain. But how do we respond until then?

He gives Lago a subtle wink.

Ah, good thinking. Best to play it down for now.

Grak proceeds with caution. "Well, I'm not surprised you know about it. Simple theory, really. Obvious, once we noticed the river was drying up. Something anyone could have figured out."

Kunthar thinks for a moment. "Yes, certainly. But you should still tell us more about it. Everything you know would be good. And be specific. Just so we can see if your information is accurate."

Wait a moment. That doesn't make much sense, does it Lago? Why would they need to know—

Of course! They didn't actually know about it yet. Not until they stole the information from me just now. Those fiends! Those clever fiends! We need to stall! Throw them off the trail until Frolan gets back.

He thinks quickly, desperate for a solution. "Well, it takes a while to explain. With all the numbers … and such. Wouldn't expect your people to understand in one sitting."

Kunthar returns to fervently whispering with Dernue. They're a little too good at that. Grak can't tell if they bought the excuse.

He leans in to Brak and tries his best whisper. "I need you to casually walk behind them and listen to what they're saying. Then report it back to me."

Brak looks confused. "But won't they be suspi—"

Frolan storms into the tent, breathing hard. He takes a moment to catch his breath before leaning in and whispering to Grak. Kunthar stops his own conversation to watch these new proceedings with great concern. As Frolan completes his report, Grak's eyes go wide.

His breathing grows ragged and furious. "So, Kunthar. I've asked you twice now, and both times you've lied to me. I'll give you one more chance to tell the truth. Have you met anyone outside of your tribe recently? Before the event at the river today?"

Kunthar's eyes dart back and forth between Grak and Frolan. He's obviously considering the possibility of keeping his lie going.

But Grak doesn't let him make that decision. He stands, full of rage. "Let me put it another way. Frolan has just confirmed it for me, and I'd like to hear your explanation of the matter. Why are you hiding Jafra and Groka among your people?"

Kunthar grows bewildered. "How …? You stalled! You stalled while your brute sneaked off and secretly espied my encampment!"

Grak likes the sound of that word. Though it's a little too bulky.

Espied. Let's keep that one in reserve and work on it. Maybe we could whittle it down for regular use.

Trusting Lago to commit it to memory, Grak returns to the conversation. "Don't change the subject." He remembers his anger. "That woman has committed heinous acts against our people. Return her to us so we can have our justice!"

Kunthar allows a slight smile. "Hmm. So it seems I have something you want. That just leaves me to wonder one thing. What do you have that *I* want?"

Grak ponders it for a moment.

What's the fool getting at? Does he want something in particular? Or is he just asking me to make an offer?

He taps his lips and sneaks Lago a slight nod.

Yes, you're probably right.

He puts on his nonchalant voice. "I suppose I could trade you one of my people. Brak here, for example. If you'd like."

Brak is outraged. "What?"

And Kunthar is offended. "What kind of an offer is that? For something as important to you as your justice? You'd have to at least trade … maybe the big fellow. And then I'd still have to be talked into it."

Brak's anger redirects toward Kunthar. "What does *that* mean? I'm an excellent offer! If I were up for trade! Which I'm not!"

Grak rolls his eyes. "Alright, clearly no one's pleased with that deal. So, Kunthar, what would *you* like in exchange for Jafra? Other than Frolan. He's out of the question."

The man ponders it for a moment. "Well, maybe twenty of your finest guards then."

Grak's anger surges. "*Twenty*? Have you gone mad? I would sooner send them to be slaughtered in taking her. Which I have half a mind to do if you won't be reasonable. I demand justice! I demand that you return her to me!"

Kunthar takes insult. "Demand? What puts you in a position to demand anything? We have the greater numbers. In fact, I demand that you …" He thinks for a moment. "I demand that you dance for me."

Now it's Grak's turn to be insulted. "What do you take me for? I'm not your Brak, to just fulfill your every whim. Quit stalling, Kunthar. And stop getting in my way. Give me the justice that I'm due!"

That aggravates the stranger far more than expected. "Getting in *your* way? It's *you* that's getting in the way, Grak! In the way of my *leadership*. My tribe is mine to lead how I see fit. I provide benefits to my people, and anyone who joins my tribe receives the same!"

Dernue whispers something to him, and he whispers in reply.

Kunthar turns back to Grak. "Alright, maybe not the *same* benefits. But *nearly* the same." He glances at Dernue, who just shrugs and looks away in disagreement. "Well, the same protection at least. More or less." That statement passes. "So it's not like I can just give you any of my people without cause. Or without a decent trade."

Grak is barely suppressing an outburst now. "Kunthar. I'll give you one last chance to accept a simple offer. Turn Jafra over immediately or

I *will* take her by force."

Kunthar's face twists with rage, but he restrains himself. The man takes a calming breath, then gestures to his companions. Dernue and the bald man rise while the tea bearer gathers cups and readies his tray.

Kunthar speaks with a controlled fire. "Try it. Test our strength." He pauses for a moment. "And if you'd like to apologize, I'll be waiting at the river. Drinking water at my leisure. Might even hoard some of it."

Without another word, they exit the tent. Grak begins to wonder if he should have taken a gentler approach.

18 - And Those Seeking to Steal What's Rightfully His

Grak retains an exclusive type of fury for people who try to take his things. Especially his valuable things. For example, having arrived at the river first, he feels his claim to it is obvious. And given the tribe's panic, his need for the water is equally evident.

But far more important is his long overdue justice for Jafra. Grak considers his claim there to have less room for disputation. And far more value. And Kunthar's threat to steal it, along with the water, is so infuriating that Grak was unable to find any rest last night.

He rubs his brow and yawns. "I don't understand how there's any disagreement on this one." Grak signals, and the guards stop beating Loren.

Not such commanding ears after all, eh Loren?

Brak rushes over to cradle her head. "Sir, she meant no dissension. Please. It's just that we've all seen so much bloodshed lately. Everyone's on edge. It really doesn't seem like anyone would want another battle. Especially when the fight has such a potential for loss."

Kando nods. "He's right, Grak. There's no way around Frolan's report. We're outnumbered two to one. The odds just aren't in our favor."

Grak sighs in frustration. "Alright, sure, the numbers don't look so good. I'll give you that. But our people have been training longer. And we've fought before. In a way, Cordo's rebellion was a good thing. It prepared us. I doubt *they've* gone through anything similar. *We* know what to expect, but *they'll* be too busy vomiting at the first sight of blood."

Grak immediately regrets having brought up the imagery. Memories from that day flood through the council. Many look uncomfortable, even ill.

Kando shrugs. "Well, that might be true *if* the whole tribe supported it. But the reality is that most of our people just aren't willing to fight."

Grak turns to the other council members. "Do you *all* feel this way?"

Olive Thirteen nods. After a tense moment, the rest do as well.

Grak rolls his eyes. "Then do you have any *other* suggestions?"

Frolan raises a hand. "Sir, perhaps instead of attacking their camp, we could simply send a small team to sneak in and take her. Not as risky that way."

Grak nods thoughtfully. "Sure, that *might* work. But there's no guarantee. And the strangers would still be around to drink up our limited water supply. I see no other choice. We have to fight them."

Kando shakes his head. "That's another thing, Grak. The tribe doesn't care enough about Jafra, and we've made it clear that the water shortage doesn't even exist. What else can we use to motivate them? Very few are still willing to follow you to death over a vague sense of danger.

"Take the Vast Oceaners, for example. We make up a good number of able-bodied fighters, but most of my people are tense. Certainly not in the mood for another battle. Then you have the offshoots. They're even more on edge. I *might* be able to gather them under common ideals, but that would be no small task."

Grak sighs in frustration. Kando is proving more of a headache than usual tonight. But since Grak can't risk punishing the man, he's forced to reason with him. Unfortunately, discussion alone is getting nowhere.

Grak rubs his brow and takes several calming breaths. After a moment of this, he dons his friendliest face. "Alright, so everyone's concerned about the plan. I get that. And it just so happens we're about ready for another break. So, why don't we all take the opportunity to stretch and relieve ourselves? Think about what I'm proposing, and take some time to calm down. We'll meet back here in a few moments."

The council rises enthusiastically and files outside with haste. Except

Kando, that is. He's pacing slowly with his hands clasped behind his back and his chin turned slightly upward in thought.

What's this fool up to? If he thinks he can wait until everyone returns before excusing himself, he's sadly mistaken.

Grak tilts his head in fascination.

Oh my, you're right, Lago. That is a nice posture. Relaxed, yet confident. Even his nose looks better at that angle.

Grak strokes his chin thoughtfully. "Commit that posture to memory," he says. "Might prove useful."

Kando pauses. Confusion flashes in his eyes, but quickly resolves into considerable calm.

He clears his throat. "You know, Grak. I imagine I could be of assistance to you here. And in getting the whole tribe to support your plan."

Grak raises an eyebrow. "And how exactly?"

"Well, the way I see it, the council is simply worried." Kando's tone proves remarkably soothing. "They're concerned about our numbers. And, subsequently, about our chances in battle. Especially against a force so much larger than our own. And it seems to me they're just looking for confidence.

"So I believe it would only require one more voice. If just one of us with enough clout were to support you, the rest of the council would follow. And so would the tribe." He pauses for half a heartbeat. "I can be that voice."

Grak's expression turns to exasperation. "Then why haven't you done it yet? Must I prod you along? Goodness, man! Speak up the moment they return!"

Kando smiles. "Good. I'm glad you see how simple the matter is. And how so much of it depends on me." He pauses for effect. "And, ultimately, how the tribe's support also depends on me."

Grak's eyes go wide in realization. "What are you after, Kando?"

The man shrugs. "Nothing. Nothing at all, Grak. I'm simply pointing out how crucial I am to your plan. Just thought you might appreciate knowing that."

Grak is both nervous and upset about this turn of events. "Sounds like you're threatening me, Kando. And you, of all people, should know

I don't tolerate threats. That offense calls for execution, you know. Remember the Cordo!" He points to the tent decoration.

Kando's smile doesn't fade. "True, you could *attempt* that. Though I have far too many people in camp who support me. And they're a loyal bunch—your punishments have beaten that quality deep into their bones. They'd fight for me. Much like Cordo's people fought for him. And win or lose, you'd be too weak without us. You'd never get Jafra back, and worse still, the tribe would be open to a quick slaughter."

Grak considers the point. It seems true enough. "But you'd be even weaker. You need the tribe more than we need you. I have to say, I would have thought you'd come up with something better. This is a pretty poor attempt to steal power."

Kando shrugs nonchalantly. "But I'm not looking to take *your* power. I only want some of my own."

Grak raises a cautious eyebrow at the man. After a moment of consideration, he turns to Lago.

That's certainly an intriguing concept. What do you think, friend?

He purses his lips and nods.

Hmm, I thought so. Seems we're of the same mind on the matter.

He gives Lago a warm smile. "As usual, I might add," he says with a jovial tone.

Grak turns to Kando. "Go on. We're listening."

Kando shoots a nervous glance at Lago before focusing on Grak again. "I … um … Yes, I simply ask that you declare me the supporting leader. You would retain full power, and I would merely be your second in command."

Grak drops a shred of his guard. "So what good does that do for *you*?"

Kando shrugs. "Well, not much, really. Or rather, not as much as the good it would do for *you*.

"Really, I just want to help. I want to make matters easier on you. And I want the freedom to make decisions without having to worry about the threat of punishment. Decisions I know you would approve of. Like the Hambo decision, for example.

"Essentially, I would speak for you when you're unable to. Or when other concerns are too pressing. And then you wouldn't have to bear the burden all alone."

Oh ... well ... that certainly sounds nice. See, Lago, I always knew Kando was a good fellow. He consistently has my best interests at heart. Good thing I didn't give in to your paranoid fears about the man, eh?

Don't get me wrong, though. You're a wise fellow, my friend. But sometimes you fail to pick up on the more important things in life. Like this offer, for example. Could be just what I need.

I don't know if you've noticed, but leading has taken a toll on me recently. Really, between you and me, I've even been dreading it of late. Giving him a portion of the burden would certainly relieve some of the pressure. And it would give me more time. Time to take up some new hobbies.

He gazes ardently at Lago. "Time to spend with *you* like we've been discussing. What do you think?"

Grak gives his friend an enthusiastic nod. "Yes, I thought you might. Then it's decided."

He turns back to Kando, ignoring the man's awkward gaze. "Very well. You can have your heart's desire. I'll allow you to be my supporting leader."

Kando quickly regains composure. "Wonderful," he says with a slight nod.

Grak opens his mouth to speak, but stops short at the sound of the other council members mingling just outside. His mind races with nervous thought. There's still so much to discuss, but so little time.

He opts for a quick finish. "What about all your offshoots? I need them too."

Kando isn't fazed by that request. "I'll take care of them. Make the announcement about my new role by nightfall. Do that, and I can guarantee every able-bodied tribe member ready to enact your plan before dawn."

The tent flap opens, leaving no time for further consideration. Grak nods his assent.

Grak traverses the stony riverbank, taking extra care with his footing given the moonless night sky. He pauses to glance at the horizon, and his heart sinks—a faint glow whispers of dawn. The idea was to strike while the strangers slept, and each passing moment lessens that likelihood.

Grak shakes his head and whispers. "Would have worked too. If Frolan hadn't gotten us lost in the woods for so long!"

He looks at Lago with shock. "What's *that* supposed to mean? Well, sure it was my idea to go through the woods, but that was a good plan! Would have flanked their whole encampment. They wouldn't have known what was happening."

Several disturbed glances remind him of the need to be quieter. As much as Grak hates their silent reproach, he's inclined to agree with them. After all, too much noise would alert the strangers far quicker than the light of dawn.

Grak softens his whisper. "If I could have led us all the way there, I would have. But I don't know this side of the river. Frolan is the only one who does. And if he had a halfway decent memory, it would have worked wonderfully. What kind of fool can't remember the way to a camp he just visited the day before?"

He turns to Lago with a look of indignation. "Well, so what if he's tired? I'm tired too! I haven't slept in days!"

That's painfully true. And obvious. Though it can't rightly be said that Grak's lack of rest stems from an absence of effort. Quite the contrary, in fact. He even made a valiant attempt earlier this evening after the meeting. It simply proved unsuccessful, is all. Every time he closed his eyes, he saw rage, full and perfect.

That reminds him, and he once again settles into warm thoughts of vengeance. "Mmm. But don't worry, we'll sleep soon enough." Grak allows himself a smile. "Once I have my justice. Once Jafra has answered for her treachery."

He turns to Lago. "Hmm? Oh yes. And once Kunthar is dead too. Thank you, friend."

Several more troubled glances come his way. Grak replies with a menacing glare, certain that he was quiet enough this time. The visual chastisement does the trick, and all eyes avert instantly.

He smiles, satisfied with his accomplishment. "Good to know we still wield such power, eh, friend? Strike fear with a glance. You don't see that with Kando." His face twists. "Or with Umo."

He's particularly sour with those two at the moment. Once the supporting leader role was announced, Kando immediately freed Umo, ignoring Grak's objections. And if that wasn't bad enough, the pair instantly began working together in a secretive and suspicious manner.

"As though old friends." He shakes his head. "And neglecting *me* in the process! As though our friendship means nothing to Kando anymore!"

Grak spots them up ahead, conversing quietly as they walk. "Not sure I trust those two, Lago. Seems like they're up to something. Keep an eye on them, would you? Not sure I trust them at all—"

An abrupt halt ripples through the tribe as they crouch in anticipation. Looking about, Grak quickly identifies the cause: Frolan is holding up a hand and peering across the river.

Grak follows the man's line of sight, but a moment of careful scrutiny reveals nothing out of the ordinary. The obvious form of Brownhand looms up from the opposing bank, but that shouldn't have caught anyone by surprise.

Although ... hmm. Yes, that's quite interesting. The rock bears an unusual likeness to a fist when viewed from this angle. You don't supp—?

Grak gasps and points across the water. "There!" A number of alarmed glares remind him of the need for silence.

He pulls Lago closer and whispers into his ear. "I saw shapes moving among the trees. I swe—

"Yes! There they are again! People. A large number of them too. But who? That's our tribe's side of the river, but nearly every member above the age of twelve is already here with us. I doubt we left that many behi—"

Grak shivers at the realization. Unwilling to risk any more noise, he updates Lago with a quick signal. But while he was hoping for some sort of comforting reply from the man, all he receives is a stiff, almost fearful look.

Though I suppose it isn't the leader's place to be comforted, is it, friend?

No, it's my duty to bring comfort.

Then it's settled. Grak dons a courageous face and assesses their options. But when nothing sensible comes to mind, he decides to get Frolan's opinion instead. Scurrying forward, he finds the brute already involved in a quiet conversation with Kando and Umo.

Grak's attempt to join in comes louder than he had hoped. "The strangers are on our side of the river! How did they get past us?"

Kando holds a finger to his lips and speaks in a gentle whisper. "Yes, Grak, they are. Must have crossed while we were lost in the woods. But no matter, we still have the element of surprise. If we can slip away from here quietly, we should be able to cross the river and take them just after sunrise."

Grak nods. "Yes. My plan exactly. Let's get moving then."

The three men shoot awkward glances at each other before Kando speaks again. "Say, Grak, I was wondering something. If we're trying to meet them in battle just across the way there, then perhaps it would be best if you remained here. To command things. And to sound the alarm should they move from that spot."

Grak considers the point. "Hmm. I suppose I wouldn't be out of the fight. If anything, I'd be at the true front, since I'm the one staying to keep an eye on them. So that sounds good. But I'll need a few guards with me, an—"

"Yes. Of course. Of course." Kando nods reassuringly as he pats Grak's shoulder. "Don't you worry. I'll see to everything. Frolan. Umo." He gestures for them to follow.

The three men fall back and soundlessly dispense orders. Kando separates nine guards, and the rest silently gather in formation. In all, the process takes no more than a few moments before they set off, moving rapidly, yet quietly, over the stony ground.

Grak watches with awe as the tribe retreats into the distance. The speed. The agility. The strength. A dreadful force, to be sure.

Turning about, he assesses his own security team with a sigh. Brak has the most impressive stature of the group, which isn't saying much. Worse still, courage seems to be avoiding them as they huddle behind a rock formation at the water's edge.

"Well, I suppose I'll have to make do," he whispers to Lago.

Grak strolls over to join them, reviewing their cover in the process. It's much smaller than Brownhand—maybe only a third the size—and bears no likeness to any human feature. But all that matters is its ability to provide protection if any arrows come their way, and he deems it "sufficient" in that regard.

Grak reaches the group and settles in. After a moment of silence, he grows bored and peeks over the rocks. The strangers are a little easier to see now, though it's unclear what they're doing.

He shrugs. "They seem to be waiting. Maybe they're lost too."

He turns to Lago in shock. "What? No! I don't see how th—"

He's interrupted by panicked hushes. Brak peers out with an anxious look on his face.

Seeking to calm them, Grak holds a finger to his lips. "Shh! Can't let them hear us. Not until we strike." In hindsight, that probably should have been quieter too, but he had to be certain all nine could hear him clearly.

"Grak? Is that you, Grak?" Kunthar's frantic voice rings out from across the water. "Stop toying with us! Show yourself, Grak!"

Grak considers his options. Now that they know he's here, choices are limited. If he stays hidden, the strangers might head back to the crossing and spoil the plan. But if he can keep them talking, they might be distracted long enough for Frolan to strike.

Well, I suppose the decision is a simple one, friend.

Grak sighs. Putting on his most courageous face, he stands, straightens his tunic, and steps out.

The early dawn sky is just bright enough to illuminate a discomforting number of people on the opposing bank. But, strangely enough, they're all looking about in the forest on that side. As Grak ponders what this might mean, a woman spots him and cries out. They all turn in response, wearing complete shock.

Grak gulps. "Hello, Kunthar! Lovely time for a stroll, wouldn't you say?" He feigns surprise. "Wh … why do you have so many guards with you? And on my side of the river?" He remembers to show a bit of anger. "Are you up to something nefarious?" He gasps. "Were you trying to kill us while we slept?" Not bad, given the lack of preparation.

Kunthar looks about nervously. "No. Obviously not." He suddenly grows indignant. "But wait. What are *you* doing on *my* side of the river? Were *you* attempting to kill *us* while we slept?"

Now Grak is nervous too. "What? Why … where would you get an idea like that?"

The two men stare at each other for a long moment, unable to come up with a valid alternative. While Grak considers this a decent method of stalling, he'll need some noise if he hopes to mask the sound of his approaching forces.

He needs to keep them talking. "Alright, look, enough with the back and forth. Yes, we were both trying to kill the others in their sleep. Can either of us take it back? No. But we need to move forward now. So I suggest we leave all of that behind and start fresh. What do you say to a second meeting?"

Kunthar hardly acknowledges his words. He's too busy scanning the trees behind Grak.

The man's tone is full of alarm. "Where are the rest of your people, Grak? I don't hear screaming, so they can't be at my camp, killing our innocents. And they're not at your camp—I was just there. So where are they?"

That takes Grak by surprise. He looks around awkwardly for any excuse to keep the man talking. Brak simply shrugs, providing no help. Lago also seems to be out of advice.

Grak looks down the river, pondering how much longer he needs to stall before his people arrive and attack. "Too long" is his estimation. He turns back to the stranger, ready to give whatever excuse he can muster in the moment. Too late.

Kunthar is looking down the river now. He must have followed Grak's line of sight. And apparently his line of thought.

A frenzy builds on the man's face as he bellows to his soldiers, "They're trying to sneak up on us! As we speak! Move into action! Time is precious! Head down the river to the crossing and attack these cowards!"

Dernue runs to the lead, and the others fall in behind. They're moving with impressive speed, especially given the stony ground being traversed. Before long, only Kunthar remains with a small team, presumably to guard against Grak's group.

Brak tugs frantically at Grak's sleeve. "Sir! Should we warn our people? Should we sound the alarm?"

Grak is peeved, both that he forgot such a simple responsibility and that the man reminded him. "Yes. Patience, Brak! I was just waiting. For the right time."

He pauses for another long moment. "Now would be a good time. Go ahead."

Brak nods. He pulls the horn from his belt and presses it to his lips, sounding a single, long call. Grak sighs.

It's up to Frolan now.

Grak peers across the river again, thankful for the morning sun providing a clearer view. The strangers aren't doing anything active over there, but he still doesn't trust them.

Grak spots an eye peeking around Brownhand. "I see you there, Kunthar! And if you're planning something, you should know that we're ready for it!"

Kunthar's head bobs as he shouts, "How could you be ready if you don't even know what I'm planning?"

"Oh, don't think I don't!" That sounded better in Grak's head.

The strangers' muffled voices carry across the water as they discuss something among themselves. Grak is tempted to describe their tone as "excited," but prudence suggests holding off on such a bold claim just yet.

He looks at Lago. "What about you, friend? You have better hearing. Can you make out what they're sa—"

"Sir!" Brak points excitedly. "A body! There in the river. It's heading this way."

Grak is indignant. "Did no one ever teach you simple manners! We're in the middle of a conversation!"

Brak looks around awkwardly. "Sorry, sir. I didn't ... um ... sorry."

Grak raises his hand to strike the man, then abruptly turns toward Lago. A moment later, his arm lowers.

He turns to Brak. "You're fortunate he stayed my hand. You should thank him for that."

Brak looks even more disturbed now. "Uh, yes sir. Thank you."

Grak rolls his eyes. "Did I say to thank *me*?" He gestures toward Lago. "*Him*. Thank *him*!"

Brak gulps slowly and looks up at the staff. "Thank you ... Lago ..."

Grak nods. "Good. Now, what was so urgent that you had to interrupt our meeting?"

Brak's voice trembles. "Th ... there's a ... um ... a body ... in the water, sir. It's floating this way."

Grak whirls about excitedly and squints down the river. Yes, he can see it now. That certainly seems to be a body, but at this distance it's impossible to tell who it might be.

He turns to Brak. "Do you think you can reach it? As it floats by?"

The bald man shakes his head. "No, not without leaving the safety of our cover."

Grak rolls his eyes and lets out an exaggerated sigh of annoyance. He turns to Lago for a moment in relative silence with lots of nodding and an occasional shrug.

With a final nod, he turns to Brak again. "He's right you know. We're all making sacrifices for the tribe. It wouldn't hurt you to make one yourself."

Grak glances at Lago and shrugs. "Well ... that's true. Alright, so it might hurt, but it wouldn't be in vain. We'll remember you for this, Brak."

The man casts his eyes to the ground. "Yes sir." He pauses. "If I don't make it, though, please tell Loren that I love her. And if she doesn't make it back from battle either, can you see to Oli—?"

"Brak!" Grak rolls his eyes in frustration. "We haven't got time for this nonsense. The body will be here any moment!"

Brak nods and chokes back his tears. He crouches in preparation, waiting as the body creeps closer.

"Grak!" Kunthar's voice rings out. "What do you say to a ... cessation of hostilities … of some sort? Just until we can grab that body and verify which tribe it belongs to."

Brak breathes a sigh of relief. Grak turns to Lago for several more silent nods and shrugs.

He shakes his head and calls back, "I'm not so sure that's necessary!"

But Brak interjects, full of hope. "Sir, if we do, it'll ensure that we can grab the body. Otherwise I might be shot trying to retrieve it, and then we'd never find out who it is."

Grak turns to Lago. "What do you think?"

He shrugs. "Yes, well of course. But his cowardice aside, he does bring up a good point."

Grak nods, then lifts his voice for a reply. "What exactly did you have in mind?"

Kunthar's reply comes without hesitation. "Here's my proposal. We'll each send out one person. Whoever can grab the body, does so. If it's not from that tribe, just push it toward the other side of the river. Once the body is with its rightful people, everyone can go back behind their rocks, and the hostilities can resume."

Grak looks to Lago for a moment, then shouts, "Very well!" He nods to Brak.

The man flashes a wide grin before abruptly switching to a somber expression. He takes a deep breath, then creeps out from behind their cover. Caution soon fades as he makes his way forward unharmed. A moment later, he reaches the river's edge. And just in time too. The body is close, and it's drifting straight toward him.

Brak calls out, "It's one of ours! It—" He goes silent.

Grak peeks out to check on the man's status. He's still there, staring down at the water.

Brak lifts his voice again. "Sir! I think you should see this!"

Kunthar calls out, "What are you up to, Grak? Just pull the body behind your rock, and let's get on with this fight!"

But Grak is just as perplexed. "I … uh … don't exactly know either," he replies. "What are you up to, Brak? Just pull the body behind our cover, and let's get on with this fight!"

"I have the body, sir." Brak's enthusiasm is growing. "But you should see the water. It's higher now."

Grak is confused. "Why would I car—"

He turns toward Lago with a look of surprise, then turns back. "Oh, the water, you say? How much higher?"

Brak yells, "It's higher than the mouth, sir. By maybe a foot or so."

Kunthar calls out, "What, in all the land, are you two talking about?"

"Kunthar!" shouts Grak. "I propose an alteration to our agreement. I need to see the water with my own eyes. Just to confirm that my man isn't hallucinating. If you wish to join me, you can. As soon as I have verification, I'll return to my cover, and we'll continue."

After a long pause, Kunthar yells, "Agreed! I'm coming out!"

Grak peeks around the rocks and spots his opponent doing the same. After a moment, they both step out and cautiously approach the river, scanning for danger as they walk. When he reaches the water, Grak kneels down next to Brak and peers across at his old, peculiar rock. He's forced to squint from so far away, but still manages to see the thing clearly.

Grak is stunned. "He's right, Lago! It's higher now! Lapping at the rock's mouth! What might be causing this?"

Kunthar calls out, "Well? What's going on?"

Grak is speechless. All he can do is kneel there, pondering the situation for a moment.

Finally, Brak speaks. "Do you suppose the water just goes up and down?"

Evidently, Kunthar heard that. "It suddenly strikes me, Grak. What's this water shortage theory of yours based on?"

Grak calls out, "Well, the water was at a certain point previously, then when we checked later, it was significantly lower. But now it's back up. Even higher than before. It's the most peculiar thing, no?"

Kunthar pauses in obvious frustration. "That just sounds like the tides, Grak!"

Now Grak pauses for a moment. "The what?"

Kunthar is furious now. "That's the *tides*, Grak! Our theorists have known about them for some time. The water gets lower, then it gets higher. It's just what happens. Are you telling me we're fighting over the tides? You fool! You bumbling, moronic idiot!"

Grak is insulted by the man's crass choice of words. "Well, when you put it *that* way, anything can sound dumb. How were *we* supposed to know? Did you bother sharing your information with us? Sounds to me like this is all really *your* fault!"

Kunthar's voice is full of fury. "You'd better get behind your rock, Grak! Our agreement is over! You mind-numbing moron!"

Fairly certain of the man's intent to follow through, Grak scrambles for cover. And just in time too, as several arrows whistle through the air an instant later. After another moment, Brak comes around the corner in a panic, dragging the body with him. He's shaken, but unharmed.

Grak bites his lip thoughtfully. "Well, I don't know about the rest of you, but I would count that as good news."

Brak settles down, breathing heavily and glaring fiercely. The other guards also show clear annoyance, but no one speaks.

Grak shrugs and looks to Lago. "Any ideas on what to do next?"

Brak rolls his eyes. "We need to send a runner, Grak! To inform the tribe. To stop this idiotic battle! To tell them we're fighting over nothing!"

Grak is caught off guard by the man's tone. "What's with this childish grievance against *me*? Huh?" He looks around at the other angry faces. "I never said there was a shortage in the first place. That was Hambo. I ordered his execution. I said there *wasn't* a shortage. So if everyone had listened better, maybe this whole battle wouldn't have been necessary!"

"*Listened* better?" Brak's tone is uncharacteristically frantic. "*Listened* better?" He's almost shrieking now. "We've done nothing *but* listen to you, Grak! Listen and follow!"

He pushes Grak. "And *you're* the one that broke the water shortage news to the entire tribe in the first place!" Brak shoves him again. "And *you're* the one that told the strangers!" Again. "And *you're* the reason why my wife is fighting for *no* reason! In fact, *you're* the reason—and the *only* reason—why we've even been having troubles at all!"

Brak gathers his weight and sends a powerful kick into Grak's chest. Stumbling backward from the blow, Grak trips and tumbles uncontrollably. He scrambles for a grip or foothold—any stability would do right now—but none comes. He loses orientation, followed by sense, then hits the water hard. Liquid rushes in before he has the chance to hold his breath. His vision begins to fade from lack of air. Panic sets in.

19 - And Hotheads

Grak describes hotheads as both "irrational" and "infuriating." And they're consistent classifications too. So regular, in fact, that he once considered creating a new category combining the two. Fortunately, prudence triumphed in the end, and he decided that would be far too brash a move. The kind only a hothead would make.

A hothead like Brak. That vile, stinking rat, Brak!

Grak once again attempts to banish that line of thinking and concentrate instead on the task at hand. After all, conventional wisdom would suggest that one focus on avoiding drowning in a situation like this. And yet, as reasonable as that sounds, plans of vengeance continue to force their way back in.

Though, if he's being honest, such thoughts aren't altogether unwelcome. In fact, Grak might even describe them as "comforting." And he's fairly certain they're helping him stay lucid at the moment. However, the lack of air still seems to be prevailing in that particular struggle.

Need ... air. Need ... surface.

Completely disoriented, Grak makes his best guess at the surface and scrambles for it. He slams into mud and rock, taking the brunt of the impact on his face. The pain is nearly overwhelming, but on the bright side, his bearings are now firmly established.

With clarity and strength rapidly waning, Grak quickly reorients and kicks off the riverbed. In a moment that feels unending, he struggles against both a lack of air and the strong current. Suddenly, he breaks free. Then he's under again. And above again. And several times more before his wits recover enough to stabilize himself.

He looks around for the nearest shore. It isn't far off, but the water is moving too quickly. Worse still, the surrounding land is unrecognizable. That is, until the river begins to bend west around a hill. Grak panics at the realization of his location.

"Hurry!" he sputters. "We have to make it to shore … before we reach the strangers beyond the hill! Bu—"

It dawns on Grak that his friend is missing. "Lago! Lago!" he shouts between breaths.

No! Pull yourself together, Grak! For Lago. For your children!

He spots a rock jutting far out into the water. The river should sweep him close enough. If he can just grab hold. Grak reaches.

Yes!

But also, no. The current shifts unexpectedly, slamming his chest into the rock's face. This creates two substantial challenges: staying conscious and maintaining a grip. Yet, despite remarkable weariness, he somehow manages both. Better still, these successes prove rather invigorating.

With renewed energy, Grak slowly pulls himself, hand over hand, toward shore. His arms burn with strain as he battles the river. Some stretches require long moments to move a mere foot, yet he presses on. The rocky ground beneath his feet is an ever present remin—

Hmm.

Grak stands. The current is still strong, but the water only reaches his waist. A nagging feeling tells him it's been this way for some time. He ignores that thought and slogs the remaining distance to shore.

Once there, he collapses onto his back, sucking in as much air as he can manage. But breathing feels ragged. And it sounds even worse. He tries for a deeper breath, but finds tremendous pain. He attempts to push past it, but only meets resistance.

Rolling onto his side, Grak heaves with uncontrollable ferocity. Water rushes out, along with no small amount of blood. After a moment of this, he collapses again and returns to labored breathing. A little less labored now. He's grateful for that.

"For a moment there, thought I mi—"

Realization hits again, and Grak sits up abruptly. He waits a moment for the rush in his head to settle, then looks about frantically.

"Lago?" His question is drowned out by the river's noise.

He raises his voice. "Lago?" Still not loud enough.

"Lago!" It's nearly a shout now, but Grak doesn't care anymore; he just wants his friend back. "Lago!"

There, just a bit farther south, stuck in a thicket of rushes. He strains to listen. Yes. It's faint, but Grak can hear the man's unmistakable voice.

He does his best to ignore the full body ache, and stumbles in that direction, pausing regularly to steady his sight. It's a curious, dizzy thing right now, his vision. It betrays him when he moves too quickly and entices him to rest when he moves too slowly.

After several moments of painful lurching, Grak pauses at the water's edge, fearing the worst. His friend is stuck there, around eight feet out, and he's completely silent now.

"Lago!" His voice cracks with emotion. "Hold on! I'm coming for you!"

Without another thought, Grak plunges in. Though he soon regrets the lack of planning. The water is too deep for him to stand, and the vegetation restricts all but the strongest of movements. But he can't let that stop him. Not with his friend's life on the line.

He forces his way through the rushes, pushing himself, exhausting every last bit of strength. Finally, he grabs hold of Lago, and a wave of relief washes over him. But they're not safe yet.

Grak desperately pulls his way back to shore with one hand while dragging his friend along with the other. But this proves more challenging than he anticipated. While his entry cleared a return path, his strength is nearly gone, and the strain is all-consuming. And yet, somehow, he finds the energy. He presses on. And on. And on.

At last, Grak pulls Lago to shore, and they collapse together. Breathing is deep and labored, but thankfully, unencumbered. He lets himself relax on the wet ground, grass and mud and all. His eyes shut. Gently. Deeply. Sleep whispers to him.

But his thoughts fight back. The day's memories flood in. The battle.

The water shortage—or lack thereof. And Brak. Grak opens his eyes with a start.

That traitorous … wretched … bald-headed … bald-brained fool! He'll get what's coming to him. And then some!

His body aches as he rises to a seated position. "No time to rest, Lago. We've go—"

Grak's heart sinks. Lago isn't moving. He shakes the man, hoping to find him merely sleeping. But to his dismay, there's no reaction. Too gentle, perhaps. He tries a little harder. Relief settles in.

Grak smiles. "You were starting to worry me there, friend."

He chuckles. "Well, that was an unexpected bit of humor. But nice. Thank you. I needed a good laugh. Something to distract from all the pressures of late."

Grak gently brushes mud from Lago's cheek, careful not to tear any skin this time. "Look at you. You're a mess!" He removes an assortment of moss and twigs from the man's scalp. "You really must take better care of yourself, friend." And several maggots from the left eye cavity. "I swear …" He shakes his head playfully. "If I weren't around, you'd fall to pieces."

Grak chuckles, but Lago's lack of expression reminds him of their current difficulties. The pressures aren't gone yet. In fact, there are more now. And they're far too daunting to ignore. No. No escape from pressures for him.

Grak frowns at those thoughts. "Well, we've got work to do." He checks his shadow. "Not much time left. No telling how long this Brak matter might take." His demeanor grows grim. "And he's just the first. Lot of people to kill before dark."

He nods. "True. No harm in a few night killings, I suppose."

He surveys the area around them. "Well, we managed to come up on the same side of the river, so that's fortunate. Let's hope things keep going our way. Shall we be off, then?"

Grak carefully rises to his feet. It's a wobbly affair initially, but he eventually succeeds. Recognizing his friend's difficulty in doing the same, he pulls the man up, then pauses for a moment to review the area.

He motions up to the trees. "Seems best to take the woods since we're so pressed for time. The riverbank is too stony. And steep. Too slow that way."

He nods, doing his best to provide comfort. "Absolutely. We'll stay close to the water. Within sight at *all* times. Shouldn't get lost again."

Grak rolls his eyes at Lago in frustration. He's growing tired of the incessant nagging. It seems to be getting worse the longer they wander. And the insults are becoming more obscene.

He takes a calming breath. "No, we already tried *that* way. I'm certain it's *this* way."

Grak tries not to take offense. "Look, I know how to get back to the river. I'm not a fool!"

His expression turns to indignation now. "Just who do you think you are? You're my adviser. That's all! *I'm* the leader! You'll listen, and you'll obey, or you'll face the conse—"

Grak crouches, gazing intently at the movement up ahead. Although, if they heard him, they'd be reacting right now. After a careful moment of observation, he's confident they didn't. He turns to caution Lago, but finds no need; the man's expression is stony and silent, even piercing.

Grak returns his focus to the humans moving about beyond the brush ahead. Squinting also reveals tents behind them. He can't make out faces, but there's no doubt in his mind: this is Kunthar's camp.

He pulls Lago close and whispers, "No more playing around, friend. Complete silence from here on out. We'll sneak wide around them, an—"

He turns to Lago in shock. "Why would you want to do that? No. Absolutely not. We can send someone to espy the camp later. There's no reason for *us* to do—"

Grak tilts his head in thought. "Oh? You think? Hmm, well, perhaps you're right. I suppose Jafra *might* be there."

He ponders it for a moment longer. "Very well. We'll *look*. But that's all. And from a safe distance. If we don't see her, we can't risk trying anything more."

They creep forward to the tree line, and Grak pauses, signaling for Lago to do the same. They're close enough now—around nine paces from the camp perimeter—to see the situation clearly. Something seems off, though. The strangers are buzzing with movement. Even panic.

Perhaps they know something I don't.

Grak carefully reviews the faces before him. "Well, I don't see her."

He grows apprehensive. "You think so? I suppose we could *try* to sneak in for a closer look. Given all the chaos, they might not notice."

Grak shakes his head. "Mmm, no. I'm not comfortable with that suggestion."

He rolls his eyes with an exaggerated sigh. "Alright, I'll tell you what, if we spot a smaller one, then we'll see about killing them along the way."

He turns to Lago with a look of shock. "What? No! Not *children*! I'm not a *monster*! I meant someone short. Or skinny. But not wiry—that's where I draw the line."

He notices a particularly small fellow. "Like him. Not too young. Would probably fight us if he had the chance. And killing him now would help our tribe. A little. Or that wom—"

Grak freezes. Her face is more than just recognizable. It conjures old memories. Memories of love. And memories of loss.

He sighs something deep and despondent. "Groka," he whispers.

He looks at Lago with dismay. "No! We can't kill *her*!"

He takes a deep breath, attempting to control his rising anger. "Because I *said* so!"

Now Grak is furious. "Stop it, Lago! You'd best be careful, friend. I'll admit, I like you, I do. And I appreciate your advice as well. But never forget who the leader is! If I say she lives, then she lives! Now silence!"

Lago gives no reply. Even his face is cold and expressionless, revealing nothing. Grak considers the man's demeanor.

Sufficient, I suppose. For the time being. At least he'll be subdued for a bit.

Satisfied, Grak returns his focus to the camp. And Groka. And—

He stifles a gasp. "How did we not see her sooner? Obvious brow and all."

It's true. She's standing next to Groka, after all. And they're not so far away, either. The two women are conversing together, no more than thirty paces from the perimeter.

A calm, steady rage consumes him. "Jafra! Now *there's* one we could kill three times over. If you want blood, take *that* one."

Grak turns in astonishment. "Oh, now you're not talking to me? I swear, Lago, sometimes you're such a whiner. This is our chance! Why bother trying to kill *Groka* when we can have *Jafra*? She's all that matters. She's the one who needs to die."

Grak purses his lips with indignation. "*Both*? You want *both*? So you're whiny *and* greedy? Well you don't get everything you want! I'm telling you, Lago, I'm beginning to regret even saving your life back there at the river. Or taking you in and grooming you as my adviser. If arguments are all I get from you."

He waves the man off. "Good! Go silent! I was about to tell you to do just that!"

Grak once again turns his focus to the camp. He's furious now. At Jafra. And Lago. And even Groka, for coming between him and his friend.

Still, though. Lago should know better than to defy me like that. I hope this chastisement does him some good. Then maybe I won't need to have the fool whipped.

Grak decides to ignore the man; he's too upset at him in the moment. Instead, he turns his focus to the task at hand, busily surveying the camp's layout. Yes, he's fairly confident now: the current chaos should provide adequate cover to slip in unnoticed.

He considers his options, and a plan clicks an instant later. Before Grak can even examine its sensibility, his feet are moving, pulling him out of the trees and down the small slope. From there, he circles west around the perimeter. Aside from unavoidable stretches behind obstructions, he never takes his eyes off Jafra. In another moment, he reaches a spot with a direct line to her back. He pauses there and allows himself a silent chuckle.

She won't even know what's happening. Not until it's too late.

Grak creeps forward, hardly bothering to soften his steps amid the chaos all around. He draws closer, passing several panicked individuals who pay him no mind. Closer. He reaches the tent where he spotted Jafra, and peers out from behind. She's still there, talking in hushed and concerned tones with Groka.

Grak takes a moment to consider his current options.

Can I handle both of them at once? By myself? I can't imagine Groka would stand aside and watch. She'd try to protect Jafra. After all, what do they care about a fair fight?

If only I had someone to fight by my side ... If only I hadn't left Lago behind. Perhaps I shouldn't have been so hard on the fellow. I mean, he was just trying to help. And he sure would come in handy right abou—

Grak turns in stunned silence. "Lago! You loyal fool," he whispers while caressing the man's cheek. "You followed the entire way!"

This brings a distinct comfort to Grak's heart. Despite Lago's previous transgressions, one thing is certain: he can always be counted on. Especially in a pinch.

Grak allows himself a few grateful tears. "I'm glad you came, friend. And not just because I could use the second person. I want you by my side. In *everything*."

He takes another moment to gaze longingly at the man. Though it doesn't last long. The burden of their task weighs on him, demanding immediate action.

Grak chokes back emotion and clears his throat. "Shall we, then? Two of them, two of us. Sounds like decent odds to me."

He takes Lago's silence as acquiescence. "Good. Now, Groka's on the left. She's yours." He points a cautious finger at his friend. "To *distract*. Nothing more."

He unsheathes Slicer. "And Jafra ..." he says with a grin, "Jafra's mine."

He takes one last deep, steadying breath. Then he gives the signal.

Grak charges valiantly around the tent with Lago at his side. "For justiiiice!" he cries.

Then they're on the enemy. Lago flails wildly to the left, while Grak reaches for the long hair to his right. She's already whirling to face him, but it's too late. He thrusts Slicer with all his weight, and the blade finds a convenient target between two ribs, lodging deep in the woman's side. Only then does he realize the error.

Off to his left, Jafra freezes in shock. Before him, Groka grimaces. She looks up, into his eyes. Grak's stomach sinks. He sees confusion in her. And pain. And betrayal. Mostly betrayal. Anxious to take it back, but unsure how, he pulls the weapon free, and she crumples to the ground.

"Groka!" screams Jafra, as if broken from a daze.

She rushes over to kneel at the other woman's side. Removing her tunic, she presses it to the wound in desperation. But the cloth hardly helps. She pleads fervently … with Groka … with the wound … with the blood. But it's still flowing. And far too rapidly.

Groka tilts her head toward Jafra, her neck straining at the effort. Her eyes wander, unable to focus, already fading. She attempts to speak. A weak gurgle is all she can manage. Then she's gone.

Jafra goes silent, motionless. She's stunned by this turn of events. A spark of comprehension lights in her eyes. It slowly grows. As does fear. Then it hits, all at once. Her lip trembles. Her eyes water. She erupts into uncontrollable sobbing, cradling Groka's head and gently stroking it.

This continues for some time until Jafra seems to run out of energy. Her weeping slowly loses vigor, though only externally. All that strength seeps into the cracks, gathering inside, until her whole body begins to shudder. Periodically, a quiet, lonely whimper escapes. And in this moment, Grak feels more than he can take: sorrow … remorse … despair …

No, Grak. She deserved it. She did! That's not the Groka you knew. This woman was a traitor. She turned on you. When you needed her the most. She tried to help Jafra take everything from you. She deserved it, Grak. She deserved it. She deserved it! And now …

"Now you know how it feels, Jafra!" Grak is barely aware of his own tears. "Now you know how it feels to lose something you love. Now perhaps we can call it even. Once you take your punishment fo—"

Jafra screams in pure agony and rage. In one swift motion, she stands, draws her ax, and lunges toward him. Her swings are wild, with no thought for form; she just wants him bleeding and dying.

Grak reacts almost as wildly, and somehow manages to deflect the blows, or at least avoid them. Though they *are* getting closer. One misses his chest as he leaps back at the last moment. Another whizzes just in front of his face as he ducks left in sheer terror. Another nicks his right forearm amid a clumsy block. Then it happens.

His foot catches on something, and he trips, dropping Slicer on impact. Jafra eagerly rounds the obstacle—a pile of firewood, as it turns out—and draws her ax overhead. But that's just enough time.

Fear surges through Grak, and he reacts with a hard kick to Jafra's stomach. Breath instantly abandons the woman, and she crashes into the firewood, losing her balance. Flailing about in a hopeless effort to keep her footing, she loses her weapon before finally toppling over onto her back.

Even in her dazed state, Jafra has enough sense to look around for the ax. Spotting the weapon, she tries to scramble toward it on all fours. But she isn't quick enough.

Grak is already on his feet, Slicer in hand. He leaps in Jafra's way and presses the blade's point between her eyes. She freezes, staring at the weapon, contemplating her options. But realization hits: she has no options.

Jafra exhales in frustration and defeat. She looks up at Grak, her eyes cold and furious. And something else. Hurt. Yes, but more than that. Betrayal again.

She settles into a kneeling position as tears slowly form. "Why, Grak?" Her voice cracks. "Why do you hate me so much? I'm sorry about moth—"

"No!" Grak presses Slicer's point to her throat, his voice full of rage. "You know the rules! You're not allowed to call her that! She's *my* mother!" He's screaming something shrill now. "Not *yours*! You *lost* that privilege when you killed her! Or have you already forgotten?"

"I'm sorry, Grak! I am!" She's weeping now. "I wish things had turned out differently. I do. And I'll never forget. Even when I sleep, I'm reminded.

"But I've learned something. Since being away from the tribe. I've seen there was nothing else I could have done, Grak. I was just a baby. Newly born at that. I'm so sorry, Grak. I am. But I'm not at fault! No one is.

"Sometimes life just … happens. And sometimes it hurts, and we can't stop it. We can't control it, no matter how hard we try. And that hurts even more.

"But the pain you felt for her, Grak … *feel* for her … we *all* feel it. You're not alone. She was my mother too, and I never even got to know her. So please, Grak … don't take your pain out on me. For mother."

Grak isn't sure which aspect of that speech he hates most, but there's a good chance it's the glaring truth of her words that troubles him so. Or perhaps it's the woman's ability to state something so complex with such simple eloquence.

No, it's the glaring truth of it all. Far more upsetting.

Grak looks at the ground, trying to avoid Jafra's gaze. Her words echo mercilessly in his head, tugging at his heart. He's managed to sidestep the issue for all these snows, but now it's latching on and won't let go.

He wants to stop. He really does. But he doesn't know how. No, that's not accurate. He doesn't know what will happen if he stops. If he loses control.

He looks at Jafra again. She really does bear a resemblance. Down to the uneven eyebrows.

Would be a shame to lose that. The last shred of mother.

Grak lowers Slicer. "Alright," he sighs. "For mother."

He stands there in silence for a moment longer, avoiding eye contact. She remains on her knees, the weeping subsiding. But Grak isn't sure what to do now.

I can't kill her, but can I take her back to the tribe? Would that be possible? Or would she continue to fight me? Where's Lago when I need his advice?

He looks around. There, some nine paces away. But the man is lying on the ground motionless, possibly wounded. Or worse. Grak's heart quickens, and he rushes over to kneel at his friend's side.

He smiles and breathes a sigh of relief. "You had me worried, friend. Jafra must have gotten you good, eh?" He pulls Lago up and dusts him off. "We'll need to get you a good wash. And get some more jasmines. Soon as we get ba—"

Something large and heavy crashes into Grak's chest, dislodging Slicer and Lago from his hands on impact. As he hits the ground, his breath rushes out, and his vision blurs. Consciousness toys with the idea of desertion.

But panicking clearly won't do any good. He needs to remain calm. To that end, Grak focuses on his breathing. And it seems to help. After another moment, sound and vision begin to return. Another moment still, and those senses regain some clarity. Enough to see the man standing above him. And someone else. Someone he recognizes.

Grak attempts a commanding voice. "Dernue ... we have no ... further quarrel. The water shortage is over. Ask Kunthar. In fact, I need to speak with him. To officially end hostilities."

He attempts to push himself up, which proves challenging, given his current fatigue. More complications arise when the large man notices the effort and stomps on Grak's chest, forcing him back to the ground.

A slight grin flashes on Dernue's face before she can hide it. "Yes, we know about the water shortage." Her voice is dry and thoughtful. "As for Kunthar, he's not around anymore. Died in battle. So unfortunate." The satisfied tone betrays her words. "Took a knife in the back. Ironically, it happened while he was attempting to stop the battle. A shame."

Dernue spots Lago and shudders slightly. She bends over and picks up the staff. Grak moves instinctively to protect his friend, but the large man's foot proves too strong.

Dernue carefully examines Lago. "This thing is atrocious." The corners of her mouth turn down. "How can you carry it with you?" Her tone is a mixture of disgust and sincere curiosity.

She looks up at him suddenly. "Tell me, I heard a bizarre rumor. Do you sleep with this thing in your tent?"

Grak finds the woman's arrogant manner repulsive. "Yes, Dernue. I do. He is my friend, after all."

The woman stares at him in silence for a moment. Then she smiles something mischievous. Locking eyes with Grak, she steps back a pace. Her nostrils flare even larger as she slowly raises the staff overhead.

Grak's heart quickens and his eyes bulge. "No! Dernue! Plea—"

The staff strikes the ground with full force just in front of Grak's face. The wood cracks loudly on impact, but remains largely intact. Lago, however, takes the brunt of the blow and bursts into pieces.

"Lago!" screams Grak. He struggles vainly against his captor. "Why? Why would you do that? He was innocent. He never harmed you!" Grief quickly turns to rage. "I will kill you for this, Dernue! I promise! My people will come. They'll save me. They know I'm missing, and it won't take long for them to look here. And when they do …"

Somehow, Dernue's smile grows larger. "Oh, I'll be happy to tell them you're here. You see, after the battle, Kando and I had a long meeting. And while we have much more to discuss tomorrow, we've come to a *few* reasonable resolutions. Agreements that will make further meetings even smoother.

"And *you* were one of those agreements. A fairly unanimous one, really. Anyone who finds you is instructed to capture you and bring you before a meeting of our tribes. To face our united justice.

"Then we'll punish you. And execute you. But publicly. Unitedly. Properly." She rolls her eyes. "Procedures."

The weight of her words hits Grak hard, and a response fails him. He stops struggling and drops his head to the side, unable to muster the energy or will for anything else.

His gaze falls on the remnants of his dearest friend. He couldn't save the man. He couldn't save his mother. And he can't save himself. Too much tragedy to bear for one day.

Grak begins to weep. From fear. From exhaustion. From loss. The sobbing is deep and quiet, slowly draining his energy. Soon, it softens, calmly fading into a whimper. His eyes shut. Gently. Deeply. Sleep whispers. Grak gives in to it.

20 - And Resolutions

In spite of the utter despair enveloping Grak, he's fairly certain of one thing at least: he detests resolutions. Truly. And it's not just a sudden realization either. He's given it a great deal of thought. Thinking, of course, being one of the few ways to pass time in his current predicament.

Rather cruel treatment when you think about it. Nothing to do. Not even a chair for comfort. At least I'm not tied up. Yet.

Grak peers out through the tent flap. He can't see any shadows from here, but the abundance of light tells him it's about halfway through morning now.

That's another way he's been passing time: by keeping track of time. As best he can without shadows to aid him, that is. Though it's been especially difficult today, since his late rising gave no point of reference to start from.

Slept past dawn. Quite a bit, it seems. Suppose I was still fairly tired.

That's true. He was. Though it's also just another good way to pass time. The best, really. So he's been sleeping more than anything else.

After his capture, Grak slept straight through that first evening. He woke up in this tent the next day, though only because of the sudden light when a soldier entered to bring him stew. Of course, hungry as he was, he devoured the food. Then, with little else to do, he thought about his difficulties for a bit until falling back to sleep. And aside from the few times he woke up to relieve himself and think a bit more, he continued to sleep until today.

And he's found, to some surprise, that his sleep has been quite sound—in spite of the stony ground and lack of a bed roll. And better still, for the first time in a while, he hasn't been dreaming. Just sleeping. Deeply. Sweetly. And he only recently woke up, feeling well rested at last.

Must be due to the lack of worries. I mean, sure, there's the impending execution, but other than that. In a strange way, I'm glad I'm not leading anymore. So glad, I don't even really mind what happens. They can go ahead and kill me for all I care. I've lost everything else, what does my life matter anymore?

Despite his melodramatic nature, Grak is being fairly honest here. He's so relieved to be rid of the burdens that he truly can't muster up any fear over his execution. And everything else, including his former prestige, simply pales in comparison.

Though the waiting is annoying. And the lack of a chair. It's really only common decency to bring a fellow a chair when he's detained. I would have done it if Cordo had asked.

Grak sighs. In all honesty, he knows that would have been improbable. But still, he likes to think it might have happened.

I'm not a monster, after all.

He sighs.

Or am I? Suppose it depends on who's asking. And who's answering. Not sure many from my tribe would answer with 'no.' And I can't really blame them. Next time ...

No. Who am I fooling? There won't be a next time. Might not even be a next day for me.

Again, very true. Lakar, the soldier who brought his food yesterday, was kind enough to also provide some information. Apparently, representatives from both tribes met all day and came to a number of agreements. And it seems they were so efficient that the meetings are projected to conclude sometime today.

Decent fellow, that Lakar. I imagine we would have been friends if circumstances had been different. Although ... he might just be taking pity on me ... given my fate.

Grak sighs once more. While he doesn't fear his impending doom, he does find himself deeply saddened by it. And not for the loss of his life, either, as he initially thought. Nor is it due to the extraordinary pain he imagines will accompany the event. Even the feeling of defeat no longer rankles him.

No, it's none of those things. Just ... perhaps I should have ... maybe done things ... better.

As difficult as that is to admit, it feels good. Grak smiles weakly.

Hmm, I suppose that's it. Would be nice to ... well ... fix, I suppose ... a few of my ... poorer decisions. Best I can at least.

But Grak knows how unrealistic that sounds, and he feels all the more saddened by this knowledge. No, that's not quite right. It's not sadness he's feeling. Not exactly. "Remorse" would be more accurate.

Sounds about right. Remorse.

Grak rolls the word around in his mind. This inevitably leads him to thinking about the situations currently inspiring that feeling. And the people. He sighs.

The people. Now there's something I could fix. Would fix. Maybe ... well, find a way to apologize ... to my friends. My former friends. Though I can't imagine anyone's still willing to speak to me.

Grak thinks about that further. Try as he might, not a single name comes to mind without exceptions.

No. Can't imagine there's anyone left. If anyone's still alive, that is.

Grak peeks back through the tent flap. He hears the shuffling of his guards, but can't see much. He's certain of their presence, though. Nearby camp fires were casting silhouettes all around the tent last night, making it clear he was surrounded.

Wise, I suppose. Though it'd be nice if you didn't need so many people to stand guard. But then the detention tent would have to be stiff, I guess. Impossible to break out of. Then you'd only need one guard. And only as a final precaution. Next ti—

Grak catches himself. He sighs and relaxes into one of his old thinking postures.

Grak shields his eyes from what he's guessing is the late afternoon sun spilling in through the open tent flap. A moment later, his vision adjusts, revealing an expressionless Lakar standing there with a dish of food.

The man covers his nose at the stench of Grak's waste. "Eat up. I'll be outside. When you're finished, let me know. They're announcing the agreements soon, and I'm supposed to take you there." He pauses and gives a slight shake of his head. "I don't imagine it's to exchange pleasantries." With that, Lakar exits.

Grak eats. Slowly. He's not stalling, though; his mind is just preoccupied with what's to come. He continues on at this pace for a while until his focus turns toward scraping the bowl clean. That's when he spots them. A slight smile creeps onto his face. This is followed by a chuckle.

Olives. And finely chopped.

He ponders them for a moment longer, then shrugs and takes the final bite.

All things considered, not such a bad addition to a meal. Could be worse, I suppose. Still … can't say I like them. I suppose 'tolerable' would be most applicable.

Grak sets the bowl aside. For one final moment, he sits in silence, breathing deeply, calmly. Curiously enough, he still can't muster any fear.

Hmm. I suppose it's the finality of the matter. Nothing left but peace.

He takes one last deep breath, then calls out, "Lakar. I'm ready."

The flap opens, but no one enters. Grak waits a moment, then exits timidly. In less than a heartbeat, he's surrounded by soldiers, two of them placing a firm hold on either arm. Wasting no time, they lead him off like this at a brisk pace.

Once his eyes fully adjust to the brutal afternoon sun, he surveys the area. In the tent, he had found it difficult to smell if this was his camp, but now he's certain it isn't. Still, he would have expected to recognize at least a few faces.

Grak clears his throat and ventures a timid question. "Lakar … what I asked about yesterday … were you able to find that out for me? Are any of them still alive?"

The soldier nods. "Most of your council survived. Except Aza. She took an arrow to the side and bled out. And the other one you asked about—Sando—he didn't make it. I'm told he probably shouldn't have been in the fight, given his age and poor health. Took an ax to the stomach. Died pretty quickly. Rather unceremoniously."

Grak sighs in deep despair. His heart shivers. The emotion is as surprising as it is painful. Must be the memories. They're flooding in now, reminding him of happier times. He hangs his head, letting silence take over.

Father ...

Grak is so consumed by these thoughts that he hardly notices when the babbling of a nearby crowd comes into hearing. Soon after, the soldiers halt. They open their circle just enough to give him a clear view of the way ahead.

He and his escorts are standing off to the side at the front of a small gathering. Most of the faces belong to strangers, though Grak is relieved to recognize many of his own people too. But something curious about the group suddenly strikes him, and he lets out a gasp.

Is this everyone that survived? From both tribes?

No more than eighty, he estimates. Their clothes are unusually tattered, and covered with more blood than he would have expected. Most of the attendees are conversing together, and many are staring at the newly erected whipping post before them. A few notice him and promptly sling insults in his direction.

Suppose I deserve that. And more.

Grak takes their abuse for several moments longer until Kando walks into view, causing the noise to abate. The man's clothes are fine, fresh leather—a stark contrast to those of the tribe. He takes position in front of the post and is soon followed by Dernue, who pauses a few feet behind him.

Kando waits until the final murmurs subside. "My people!" His voice booms clearly across the crowd. "We have good news. Our meetings have concluded, and we've made a number of resolutions. Thank you for your patience during this time. It's what made the process possible."

He pauses to wait out an unenthusiastic and spotty cheer. "So, on to the announcements. The chief decision we made deals with our weakened numbers. In both tribes. There's no doubt in any of our minds that we will not survive without greater strength. So, with that in mind, we've resolved to join the two tribes."

A hesitant applause slowly forms. At the least, people seem relieved that more fighting is out of the question.

Kando waits for the noise to die down. "But that does raise some complications. We'll have a daunting task ahead of us if we hope to truly unite as one. New organization is needed. New role assignments as well. And, of course, new guidance so we can all sleep easy at night knowing that someone watches over us. So we asked ourselves, who should lead this new tribe?"

A curious, yet subdued murmur ripples through the crowd.

Nervousness flashes in Kando's eyes, but he stuffs it down and moves on. "And after careful consideration, we've come to what we believe is the best possible solution. My people ... *I* am to be your new leader!"

As if on cue, Brak walks forward, carrying Grak's cap. But the thing is different now, clearly altered for the occasion. Bright yellow threads have been woven in, forming a shape or symbol of some sort.

Branches, it looks like. How odd. But what type?

Grak continues squinting until realization sets in a moment later. He rolls his eyes.

These people and their obsession with olives.

With great flourish, Brak places the hat on Kando's head. The crowd's conversation slowly turns toward general acceptance. Soon, they begin applauding with mild enthusiasm. Though several faces still wear obvious disapproval.

Kando raises his hands to signal for quiet. "Thank you! Your love and support mean so much to me. And in return, I will not disappoint you, my children. I promise to be a fair and just leader. One who handles all matters with wisdom and care. The tribe will *always* be my *highest* priority!"

He pauses as lukewarm assent rises from the crowd. "Now, there was some concern that my former tribe would be favored as a result of this.

And we want you to know that we've anticipated this need, and that we intend to strive for equality for all members of the united tribe. Thus, we have decided that Dernue will be my supporting leader."

The crowd responds well to that. This time there isn't even a hint of dissension. Once again on cue, Brak brings a cap forward: Kunthar's old hat. While it has the same yellow threading, the shape isn't nearly as elaborate. It's just a circle. And not even a very round one. Brak quickly places it on Dernue's head and strolls back to his spot.

She opens her mouth to speak, but is interrupted by Kando. "And it gets even better. We've learned how important it is to listen to what you have to say. We won't repeat previous leaders' mistakes by silencing your voices, my people."

Kando smiles at the enthusiastic response. "And so, my children, I'm pleased to announce that you will have representatives! And they will be chosen by you, according to your area of the camp."

A unanimous and resounding cheer breaks out. This is easily the most popular announcement yet.

Kando allows a little more time for the applause to die down. "And I know many of you are eager to hear about the water shortage." That elicits some approval. "Well, I have good news for you. The best surviving theorists from both tribes have put their minds together, and it turns out we're *not* running out of water. They've concluded, without a doubt, that the tides are a natural occurrence and shouldn't be feared."

Again, the crowd cheers. Though it seems many are still a little begrudging about that issue. A number of heads shake, and plenty of tears fall.

Kando spots this and hurries on to his next announcement. "And with that news, I'm thrilled to inform you that we also have the ability to move. We'll begin packing tomorrow."

More approval comes from the crowd, though many simply appear to be cheering at anything now.

Grak shrugs.

At least I won't have to endure another packing day. So, that's one positive outcome from this whole execution thing.

Kando quickly jumps to his next point, seeking to keep the remain-

ing momentum alive. "And for those of you wondering where we'll
be moving, take comfort. That was discussed too. And in great detail.
Many factors were taken into consideration, including growth, shelter,
herd size, and herd predictability. And, in the end, we decided that
the best choice was to head for the hot springs and follow the travel
patterns of my old tribe."

More absentminded cheers rise up. Clearly, the crowd feels that the
important announcements are over. Now they're just hoping to dis-
perse soon.

Kando pauses for a moment, then switches to a grimmer tone. "And
now for the two closing resolutions. To dispense justice and attain
finality for recent events and abuses."

He turns and points at Grak. "Grak! Step forward! Receive the tribe's
punishment!"

Grak gulps as fear threatens to take over. All the formalities are making this far more difficult to bear. He takes a deep breath, which proves
calming.

*No matter, Grak. It'll be over soon. Just one more task. And a simple one
at that.*

He takes a step. Then another. Surprisingly, walking to his death is
far easier than he imagined. Before long, he's at Kando's side.

The man whispers, "Seven feet, Grak."

It takes him a moment to realize what Kando is referring to, but when
it finally clicks, Grak nods. He moves back to the required distance and
hangs his head, waiting for the pronouncement.

Kando turns to the crowd. "Grak! For your abuses of our people and
wanton destruction of our way of life, you deserve nothing less than
execution!"

A hearty cheer erupts, which stops the speech. Kando attempts to
gesture for quiet, but to no avail. He's forced to wait it out.

After another moment, the noise dies down enough for him to proceed. "And many wanted that execution. In fact, many even pleaded
with me to let them be the ones to do it."

More elation rises from the crowd, though it's much easier to stop
this time. "But many didn't. In fact, a significant number *insisted* that

we *not* execute you." He shrugs. "For some reason. Not entirely sure why."

This elicits some dissension, though not as much as Grak would have expected. But that really doesn't concern him right now. Instead, he's occupied with what this might mean.

What, in all the land, is the fool getting at? Could there be a chance to keep my life? To stay? To make amends? And new friends? Would I even want that anymore?

Kando continues. "So we discussed it at considerable length—nearly all of our meeting time, in fact. And after hearing the desires of our people ..." He's noticeably disappointed now. "We've decided ..." He sighs. "Grak, you will *not* be executed."

Grak's eyes go wide with shock. All he can manage is to stand there in bewildered silence. The crowd, on the other hand, shouts their vehement disapproval. Apparently, anyone who defended him isn't prepared to declare it openly.

Kando holds up his hands in a vain effort to calm the tribe. "But wait. Don't worry, my children. There's one more! A ninth and final resolution!"

The noise drops enough for him to be heard clearly. "Those of us who demanded his execution only relented in the face of an alternative punishment. So, without further hesitation ..."

He lifts his voice even louder and adds a commanding tone. "Grak! For your abuses of our people and wanton destruction of our way of life, you are officially expelled from this tribe. Additionally, you are banned from ever returning, on pain of immediate torture and execution!"

The crowd takes a moment to ponder that one. A cheer slowly builds as they realize its significance. But Grak understands too. His stomach sinks.

Hadn't thought about that possibility. Not much better, really. Rather than a quick and painful death here, slow and agonizing starvation out in the wild on my own. Hunting will be too difficult without a team.

Grak gulps. It's a highly unpleasant prospect, to be sure. Much to his dismay, however, he's clearly not in a position to negotiate the matter.

But what else can I do? Nothing. Nothing at all.

Grak's head slowly lowers under the weight of this new burden. He sighs something deep and pitiful.

Grak looks around at the gathered crowd. It's a measly showing. And fairly discouraging as well. Though he does take heart that two tribe members just arrived.

Perhaps more will come. Perhaps.

But reality doesn't bode well for Grak. Around half of those present are soldiers, and it's unclear whether they're here to protect him or the tribe. The rest are mostly strangers, clearly here out of curiosity alone.

At least some of my friends showed. Former friends, I suppose.

Grak attempts his best smile. Frolan gives no response, save for a slight nod. Brak and Loren reply with awkward avoidance. Even Olive Fifty-three seems to be ignoring Grak.

Can't blame her. Can't blame any of them. At least they dressed up for the occasion. Obviously tried to wash out those blood stains recently. I imagine that was for my benefit. I hope.

Brak finally manages eye contact. "Well, I suppose this is it, Grak." There's no warmth there, but neither is there any hate. "I won't be needing this anymore."

He passes a wadded piece of soiled leather, his eyes trying not to reveal emotion. Grak unfolds it for inspection, though there's little doubt what's in his hands. He gently dusts off the cap and puts it on, careful to flatten the point.

He turns to Brak and smiles. "My *good* hat. Thank you."

Brak shrugs, a touch of compassion showing in his eyes now. "You're welcome."

Grak would like to say something, but he's certain his voice would crack if he tried. Besides, it's too late. Brak and his family are already leaving.

Grak shakes his head thoughtfully.

Can't blame any of them.

He looks to Frolan now. The man softens slightly, and the faintest hint of a sad smile forms.

He pities me, I suppose. Can't blame him for that, though. I imagine I look quite pitiful.

Frolan unwraps the bundle he's been carrying, revealing the statue he made for Grak so long ago. Several recent nicks and gouges are present in the otherwise rich, red wood, but aside from that, it's still in good shape.

He passes it over. "This belongs to you. Even if you didn't earn it."

Grak nods. "Thank you." He clears his throat. "I ... um ... I never told you how much I appreciated the effort you went through to carve this. But I did. And still do. So, thank you."

Frolan nods in reply, then breathes deep and sighs. "I suppose this is farewell, Grak. Can't say I disagree with the decision ... but I will *miss* you. Sort of. A part of me. We had some good times at least." He pats Grak on the shoulder.

"Frolan ... I ... well ..." Grak digs through his memory for an example of how to say this sort of thing. "I probably should have handled things differently. I'm sorry. I hope you can get on in the tribe without anyone holding a grudge. Because of the things I ordered you to do, that is."

Frolan's smile is gentle and warm now. "Well, I suppose I forgive you then. But don't worry about me. I'm leaving too."

Grak's eyes light up. "Really ...?"

Frolan responds hastily. "Well, not with you. I'm sorry, Grak, but that wouldn't work. I can't really trust you. But I don't trust Kando either. Never did. I always felt he was just seeking power. And Dernue isn't any different. I fear bad times are coming for our people. I hope not, but ..."

He shakes his head. "Anyway, I'm going with several of the old hunting team. And Opa. We're sort of ... together ... now. So that's nice. We'll see how it turns out."

Grak smiles, sincerely happy for the man. "Well, congratulations, Frolan. She certainly has good hands." He looks around. "She ... um ... didn't want to come, then?"

Frolan shrugs. "Well, no, she did. Sort of. Just, Kando has been keeping her busy. You know, maps and such."

The man looks about awkwardly, then suddenly gets excited. "But Doran said he'd be here." Realization hits, and he frowns. "So, I don't know why he didn't show. Suppose Kando might have him busy too. With something."

Grak nods sorrowfully. "I see." He pauses for a moment. "I ... um ... don't suppose you know about ... well ... Jafra? Do you thin—"

Frolan shakes his head. "No. She's ... I don't think she's ready to see you. Certainly not while she's still grieving. Maybe if you give it more time."

Grak nods. "Well, thank you. For notifying me." He pats the man's shoulder. "And for seeing me off."

The two stand in awkward silence for a moment. Finally, Frolan nods his farewell, then turns and ambles off. Grak sighs at the man's retreating form.

Can't blame him, really.

He looks around. No other familiar faces. Except for Lakar among the soldiers. That reminds him.

Grak approaches the man. "Did you happen to hear anything? About my request?"

Lakar shakes his head. "Sorry. I haven't. Kando's been busy, so I don't even know if he was able to review the matter."

Grak nods. "Of course. Of course. Well, just thought I'd try. Thank you, though. For carrying the message."

The soldier replies with a kindly nod, but says nothing. No matter. Grak has nothing more to say either. And nothing more to do. Not here at least. With a heavy heart, he shoulders his pack, turns, and slowly walks away.

Well, can't really blame them. Can't blame any—

"Grak!" calls an unmistakable voice.

Grak whirls in excitement at his old friend's shout. What he finds, however, takes him by surprise. Doran isn't alone. He's leading Patyr along behind him, the pony's fur glistening from a recent wash.

And a brushing too, if I'm not mistaken.

The man dons a reserved, yet friendly smile as he approaches. "Hello, Grak. I'm glad you didn't leave yet. Or rather, *we're* glad you didn't leave.

"Sorry about the timing. It took me a while to push your request through. Kando felt apprehensive about granting you anything. He thought it might reflect negatively on his leadership. But I pointed out that we don't need the pony. It actually gets fairly neglected around here." He shrugs. "Also, I know how much you love this little fellow."

Tears stream down Grak's face. He gives the man an earnest embrace.

"Doran ... I ... um ..." Grak digs through his memory once again. The words come easier this time. "I'm sorry ... I'm so sorry. I treated you poorly. And you were always a friend to me. Even when I was treating you so poorly. I don't know how I could have done that. You were the only one, you know. Who never called me names."

Doran nods sadly. "I know, Grak. I know. I would have liked things to turn out differently. Truly. But, this is the tribe's decision. I hope you understand."

Grak nods. "Yes. I do."

He ponders whether to ask. "So, Doran ... I don't suppose you ... um ... want to com—"

Doran slowly shakes his head. "No, Grak. I can't do that. We don't have the friendship we once had. It would take a lot to get back to that point."

He shrugs. "Besides, Kando's asked me to head up the Vast Oceaners again. Well, under him. He's still leading them, but says I can be his supporting lead for the group. So that's nice."

He pauses for another awkward moment. "A lot of interesting new theories. More fracturing, of course, but Kando's fine with it if they're all reporting to him.

"I'm leaning toward one group called the Earth Talkers. They're proposing that the thing in the ocean was the earth itself, reaching up out of the water to communicate with us. We have a few followers so far. Sounds like it makes sense."

Confusion spreads across Grak's face. "Oh ... I see. But don't you *know* what you saw?"

Doran shrugs. "Honestly, I don't really remember anymore. It's been a while."

Grak nods, and the two men hang their heads in silence. And even though this quickly grows awkward, it somehow seems better than parting ways. At least for now.

Doran clears his throat timidly. "Well … I have to get going. But with any fortune, perhaps we'll see each other again. If you stay in the area, I might be able to find you the next time we pass this way."

Grak nods. "That would be nice … friend."

The two embrace one last time. With obvious hesitation, Doran turns and slowly walks away. And that's when Grak feels it. A wave of overwhelming sorrow suddenly washes over him as he watches his oldest friend depart.

Should have handled things better. Should have done things differently.

He strokes Patyr's head, hoping the distraction might avert oncoming tears. The pony gives a sympathetic look in reply, which brings a smile to Grak's face. A sad smile, but it's something.

"Well, friend," he whispers with surprising skill. "Seems it's just you and me now."

Grak exhales in frustration. He checks his shadow. It's been far too long already. He was hoping to have this fire started before nightfall, but that's looking less likely by the moment.

With a sigh, he turns to gaze back at the camp. His hilltop position provides a clear, almost serene, view of the tents below. But the sight tugs at his heart. And at his memories. The dull sea of mottled brown leather with patches of grey smoke reminds him of so many snows gone by.

Of mother. And father. And Jafra.

The forest surrounding him now, while relaxing in its soothing greens and gentle browns, is too sharp a contrast. It feels almost like the detainment tent, separating him from the people he once called his.

I wonder if I could get someone to help me with the fire. No, that's right—the whole 'on pain of immediate torture and execution' thing. Can't blame them, really.

Grak sighs. He thought it would be best to sleep nearby tonight as a practice of sorts before the tribe leaves. But so far, it's only been a reminder of what he's losing.

He turns to Patyr. "That's probably why I'm having trouble with the fire. Just distrac—"

A branch cracks somewhere off to the left. It sounded like a footstep. Grak's spine tingles as he peers intently through the brush. Nothing.

He tries calling out, "Hello? Who's there? I have a knife! It's very sharp!"

That's not entirely true. The council *did* give him a knife, but the thing is old and rusted and obviously hasn't been considered sharp for quite a few snows.

Still, he was grateful for it after losing Slicer. Initially, they considered letting him keep the longer blade for his travels. But in the end, they deemed the thing "too foul to exist" and destroyed it, giving him the knife instead.

A familiar voice calls back, "Put that away. I'm not here to hurt you."

A woman steps into view, freshly washed with a new tunic and trousers. She's carrying a sack and doesn't appear to have any weapons at the ready. Grak's mind races at what this might mean.

He clears his throat. "Olive Thirteen?"

She rolls her eyes. "Please … for the last time, Grak. Can you just call me Olive? I've never understood this nonsense with the numbers."

He nods in shock. "Alright. I can do that. But … what …" He clears the crackling in his voice. "What brings you here?"

Olive smiles. "I thought we were friends, silly." She pauses. "Or was I wrong?"

Grak smiles tentatively. "Well … yes … we were … *are*. But … don't you hate me? Like everyone else?" He shakes his head. "Can't really blame them."

Olive looks him over inquisitively. "I don't think they truly hate you, Grak. Not for the most part. Look, you did some awful things. And you caused a lot of pain. And when people are hurting, they tend to react with strong emotions.

"The tribe may think they hate you, but it's just their reaction to the pain. Give it time. They'll soften. Maybe not enough to let you return, but enough to stop hating you."

Grak nods, still somewhat confused. "And you?"

Olive raises an eyebrow. "Didn't I just say we were friends? I think I know the real you." Her expression turns to concern. "But don't get me wrong. You know how adamantly I disagreed with most of your policies. Especially the ones that hurt people." She shakes her head. "Those were ... terrible."

Grak digs through his memory. "You did? I ... can't seem to recall that."

Olive's expression turns to shock. "Of course I did! Though I'm not surprised you don't remember. Listening was never really one of your strengths. And your memory has always been rather selective."

Grak nods in shame. "I suppose you're right." He grows puzzled. "But, that still doesn't explain why you're here. Even less so. Seems like I should have driven you away. Given how horrible I was. Am."

Olive pauses in thought. "Well, Grak, you did a lot of terrible things, that's true. But I always felt you did them because you were blinded by selfishness. Disgusting, yes, but something you can change. And something I can forgive. It doesn't have to be a part of you any longer." She shrugs. "So if you'll work on not being such a selfish prick, I'll keep trying to see the good in you."

Grak clears his throat again, though it's far more challenging this time. "And you would do that? You would forgive me? And ..." He looks at her pack. "And come with me?"

Olive nods and smiles something warm. "I would. And I do." She shrugs. "And the way I see it, we're both better off away from the tribe. I don't really trust Kando. Never did. He always struck me as someone who was just out for power. That's why I was always warning you about him. Not sure why you ignored those concerns." She thinks about it. "Though, I suppose your listening skills might have had something to do with it."

Grak is nearly at a loss for words. "Well ... I guess ... you might be right. Perhaps I should have paid closer attention to your advice, Olive Th—" He clears his throat. "I suppose I just always thought you were sort of hanging around because you lacked the sense to do anything else."

Olive stifles her annoyance. "Well, don't mistake kindness for stupidity, Grak." She pauses in thought. "And just so you know, it'd be best if you stopped thinking like that about me. We won't get along very well otherwise. Friends aren't supposed to put each other down, Grak. Friends are supposed to be a support for each other."

Grak smiles. "I like that saying. I'll have to remember it. Alright. I can do that."

His smile widens as he looks at his friend. His *good* friend. He mulls her words over.

Remember that saying, Grak.

Epilogue - But Not Olive

Grak has never disliked Olive, though now he's beginning to feel something new for her. He glances at the woman seated to his left. In this light, approaching dusk, the green of her eyes sparkles just so. It's a curious feeling he gets when looking at her, though he's not quite sure what to call it.

Admiration? Maybe. Respect? I could see that. Hmm, something else though.

From the corner of her eye, she catches him staring, and turns her head. He looks away abruptly, suddenly entranced by the meager wisp of a cloud off to his right.

That was close. Can't let on. Don't want her to get nervous.

Grak casually looks to his left again, pretending to suddenly notice her. "Oh, hello."

Olive smiles and rolls her eyes. "You don't need to pretend, Grak."

He puts on his confused face. "Oh? Pretend what?" His voice cracked at the end there, betraying his nervousness.

Olive shakes her head and smiles wider. "What do you have so far?" She looks down at the clay tablet on Grak's lap.

While he's thankful for the change of topic, he's left wondering what that whole "pretend" comment might imply. He opts to set the issue aside for the moment and ponder it later in private.

Grak clears his throat and puts on a thoughtful voice. "Well, I'm stuck on the beginning."

Olive leans back in her seat. "Read it to me."

He's nervous at that prospect, but finds it difficult to deny her anything. "Sure … I mean, it's short. It's not much. Just says, 'I hated olives.'"

"Not bad. Not bad." She raises an eyebrow. "Though you will make it clear that you differentiate between the fruit and the people, right?"

Grak nods. "Oh yes. Of course. Of course." He shrugs. "Though it's not quite right. Doesn't sound so great."

He scratches his chin with the stylus. "Maybe if I write it as though in the present. And from someone else's perspective. Would look more prestigious that way. Like someone else is recording my history for me. The reader might even assume I've never seen it."

Olive taps her lips thoughtfully. "So how would that sound?"

Grak shrugs. "Well, it would just say, 'Grak hates olives.'"

She nods. "I see. Interesting. Has a nice ring to it. Though maybe it needs something more."

Grak ponders it for a moment. "'Truly.' I kind of like that. 'Grak hates olives. Truly.' Makes it more definite. Makes it clear where I stood on the issue."

Olive gives a hearty and approving nod. "Yes. I like it. Why don't you go with that?"

Grak smiles and quickly scribbles the words down. Once finished, he leans back in thought. "I think that's enough for today. I'm getting hungry." He sets the clay on a scrap of leather to dry. "Hard to think clearly when I'm hungry."

"Should we head down, then?" Olive sounds truly concerned. "Get some food?"

He shrugs. "Might as well."

As they stand and stretch, Grak takes a moment to bask in the array of brilliant colors before them. Draped across the hillside is a vivid bed of green grass, dotted about with the intense reds and oranges of maturing leaves. Above, the deep blue, nearly cloudless sky envelopes all in its soothing embrace. Below, between the river fork, the fields of golden wheat stand in bold rows, taking on an even more radiant hue in the setting sun.

In those fields and in the neighboring "village," as they call it, Grak's new people are bustling about. Activity tends to pick up like this at the end of the day. Even more so in this part of the "year," as they refer to it. "The harvest," they say, is a very busy time. Although, from what Grak has noticed so far, it's a little *too* hectic. Disorganized, even.

They could use some tips, really. On organization. Just a few. To show them how to make things run more efficiently. Before you know it, they won't be such an uncivilized people.

Olive begins to leave, so Grak stores that thought for another time. He starts to follow her, then pauses abruptly.

He looks at their seats, then back down to the village, estimating the distance. "Olive. Should we take these with us?"

She checks the sky. "Well, it doesn't look like rain. I think they'll be fine for the night. They're too big to carry every time we want to come out here."

Grak takes offense at her comment. "What does *that* mean? You *agree* with everyone else? That my work is a monstrosity? Because you know how I feel about that."

Olive smiles. "No, Grak. I'm simply stating the truth. They're too heavy. If we don't have to carry them, let's not bother with it."

But he's still offended. "Because you, of all people, know that I put a lot of work into them. And the extra supports were simply for necessity. And I don't think all the extra wood makes them ugly. Not at all. I think it even adds some character."

Olive touches his cheek with a gentle smile and looks deep into his eyes. "I like our chairs, Grak. Well, now that the splinters are all gone. And now that we've taken care of the nails that were poking through. I just don't want to carry them. That's all. And what does anyone else know?"

Grak melts. She has a way of stopping him before he goes too far.

He smiles and nods. "Alright. Let's go get some food."

As they head down the hill, Grak looks back one last time. He's quite proud of his handiwork. Definitely his best ever. Very solid. Very sturdy. He had to make them rather large, though. With lots of wood. But no matter. He likes them. And so does Olive. And that's all that matters.

She catches him looking back and smiles. "Still thinking about your chairs?"

Grak shakes his head. "No. And you know, I wish you would stop calling them that. They're better than normal chairs."

She rolls her eyes in reply. "Right. Sorry, I forgot. What was it you wanted me to call them?"

"My thrones," Grak says with a gleam in his eye.

Thanks

Alvi, you are priceless to me. Your help and encouragement while I wrote this book have been what made it possible.

Andy Peloquin, thanks for being a support and inspiration during the writing process.

And special thanks to everyone else who has indirectly contributed to my writing over the years.

About the Author

Peter J Story lives in San Antonio, Texas with his wife and their two pugs. He writes code by day and fiction by night, considering himself an author of deliberate, genre-free stories with a soul. While his is not a pen name, he does enjoy chuckling to himself about how well it suits his passion.

Being extremely shy as a youngster, Peter spent his days in two primary hobbies: studying people and reading. He found both pastimes equally fascinating. Among his favorite characters were Encyclopedia Brown, Sebastian the Super Sleuth, and Sherlock Holmes. When in search of new mystery stories, he read *Murder on the Orient Express* and found the tale intriguing. Unfortunately, he felt that the name "Hercule Poirot" was unseemly, and abandoned any further inquiries in the character's direction.

Then one day, at the age of ten or so, Peter's uncle introduced him to the work of J.R.R. Tolkien, and his world changed forever. He was carried away by the story and tried his hand at mimicking the epic. Unfortunately, due to his existing love for *Star Trek: The Next Generation*, this took an unholy turn toward a hybrid of the two worlds. But he enjoyed it, nonetheless, and isn't that what matters most? Of course it is.

As he grew, Peter learned to enjoy a variety of new writers, such as George Orwell, Leo Tolstoy, Herman Melville, Ernest Hemingway, Fyodor Dostoyevsky, Stephen King, Dave Barry, and C.S. Lewis, all of whom had a tremendous impact on his writing style. He planned to go to college (with a vague notion of majoring in something to do with literature), then decided to instead spend seven years as a missionary (mostly in Mexico City). The time paid off, however, and taught him even more about human nature and the art of telling a subtle, character-driven story.